SUNSET DISTORTION

SUNSET DISTORTION

THE PYRAMID AT THE END OF THE WORLD

PAUL BAHOU

Grateful acknowledgement is made to Writer's Therapy for helping steer my ideas into a stronger finished product. My wife Melissa for putting up with me disappearing for hours at a time to write this thing. Nick Bennet, for reading multiple iterations of the book and giving invaluable feedback. Wesley Strawther, for making the story visually come to life and David Blau, for legal advice and for being an all-around good dude.

Author website: SunsetDistortion.com

First Paul Bahou printing 2021.

Digital Edition ISBN: 978-0-578-80419-4

Print Edition ISBN: 978-0-578-80418-7

Cover Design by Wesley Strawther

I dedicate this book to my wife Melissa. Babe, babe, babe.

TABLE OF CONTENTS

PART 1

LIVING THE DREAM IN 2015

THE AIR-CONDITIONED OASIS OF LOVE ON THE ROCKS WAS A WORLD away from the late-August swelter suffered by those just outside the bar's black vinyl door. For an aging watering hole in West Hollywood, that was all it really needed to be: cold, dark, and open for business. Sure, like more than a few of the Rock's regulars, this place peaked in the late '80s. Yet despite the fading fluorescent beer logos flickering on the walls, scuffed and stained concrete floors, and bathrooms that looked grimy even after being cleaned, it had its charms. There was also something to be said about a place that made no fuss over a patron wearing leather pants at noon on a Tuesday. One such man who came as close as one could get to abusing such a privilege was Georgios Hassan.

Georgios was not necessarily the most heavy metal of names, he felt, but he was in the land of self-invention. Identity was a little more flexible in Los Angeles; it bended and melted in the heat like a poorly tended record collection. Sometimes, it was hard to tell where the persona ended and the person began; others were who they were twenty-four-seven. Georgios could be fairly counted among the latter. He was just a man with a guitar and a van, living in equilibrium in this neon fishbowl called life. He swam in circles but enjoyed the view—day after day, month after month, year after year. Though you could call him Georgios all you'd like, if you cared for a response, he only answered to . . .

"LAZER! Great set last night, man!" a nameless barfly called out to the lanky black silhouette cast against the blinding white glow of the real world behind him. The door swung closed, enveloping the room once again in its more comfortable shade of darkness. Lazer gave the man a subtle nod as he stepped up to the solid oak bar while rubbing his hand across his still-waking face. He pulled his wavy salt-and-pepper mane behind his ears with an olive-tanned hand and claimed the first open barstool available. Rebecca, the tatted and youthful bartender, placed a frozen glass of pale liquid sunshine before him.

"Breakfast is served," she said with the same wink of familiarity she gave him every time she dropped that line.

Lazer thanked her with a grunt and a smile, then chugged half of his beer without breathing. He set it back down with a clack as the thick glass hit wood. A tiny splash ran down the side, pulling beads of frost with it into a small pool on the ring-stained bar top. Lazer wiped the foam from his weeks-old stubble with his forearm, collecting a layer along its curly black fuzz, while the remainder dripped down onto his chest and yellowing undershirt. He grunted a hearty morning cough and looked at the clock on the wall. It was a little after noon.

A laser is, by definition, a narrow and focused beam. It's an instrument of precision. Another drop of beer dripped from Lazer's stubble to his chest. Perhaps it wasn't the most accurate of monikers. Lazer wiped his mouth and dried his hand on his vest. He cleared his throat and took another sip.

The road that led to this point in Lazer's life on planet Earth read like the typical *Behind the Music* bacchanal. There were women and drugs and such. Some memory loss, some hearing loss, some memory loss, and a well-used liver. It was a lifestyle of glorious inertia. It was a song on repeat, one he had no intention of turning off, even as it showed its age a bit more with each passing year.

Lazer hadn't always lived in a van behind a bar, playing dives and Bar Mitzvahs. He was once the lead guitarist for the thrash metal buzz band Killer Orca. Lazer and his bandmates were kings of the West Hollywood metal scene in their prime, a local favorite who packed every show they played. The crowds sang the songs, some of which were in regular rotation on local radio. Everyone in the scene was sure of the band's trajectory. Ask anybody, and it was always the same answer: to the top.

Sunset Distortion magazine called them "Black Sabbath with the immediacy and rage of punk rock paired with the virtuosity of the classically trained." Their single "Run! Punch! Smash!" got them some traction overseas. To everyone who knew them, they were an inevitability . . . an inevitability that never happened.

One day, it just fizzled. The van ran out of gas. Everyone in the band had someone to blame. The drummer, Roy, founding member and generally responsible guy, had a baby with his girlfriend. Maybe he had lapses in judgment here and there—like not using condoms consistently as an obvious example—but this new reality meant Roy stopped showing up to practice every time. When he did come, he'd leave early. His playing got sloppy from the lack of sleep that came with having a newborn. His attention scattered. He said he needed more money and could only play certain gigs. He took a second part-time job, and things never seemed to get better. He drifted further and further away.

Bassist Sid, who was a year older than everybody else and the principal songwriter of the group, took it personally that the label, who always seemed so eager for meetings and dinners and pep talks, stopped returning calls. One day they were drinking whiskeys at the Rainbow, talking about what they were going to name their boats, the next they were strangers. The release date for the record kept getting postponed. So did the meetings. It just never seemed to be a good time. After a while, it didn't seem like it would ever be a good time.

Then there was singer Javier, a wiry suburban nihilist with a shock of bleach blond hair who drank too much. He was pure electricity on stage with moves that made Mick Jagger look like a corpse. He was also an asshole.

Lazer drank too much too, though never enough to affect his playing. It was just to keep him at his level. On *the* level. The problem was that he was always on that level. He never really found the balance, though he was never really in any hurry to find it either. Still, while he was the one who tended to drift through the clouds, Lazer was the only member who saw their situation for what it was: bad timing. Call it the universe if you'd like, but this was the '90s. Their fans stopped wearing black and started wearing flannel, then they showed up less, then not at all. Sometimes life just found a way to kick your soul in the balls.

Killer Orca was officially dropped from their label in the spring of 1992. Adrift and in need of money, they played any show they could, which were in smaller and smaller venues for less and less pay. Roy left and was replaced. Sid left, got kicked out of his new band, then came back. Javier was Javier. His parents were old and rich, so he did whatever he wanted. The years passed, grunge died, then nu metal came up in its place, which also died, and then something else came up and so on and so on . . .

Still, they never stopped playing, even though the money from birthday parties, pay-to-play ticket sale shows, and Bar Mitzvahs wasn't great. A show was a show, and paying rent was the new record deal. The fans were gone. The scene was gone. The high-pitched squeal of tinnitus was still there though—the collateral damage of following his dreams. Even still, they played.

Twenty-five years later and they were clinging to the music in their hearts and the hair on their heads, except for Lazer. His hair was glorious. He may as well have been genetically engineered to have the hair a guy in a heavy metal band is supposed to have. There were streaks of gray among the wavy black mane, but even those were finely placed. The women all noticed. No matter their age, they all wanted to touch it. He usually let them.

Killer Orca eventually retired the originals and swapped out their set for heavy classics from bands like Black Sabbath, Motorhead, and Judas Priest. They landed Sunday through Wednesday nights as the house band at Love on the Rocks. It was the final retreat for the ride-or-die holdouts from the old scene and tourists who couldn't get into the Viper Room. Worldwide fame was out of the question. They weren't rock stars, or at least not on paper, but on Sunday through Wednesday nights between nine p.m. and midnight, they were nothing less than gods.

THE GIG THAT NIGHT WAS like most—hot, loud, and blurry. The energy of the crowd of cougars and barflies reliving the glory of their youths was the last bit of substantial meaning Lazer's life still possessed. His bandmates weren't as tight as they used to be. They were more than coworkers, but somehow a step removed from the brotherhood they had once shared. They had stopped talking about their future a long time ago. For a while, it bothered Lazer, until the day it didn't.

Lazer had no wife, no kids, no siblings, a deceased mother, and a dad who left when he was in middle school. For Lazer, it was just his guitar and the women who loved hearing him play it. The older women loved him because he reminded them of their youth. The younger ones loved him because he was the right amount of trouble as they pushed deeper into their twenties. On this cloudless night however, he was alone.

The leather-vested rocker staggered out the back of the employees-only exit into an oddly silent night. The air was crisp for summer, only slightly polluted by the alcohol quickly dissipating through Lazer's pores. He stumbled past an overflowing trash bin and took a large, careful step over a puddle of urine using his drunken agility. He moved past a man busy excavating the recycling bin and shimmied between several cars, taking care not to spill the final swig of Jack swishing around the bottom of his bottle. A few more steps, and he was there—home.

Lazer's dark blue 1988 Ford Econoline was his transportation, his apartment, and his most prized possession. It had a custom-built bed in the back and a howling space wolf airbrushed on the side. It was based on a sketch he came up with for an old album cover. The drawing got shut down by band vote, but it looked pretty good living on as van art. He called the van "backstage." He never got tired of telling that joke and suffered no pretenses regardless. Some women picked up on that. He picked up on them. Everybody won.

Lazer hadn't always been in this situation though. He had a girlfriend he'd lived with up until recently. She wasn't a regular at the Rocks, but they had met there. She was in a bachelorette party that had hit its final stop during the last hour of Killer Orca's set about a decade before. They had a backstage tryst that led to Lazer moving in several months later. For a while, it was good. They could have gotten married, started a family, moved to the Valley, got a minivan, the whole deal. But like most other things in Lazer's life, it seemed to fizzle out. It was less of an abrupt bang than a middling disintegration into oblivion that led him to here, drunk, stumbling to his van. But what was oblivion to the oblivious? It probably looked something like Lazer's current lot.

Lazer sidled up next to the passenger side door of his van. He rested his forearm against the window, smearing the dew that had accumulated in the wee hours of the morning. He fumbled through his keys between boozy exhales, looking for the right one.

"Nope. Nope. Nope," he murmured as his keys dropped his feet. "Ugh." He reached down to pick them back up with a displeasured grunt. He lowered slowly, hand on the van to steady himself. For a moment, his hand floated, halfway between picking them up and falling over. He swiped them and rose back up, flipping through the ring once more.

"Nope. Nope. Nope. Bingo!" Lazer mumbled as he took the right key and slowly pushed it toward the lock. He paused. *This would be much easier if the lock would just stop moving*, he thought. He closed one eye and repositioned his feet. Slowly and with a subtle groan, he lined up the key, slid it in, and turned. *Click.*

Success! Beyond the applause and beyond the music, this was the most beautiful sound he had heard all night. Before he could open the door, however, a blinding spotlight enveloped Lazer, casting everything beyond his van in shadow. He glanced upward into the abrasive gleam, dew-smeared forearm over his eyes. He reached into his pocket and put on his aviators, glancing upward a second time.

He flashed back to that night's show—the bright lights, the cell phone cameras . . . Was this an encore? Was he still on stage? With a nearly empty bottle in his right hand doubling as a pick and an invisible fret-board in the other, Lazer took his best rock stance. He strummed a mighty power chord across his air guitar as the roar of a crowd erupted, passionate and present only in his head. He mumbled incoherently and sloppily headbanged, his hair whipping back and forth in a bouncing flop.

Lazer began to float. He reached for his door but was only able to grab at his key ring. The key to the van slid back out of the van's lock as Lazer ascended toward the beaming source of light. It was the great gig in the sky, and Lazer submitted. He released the bottle, which fell to the ground and shattered on the concrete as he vanished into the night sky. A warm feeling rushed over Lazer's body. It was warm like stage lights. It was warm like whiskey. Then darkness.

LAZER OPENED HIS EYES TO find himself in a white room with cushy white carpet, sitting in a white metal chair at a white table facing two blurry blue objects. He blinked several times, digging out whatever crusty matter had accumulated in the corners of his eyes while he was out. He scratched himself below the table while releasing a series of grunts.

"Georgios . . . Georgios . . . ," a calm female voice echoed. Lazer mumbled inaudibly. The voice sounded like it was at the end of a tunnel. "I suppose you're wondering where you are."

"Vegas?" Lazer replied, still rubbing his eyes.

"No. Even better," the voice responded with reserved enthusiasm, becoming clearer as Lazer's eyes focused. The blurry images merged into a single powder-blue-skinned woman wearing a crisp white dress shirt, skinny black tie, and black slacks. She was short and squat, which was evident even though she was sitting, her chubby fingers earnestly folded between each other. Her face was filled out, though youthful, slightly reflecting the fluorescent light beaming from above. Small ridges pushed up around the edges of her platinum blond hair, which was kept in a tight bun. Similarly dressed powder-blue men and women scurried about their desks; some wore bicycle helmets with the chin straps fastened.

"You are on the *John Smith seven*."

"The what?" Lazer groaned.

"Our missionary ship," she said, tapping on the table. "Tell me, Georgios, have you ever heard of—"

"Lazer," he cut her off.

"Excuse me?"

"My name's Lazer," he said with a hiccup as he slid down in his chair.

"Oh, I'm sorry," she apologized, punching several times into an invisible prompt. "Your identification labeled you as being a Georgios Nicholas Hassan, from 3577 Ridgecrest Drive, Hollywood, Califor—"

"Nope, just Lazer," he said with a quiet burp.

"Very well, Mr. Lazer. I will—"

"With a *z*, not an *s*. Zzzzzzzzzzz," he slurred, leaning forward in his chair. Bits of spittle flew toward the blue woman as she moved her chair back several scoots.

"Noted," she said with professional reserve as she punched at several more invisible buttons.

"What are you pointing at?" Lazer asked with a head tilt.

"Oh, sorry. It's these silly visual overlays they make us use. Here, I can take it off private mode. I'm just going through your file," she said as a hologram appeared from the table, bearing a scroll of information.

Lazer stared at the woman for a moment with a confused look on his face. "So is this a dream? Usually the girls are hotter—*hic*. But I guess I . . ." Lazer reached down and fumbled with his belt.

"My, aren't you . . . charming."

"*Hic*—Are you coming on to me?" Lazer asked as he glared at her with a single bloodshot eye. There was another slight and awkward pause.

The woman continued, "I was hoping to talk to you about church."

"The chicken place?" Lazer asked with another hiccup.

"No, not the . . . The Church of Jesus Christ of Latter-Day Space."

Lazer shrugged.

"You know, the Smormons!" she said with a reassuring smile, turning off the hologram as Lazer wobbled. "Tell me, Mr. Lazer, do you know where you'll go when you die?"

"I'm dead?" Lazer patted up and down his chest in a confused panic. He squirmed in his chair, looking for a gaping wound of some sort, ultimately finding nothing.

"No. You are very much alive. My apologies, Mr. Lazer. This is my first day on this ship, and I don't have much experience speaking to humans. You know, you are actually my first potential," she said, steering the conversation.

"Potential?" he asked with another heavy burp under his breath. He blew the noxious air sideways.

"Yes. This is new for both of us," she said with a smile.

"Hey, I don't know what you've heard—*hic*—but I don't have any money." Lazer patted at his pockets and shrugged. The woman paused.

"Potential convert. Sir, please, I wish to tell you about our Lord Jesus Christ. But first, it appears I have broken protocol. Like I said, first day." She chuckled apologetically, punching at a few more buttons.

"You look dehydrated. I mean, that *is* what humans look like when they're thirsty, right?" she said, looking him up and down. "What can I get for you?"

"Jack and Coke," he stated with a mild shrug.

She typed into her prompt. "I'm sorry, but we do not have any alcoholic beverages aboard."

"I thought you said this was Vegas."

"*You* said this was Vegas!"

"So we're not in Vegas?"

"NO! WE'RE NOT IN—" the woman responded in elevated frustration before cutting herself off. She paused once more, straightened her tie and posture, and replaced her tense reserve with her previously chipper vibe.

"Can I get you something besides a Jack and Coke?" she asked without a hint of her prior irritation.

"You're proba . . . probab—*hic*—probably right. It's cool. I shouldn't drink more. It's . . . Do . . . you . . . Uh, coffee?" Lazer mumbled incoherently as he wobbled again.

"I apologize, but we do not have any caffeinated beverages either."

"What kind of restaurant is this?" Lazer asked, scratching under his shirt.

"It's not a . . . How about I just bring you some water, OK?" she said as Lazer slumped back into his chair and began to doze off.

"Moons over my hammy..." Lazer mumbled beneath whiskey breath, trailing off in an incoherent babble for a few seconds before falling into a snore. The woman hopped off her chair, walked around her desk to Lazer's side, and poked him with her finger, giving him a slight shock. Lazer jolted awake.

"I want a paternity test . . . Oh, um, what?" Lazer looked directly at the woman with squinted bloodshot eyes. She looked eye to eye with Lazer even though he was sitting.

"My name's Qiti," she said, pointing to her name tag. She smiled and held out her hand toward Lazer, waiting. Lazer shrugged and clasped her hand, shaking in a temporary moment of understanding. Up, then down, up, then down.

Qiti continued smiling as Lazer hiccupped once, twice, then proceeded to throw up a night's worth of whiskey and bar snacks all over Qiti's chest and pants. She stopped shaking and took register of the watery brown mess splattered across her body. Lazer groaned as he wiped his nose with the back of Qiti's sleeve, leaving a snail trail of viscous remainder. He released her hand and slumped back into his chair, pieces of half-digested peanuts littering his face.

"I think we'll try again in a few hours," she said as she motioned to another missionary.

The man had a trim white beard and soft, friendly wrinkles around his eyes that were visible beneath the slight shadow of his helmet. He smiled and took Lazer's forearm, helping him out of his chair. Qiti walked away as this new person led Lazer into an adjacent room through an automated sliding door.

This area was stark white and windowless, simple and minimal like the first room. The doors closed behind them as the seams vanished into the walls. Within the space were rows of white recliners, twenty in total, about half of which were occupied by other humans. Most of the people were dirty with heavy clothing lying folded on short white tables beside the chairs. All of the people were asleep and had shimmering aluminum tubes running directly into their chests from toaster-sized white boxes that sat on their own small white tables. The missionary led Lazer to a chair near the center of the room. He pointed to Lazer's chest.

"Shirt, please," he asked Lazer, who wobbled some more before catching himself on the chair. Lazer pulled off his vest and held it toward the powder-blue man but dropped it. He pulled his shirt above his head and became stuck, his arms hanging bent out of the top. He leaned forward, gazing at the missionary from the hole in the collar.

"Sorry, one sec," Lazer apologized, bending over and picking up his vest with his still-tangled hands. He rose to a ninety-degree angle and handed it to his waiting nurse before straightening back up and removing his shirt the rest of the way. He wiped his face with the garment and handed the soiled article over.

Lazer fell into the recliner and stretched his arms behind his head. The powder-blue man slid a length of tube from the box, planted the end just below Lazer's sternum, and twisted. A soft purple light emitted from the tip as it attached to Lazer's body. The man pressed the top of the box, causing it to emit a low purr. Lazer looked up and took one last look at the ceiling before drifting off to sleep.

LAZER AWOKE TO A SERIES of distant thumps. He sat up and ran his hand down his face, catching whatever crust remained stuck to his stubble from his still-foggy evening. He slid off the recliner, peeling the skin of his back from its textured surface, and stood. He inhaled deeply, stretched his arms high above his head, and took a diving exhale forward. A chorus of pops from his spine thanked him in rapid succession. Once at the bottom, Lazer hacked a phlegmy cough, clearing his throat as he became aware of the tube still planted firmly in his chest. He straightened back up and looked down, inspecting the aerodynamic object attached to him by the thin, shimmering hose.

Everything between walking off stage and now was a blur. It was a fragmented series of images and sounds, jumbled, shaken, flipped upside down, and placed out of order. There were lights. And a woman. Two women? No, a single blue woman and a short man . . . They were all short . . . right? Where was he again? Something about Mormons? Smormons? This room didn't look like any drunk tank he had woken up in before. Was this the hospital? But what was this tube, these chairs, these people? Everything was off. Didn't he talk about Vegas the night before? Had he agreed to a road trip while blackout drunk? It wouldn't be the first time . . . or the second.

Another thump, muted but inescapable, came from somewhere. But where? Lazer scanned the room to see what hadn't even registered the night before. Was this Vegas? Why did he keep thinking of Vegas? Some trendy new detox bar in Silver Lake maybe? Lazer did feel strangely renewed. He wasn't hungry, thirsty, or hungover. This was actually the best he'd felt in years, decades even. He looked at his reflection in the casing of the toaster-sized box. There were no buttons or levers or logos of any sort, just a sleek, uninterrupted surface that wrapped around the entirety of this odd rounded object.

A series of thumps rumbled somewhere nearby. They were closer. It reminded Lazer of that mariachi band that used to practice on the floor above him at his last apartment, though with less accordion. Lazer always thought their late-night jamming was one of the reasons things failed with his last girlfriend. She was always so sleep deprived, so on edge. Lazer's hearing had taken a hit over the years, so he slept right through it most of the time.

Another rumble, then a loud bang.

"Hello?" he called out.

The room shook as Lazer braced himself on the recliner beside him. A middle-aged woman wearing a dirty beanie at the far end of the room sat up, startled. Lazer looked down at the tube attached to his chest again and gave it a slight tug. Nothing. He looked back at the box and poked at it in several places, hoping to activate an off switch or something. Still nothing. He picked up the device and gave it a shake. Nada. He tapped it on every conceivable part of its surface, but the box continued on with its low purr, entirely unresponsive to Lazer's efforts. A crash from the room over shook several of the people out of their chairs as a larger man in camouflage pants hit the ground with a thud and a groan. Several of the others sat up; one was crying.

"Hello? Papa Smurf? A little help, please!" Lazer called out.

An explosion, loud and forceful, rocked the room again, sending Lazer and his medical appendage to the floor as a crack climbed up the wall on the far side. At this point, everybody who had been asleep was now awake and in various stages of panic. Lazer stood back up and placed the device back on its stand. He looked down at the hose, grabbed it firmly near the base of his sternum, and took a deep inhale, muttering under his breath, "OK, Lazer, you can do this. Just like the time you had to get waxed for that photo shoot. Super easy. On the count of three. One . . ."

Dust fell from above. The crack in the far wall extended from floor to ceiling. A woman near him was sobbing, confused and frightened. Beyond her, two people were yelling at each other. He couldn't tell if they knew each other or were just scared.

"Two . . ."

Another bang, followed by screams. Some sounded human; others didn't. Lazer tensed up and yelled, "Thr—"

The far wall crumbled as a cloud of dust filled the room in a rolling wave. He looked down once more, gritted his teeth, and yanked with all of his strength. Nothing happened, not even the slightest budge. He pulled again and again, furiously with no luck. He coughed and wiped the sweat accumulating on his brow as sets of red dots beamed through the floating haze. They were eyes. Figures moved in the distance.

It was difficult to say who or what they were, though Lazer had no intention of waiting to find out. He picked up his vest from the floor and threw it on, grabbing his aviators and leaving his crumpled, vomit-crusted undershirt behind. He picked the machine up off its stand and tucked it under his right arm. He ducked and hurried to the other side of the room, as far away as he could get from the collapsed wall and shrouded intruders.

A high-pitched whistle streaked by Lazer's ear. Several more followed, buzzing by. They were single notes, all abrupt. *Is that an F or F sharp?* Lazer thought, trying to pin the frequency. A person nearby gurgled as a purple streak hit him directly in the chest, sending him backward and to the floor. There was no time to test Lazer's perfect pitch. This wasn't music. It was gunfire.

More people fell to the ground, their wounds smoldering. Screams of terror were muffled in the dust as people ran in panic. Lazer wiped manically at the wall, searching for any kind of door or button or switch. With nothing to find, he punched the wall in frustration, immediately regretting it. Lazer shook his pained hand and continued his search for a way out.

Another passenger ran up to Lazer. He was a young man, drunk and disheveled with a scraggly beard. He was confused as he ranted, his missing front tooth squeaking out bits of spittle. "Where are we, man? What is this? What the f—"

And just like that, a softball-sized hole was punched directly through the man, covering the wall before him in splatter and gore. Lazer crouched and put his arms over his head while looking back at the wall. The blood had revealed a small circle about three feet above the floor.

"They were short! Duh!" Lazer said to himself as he reached over and pressed the button.

A vertical line of light split the circle and traveled from the floor to a point slightly above his head. It slid open silently, presenting the room Lazer had his first encounter in. He took a single step forward through the exit when he heard it—a growl, guttural, wet, and dripping right behind him.

Lazer froze as the hairs along his neck stood up. This wasn't fear. It was primal—the genetic response passed down the generations by cavemen clever enough to avoid getting eaten by saber-fanged megafauna. He turned slowly . . . or maybe quickly. To Lazer, all time had frozen, and such distinctions were meaningless now.

The creature was obscured by dust, save for the eyes, piercing and red and burning with the subtle ember of a waning cigarette, and its mouth, opened to fangs beyond fangs, serrated and dripping. Its teeth glowed a fluorescent white, brilliant in its bold luminescence. Beyond the horror and the shocking dread fully enveloping him, Lazer knew in his heart that if he survived, if he managed to outrun this thing, whatever it was, that this would be his new band logo.

The door finished opening behind Lazer as the eyes of the shapeless beast rose to nearly ten feet. The dust thinned for a moment, revealing a shaggy, blizzard-white coat of fur covering a hunched but upright canine. The lower half spread out wide with the thin and sharp legs of a spider, moving like fingers on a piano. Subtle thumps rumbled underfoot as the monster tapped the floor with shifting scopulas, searching, hungry. The fleshy nubs near the creature's shoulders were outfitted with shimmering metal hooks. The beast raised one, hoisting a powder-blue woman who was impaled through her thigh. She writhed as she cried in terrified desperation.

The creature sniffed the woman, bit down firmly into her nonskewered leg, and flung her back and forth violently by the mouth. The monster growled as the woman whipped like a set of keys being spun around a finger. She jostled and snapped until her leg detached, sending the rest of her crashing into the mist of debris. The monster stomped around in a circle and let out an earsplitting roar between fits of chewing. Lazer looked upon the beast as its teeth gnashed on the crushed femur in its mouth.

"Nope!" he said as he turned and sprinted.

Lazer ran with no direction. It was flight in its purest of forms—elegant, vital. He hurried into the interview room and noticed an opening at its far end. He pushed ahead with single-minded cause, clearing a knocked-over chair as he took a hard left turn down a white hallway.

It was empty, stretching before him with a slight curve without doors or windows of any kind. He ran, carried on the wings of adrenaline, measuring his current situation against the scenario he always hoped to die in: suffocated under a large pile of naked women. Sadly, for Lazer, it dawned on him in this moment that that was now, most likely, not coming to pass.

The long curved hallway seemed to stretch forever as Lazer's legs got heavier. His mouth tasted like copper, and his side punished him. Lazer couldn't remember the last time he actually ran, though he couldn't remember many things. He huffed and puffed and hacked, but continued moving. He had to. His mind churned as the pain got sharper. Maybe it was time to quit smoking—maybe.

Lazer turned a corner and knocked into two of the little powder-blue people from the night before. The three collapsed to the floor with a thud. Both of the small men stood quickly, angrily huffing a string of clicks, punctuated by a whistle. Lazer climbed back to his feet as the wall behind his hosts crashed into rubble. The monstrous beast slid into the hallway, crushing one of the diminutive men into the side of the hall, leaving nothing but a bright purple smear and a rumpled mess of clothes, skin, and bones.

The beast bent over and drove its hooks into the shoulders of the other missionary, who squeaked out more clicking noises. The multilegged behemoth raised the man up face-to-face and released an earsplitting roar. Lazer scrambled as fast as he could farther down the hall. His lungs heaved as the beast roared again behind him. The sounds of it feeding on the still-living crew member chased him as echoes.

Lazer turned a final corner and came abruptly to a set of white doors that slid open just in time for him to run through them. The doors hissed and slowly shut behind him with a click. He ducked behind a flipped-over table to the side and collapsed, catching his breath between wheezes.

Breathe in, then out. In, then out. He remembered the advice his dad gave him at his first gig. It was a local talent show, and he was ten years old. Lazer didn't even know how to tune his guitar yet, let alone work a crowd with the raw power that carried him on stage today. The butterflies were excruciating, like the overwhelming urge to run away and vomit and hide in the closet. It all came back. He remembered his dad, hand on Lazer's shoulder, looking down slightly as he spoke.

"It will all be all right, Georgy. Just breathe—no matter if you mess up or break a string or even piss yourself right there on stage. Just breathe and you'll get through it, I promise."

It was the first time Lazer had really thought about his father in years. His breath returned, and he slowly made his way back to his feet with the help of the downed table. He was in some type of dining hall. The lights were all off, but the room maintained a soft blue hue that emanated from long tubes that ran above the series of windows off to the side. Nothing was white here. The tables were metallic and black, and the flooring was dark. Tables and chairs were a mess; cups were tipped over with their contents spilled out. People had left here in a hurry.

Lazer crept to the nearest window and looked out. He stopped, removed his sunglasses, and rubbed his eyes. He gazed out into the vastness of space as bits of debris floated by in silence. Deep purple, atmospheric pink, and the orange brilliance of a yawning galaxy that was flush with tiny twinkling specks of white stars populated his view like splashes of paint. He was minuscule in its grandness. No, this was definitely not Vegas.

In his notable history of brain-melting benders, Lazer had found himself in several unique locales. The greatest hits included his neighbors' bathtub, pants only; the trunk of his drummer's Chevy Impala, missing only his pants; and a Tijuana jail cell, wearing somebody else's pants. But this . . . this was the "Bohemian Rhapsody" of mornings after.

A clatter of utensils alerted Lazer to the kitchen that resided deeper into the commons. He crept slowly toward the back of the room, doing his best to keep his breathing as quiet as possible. He stepped over littered trays and spilled food, careful not to slip. He moved quietly, with intention, reaching the cooking station that separated the dining area from where the noise came from. Lazer squinted and ran his hand along a low metal counter for guidance, passing cabinets until he reached the open door to the pitch-black space. He peered around, eyeing for movement, but saw nothing.

He stepped back and opened one of the cupboards. He felt something small but weighted and pulled out a stubby, knife-like utensil. He set it on the counter and opened a second cabinet. From there, he pulled out an even larger knife, curved and elegant, its blade and handle all one conjoined piece of glistening alloy. He set this knife next to the smaller one and continued searching.

He reached into a low cabinet and touched his hand around until he felt something larger, heavier. He put both hands under it and removed a thick chopping utensil with a wide blade. He pressed a round red button on the side, which triggered two tiny knives to come out of the base of the handle. Once fully released, they began to spin as smaller knives came out of those knives and whirred in a blending motion. Lazer pressed the button once more and retracted the blades.

He smiled and stood, confident in his weapon. He turned around, took one step, and immediately dropped the knife, which made a quiet rattle on the floor. Before Lazer hung a large black pan with gleaming spiked edges that twinkled in the darkness. *It would probably make a pretty decent omelet too,* he thought.

Lazer set his still-attached medical toaster on the counter and pulled the pan down with both hands. He turned it and made sure he had a solid grip on the handle. He gave it a few good practice swings, then nodded in approval. This would work. He picked up the toaster from the counter and tucked it back under his arm, tiptoeing in his continued attempt at stealth as he backed up against the near wall beside the open door. His heart beat like it was being played by John Bonham. *Bump Bum, Bump Bum, Bump Bum . . .*

Lazer took a big breath and let out a scream. It wasn't fearsome, but it was loud and startling and wavering in pitch like a tone-deaf drunk at a karaoke bar. He swung the pan into the open darkness and connected with something with a clang. The something then landed on the floor with a thud.

Bump Bum, Bump Bum, Bump Bum . . . Lazer's heart raced. He ducked and reached around along the inside wall, finding the small button and pressing it. The area lit up to reveal a storage pantry with open cabinets full of bins and cylinders containing various colored liquids. The older missionary from the night before was sprawled out on the floor, unconscious but breathing. It was good he was wearing his helmet.

"Mr. Lazer with a *z*," said a feminine voice from behind him.

Lazer spun around, flailing his weapon. It narrowly sailed over Qiti, who even standing upright was diminutive enough to avoid Lazer's spiked pan. She didn't react to almost being brained but rather just stood there, stoic, waiting. Lazer looked down.

"Oh, sorry, I almost got you," he said, his heart slowing to a more manageable rhythm.

"We're under attack," Qiti stated matter-of-factly, her tight bun not even showing a single stray hair.

"Yeah, so what's the deal? Someone forget to pay their tab?"

"Pirates," she replied.

"Pirates forgot to pay their tab?"

"No, we are being boarded by pirates, as pirates do."

An explosion blew the entrance door open at the far end of the room. Qiti quickly turned off the pantry light as they ducked behind the cooking station.

"So what do we do?" Lazer whispered with urgency.

"Just keep your voice down and let me do the talking," she replied.

"Talk? I just saw two of your buddies get torn to pieces by a monster," Lazer barked in a whisper.

"Shh," Qiti hushed.

"You shush!" Lazer whispered back with a little too much volume. "Do you have one of those laser weapons?"

"I'm sorry, I am not a security technician. I just teach the word."

"Word?"

"Of Joseph Smith."

"Oh, you mean like The Cure? That band's horrible."

Qiti gave Lazer the same look he had received from many women over the course of his life—a displeased grin somewhere between confusion and pity. Lazer missed it entirely as his attention remained firmly in the direction of the demolished entrance.

"OK, be quiet. Someone is coming," Qiti whispered.

Lazer peeked around from behind the counter. There, emerging from the end of the commons, stood a bird-man with black, white, and neon-green feathers. He resembled an ostrich with a sharp turquoise beak, a shaved human torso, and slightly smaller but muscular human arms. He was definitely more bird than man—or maybe calling him a bird-centaur would be more accurate. Was there such a thing as a bird-centaur? Would it lay eggs or what? Lazer pondered this as the pirate moved farther into the room.

The man-bird-centaur wore a black bandanna around his head, a ruffled pirate blouse, a red sash around his waist, and held a sleek gray cutlass in his hand. He was dressed like a child who had gone through the Pirates of the Caribbean gift shop with his mother's credit card.

"OK, why is he dressed like a—" Lazer began.

"Shh," Qiti cut him off.

Two more pirates entered behind the first one. They were both hulking bipedal brutes about a head taller than the man-bird-centaur-pirate. They were translucent pink with flushes of red. Writhing, fleshy tentacles arose from their backs as a soft slithering noise underpinned the stomping of their thick, flat feet. Both pirates had a single nubby appendage with two fingers coming from the center of their torsos. They wore matching black leather pants, black boots, and open black blouses, giving their respective nubs the unencumbered space to swing around their matching swords. Also, one of them had an eye patch. It had a skull on it. Lazer thought it was pretty cool.

"We need to get out of here," Lazer whispered to Qiti.

"That would prove to be a little difficult, Mr. Lazer with a z," she replied.

"Just call me Lazer," he said before looking around the counter at the incoming pirates again. They approached slowly as they searched the disordered cantina.

"OK, Lazer," she said.

Lazer turned back. "Yeah?"

"Yeah what?" Qiti asked, unsure.

Lazer looked side to side and shrugged. "You asked me something?" He scratched at his chin.

Qiti raised an eyebrow as both of them remained crouched in a moment of awkward confusion. "No," she said slowly, breaking the impasse. "You asked me about escaping. I was telling you that such a request was not possible."

"Oh yeah. Why not?"

"Well, to begin with the obvious, we're in space."

"Right."

"If you tried to leave the ship, you would asphyxiate," she continued. Lazer shrugged and waited for more. "Asphyxiate means you will die a very painful death due to your cells starving of oxygen," she elaborated.

"Oh, that's not good. Well, don't you have escape pods or space suits or anything?" Lazer asked with a slightly nervous shrug.

"Disabled. Do you think this is the first time these pirates have raided a ship?"

Lazer shifted in a moment of contemplation. "Yes?"

The pirates fanned out and moved toward the kitchen.

"So what do we do?" he asked.

"We are going to give ourselves up," she said, taking Lazer's hand and opening his fingers.

Qiti pressed her hand, which fit entirely within Lazer's palm, against his own. A blue flash of light glowed from the crease between them. There was no physical sensation, but Lazer pulled his hand back in reflex anyway. He looked at his palm to see an emblem with a rose tattooed into it. The rose had closed, pillowy petals and a thorn that dripped a single drop of blood. Lazer felt the minor embossing on his skin and looked back to the blue woman who sat next to him.

"Does this mean I have to listen to The Cure now?" he asked.

Qiti looked at Lazer with a confused tilt. The silver ring around her black pupils shimmered in the dim lighting. "No. This has nothing to do with the popular Earth-based music group," she said, taking his hand between hers. "This will save your life. It will brand you as an employee of the ship and ensure your freedom after we are apprehended. Just please try not to die before that happens."

The pirates edged closer to Lazer and his host.

"Yar, ye find anything?" one of the larger pirates spoke out in a gravelly baritone.

"Nothing, methinks we've gotten them all," the man-bird-centaur-pirate replied.

The third pirate clicked a button on his open blouse, its voice in an equally low pitch. "Any word be on if the asset has been found?" it asked, followed by a chirp and a quick hiss.

A voice over the comm responded, *"Nay, keep searchin', ya salty dog."*

Lazer turned back to Qiti and whispered, "So, does everybody in space speak English or—"

"Who be there?" squawked the man-bird-centaur-pirate, cutting Lazer off.

Qiti gave him a stern look, holding up her pointer finger signaling for him to stop talking. She leaned in. "You are going to put down that cooking implement, and I am going to step out and surrender. I do not want to be shot. So please, Lazer, I will need you to not do anything that may increase the odds of that occurring. You just need to stay here and remain quiet. Can you agree to those terms?"

Lazer crouched silently for a moment, staring off into space. "Hey, where does that go?" he asked, pointing to a small button on the adjacent wall.

"That hallway leads to the bridge. But it doesn't matter. The pirates have captured this ship. Surrender is the only option."

"I think I could make it."

"You won't make it. Even if they miss and you get through, their armaments use the surrounding electrical charge in the atmosphere for ammunition, which is infinite. They can fire until they hit you, for as long as that takes."

"But they only have swords."

"Their swords shoot."

"Their swords shoot? That's awesome!" Lazer said as he peeked around again.

"Lazer, I need you to focus," Qiti said, redirecting the conversation. "You will not make it to the door. You cannot fight your way out and you cannot get off the ship. My plan is the only reasonable course of action. Do you agree to—"

"I don't know. I'm still pretty sure I can make it," he argued, cutting Qiti off.

"It is not feasible. The likelihood of your demise is probable to the point that it falls into the margin of error of certainty, and if that happens, you will be dead, and I will have failed in my mission to bring you to the Lord," Qiti said as she looked at Lazer, waiting for a nod or sign of agreement.

"Agree to disagree," he said.

Qiti paused for a moment, giving Lazer *the look* once more. "All right, Lazer. How do you intend to reach the door before you are robbed of the spark of your existence and sent to the outer darkness?" she asked with a hint of dissipating patience.

"With this," Lazer said, setting down his pan and holding up a small silver spoon. "It's a distraction . . . you know, for distracting. I throw it over there, and when they are trying to see what it is, I nail 'em with the pan and make my escape."

"Bu—"

Before Qiti could finish, Lazer threw the utensil over his shoulder toward the crumbling hole where the door once stood. The spoon sailed high in the air with the gentle rotation of an Olympic figure skater, a music box ballerina, or a well-rehearsed veteran of the pole at Lucky Seven Gentlemen's Club on La Brea Avenue. Lazer played a show there once. He had played more bad notes than usual.

The spoon caught a slight glimmer from the dim lights around the windows on its way down, clattering on the floor as it bounced across the feet of the nearest pirate. The man-bird-centaur-pirate stooped down and picked up the spoon with his free hand, raising it to his large, avian eye. Vertical eyelids narrowed, then blinked, exposing his bright red-and-black pupil.

Lazer grabbed the pan, sprang to his feet, and chucked it like a Frisbee. It spun around and around, spikes then handle, spikes then handle. It moved in perfect trajectory as it planted directly into the silver beak of the man-bird-centaur-pirate. Its head flew back as several neon-green feathers popped into the air and gently sauntered their way to the floor. Lazer sprinted toward the button, clutching his medical toaster like a football.

He had never played sports, but in this moment, it didn't even matter; he was in survival mode. It was an impressive display of dexterity as Lazer leaped, turned, then lunged with a single calloused finger extended. He flew and pressed the button, looking back to see the two fleshy brutes pointing their cutlasses at him, white and charged and emitting a low-pitched hum. Qiti remained behind the counter, covering her head. The swords fired, sending glowing white bolts of energy that hit the wall. The door slid open.

Lazer stood and turned forward, then stopped. He was face-to-face with a dozen more pirates in a variety of shapes and colors, all wearing Halloween costumes, all with weapons drawn. Some of the costumes still had the tags attached. One resembled a costume he himself had purchased about a decade prior.

"Weird," Lazer said to himself as a blast rang out. He dropped to his knees, then fell to the floor, smoke rising from the cutlass of the brute that shot him.

The world turned black for Lazer, who sank deeper and deeper into himself. It was the soft release of leaving one's body. In the fading darkness, he heard a voice, gravelly and wet.

"It's a positive read, Captain. We've located the asset."

Another sensation passed like a wave over Lazer's body. It felt like he was on fire, like a pair of leather pants on the Las Vegas Strip at one in the afternoon in July. It was the all-encompassing burn that silenced everything else. It was nothing but fire, then it was nothing at all.

PART 2

THE UNKNOWN ORGANISM

ONE WEEK EARLIER

QITI PULLED THE FINAL SCREW FROM THE HEAVY METAL PLATE COVering the private server stored within the antiquities vault of the University of Xyzor Adjacent. The plate wobbled as she propped it against the wall, making sure to keep it from sliding down to the floor. She looked around her surroundings, inserted a line of cabling into the server, and initiated the interface. She scrolled through a series of files, ending at one that said "Bakuma Key." She engaged the option and began to download the folder's contents. As she waited, she scrolled through other files on the server.

"Nope, nope, nope," she said to herself as she casually sorted through the information. "Hmm, what's this?" Qiti stopped. It was a file titled "Dex Rotho."

"Mom?" she said aloud as she opened it. There was a list of categories with such entries as "Piratech" and "Off-Book Receipts." She scrolled through the information and stopped. She opened the file titled "The Olympian Case Study of the Unknown Organism."

She moved through various documents and video files and opened one that was titled "Logs: Dr. Borgia Quant." She played the video. The footage began with a woman sitting at a desk with two clear holding cubes before her. She had a slight frame and light skin. She wore a standard-issue gray medical smock and red glasses that were boxed in by a curtain of straight black hair that was chopped even at the shoulders. She appeared human but was actually a member of the species known as the Olympians.

Her species had descended from human ancestors that had been abducted tens of thousands of years prior by a more advanced race. They were genetically modified to be better suited for mining precious metals on a wider variety of colonies as cheap labor. Before being taken, Dr. Quant's ancestors were from a village located in southern China. The doctor had never heard of the Earth-based nation, though in her defense, it didn't exist yet.

The abductors of early Olympians were a race of terrestrial fish that made bong-water noises when they spoke from behind their glass-bowl helmets. They were also terribly awkward for a race capable of enslaving others, frequently bumping into each other and apologizing profusely. Their bodies faced forward while they could only see sideways, making close-quarters maneuvering a dicey endeavor. This aspect of their evolution seeped into their culture, making any type of direct conversation faux pas. They preferred euphemisms and downward glances. It would be their undoing.

The frequent use of gene editing, while enabling the spread of humans across the galaxy, had the byproduct of creating a superbug that turned one's cloaca inside out. With the rapid proliferation of the disease, the fish-people were completely unable to reproduce within a few short years. They were certainly savvy enough to have developed a way to grow fetuses in a lab or some other work-around, though because they were all too embarrassed and anxious, they collectively preferred to ignore the whole mess until everybody died out.

As mammals do not have cloacae, the off-world humans were unaffected and subsequently left to their own devices, surrounded by technology beyond their means just lying about. The first years of liberation were akin to handing a toddler a handgun, though better fortunes prevailed. At this particular juncture, the Olympians had only just begun colonizing the worlds beyond their own and expanding the bounds of their understanding of the universe around them. In her own way, Dr. Quant would make an important contribution to this endeavor.

Dr. Quant looked straight into the camera, cleared her throat, and spoke. "This is Dr. Borgia Quant, chief medical officer on the *Star of Zeus*. Our ship is currently carrying one thousand children stricken with the Ravage virus in cryogenic sleep pods. They are all wards of the state with no next of kin. We are en route to the Eir Pharmaceuticals research facility at the Zeta-Olympus settler colony and expect to reach our destination by month's end. This trip had been uneventful—until this morning, when we found this . . ."

Dr. Quant angled the camera down toward the two holding cubes before her. In one was a small metal pyramid, partially crushed on the side, no larger than a toaster oven. It was charcoal black and had the waves and grooves of uneven fabrication. In the other lay a small creature that resembled a fleshy square. It had a dull-hued amber tone with flecks of gray scattered across its body. It looked sick. Both the object and the creature were covered by a clear plastic lid.

"If you look in my first holding cube, you can see what appears to be some kind of rudimentary spacecraft. We found it adrift while on our course. It contains no steering mechanism or means of propulsion. It did possess a primitive parachute made of an unidentified form of dried moss, indicating that this is some sort of escape pod or landing vessel. What is more interesting to me is its passenger."

Dr. Quant zoomed the camera in on the creature in the second holding cube using her keypad. It shimmered like a prism reflected through soapy water when it moved. It had no eyes, ears, or mouth. There were no appendages, fins, or any sort of part obvious in enabling motion.

"Preliminary scans have shown the life-form to be carbon-based and in possession of a neurological web that is sprawled in a veiny network housed within its stretchy, photovoltaic skin. It does not appear on any database of life Olympians have encountered so far, nor does it resemble anything on said databases. As the creature is still exhibiting signs of life, I will conduct my first experiment on nutritional intake," she said as she pushed a button.

A series of tubes, ten in total, rose from inside the creature's cube, each marked with identifiers of their respective contents.

"Each tube contains a sample—the first being fresh water, the second salt water, three through five various minerals, six through eight are types of plant matter, with nine and ten being raw meat and a live grasshopper."

She looked down and tapped at the cube.

"Hey, little fella, I wonder what story you have to tell. I suppose a good start would be letting me know what to feed you." Dr. Quant looked back up into the camera. "I am going to step out and conduct my rounds on my patients. I will return in an hour to see what, if anything, has been consumed by our new passenger. Logging off."

The video ended as Qiti paused for a moment in thought. She looked around, then clicked on the next video.

PART 3

ON THE MARKET

LAZER AWOKE WITH HIS FACE AGAINST A COLD, HARD FLOOR. HE opened his left eye first, then his right. He sat up and wiped the bit of drool pooling in the corner of his mouth. A single light, dim and yellow, glared down from the middle of the ceiling, its small radius barely reaching the dimly cast metal bars of what appeared to be a jail cell.

He stood slowly and cracked his neck, then his back. He took a deep inhale, filling his lungs to the brim with stale air, and stretched his arms up. He folded forward with a deep exhale. *Pop, pop, pop.* Lazer's body was a symphonic ode to middle age and poor sleeping surfaces. He scratched his stomach and noticed that the medical toaster had been removed.

His eyes adjusted, making out the shapes of others in the shadows. They were huddling toward the edges, avoiding the light, little more than outlines in the dark. Lazer stood alone in the middle, accompanied only by the sobs and whispers of those out of view. Something moved in from the shadows.

A pig, walking upright and wearing fashionably ripped jeans, a braided brown belt, and a black glitter Carly Rae Jepsen tank top stepped out. She had brushed out, mid-length platinum blond hair that partially obscured her dangling gold hoop earrings. She made a slight tapping sound upon her approach, her manicured hooves clicking on the hard concrete. *Click. Click. Click.* The pig stood no higher than his stomach, looking up with the same starstruck gaze Lazer used to get when he was younger. She took a quick breath.

"I . . . um . . . Wow, you're, like, alive! I . . . um . . . I saw them bring you in, and, like, your blast wound was still smoking a little. You . . . um . . . You're really lucky, Mr. Human . . . sir," she stammered with a snort that blew her bangs upward.

"Yeah, it looks like I'm winning at life right now," Lazer grumbled as he patted at his vest. He coughed and spit phlegm toward an unoccupied area of bars.

"I'm being, like, totally honest. Without your teleobox, you would have sooo been dead—*snort*. Their blasters are set to stun so they don't ruin the merchandise, but like, humans are fragile. It was probably set to cellular fortify or something. I learned all about teleoboxes in my medical robotics and engineering class last semester," she continued with a nervous smile.

"My what?" Lazer asked, looking down at his now-naked sternum. "Oh yeah, the toaster thing? Yeah, where'd it go?"

"They took it off you when they dropped you in here—*snort*. They probably took anything else valuable too. It sucks, you know. You could have totally, like, had some hella awesome stuff."

"Hmm. So what are we doing here?" Lazer asked as he fished out a piece of lint from a vest pocket and tossed it aside.

"Well, I was on a class trip when our ship broke down. We, like, put out a distress signal to the district security forces, but the pirates picked us up first. It's OK, like, we'll all be ransomed and back home by the end of the day, NBD. The district insures us students for this sort of thing—*snort*. So, you know, this happens sometimes, I guess. Whatever," she answered with a shrug.

"Yeah? I seem to remember something about pirates," Lazer said, patting his back pockets.

"Yeah, the pirates, they, like, board your ship, take all your stuff, then ransom you back to your district. It's, like, all on auto-pay now. They scan your chip and send you home," she said, pointing to the pink flesh above her hoof.

"Oh, that's what this thing must be," Lazer said, holding his hand with the rose tattoo out to the girl. She took his hand and inspected it, rubbing her hoof around its edges and sniffing it with her moist snout. "The lady who gave it to me said it would save me or something."

"Hmm, I don't know. I've never seen a chip like this before," she replied, turning his hand back and forth.

"So what does that mean?

"If you don't have a chip?"

Lazer shrugged.

"Oh. Well, if you don't have an insurance chip, then they'll sell you on *the market*," she intoned with hushed seriousness.

"The market? You mean like slaves?"

"No, no. Slavery? No, that's not allowed. We're not barbarians out here. *Snort*—no."

"Phew, that's good to know."

"No, you'll be food."

"Food?"

"Yeah, probably . . . Sorry." She winced.

"Oh."

"I mean, you never know. Some pirating companies are different. Maybe you'll be somebody's pet?" she said with a shrug. "Therapy humans are totally a thing now. You know what? Forget I said anything. You'll probably be fine. I mean, like, you're a human! You're, like, practically famous. So don't worry, OK? Who would waste a human on dinner? Right? Plus, that's only if your tattoo isn't some new kind of tech I've never seen before. But hey, it's a bad day for both of us. They took my issue of *Teen People*. It cost me a whole month's allowance to buy that. It was, like, an Earth authentic, you know? Those are, like, pretty rare. Like, what the heck, right? Psh. Stupid jerks." She kicked at the floor.

"Bummer," Lazer replied as he reached into his front pant pockets and pulled out his keys, a paperclip, two guitar picks, a quarter, and several dozen bar nuts. He looked at his remaining possessions in his hand, then looked back at the girl.

"You wouldn't happen to have a cigarette, would you?" he asked, putting everything back into his front pockets.

"Ew no, smoking's for losers. Besides, they're poisonous! Duh!" She sassed.

"Yeah, that's kind of the point," Lazer lamented, though his eyes suddenly perked up as he snapped his fingers. He took a seat on the hard floor.

"You know, you're the first human I've ever actually seen in person. Like, you're a little taller than I pictured, no joke," she said with a sniff. "You smell funny too. No offense."

"None taken," Lazer replied casually.

"Hey, do you know any of the people from video-vision?"

"The what?" Lazer asked as he pulled off a boot.

"You know, video-vision. Music, movies, all the things . . . Video-vision! That's how the song goes. *Music! Movies! All the things! Video-vision!*" she chanted.

"You mean like TV or something?" Lazer asked as he turned his boot upside down. Two cigarettes and a book of matches fell out.

"Yeah! Human entertainment is hella popular! I just love it all—*snort*. My planet didn't even start getting human programming until a few years ago, but since it came out, I've been its number one fan!" She cheered enthusiastically as she held up her hoof, waiting for validation.

"Huh, no kidding?" Lazer replied as he put a cigarette in his mouth.

"Yeah, my favorite is the music videos. I love Earth music. It's, like, what I live for! If they took it away, I'd totally die!"

"You ever heard of Killer Orca?" Lazer asked, striking a match against his vest and lighting the cigarette. He waved out the matchstick and tossed it over his shoulder. He put the second cigarette and the match-book back in his boot, making sure to blow the smoke away from the girl.

"Who's Killer Orca?"

"I thought you said you loved Earth music?" Lazer replied as he put his boot back on.

"Oh, never heard of them . . . But yeah, totally, we all love Earth music in the GU!" She beamed.

"GU?" Lazer asked, looking up.

"Galactic Union. Pretty much all of the planets in a million light-years in any direction that host interstellar life are members," she replied with a wide wave of her hoof. "And all of them use Earth culture in some way. Well, except for maybe the Cloud People of Gomnitak 7 who don't really have ears or eyes or brains, and they're mostly made out of water vapor, so they're kind of hard to interact with—*snort*. I learned about them in my gaseous biology of atmospheric consciousness course. But anyways, like, some call Earth culture a fad since it's only been around for, like, thirty years or something like that. But whatever, it's huge and I love it, no apologies here. I'm even getting an A in my Earth culture class right now!"

"So that explains the English, yeah?" Lazer mumbled around the cigarette in his mouth as he climbed back to his feet.

"Oh, English is, like, the most used language in the known universe, duh." She giggled. "Some races don't care for it much though, like the Eldermoles of Tar, who communicate through a series of elaborate wiggles," she said with a snort as she did a little shimmy.

"No?"

"Nope, doesn't really work for them. I learned about them in my modern dance of subterranean vertebrates elective . . . But besides a few planets that aren't with it because they're, like, total losers, most speak it—*snort*. The Galactic Union even changed the official language to English, so, like, it's everywhere now."

"Hmm," Lazer grunted as he pondered the ramifications while taking another drag.

"My friends won't even believe me that right this minute, I'm here talking to a human. A real-life human!" she enthused as she spun around in a circle, trailing off. "This is so cool!"

This situation felt familiar—fuzzy memory, sore back, groupies worshiping the ground he walked on. It was almost like he was back on that European tour in '91. Ahh, the European tour . . . was a long, long time ago.

Lazer walked to the cell door and peered down the halls the best he could. The girl faded into white noise as she continued to elaborate on her favorite things. Cells lined the hallway as far as he could see in both directions. A random assortment of creatures occupied the jails, none of whom were particularly visible. Lazer blew a cloud of smoke between the bars and watched it expand in a rolling gray wave, out into the wider darkness, getting thinner and thinner the farther it spread until it was gone. The teenybopper stepped up beside Lazer.

"So I bet you're, like, totally freaking out right now—*snort*. Right?" she asked, looking up at him.

"I'm still figuring it out," Lazer said as he flicked at his cigarette. A bit of ash sprinkled to the floor.

"Yeah, you don't look like a leaver."

"A leaver?"

"Yeah, you know, a human who can leave. There aren't many, but like, they're out there," she said with a smile as she leaned against the bars.

"Nope, can't say that's me. I was kidnapped by little blue people," Lazer replied as he took a drag and waved his hand. "They're the ones that gave me this."

"Oh, the Clicklaxia."

"The Clicklax-i-whatnow?" Lazer asked, blowing more smoke between the bars.

"The Clicklaxia. They do that. It's totally not allowed by intergalactic law and stuff, but they do it anyways. That's sort of their thing," she said with a shrug.

An amorphous man-sized bacterium oscillated its way past the cell. It didn't wear any pirate attire so much as it had an assortment of accessories suspended in its gooey cytosol. A hook, a dagger, and some gold coins floated about as a single large nucleus hovered near where Lazer supposed its head was. It was framed in wispy mitochondria that waved as it moved past Lazer and the girl, a quarter-sized dot in the middle of the nucleus staring directly at them. Lazer maintained eye contact as the pirate glided away until it was gone. Lazer looked back at the girl.

"So why did those Clicklaxicans—" he said, getting cut off.

"Clicklaxia, it's the same singular or plural—*snort*. I learned that in my—"

"Sorry, sorry. Why did those things kidnap me?" Lazer asked with a wave of his cigarette hand. "I'm not important or anything. I mean, I was at a gig, then I was talking to this one chick on the ship about a chicken restaurant or something. I got chased by a spider dog . . . Yeah, it got gnarly there for a minute."

The girl's face contorted in disgust. "Chicken? Ew, you should try going vegan. Way better for your skin! But the Clicklaxia? Oh, that's easy," she said, resting a hoof on her hip.

"Yeah?" Lazer asked, adjusting his lean.

"Totally! They took you so you'd join their church. That's what they do. They used to be, like, explorers 'n' stuff, then they made their first contact with Earth, like, a hundred and fifty years ago . . . ish. Something like that—*snort*. But yeah, they landed in this place called Utah, like, where they met all these settler people who looked like they were from that one show . . . Oh, what's it called? That one lady was in it . . ." The girl tapped her hoof impatiently as she worked out the answer.

"*Dr. Quinn, Medicine Woman*?" Lazer asked with a shrug.

"Um. Actually, yeah. Random . . . Good job," she said, impressed. "Aaanyway, they, like, returned home, like, converted and stuff. Next thing you know, the whole planet is Smormon."

"Smormon?"

"Space Mormon. It's its own thing, I guess. I don't know if they're even affiliated with the Earth version," she said with a shrug.

"I knew a Mormon dude. His name was Elder. Weird name. Nice guy. Never tried to kidnap me, though," Lazer replied.

"Yeah, it's more of a Clicklaxia thing, I think. It was, like, one day they were known for the explorer thing, then they were Smormons. The whole planet, boom, just like that," she said with a click of her hoof on the ground.

"Boom?"

"Boom," the girl whispered back with emphasis.

"That's a lot of bike helmets," Lazer expounded, taking another drag.

"You know? I never really thought of that. They probably buy in bulk. But yeah, advanced species aren't, like, supposed to make contact with lower life-forms that haven't left their solar system yet—*snort*. No offense."

"None taken."

"But the Clicklaxia totally break the law anyways. It's not just them though—*snort*. Seriously, like, all sorts of planets have made contact with Earth. That's why, like, the GU had to step in, 'cause so many squatters were coming over, like, claiming to be the creator of the universe—*snort*—so they could get free rent. True story."

"Hmm. Not the worst idea when you think about it."

"It's actually a running joke in the galaxy—*snort*. OK, so how many humans does it take to build a pyramid?" the girl asked, trying her best to hold in her laughter.

"I don't know. How many?" Lazer replied, pulling the cigarette from his mouth and holding it in his hand, the smoke rising in a dancing wave.

"THREE!—*snort snort*. Get it? You stack them up, and they—*snort snort*—ahh, never mind." She laughed as she rubbed a tear from her eye. "Anyways, these days, that's all finished. There were too many prophets and swamis and gurus and culty people popping up. Earth's, like, a stage three nature preserve now, so there's supposed to be no funny business—*snort*. So the Galactic Union stepped in and pretty much stopped all that, but the Clicklaxia were just like, 'No!' And the GU was like, 'Yeah, that's the rule now!' But the Clicklaxia were like, 'Yeah, make us!' Then the GU was like, 'We totally will,' and then the Clicklaxia were all, 'Well, we'll leave the union,' and the GU was like, 'Ugh, fine, let's compromise.' So now they're only allowed to pick up, like, economically disenfranchised humans here and there, and the GU only charges them for a provisional license. It's catch and release only, but that's what they do. Hey! Maybe you were you drinking alcohol? They love picking up drunk humans."

"Yeah, I was definitely drinking," Lazer replied, staring off into the unreachable distance beyond his cell. "So . . . no one knows I'm up here?"

"I wouldn't know, but even if they did, could they help?" she asked with a shrug.

Lazer paused for a moment, going through his mental Rolodex. "Probably not," he lamented. "I really need to get back to my van though. It's custom. I put a lot of work into it. If I'm gone for too long, it'll get towed and then it's just, like, good luck getting it back without having to pawn my guitar—which, you know, I'd definitely do for that van, but knowing my luck, it's probably sitting in the van and wouldn't do me any good in that scenario." Lazer paused and tapped his foot while he thought. "Do you think you could help get me back?"

"Probably not," the girl replied. "I'm sorry."

"What about the Clicklaxi . . . Clickl . . . You know, the blue Smurfy dudes. What about the Clicklaxicans?" he asked with an exhale of smoke.

"You mean them?" the girl asked, pointing to the back of the cell.

Lazer stepped to the center, reached up, and tilted the overhead light. It illuminated a few Clicklaxia huddled in the corner. They were banged up, bleeding, and scared, desperately holding their open hands up to block the glare and whatever else came with it. He released the light with a sigh. It swung back and forth, eventually losing momentum and coming to a standstill. Lazer turned back to the girl.

"So, um . . . girl . . . You're a girl, right? What are they going to do to us?" he asked, looking down.

The pig girl chuckled at the question. "Well, for your information, Porcli have four distinct genders, thank you very much," she said, holding up a single cloven hoof.

"Oh, my bad."

"No, it's fine. My style icons are all female, and you can't really be expected to know any better—*snort*. My name is . . ." The female-identifying piglet let out a series of high-pitched squeals punctuated with a guttural gurgle purged from the deepest pits of existence.

It reminded Lazer of a few of the newer metal bands Killer Orca played with at the Whiskey from time to time. The fliers were pointless—you could never understand any of their logos. *Is your band just called Sticks? There's already a band called Styx*, he'd always thought.

"But you can call me Miley Katy Obama-Kardashian," the girl chirped with an extended hoof. "You do shake like on video-vision, right?"

"Sure thing," Lazer said as he held her hoof and shook it several times. Miley beamed.

Lazer smiled back. "I'm Lazer."

"Pleasure—*snort*—to meet you."

"So what now?"

"Well, cross your hooves, but the odds are that they're going to—"

A pirate's voice came over the intercom from the light fixture, cutting off Miley midsentence. "We be openin' the doors now. Don't try anything that may get yerself into more trouble than ye already be, which be a lot, in case ye were wondering. So don't dig yer hole any deeper. I promise there be no treasure waiting for ye at the bottom . . . Just yer corpse . . . Because we'll kill you . . . Because we're pirates . . . *Yar.*"

The doors slid open with a repeated clicking ending in a clank.

"Proceed down the hallway in the direction the arrows be pointing," the voice commanded.

A series of vividly glowing white arrows lit up along the floor, starting from under the lamp and leading them toward a wider walkway outside of the cell. Lazer followed Miley and noticed a row of ears that lined her back like a rubbery mohawk, sticking out of an open slot in her shirt. Pirates watched the prisoners from fortified platforms above the cells, all armed with a wide assortment of glimmering laser guns . . . or at least they looked like laser guns. For all Lazer knew, they could shoot whiskey, which now that he thought of it, he could definitely use a drink.

Fifty prisoners, most of them Clicklaxia, made their way past the forest of bars to a pair of towering scuffed and rusty doors with copper marks scratched across the bottom of the thick gray slabs. A sharp buzzer echoed out, followed by the sound of metal on metal as the doors opened slowly, grinding. The herd filed into a large, brightly lit loading dock. It was about the size of the Long Beach Arena, which was a mixed sports venue Lazer's dad had taken him to when he was fourteen to see Iron Maiden. It was one of the last times he had seen his father.

A wide assortment of small ships occupied the edges of the hangar, all parked in neat, even rows. There were sleek saucers, shimmering aerodynamic disco balls, and no-frills shuttles layered in the grimy sludge of space travel. A yellow school bus with a pair of stubby, semifolded wings hugging its sides sat at the end, an obfuscated driver still sitting in the front.

The prisoners made their way to a large black stage that stood toward the back of the dock. The pathway to the wide metal ramp was lined with pirates, most of whom held some firearm or another. A rail-thin purple meerkat with teal spotting held a rocket launcher. Its frazzled red mohawk and twitchy eye made Lazer wonder if it was the best one to be holding it. The creature blinked violently several times.

In the center of the stage was a large serpent with blood-red scales etched with soft white lines. They popped in stark contrast to his black pants, black shirt, and black buccaneer hat. Leathery hands with sharp ebony claws extended from the sleeves of his crushed velvet blazer, which had coattails that rode down to the bends in his knees, parted by a thick muscular tail. His head, imposing with a strong jaw, was lined with wide black lips. His menacing yellow eyes were recessed within his angular face, which rose above his body with a winding, serpentine neck that ran down into the black frill of his collar.

A small barricade separated Lazer and his fellow kidnapees from a second grouping of aliens sitting in rowed seats. These were not captives; they were buyers. The serpent leaned into a golf-ball-sized microphone on a stand and addressed them with a menacing piratical brogue.

"Welcome, guests, to the *Jollier Roger*, the flagship of Buccaneer Enterprises, subsidiary of the Piratech Corporation. As ye may or may not be aware, I am yer trusty first mate, Red Scale, second in command to the one and only Captain Izzit." He cheered as the crowd applauded. He waited for the clapping to die down and continued, "I know, I know. We'll get to the bidding soon, but first, we got to do the legal part. Can I get the insurance adjuster from the local district office to claim all Galactic Union employees, students, and any of those carrying thar own private abduction insurance?"

A pudgy, brown, carpet-skinned mole-man with a rumpled tan suit, tan shoes, white dress shirt, and slightly darker tan tie scurried forward. He procured a small handheld device as he pushed his glasses back up to his sweaty face, nervously muttering to himself in an unfiltered ramble. He stepped up to the first captive on the stage. It was the female Clicklaxia who had been mangled by the monster that chased Lazer back on the ship. She looked terrified and was missing one of her legs but was otherwise very much alive.

The adjuster held the device and looked toward the towering serpent before him, quaking slightly. Red Scale gave the adjuster a nod with a grumbled exhale and took a swig from his canteen. The adjuster held the device to the woman's right wrist. He continued down the line and repeated the process, captive by captive. A batch of students checked out and made their way to the winged bus. The survivors of Lazer's ship raid and a few others remained standing. The adjuster made his way through the line. *Click, buzz. Click, buzz. Click, buzz.*

Miley turned to Lazer with a wistful smile, looking up. "Well, Mr. Lazer, um, Human, sir. It was really nice meeting you. Like, you've been super nice and totally chill and I can't wait to tell all my friends about you. I also hope, like, you find your way back home and that nobody eats you. That would suck," she said with a smile, snorting lightly.

"Thanks, Miley. Be safe out there," Lazer said as he pulled one of his guitar picks from his pocket and handed it to the girl. "Here, since you lost your magazine."

Miley squealed and gave him a powerful hug, pushing the air out of Lazer with the unbridled excitement of youth before bopping along toward the school bus, inspecting her prize.

The adjuster stepped up to Lazer, looking him up and down as he breathed in an audible pant. He pointed the device at Lazer's wrists. Nothing happened. He knelt down and pointed it at Lazer's ankles. Still nothing. He tapped it a few times to make sure it was working. Lazer put his hand on the adjuster's wriggling shoulder.

"Are you looking for this?" Lazer asked as he held out his palm.

The inspector pointed his scanner at the tattoo. Nothing happened. He pointed around on both sides of the hand and at the tattoo from several angles. Still nothing.

"Hm, I should switch to cavity mode in case you have an internal chip," the adjuster said as a garden-hose-thick silver probe slithered out of the handle like a hungry snake.

Lazer casually clasped his hands behind his back and rocked back and forth on his heels. "I think I'm good," he replied with a sheepish smile.

The adjuster smiled back and continued on, waving and scanning. When he had processed the last of the prisoners, he gave a nod to Red

Scale and scurried back to the bus. The serpentine first mate stepped back up to the mic, his boots rattling the floor beneath him. He eyed the captives, his neck slithering slowly.

"Now then, for the rest of ye with no chip, may the fortune of the seas be with ye on yer new adventure," Red Scale exclaimed with a thump of his tail for emphasis. "It is now my pleasure to introduce yer host, auctioneer, and the fastest gun this side of the Andromeda, my best friend and yers: Captain Izzit!"

A small gray alien took quick tiny steps to the microphone stand amid cheers. He wore a black button-down shirt, black pants, a red waist sash, and a shiny golden coin with an engraved skull pinned on his cloak like a protective broach. He blinked with flat gray eyelids over infinitely black almond eyes that pooled into their own abyss. The alien pressed a button on the side of the stand and stood expressionless, facing the seated guests as the mic slowly lowered halfway down to its small, ill-defined mouth. A tiny smile cracked as it spoke with an animated squeaky rasp that blasted out of the speakers.

"All right, everyone! Who's ready for a deal?" he said enthusiastically to a wave of applause. "I see some big spenders in the crowd. Hey, Torbor!" He pointed to a lean, pea-green man with clusters of small mustard-colored freckles sitting at the end of the front row. He had short ivory tusks and a bony ridged forehead that stretched back like a boomerang. He wore a dark, tie-dyed maroon toga with purple trim that hung over his shoulder. A large brown sack sat tied off beside him.

"Is that sack full of credits or have you already been shopping?" Captain Izzit joked. The crowd laughed with scattered applause.

Torbor placed his hands open, palm toward his face, and bowed with the slightest tilt.

"It's OK, I've been shopping too," Captain Izzit said as he swung his cloak. "It's vintage. Neat, right?" A single hoot came from the back. "Anyway, it's good to see you. Glad you could make it out. We've got some great product today, really. I'm excited about this batch and I know you're all excited for some bidding!"

The crowd got louder. The Clicklaxia woman with the missing leg was brought to the front of the stage and made to stand on a short riser, propping against her crutch. She was shaking in fear, sobbing with squeaks that were pitched so high they were nearly inaudible.

The gray alien continued, "Here, we have a fine female Clicklaxia, only slightly damaged during procurement by our Vithrax puppy. I know, I know, they can be rambunctious, but he's a rescue." He looked back at the monster, who was at the back of the stage on a leash held by one of the fleshy one-armed pirates Lazer had encountered back on the Clicklaxia ship. Captain Izzit smiled once more and baby-talked toward the spider canine, who panted in contentment. "Who's a good Vithrax? You're a good Vithrax! Yes, you are! Yes, you are!"

The Vithrax barked back with a toothy grin.

Captain Izzit turned to the crowd and got back on topic. "But not to worry, this will not affect her egg output, which as we all know are fantastic with a little salt and Cholula. Very space efficient, and they never complain. Cheap to feed and incredibly docile, so no pesky uprisings. I'm looking at you, Botonortz!" Captain Izzit chuckled, wagging a finger at a pale-pink equine with a mane of magnificent rainbow feathers.

The horse tilted back and whinnied. His bloodshot eyes went wide as he cocked his head. His crushed orange velour tracksuit reflected under the lights above. "You're right! I had to kill them all!" Botonortz called out in manic agreement. A smattering of laughs followed.

"Yes, Botonortz, we all remember. How could we not? It was all over the news!" Captain Izzit yelled in jest to his captive audience, who continued clapping. "OK, OK, but seriously, guys, on to business. Time is money, and these crew salaries ain't cheap. Bidding starts at two thousand GU credits, do I hear two thousand?"

An opaque and amorphous blob of sentient goo raised a paddle with a stubby, moist appendage. Swirls of murky brown muck shifted about under its thin, filmy skin. It wobbled in place like a van-sized Jell-O mold as it belched out a series of audible gurgles. The Clicklaxia woman's eyes widened as she cried out a string of clicks and whistles in protest.

Captain Izzit continued the bidding. "I have two thousand, do I have two-five?" he said, surveying the audience. A female Clicklaxia in a sharp black suit and wraparound shades lifted her paddle. "Two-five, do I have three thousand?" Nobody raised their paddles. "Three thousand? Nothing? Come on, guys, it's not like her eggs'll be any different. If anything, she'll take less space." The room stayed silent save for a cough from the back. "All right, fine. Going once . . . Going twice . . . Sold to the lady in the back," Captain Izzit called with dampened enthusiasm as the

Clicklaxia woman moved off the stage slowly, hobbling on her crutch. "Now then, our next offering . . ."

THE AUCTION ONLY LASTED ABOUT an hour, though time does slow down for those in the midst of an existential crisis. Every Clicklaxia taken from the missionary ship was purchased by the woman in the black outfit. She remained in the back, emotionless despite her successful bidding.

A burnt-orange slug, oozing with a syrupy sludge secreted by the small teal nipples dotting its back, nudged Lazer in the butt with its cutlass. It was bulky but short to the ground, its moist antennae coming only to Lazer's waist. It wore nothing but a black belt with a large silver buckle emblazoned with skulls and salt shakers. It motioned for Lazer to move, leading him to a taped-off square near the bottom of the riser.

A seven-foot-tall grasshopper, brilliant in olives, peaches, and Bubba Kush green, stood in front of him, shivering in his business-casual clothing. The nervous twitching and sporadic flutter of the paper-thin wings beneath the hard casing on his back sounded like knocking on an acoustic guitar. He sobbed as the dripping slug poked the back of his leg.

"Onto the platform with ye," it gurgled with a mild jab.

"No, you don't understand, I'm protected," the grasshopper pleaded with the slug. He turned to the crowd. "This is all a mistake. It's just that . . . that my chip . . . it isn't working for some reason. I shouldn't even be here. My name is Milton G. Hopper. I . . . I work for the GU. I have clearance. Just let me go and I'll give you whatever you want. Please," the frightened insect pleaded. He looked over to a distracted Captain Izzit, who had been typing something into a hologram projected from his wrist.

The pirate captain looked at the slug. "What's the holdup?" he asked with mild impatience.

"He doesn't want to go," the slug pirate replied with a shrug.

"Please, please, you're supposed to let me go. That's . . . That's the rule, right?" Milton stammered.

Captain Izzit afforded no patience. "Get up here or I'll buy you myself and feed you to the Vithrax," he said, nodding back to his pet, who was busy scratching behind his ear with a scythe arm. "Get. On. The. Stage," the gray alien demanded, his elongated finger pointing to the empty riser.

"No, I can't," the grasshopper said, quaking, his multitude of eyes darting around the room.

Captain Izzit looked directly at Milton, blinking without expression as he flashed open his coat. He snapped his fingers twice, pulling the exasperated grasshopper's gaze to the silver pistol in a holster on his waist. "Last chance," Captain Izzit intoned.

"Please . . . Just let me . . . Just let me leave! Wait . . . Wait! I know, I'll buy myself. I have money. I can afford it. Let me scan you the balance from my chip. Maybe it will work with a different scanner. If you bring the adjuster back . . ."

Captain Izzit pulled the pistol in a single quick motion and pointed it at the wiry insect. Milton darted into the air as he flew with a buzzing flutter to one of the large light fixtures hanging from the bay ceiling. The pirates all looked to Captain Izzit, waiting for orders as he deliberated with a sigh. The gray alien waved his pistol in a small circle in resignation.

"Just try and wound him a little."

The pirates all turned and fired toward the insect as he jumped from light fixture to light fixture to spaceship to wall. He bounced and buzzed through the air, dodging streaks of light with panicked agility. The glowing projectiles all came close but always missed. He zoomed toward another flat and silver light fixture. A warm *kapink* rang out, bathing the open space in steel-drum overtones as his legs brushed up against it. Milton hung on as the fixture swung back and forth. The firing stopped.

"Stop embarrassing yourself. You're acting like such a larva," Captain Izzit taunted.

"Just let me down. I have credits. I can pay for myself," Milton shouted back.

Captain Izzit paused for a moment, pondering the offer. "Fine. If you come down, I'll let you bid on yourself. I'll recheck your chip if it's *that* big of a deal. Jeez," he replied with an overt hint of annoyance.

"OK. Thank you. Thank you. I'm coming out," the grasshopper said, slowly creeping down from behind the fixture.

Without hesitation, Captain Izzit pointed his pistol and fired a single shot, the blue beam of energy striking the grasshopper directly on one of his lower legs. Milton plummeted with a screech, landing directly on the single-celled pirate that had walked past Lazer's cell earlier. Wavy mitochondria and inner fluid splattered across the floor in all directions, as the collection of random pirate accessories now lay about scattered.

Milton sat up to find one of his legs snapped, hanging by a flap of tissue. He screamed. He screamed like he had never considered that such levels of pain could even become a part of his condition. He gritted his teeth and climbed back up, grunting all the way. His wings fluttered as he launched himself vertically toward a different light fixture, his leg hanging like a loose tooth, flopping with every motion. A flurry of shots lit up the hanger, all missing. Milton reached the light, screaming as he ripped the flat metal disk from its base. He jumped to a separate fixture, carrying the first one under two arms, swinging wildly as he avoided some shots while deflecting others with his new shield. He positioned himself so he was blocked from below and the side, now nearly untouchable in his makeshift fortress. A few more shots went out. *Kapink. Kapink. Kapink.* All deflected. The firing stopped as the room settled into anticipatory silence. There was no shooting and no talking. It just stopped.

Captain Izzit shielded his eyes from the lights as he looked up. "Look, I get it. You're scared. You're worried whether you'll see your family again. Also, you are most certainly suffering from low blood sugar right now. It's OK, we've all been there, pal."

"You said I could bid on myself!"

"Well, yeah, I say lots of things. This one just happened to not be true. What can I say? It happens sometimes."

"But you shot me! My leg is real messed up. I need a doctor."

"I did, I did. I shot you. But to be fair, you were kinda asking for it. Now come back down here and get on the stage before you decrease any more in value. I've got clones to feed, you know."

"I just want to go home!"

"Well, so do I, but the longer you stay up there, the longer until that's a reality. Now stop being rude and come down here so I can sell you to one of these nice people. I mean, have some self-respect, man!"

"NO! I'm not coming down!"

The gray alien sighed and motioned toward one of his subordinates. He waited a beat as the twitchy meerkat with the mohawk handed him his rocket launcher. Izzit hoisted the launcher onto his shoulder and peered through the sight. Slightly up. A little more. He pressed the button. A rocket flew across the room with a whoosh as a cavalcade of sparks followed. It shot straight toward Milton, who jumped away as the rocket connected. The room shook, bits of plaster raining below, as ash and smoke drifted down slowly.

Milton spiraled down and crashed to the floor near the bidders. He lay among the rubble for a moment—twitch twitch—moaning as he sat up. He looked down to see that his bottom half was missing. Clusters of royal-purple orbs spilled out of his body cavity and landed with a squish as they flopped onto the floor. He picked up a severed leg and looked at Captain Izzit—*twitch twitch*. He grimaced as he struggled to stand but was unable, grunting and squirming in vain.

A shadow cast over him. Milton looked up to see a massive black and gray monstrosity of thick brute muscle, its chest heaving with each breath. Its face was smoky black leather with a trio of forward-facing horns, ivory and serrated, protruding from a short snout above its cavernous mouth, which dripped with thick saliva in eager anticipation. It was covered in short coarse fur that emitted a muted glow, which come out in patches between the beast's flawlessly polished medieval-style armor. The protective coverings were black with magnificent jade etchings of pain and violence that twinkled faintly under the lights. The armor covered its chest in broad plates with matching bracers, shin guards, and codpiece, all perfectly crafted to the beast's form without imperfection. The small giant bent down and picked up the remaining half of the still-conscious grasshopper and held him face-to-face. The beast's pupils dilated with holes like dinner plates. Inside, a pair of small pale-white creatures slowly peeked out of the infinite blackness. They hissed.

"What are you . . . What are you doing? What are . . . ," stammered Milton.

The monster slowly opened its mouth wide and bit off the top two-thirds of the grasshopper's head, leaving the neck and lower portion of the jaw. It let out a grunt of satisfaction, chewing, grinding with dull flat teeth. Milton's exoskeleton snapped like dry branches. The monster swallowed loudly with a moan of satisfaction, followed by another grunt and some heavy breathing. It took another bite, this time getting halfway into the torso as lime-green fluid dribbled out onto its face. Several more clusters of purple orbs fell out of the bottom, landing on the floor with a mushy splat. A multijointed leg hung from the behemoth's mouth as it exhaled a satisfied, gravelly rumble.

Captain Izzit yelled, tapping into his mic, "Hey! Hey! No such thing as a free lunch, buddy."

The beast grimaced at the gray alien on stage as it maintained eye contact. It took another bite, slurping the remaining innards with sloppy satisfaction, then dropping the last bit of husk to the floor. The behemoth sat back down, pulled the twiggy limb from its mouth, and tossed it aside.

Izzit threw his hands in the air. "Fine, you can pay for the half you ate. I'm putting it on your tab!" Captain Izzit yelled as he looked around before stopping to let out a sigh. "Are we done? Do we have more? Ugh. Let's keep this going here."

The orange slug poked Lazer in the back, pointing its antennae with a nonverbal cue. Lazer climbed to the stage as the Vithrax sniffed the air and let out a subtle growl. Lazer looked out at the gathered buyers and their hungry stares. This crowd was officially worse than the time Killer Orca played that roadhouse in Memphis and got more bottles thrown at them than applause. For as brutal as they were, those country fans at least had the decency to not eat anybody.

Izzit's face beamed upon Lazer's arrival, abandoning any hint of his prior frustration. "Ahh, a human, I thought they all died. Awesome!" the captain exclaimed in marvel as he reached an elongated finger into Lazer's mouth and inspected his teeth, the gray alien's short knobby nail running around Lazer's gums. "Who needs fish bait when you've got someone from the entertainment capital of the universe?" he asked enthusiastically, looking Lazer up and down, who was busy gagging and spitting to the side.

"This one appears to be in fairly decent shape . . . although his best days are evidently behind him," Izzit joked, poking at Lazer's belly. The crowd laughed. "But nonetheless, a creature good for blood-farming. You can also use his bones for putting a little extra zip in the bedroom, if ya know what I mean." He laughed before leaning into Lazer, giving several sniffs. He looked back out to the crowd. "Also makes a good stew . . . Sold as is. Do I have ten thousand GU credits for such a rare find? Ten thousand credits."

Several paddles went up.

The armored beast who had consumed Milton the grasshopper stood back up, raising his paddle. "Gorlak the Magnificently Amazing has decided to put this poor creature out of its misery. It has been some time since Gorlak's last man-kabob!" the beast exclaimed with a wailing growl.

"Heh, man-kabob." Lazer chuckled to himself.

"You know you have to pay full price for this one, don't you?" Izzit said sternly, pointing at Gorlak. Lazer stopped chuckling. "So we have ten thousand for the human nabbed off the Clicklaxia ship. This one even looks pretty good, considering the flotsam those Smormons tend to pick up. Do I hear fifteen thousand?" Izzit called out, looking around the room.

Gorlak remained standing, releasing a mighty roar as he turned about in several directions. All but one of the paddles went down. Only the Clicklaxia woman sitting in the back kept her paddle up.

Gorlak looked back at Izzit. "Twenty thousand!" he barked with thunder, a quick spark of lighting shooting across his fur.

"I hear twenty, do I have thirty thousand?"

The Clicklaxia kept silent and raised her paddle.

"Thirty thousand, do I have forty?"

"Forty thousand!" Gorlak roared.

"I've got forty, do I have fifty?"

The Clicklaxia woman raised her paddle again.

"I've got fifty, do I hear seventy-five thousand? Seventy-five for this rare treat!"

"Seventy-five!" Gorlak bellowed as he turned around to make eye contact with his competitor, heaving in ever-increasing rage.

"Seventy-five, can I get a cool hundred?" Izzit said, keeping the pace of bidding flowing.

The Clicklaxia woman in the back kept her paddle raised.

"ENOUGH! THREE HUNDRED THOUSAND GALACTIC UNION CREDITS!" Gorlak screamed as he crushed his paddle in his hand. He roared across the crowd of fellow bidders in the audience and grabbed the anthropomorphic lobster wearing a fancy blue suit who was sitting next to him. He raised the squealing crustacean above his head and ripped it in half, cutting off the creature's high-pitched wail. Milky-white goo exploded from its body as it showered all over the raging beast, mixing in with the smeared gunk from Gorlak's previous snack. Everyone sitting by the behemoth stood and moved several chairs over, getting away from the blast radius of soupy innards. Gorlak turned and made direct eye contact with Lazer, staring him down and huffing violently.

"Three hundred thousand, going once . . . ," Izzit said.

Lazer swallowed hard.

The Clicklaxia woman in the back lowered her paddle.

"Going twice."

A bead of sweat ran down from Lazer's brow.

Gorlak heaved in bloodlust.

"Sold! To the rage monster covered in the entrails of two different people!" Izzit called out as he banged his gavel.

Gorlak roared in triumph. The two small demons living in his eyes burst out like Pac-Men with their stubby feet dancing upon Gorlak's snout. They were connected by stretching bungee cords of nerves and tissue, intertwining like braids going all the way back into the deep chasm of the beast's pupils. They released a high-pitched roar that harmonized with Gorlak's, their rows of tiny pointed teeth like the edge of a bread knife.

Lazer looked to his left, then his right, then straight ahead. "Balls."

PART 4

FOUND FOOTAGE FROM THE STAR OF ZEUS

QITI'S NEXT VIDEO FROM THE SERVER BEGAN. IT WAS A SERIES OF clips from the security cameras on the *Star of Zeus*. The footage picked up from where Dr. Quant's video log ended.

She left her lab and walked down a hallway lined with silver panels and glass. She passed through the automatic doors and was greeted by the subtle beeps of brain patterns and heart rates. She picked up an electronic tablet and stylus and took a seat in a firm metal chair beside a patient encased in a transparent tube. She checked through some of her notes and logged information before leaning in toward her patient.

"Good morning, Dex. Let's see how your vitals look today," Dr. Quant said to herself more than the vegetative child lying motionless in her preservation capsule. She read through the stream of information on the monitor on the terminal beside the enclosed bed.

"Hmm. Levels seem really low across the board. You feeling all right? Maybe the electrodes are crooked? Let's see," she said, clicking on the keyboard. The glass casing slid open, exposing Dex's head and chest, allowing the doctor to check and adjust the smattering of pads taped to her patient. She moved several raven-colored braids and touched the pads; they were properly affixed.

"No, maybe interference of some kind . . ."

A loud boom was followed by a brief interruption in audio and video. When the cameras resumed operating, the emergency siren blared as red lights flashed. The force had shoved Dr. Quant, who caught herself by gripping the side of Dex's pod. Cabinets had swung open, spilling medical supplies across the floor. The doctor made her way to the terminal and paged the bridge.

"This is Dr. Quant in medibay. What happened?"

"Nothing to worry about, Doctor. We hit some kind of magnetic field that kicked us off main power for a moment. It looks like systems are fine. Everything should be back up shortly. Are the patients still stable?"

"Yeah, it looks like everyone's OK. Just going through my checkups. Maybe send custodial to help with the cleanup, please."

"No problem, Doctor. I'll get someone sent your way."

"Thanks."

Dr. Quant pulled her hair behind her ears and checked back on her sleeping patient. The monitor was blank. She tapped it several times with no effect. She paged the bridge once more.

"Hi, Dr. Quant again. Could you send the technician to fix my monitor?"

"Sure thing, Doctor. She's busy with some of the equipment up here at the moment though. You're going to have to wait a while."

"Understood, thank you."

"No problem."

Dr. Quant lightly tapped the monitor in thought.

"Shoot," she said to herself. "Have to do this manually. Great."

She got up and went back down the hall to her lab. She entered the room, opened a panel, and rifled through packages of gauze and splints before finding her stethoscope and blood-pressure gauge. She grabbed them and headed back toward the door but stopped, frozen where she stood. She dropped her items and approached the holding cube that housed the alien flap of skin found on the tiny craft earlier in the day. It was empty.

She frantically looked around, under the table and along the other surfaces. Nothing. She opened every cabinet, every drawer, tossing items on the floor in a hurried search for the missing creature. Nothing. She looked keenly, sweeping her gaze methodically before she saw it, a small sticky spot on the side of the table. She put on a pair of gloves and grabbed a handheld black light. She flipped it on and gripped it over the holding cube.

A streak of sludgy film illuminated, revealing the escape route of the missing creature. She walked slowly in a crouch, following the trail of slime across the floor, under the tables, and into a tiny crack near the bottom of the far wall. The next room over was the neurology ward. Dr. Quant jumped up in panic and grabbed the empty cube. She raced out the door and down the hallway, back to where her patient lay sleeping. The automatic doors slid open, and Dr. Quant ran inside, only to come to an abrupt stop.

Dex was awake, standing beside her pod in her patient gown.

"Where am I?" the girl asked.

"Dex? Oh my God." Dr. Quant exhaled as she raced over and hugged the girl. "Are you OK?"

"I think so. Where's my mommy?"

"Um, we can talk about that in a little bit, OK? Hold on, sweetie." Dr. Quant pushed a button on the terminal. "Dr. Quant to bridge, there's been a development."

The video ended.

Qiti furrowed her brow.

PART 5

THE RECIPE

THE CARGO HOLD OF GORLAK'S SHIP WAS CRAMPED, CLUTTERED, AND exuded the dank miasma of a tour van that'd been on the road for a month. Cages of various sizes were stacked about, some occupied, others not. Winged Chihuahua lizards screeched in their cages between fits of pulling at their sharp silver feathers. A dried smear of deep-red blood led from the center of the hold to the hatch at the back of the vessel, ending in the caked stamp of a four-fingered handprint. Lazer sat curled and contorted in his small cage, asleep, his spine resting between two metal bars covered in a layer of grime. He snorted and mumbled.

A small rock hit his cage, giving it a rattle. Lazer opened his eyes to a post-nap blur, unsure of what woke him. Another small rock lightly bounced off his leg and skipped a few times on the floor.

"Wha—?" Lazer moaned, attempting to turn.

"So you come here often?" a gentle voice with a distinctly English accent asked from behind him.

"One sec," Lazer croaked while decontorting himself. He grunted and shifted his legs, leaned back and slowly spun himself around on his tail-bone, kicking a small container of salt over in the process. A foot away sat another cage about the same size as Lazer's, this one containing a pirate. He was a bright red squid . . . or maybe more of an octopus—Lazer always had trouble remembering the difference. He was as red as a cherry Fender and the size of . . . a cherry Fender, though sans the head and fretboard. He had one bulbous eye with the other covered with a black eye patch. Smooth shimmery skin carried down to noseless nostrils and a strikingly human mouth. He was about ninety percent head, with small slightly curled tentacles hanging freely below his chin. They were thick and stubby with purple rings around the suction cups. He held a small curved hook while the remaining tentacles moved slowly and individually, undulating beneath his boxy frame as the pirate hovered slightly above the bottom of his cage. Besides the eye patch and hook, his only article of clothing was a black bandanna wrapped snugly around his head.

He repeated himself, "I said, do you come here often?"

"Often?" Lazer replied, rubbing the sleep from his eyes.

"Oh, never mind. It looks like no one appreciates a clever ice breaker anymore," the tentacled pirate opined, deflated.

"Huh? Oh, yeah, right. This is my favorite drinking spot, man. Just waiting around for happy hour. Cheap wells . . . So you're a pirate too or something?" Lazer asked.

"Was. I *was* a pirate. Let's just say my employer decided he no longer required my services," the octopus said with an air of disappointment.

"Huh?"

"They fired me."

"Oh, hard luck, man."

"Yeah, I thought I had a career there too. Bastards," the octopus said as he shook one of his tentacles in measured defiance. "I suppose it beats the plank though."

"Yeah, I used to know a girl who beat the plank pretty good, ya know?" Lazer said, resting once again against the back of his cage.

"Well, I suppose any female would beat the plank if you think about it. I mean, come on. It is *the plank* after all."

"That's what I always tell 'em. They usually want drinks first though. I guess the classy ones just wanna be romanced."

The octopus floated, his single unexposed pupil going back and forth slowly. "I . . . don't think we're talking about the same thing," the octopus said.

"Ladies?"

"No, being sentenced to death."

"Don't worry, man, just wear a condom," Lazer replied.

"No, I mean . . . space planks. You know? Angry pirate holds a sword and pokes you in the back and forces you off a . . . Look, it doesn't even really matter, space planks were banned last year. They were industry standard for a while, but the union had to finally step in. I mean, it was absolutely ridiculous how many dues-paying pirates were finding their end in that manner."

"Union?"

"Of course, friend, how else do you think we got our dental benefits? The generosity of Piratech?" the octopus said, showing off a perfect smile.

"Well, I guess . . ."

"You guess right. Those bastards had to know we wouldn't stand for it anymore."

"But you float," Lazer replied, looking the pirate up and down.

"It's a figure of speech. Were you hit on the head on your way in the cage?"

"Maybe. Are you supposed to be British?"

"Ah, yes. You must be referring to my proper pronunciation of the English language. Much more preferable to that cockney, if you ask me."

Lazer paused for a moment. "We talking about planks again?"

"No, my accent. I sound the way I do because my planet only gets British broadcasting. Some blather about licensing or planetary zoning or something. Video-vision isn't too good for you anyway, so I don't really worry about the limited channels. Although now that I think about it, I suppose sitting around on your couch eating crisps is still better for your health than pirating."

"Makes sense," Lazer said, scratching his thigh. As his nails dug into denim, a quiet clink sounded as he brushed across his keys. He pulled the keys from his pocket and studied them. There was his van door key; the key that opened the lock on Lazer's guitar case; the key for the Love on the Rocks employee door, so he could use the bathroom in the middle of the night if he needed to; and lastly the custom key chain, a miniature replica of his actual van. It was painted and decorated with the same howling wolf. Lazer spun the keys around the ring once and sighed.

"What's that?" the octopus asked.

"Just the keys to my van. It's custom. It's probably the greatest thing I've ever owned," the rocker replied, peering into the tiny scuffs and scrapes in the small totem's paint job.

"Where is it?"

"Back where I left it as far as I know. You know, I wouldn't mind being back in my van having a snack right now. I think I've still got the other half of my grilled cheese from last night sitting on the dash. You know, to warm it back up so it's ready when I wake up in the morning."

"You know, now that you mention it, I am getting a bit hungry . . ."

A crackle and hiss came from a small speaker in the ceiling. *"Attention, food. It is I, Gorlak the Magnificently Amazing. We are now entering our final descent. If you would kindly apply the salt rub provided to your bodies, it would be greatly appreciated. Thank you for flying Gorlak the Magnificently Amazing Airlines."*

Lazer and the pirate looked at each other.

The octopus spoke as Lazer resumed spinning his keys. "Well, I guess somebody is getting something to eat."

THE SHIP TOUCHED DOWN WITH a screech and a wobble, settling for a moment before the hatch lowered with the whir of moving gears and cables. Outside the ship stood another of Gorlak's kind. She was smaller and leaner but still gigantic compared to Lazer. She wore ebony armor carved with glittery magenta etchings and had coarse, sandy-white fur that had streaks of black, one of which ran horizontally across her eyes like a raccoon. Behind this hulking wall of flesh stood two fuzzy and diminutive giants, nervously peering out from each leg as they whispered among themselves. Behind them, a soft breeze blew tall velvet grasses in hazy pink daylight with a gentle hush.

The well-muscled mother entered the cargo hold and stepped to the center. She waved her hand over her watch, bringing up a holographic prompt. She tapped at a few floating buttons, which caused Lazer's cage to shake as it rose a foot off the ground. Lazer looked across to the octopus's cage. It, too, had risen upon a set of spindly metal legs. One by one, the cages escorted themselves out of the hold and toward a small gravel clearing set within the windswept grasses.

Lazer scanned the cages to find there were other large captives. There was Lazer, his new hovering octopus friend, and two adult Porkies . . . Porkine? . . . Porcli? Yeah, Porcli. Lazer was pretty sure they were called Porcli. They were bald-headed with wiry white hairs around their pointy pink ears. They wore matching blue jumpsuits with slits down the back. One had a row of hands planted along its spine, the other, a row of feet. They nervously snorted among themselves in adjacent cages.

A door near the front of the ship opened, and a long metal walkway extended down to the grass. Gorlak stepped out of the cockpit, taking a short pause to appreciate his native air as a gratified smile crept across his face. He stepped down the ramp to his female counterpart, giving her a short bow. She bowed in return.

"Spouse of Gorlak the Magnificently Amazing! Gorlak honors you and our offspring with an exotic variety of lesser beings to devour!" he exclaimed in gravelly excitement, opening his arms out wide.

"Thanks to you, spouse of Brubnub, father of Girlak and Bru, master of the realm of eternal light. Your offerings are well received. May the char of their carcasses honor your victory upon them!" the stout female said in the boisterous fashion that appeared to be the way of their people. The two smaller beast children ran and hugged Gorlak's thighs, chirping in spurts of innocent laughter.

"Children of Gorlak!" he exclaimed with a beaming smile, bending at the knees to be closer to their level. "Your father has missed your cute gnashing jaws."

"Father! Father! Have you brought us new creatures to crush and devour?" yipped one of the children, the demons in his eyes peering out of their windows to the world.

"Yes, children of Gorlak. I have done this for you."

"Are we going to turn their brains into bread?"

"Yes. Wife of Gorlak shall make this."

"Are we going to make porky smoothies?"

"If children of Gorlak so desire. Do you prefer chunks or no chunks today?"

"Chunks!" exclaimed the children in elated unison.

Gorlak smiled and placed a hand on the back of each of the diminutive giants. "So it shall be."

"Smoothie! Smoothie!" the children sang while running circles around Gorlak. The creatures in their eyes jumped out of their pupils and climbed upon their respective heads. They sang along with the children in screeches and danced. Brubnub pressed several projected buttons, and the cages stood back up. They lurched forward in their awkward gait, moving along the pebbled pathway that climbed the hill in a winding spiral.

The surrounding countryside was lush and full of life. The clearing of wild grasses was ringed by a dense forest of green and purple. The trees had thick, translucent trunks that rose hundreds of feet into the air. The sky was a soft pink with an imposing red sun that burned close but low. It breathed like embers in the ashes of a cigarette as it slowly set behind the tips of the trees. The cages lumbered slowly, plodding, their doomed cargo watching the passing scenery in silence.

A small castle of ash-gray stone and stained glass windows rose before Lazer as they made it closer to the top of the hill. A flock of birds, black and featureless, careened from the forest line to the house, circling twice, then flying beyond the horizon, their calls echoing as they vanished into the distance. The cages crawled their way to their destination, a large round extension behind the back of the fortified manor. Teal and purple stones lined a set of massive blue doors, sturdy and grand. Gorlak placed his thumb on a pad beside the door. A tone beeped, and the doors yawned wide, revealing a dank cavernous space. It was black, black like a moonless night when the power was out.

Gorlak entered first as the captives dragged along behind him, the cages shuffling but keeping pace. As he entered, his fur glowed white, getting brighter the farther he walked into the darkness. Gorlak's family began to glow one by one as they entered behind their patriarch, giving off a soft aura of electric visibility around them. Once everyone was inside, the doors creaked closed, and the ceiling flooded with light.

It was a kitchen. It was a dungeon. It was both. They were surrounded by hooks, chains, and a plethora of sharp utensils of varying sizes. There were tables with serrated saws and leather straps stained with splotches of reds and browns. Empty cages lined one wall, some with doors open, yearning for new tenants. A stone-lined firepit in the center lay cold, a tire-sized steel plate held above it by chains with fragments of charred bone poking through the soft pile of ash. Jars on a shelf held unfamiliar ingredients: leaves in indigo liquid, pickled eyeballs, a lone toe in clear jelly. The white tile floor had sections of steel grate, bits of gristle and chunks of matter wedged between the dull parallel bars. They appeared to have been hosed down but not cleaned thoroughly.

The cages, save for one holding a Porcli, crawled their way around the grates to a sizable holding cell against the near wall. They walked in, the thick metal door shutting behind them. The cages swung their doors open, tipped forward, and dropped their respective prisoners onto a straw-covered floor. A Porcli fell onto a section of dried grasses with a squeal. Lazer fell after with a thud, landing on a solid section of stone ground right beside a thick stack of hay. The octopus gently floated out of his cage last.

Lazer stood with a groan and a *pop pop pop* from his back, as his spine realigned. He pressed his hand on the right underside of his jaw in an angled and upward fashion and pushed, yielding a few extra pops from his neck. He turned back to see the walking cages collapse their bars into their bases and slide out of a small slot in the side of the cell. The three tenants approached the barred door and looked at the other Porcli, who was outside of the cell but still in his cage, shaking and whimpering, a clear liquid dripping down his hoof. One of the children took a long rod and hopped up and down by his distracted father.

"Father! Father! May I disable the creature before we devour his innards?" he exclaimed.

"Yes, child of Gorlak! Remember, if you do not press hard enough on the light stick, it will not render your prey compliant. Always press, then shock," he said, pointing to the rod.

"Press, then shock!" giggled the child.

"Yes, child of Gorlak. Press, then shock."

The child shoved the rod aggressively through the bars and into the pig's still-quivering leg; a charge of power coursed through it with the *bwap* of a fly zapper. The Porcli's fine hairs stood on end as it squealed and collapsed to the base of his cage. Brubnub pressed a floating button, and the Porcli's cage door quietly opened. Gorlak bent down and reached in, pulling the shaking pig-man out by the back of his neck and tossing him on the table.

The two children grinned joyfully as they helped hold their struggling dinner down while Brubnub tied leather straps around the Porcli's waist, feet, and head. He squealed again, immobile, terrified. Lazer looked on with the hapless stance of a man in shock. It was the detached coping mechanism people experience right before a car crash as time slows down. It was less about avoidance than inevitability.

He closed his eyes and opened them several times, hoping that each long blink might be the one to finally snap him back to reality. Lazer was not here, in a cage, on some alien planet, about to become man-sausage. He was in Mexico, tripping balls, sliding along some filthy graffitied wall in Tijuana with a bottle of something cheap in one hand and a local girl in the other. This wasn't real life. There was no way. Any minute now, he'd collect his senses. He would call his bandmates, and they would pick him up. They would get him. Again. They would do it like they had before . . . Any minute now.

Gorlak stomped his way to a shelf and pressed a spiraled button on the shoulder of his armored plate. It swirled and spun until the entire piece disassembled and turned into a shimmering black octagon no larger than a paint can. He set it on a shelf and repeated this process for his bracers and shin guards, leaving just the codpiece on his blood- and fluid-laden body.

Gorlak picked up a large red apron and put it on, tying a small string behind him as he turned around. His apron read "Kiss the cook OR HE WILL DEVOUR YOU!" in bold white font. He stepped up to one of the racks and perused his options. He ran a thick, bristled fingertip along the fine edge of a heavy cleaver. He shook his head with a grunt and continued down the line. A hide-bound glove with thick hooks on the ends of the fingers. Another grunt. He walked to the end, then back again, pacing as he mulled his options.

"Father, you promised smoothies!" cried Bru, still clutching the electrocution rod. His pupil demons pouted along with their host.

"Ah. That is correct. Gorlak apologizes," he said, smiling as he bent down and rustled under a cabinet until he met the clank of his desired object. Gorlak stood back up and turned around. He was holding a gyroscope whisk with serrated spines set within a chain saw that itself was set within another chain saw. Its sterling teeth wrapped around an elliptical wheel, the inside of which contained two horizontal rings of rotated teeth, one facing inward, one outward. They were glistening and ready to shred.

The children took a step back as Gorlak gripped the handle and pressed a small button on its side. It whirred into life, teeth spinning, spines rotating. Pleased grins spread across everyone's faces—or at least, everybody standing *outside* of the locked, hay-strewn cell. Gorlak stepped up to the restrained pig, who was squirming on his backside, struggling against the restraints. Gorlak sniffed at the Porcli and raised his arm high.

The moment floated in weightlessness, suspended from the normal flow of perception. Gorlak released a mighty roar, breaking the spell as he plunged the toothy whisk directly into the pig's chest. Dark blue blood and bits of gore flew up and out in all directions, showering Gorlak and his family in a mess of innards as they collectively howled in laughter, drowning out the continuous buzz from the saw. The other Porcli in the cage fainted, clanking against the bars on the door before sliding onto a small patch of hay.

Gorlak pulled his saw from the deceased Porcli and held it above his head triumphantly before turning it off. Once the blades stopped, he licked the sides like an impatient child slurping cake batter. The demons in his eyes rushed out and nibbled enthusiastically at the remainder, squealing in delight as they lapped up the dripping slush with their tiny tongues.

Brubnub walked to a counter and waved her hand over a black orb. It rose from its stand, hovered over to the fresh carcass, and lowered into the hole in the Porcli's chest. It emitted a hum as a dozen silver tubes slid out, three snaking to each member of the family with an additional two smaller ones going their respective eye monsters. They anxiously placed the straws in their mouths and slurped with eager violence.

The sounds of their unbridled enjoyment sent a cold wave through the hairs down Lazer's back. Maybe this wasn't TJ. Maybe this really was all happening exactly as Lazer saw it. The blood, the slaughter, the impending sense of doom barreling through his veins, triggering that rare instance of fight or flight. It was an evolutionary tool that had gone largely unused by Lazer prior to the last twenty-four hours. This could be how it ends—just a pulpy mess smeared across someone's furniture. If so, it was in times like these that there was only one thing left to do.

Lazer walked to the back corner of the cell and took a seat on a bare section of floor. He tucked his legs in and removed his boot, pulling out the matchbook and his last remaining cigarette. He put his boot back on, put the cigarette in his mouth, lit it up, and took a long, satisfied drag. He blew a large plume of smoke to the roof of his cage.

The octopus turned from the carnage and floated over to Lazer. "Saying your last goodbyes?"

"More like one last hello," Lazer replied over the relentless guzzle of liquefied organs and bone.

A metallic chirp came in bursts of threes. *Chirp chirp chirp. Chirp chirp chirp.*

Gorlak stepped away from the mess of blood and viscera. His ocular demons retreated back into their pupils as he wiped his face with the neatly folded towel he had stowed beneath the table. He wiped off his hands and pulled a small earpiece from a pouch attached to his belt, put it in his ear and pressed a button on his watch.

"Who calls Gorlak the Magnificently Amazing?" Gorlak yelled.

A long pause followed.

"WHAT? NO! No, he is not for sale! I was planning on consuming his flesh shortly," Gorlak barked as he looked over at Lazer.

Another pause.

"No . . . Gorlak does not care . . . No . . . No . . . Gorlak has had an appetite for human flesh for some time, no deal and—"

Another pause.

"NO! I don't need a new one. NO! Not even for . . . No, credits are of no object to me. Do you know who Gorlak is? Gorlak is the mightiest gladiator of all time. Gorlak is the reigning champion of the Blood Arena . . . No, Gorlak does not care about that . . . ," he argued with the stranger on the other end of the conversation.

A longer pause.

"DO YOU THINK GORLAK THE MAGNIFICENTLY AMAZING CAN BE THREATENED?" Gorlak screamed as he slammed his free fist on the table.

Lazer turned his attention away from his cigarette to the unfolding argument. Gorlak beat his chest twice and ripped a leg off of the dead Porcli. He took a hurried, angry bite, chewing as he spoke, pacing back and forth with a slight bit of juice running down his chin.

"Yes, if you come, perhaps you will be dinner as well! Your reputation does not frighten Gorlak . . . VERY WELL, THEN! GORLAK WILL SEE YOU SOON!" he yelled as he pressed the button once more and pulled out the earpiece. He threw the remainder of the leg back on the table and turned toward Lazer, who took another drag.

"It looks like dinner of Gorlak is popular today," he said with a mouthful of food, laughing as thick blue muck still dripped from his freshly used implement. Behind him, the two children reached into the Porcli carcass and picked out fresh pieces from the sizable cavity, enjoying them loudly as they traded with each other.

The eye demons sat on spikes and snouts like benches, chewing minute pieces of messy flesh, yapping along in their own indecipherable language. Gorlak took several steps toward the cage and squatted down, his imposing head pointed downward, only slightly above Lazer's. Gorlak looked directly into Lazer's eyes as Lazer looked back, deep into the void of Gorlak's pupils. The monsters within the pupils stared, waiting.

A rush of warm air wafted from Gorlak's mouth as he spoke. "Darling Brubnub, would you go inside and prepare the ingredients for the new recipe? I suddenly became hungry for man-sausage," he said with an ominous smile.

Lazer coughed with a snicker.

"As you wish, love of Brubnub," she said with a bow before exiting through a door at the end of the room.

Gorlak pressed his thumb against a metal plate that was situated a few feet above Lazer's head beside the cell door. A short beep came from the plate, and the door unlocked. Gorlak pulled the gate open and reached in, grabbing Lazer and tossing him toward the blood-covered table. Lazer slid across the floor, his jeans offering no resistance to the slick tile.

Gorlak slammed the cell door behind him and pressed the plate once more. Two beeps chirped, and the cell locked shut. Gorlak strode over to Lazer, who still lay on the floor, disoriented. The giant reached to a shelf and grabbed a coffin-sized metal tray, slamming it on a table below. He pushed the button on the handle of his contraption, and it whirred back to life. The children stopped picking at the Porcli's carcass and cheered with delight. Gorlak reached down and picked Lazer up by the back of the vest with his massive blood-covered fist. Slight twitches of static ran across Gorlak's fur as he bared a pleased grin that contained bits of man-pig wedged between his wide, flat teeth. He pulled Lazer up close to his face, his breath hot, like in traffic on the 405 in August with a busted AC. Lazer hung without struggle, cigarette still dangling from his mouth.

"So, human, you are the entertainers of the universe. Tell Gorlak a joke while you still have the use of your tongue. You shall have the privilege of amusing Gorlak before you are consumed. Tales will be told of your sense of wit as well as your mesquite flavor," Gorlak boasted with amusement, another rush of hot breath blowing into Lazer's face. The toothed whisk continued to whir. The children stopped picking at the liquefied innards of the pig to applaud their father's proclamation.

"I love mesquite! Yay, Father!" exclaimed one of the children.

"I love mesquite more," the other bickered, giving her sibling a shove.

Lazer pondered his last words. Would he use song lyrics? Something he wrote? Lazer flipped through flickers of memories of his half century on Earth. Some were blurry; others were fuzzy. One from his mother, back when he was a kid, popped into his head. It was from one of their road trips. It was summer, just the two of them, driving up PCH. He couldn't remember where exactly, but the sun was setting over the Pacific to the left. There were birds. "Here Comes the Sun" by the Beatles was playing on the radio. His mom told a joke . . . Lazer snickered and opened his eyes. He was back in the kitchen, suspended above a blood-covered floor once more. He raised his head toward Gorlak.

"OK. What did the ocean say to the beach?" Lazer asked as he hung in the grip of the hungry beast.

Gorlak thought for a few beats and shrugged with a short grunt. "Gorlak does not know," he grumbled.

"Nothin', man, it just waved," Lazer said with a smirk and a wave.

The beast paused for a moment in contemplation before erupting in laughter. Gorlak heaved in deep, heavy breaths, inhaling the stream of pollution floating upward from Lazer's cigarette. The whir of gears turning teeth continued.

"Hahaha, you are a funny one," Gorlak coughed with a smile.

"Thanks," Lazer coughed back.

Lazer took a long drag from his cigarette and blew a thick cloud of smoke directly into Gorlak's face. The ash-gray plume surrounded the giant's head and hung like smog in the LA basin.

Gorlak's laughing stopped, his face froze. He coughed, then coughed again, but bigger, louder, guttural. A small bit of maroon liquid came out from the corners of his mouth. He wheezed violently and dropped Lazer, who narrowly avoided the spinning teeth of the handheld blender on his way to the floor. Lazer landed with a clank on a metal grate and scurried back toward the cage door. He pressed his back against the metal bars, unable to retreat any farther.

Gorlak grabbed at his throat with his free hand and staggered toward Lazer, then back, coughing and choking in a confused panic. The two children ran up to their father, chirping like birds with worry. He hacked out a phlegmy cough and fell backward, stumbling, his still-whirring utensil flailing before connecting with the shoulder of his son. The young beast shrieked as the blender hacked into fur, then muscle, then bone. The smaller monster gurgled. A streak of blood projected from the wound like a sprinkler.

The other child leaped to her sibling, growling in panic. She pulled manically at the handle of the buzzing kitchenware with no success. Gorlak made an attempt to stand. He climbed back to one knee slowly, drawing in labored breath. He made eye contact with Lazer, who sat pressed against the cell door, polluting the air to the best of his ability via quick puffs of his cigarette.

Gorlak coughed and reached toward Lazer, his thick, massive hand impending. The monster wretched and shot a fountain of blood from his mouth directly atop the trapped human and collapsed, dead. Gorlak's fall ripped the saw out of his hand, leaving it stuck in the shoulder of his child, the tightly pitched whir of the saw now replaced by a slow, churning slush.

Girlak shook her sibling but got no response, her hands now covered in the blood of her brother. She turned and shrieked in anger, taking off in a sprint toward Lazer. Her steps were long and bounding as she transitioned to all fours, her eyes filled with rage and grief and the raw desire to destroy. The young giant leaped, powerful but unsure, and slipped swiftly backward upon her landing. The back of her skull hit the tile floor with a hard crack, after which she lay sprawled and motionless.

Lazer stood and looked around, a small trail of smoke rising from the nearly finished cigarette in his hand. The room was covered in splashes of blue and red, the swirling purple mess conjoining the various puddles of gore that were slowly draining out into the scattered grates. The struggling pitch of gears caught in the mounds of fur of Gorlak's dead offspring continued their low grind.

"Maybe this is a good time to quit," Lazer said as he flicked the butt of his cigarette onto the pile of motionless bodies.

"Excuse me, um, a little help?" the octopus called out from behind him in the cage.

Lazer turned and looked at his floating companion. "Sure thing, man. You wanna push and I'll pull?" Lazer asked as he gripped a bar and grunted, struggling as he pulled on the thick piece of metal.

"That won't work," the octopus said flatly, not sharing in Lazer's attempt.

"What's that now?" Lazer asked, cutting his feat of strength short.

"You need the guy's thumb," the octopus said, pointing to Gorlak's blood-soaked corpse.

"Dude. I can't pick him up. He's way too heavy."

"I didn't say the *whole* body," the octopus answered with a slight grimace. He made a sawing motion with his tentacle.

"Oh."

"Yeah."

"Um, OK," Lazer said, turning back to the scene of slaughter.

"No shortage of choices," the octopus called out.

Lazer walked his way toward the pile, taking slow and steady steps through the coagulating blood. *Shloop. Shloop. Shloop.* His feet were heavy in the muck. He reached Gorlak and climbed up to the center of the felled giant's back. Once on top, Lazer noticed the beast's face twitching in quick spasms. He clenched his fists in anticipation.

One of the eye demons dashed from its hiding place and leaped toward Lazer, its tiny mouth snapping like a famished piranha. Lazer took a swing and punched the ocular minion in the front of its orbed body, sending the creature reeling backward. It flew, reached the maximum give of its tether, and snapped forward, careening into the floor. It shook its little body and regained its senses. It climbed up the side of Gorlak's face with enthusiastic exertion and reached the summit of its dead master's head. It leaped again with miniature ferocity.

Lazer dodged to the side as the creature missed, its tether giving little elastic allowance before snapping back again. It landed and hissed like a snake, bearing rows of tiny teeth. Lazer slowly took off his vest and placed a hand out, as if to calm the little beast. The creature pounced, its mouth stretching wide, eager. Lazer held the leather article open and caught the creature. He quickly wrapped it up, tying the vest off at the ocular cord like a hobo's knapsack. The demon let out a muffled shriek as it pushed about inside Lazer's garment. Lazer dropped it to the floor and raised his foot. He grunted with exertion and brought it down with force.

The other eye demon charged out and sunk its razor jaws into Lazer's boot before he could complete his stomp. Lazer shook his foot but was unable to loosen the creature's grip. He kicked harder and fell backward onto Gorlak's soft, furry back. He bent forward while seated and grabbed the cranial denizen by the base of its cord at the back of its body. He squeezed. The eyeball monster released its toothy grip as Lazer pulled it off. He compressed the cord as hard as he could, getting tighter. Tighter. The chewing motion of the demon's jaws slowed until the little monster fell into unconsciousness. Lazer gave a final squeeze and dropped the incapacitated creature.

He got back to his feet and grabbed the stretchy umbilical cord of the other monster, which was still pushing out from inside Lazer's tied-off vest. He swung the biological rope like keys at the end of a lanyard, gaining speed as the vest whooshed by over and over. The creature screeched in helplessness, its volume gaining or decreasing as it spun. Lazer released his grip, sending the creature careening upward into the edge of the table. It connected with a clunk. The small monster fell to the ground, its tether bundling limply on top. Lazer pulled the vest back up and untied it. The little beast within lay motionless. He gave it a light kick and watched it sail over Gorlak's head and land on the floor with a squishing sound.

Lazer put on his vest and edged to one of the tables from the top of Gorlak's back. He climbed the side and pulled himself up with a bit of middle-aged struggle. Once on the surface, he was greeted by a variety of enormous knives. Their edges were sharp, their metal was glistening, and their handles were as big as bedposts as they hung from sturdy hooks. Lazer crept along the top of the table, leaving a trail of muddy purple footprints behind him.

Among the line of grisly utensils hung a smaller item, like a hacksaw with parallel rows of teeth. Lazer pulled the saw off its hook and felt the weight of it in his hands. It was heavy but manageable. He tossed it over the side onto Gorlak's body. Lazer climbed back down the way he got up, dropping from the ledge to Gorlak to the splatter-coated tile. Lazer grabbed the saw and *shlooped* his way over to Gorlak's hand. He placed the saw near the base of the monster's thumb and angled it within the small fuzzy webbing of skin connected to the creature's thick index finger. He propped his foot on Gorlak's wrist, widened his stance, and took a deep breath.

Rip. Shred. Rip. Shred. Back. Forth. Back. Forth.

Lazer carved into the meaty, fire-hydrant-sized digit. He sawed, farther and farther, tearing deeper and deeper into flesh. He looked back at the octopus, who winced in discomfort with every slice. Deeper. Deeper still. *Zip.* He hit bone. It was dead in tone and hard like wood.

"You got it . . . guy! Keep going! Only a little more," the octopus cheered cautiously from the cage, the remaining Porcli still passed out on the floor beside him.

Lazer worked harder, faster. *Zip zip zip* went the sound of blade upon bone. His progress slowed, but he pushed forward, sawing with determination. He reached the bottom of the osseous matter that gave him such resistance. He stepped back, took another deep breath, and gave the thumb a hearty stomp, splintering the remainder with the sound of snapping branches. Lazer then resumed, slicing his way through the remaining flesh.

With a final pull, Gorlak's thumb plopped onto the floor like a soggy bag of potatoes. Lazer dropped the saw, winded. With a huff and a grunt, he bent down and picked up the meaty digit, bear-hugging it first before swinging it over his shoulder. He cautiously crept his way back to the cell, making sure not to slip. *Shloop. Shloop. Shloop.* Once at the cell door, Lazer grabbed the thumb by its severed, dripping base and held it up over his head. He waved it slowly, attempting to connect the flat surface of the digit with the reader above him.

"You have to be careful to give it enough pressure," the octopus directed.

"Sure thing," Lazer said, a bit of blood dripping from the thumb's base onto his head. Lazer moved about, trying to dodge the falling liquid.

"Also, you probably want to make it quick. Who knows when the other big one will be back, right?"

"Totally," replied Lazer as he looked up, his forehead now getting a run of ruby drops falling upon it. He lined up the thumbprint with the pad and pushed. Nothing happened.

"Try sliding it around a bit," the octopus suggested with a wave of his tentacle.

"Got it," Lazer said, a steady stream of blood washing over his face. He spat out some that had gotten into his mouth.

"That's an awful lot of blood for just one thumb," the floating alien said, surprised.

"Tell me about it," Lazer replied as gushes of plasma dumped onto him like buckets.

"Are you sure you're doing it right?"

"I think so," Lazer said, swinging the thumb over his head against the plate repeatedly. Small bits of juice and matter flung out with every flail. A small drop landed on the octopus, who looked at its tentacle and recoiled in horror.

"Ew, gross!" the octopus yelled.

Lazer paused what he was doing and looked at the octopus. Blood oozed down his body, thick and slow like strawberry syrup with drops landing with a patter upon the tile.

"My bad." Lazer shrugged, looking back up into the now-lighter sprinkle. He pressed the flat surface of the thumb against the reader several more times with no effect.

The octopus raised his fleshy eyebrow. "Um, I hate to be the one to break this to you, mate."

"Yeah?" Lazer replied, still looking up.

"I think you have the wrong thumb."

Lazer stopped, looked at the octopus, then back up to the thumb. He sighed and tossed the fleshy appendage. Lazer turned and walked back to Gorlak's corpse as the octopus mildly tapped at the unconscious Porcli.

"Hey, um, excuse me. You're gonna need to wake up now," the bulbous tentacled head said politely.

The sound of carving flesh followed by the *zip zip zip* of saw on bone in the background drowned out the octopus's efforts. He tried again, lowering to the Porcli's face, floating inches off the ground. He poked him a few times in the arm.

"Hey, mate, please wake up. I think you would be most interested in not dying here," he said a little bit louder. The levitating creature shook the man-pig harder. Nothing.

The octopus looked side to side, then down at his still-sleeping cellmate. "I'm really sorry, but you've left me no other choice."

The octopus floated several feet back and tensed up. His eye bulged as a low rumble shook the space below his chin. He reached a tentacle to his underside and procured a small, smoky black orb with a gelatinous sheen. He rubbed the viscous fluid around one of his suction cups and lowered his tentacle to the nose of the comatose Porcli.

The pig-man's eyes immediately opened. He rose up halfway with a shocked squeal and shot a projectile stream of vomit to his side. With watery eyes, he looked up at the floating octopus and wiped his snout with his sleeve. Lazer returned to the cage, holding the other thumb, still coated in a coagulating mess.

"What smells?" Lazer asked, carrying the severed thumb under his arm like a roadie carrying a box of T-shirts.

"Oh, nothing. Just a thing. Good, you have the other thumb. Let's get out of here," the octopus replied as the Porcli struggled to his feet.

Lazer hoisted the thumb above him and pressed the flat edge against the reader. It beeped, and the cage door unlocked, swinging ajar. The octopus and the Porcli pushed the gate and stepped out as Lazer tossed the thumb to the side. The Porcli looked at the mess of bodies and blood and pieces and gore.

"What the Florb?" he yelled.

"Shh. The other big one is still inside. We have to get out of here. Now," the octopus hissed.

The three made their way to the grand doorway. It towered above them, looming as an impassable barricade. The octopus pointed to another plate-sized reader beside the door. Lazer sighed and went back to retrieve the thumb.

The great doors opened inward with the click of the lock. Lazer tossed the thumb to his side once more and stepped out into the world. It was dark and starless, yet everything was illuminated with the neon vibrancy of a music festival in the desert. The leaves in the trees glowed, their florescent hues shifting along the color palette. They dimmed and brightened and rippled across the tops of the forest with the rhythm of breathing lungs. The trunks spiraled upward like white ribbons looping around some unseen post. The grasses at the base and down the slope twinkled with golden warmth, as the collective glow of the surrounding woods hummed with brilliantly illuminated contours and the flickering movements of life.

Lazer looked at his fellow escapees. "Are we dead?" he asked, a drop of blood falling from his brow.

"No, this planet just glows in the dark. We need to—"

A ground-shaking roar bellowed from behind them. The three turned back to the castle.

"As I said, I think now is the time to . . . ," the octopus repeated himself before trailing off as he looked back toward the forest. Lazer and the Porcli had already taken off down the slope. The two were bounding as fast as they could, long steps, then short, taking care to avoid the rocks and bones that littered the hillside. The octopus tilted downward and sped after them in desperate self-preservation. He raced, passing the Porcli and catching up to Lazer.

Brubnub, fierce in the churning rage of a mother who just lost her family, glowed like a ghost at the top of the hill. She let out another thunderous howl, its echo scaring a flock of neon-pink avians out of the treetops. She hunched onto her knuckles, beat her chest twice, and took off running down the slope of grasses, charging toward them like a fur-laden cannonball.

As he ran, Lazer's keys worked themselves free from his pocket, landing with a soft *kachink* on the ground. He bounded along another half dozen steps before noticing they had fallen. An alert shot up his spine with the realization that all was not right. He patted at his legs and looked back, eyeing his key chain as the rage-drunk beast gained ground. Lazer looked back down the hill at the octopus and pig-man, who continued their sprint toward the tree line. He took a tense inhale and charged back up the hill with all of his strength and energy, over rocks, bones, and uneven soil. He bent down with uncharacteristic dexterity, grabbed the set of keys in a single swipe, and resumed his escape.

Lazer, the octopus, and the Porcli entered the psychedelic forest at a full sprint. Falling leaves swirled about in a dance, twinkling softly on their way down to the colorfully littered forest floor, which, at the moment, thudded with footsteps. They reached a small stream that glowed in bold teal with bubbling froth. Lazer and the Porcli leaped without breaking stride, clearing the hurdle as the octopus flew over it. They curved around ribboned bramble and slid down a grassy slope. Then they ran some more.

In the thick of the forest, they ducked behind a series of boulders covered in vegetation. The large rocks looked like moons with tiny craters speckled across their glowing off-white surface. The craters vibrated faintly, like pools of water with the quietest of ripples perpetually wrinkling out. Papery maroon kelp stretched in bloom from craggy pockets and waved listlessly in the softly stirring wind, their deep pigments nearly fading into darkness the farther they grew from the radiant minerals.

Lazer went down on one knee to catch his breath. The Porcli collapsed, wheezing, the row of feet along his back resting against a rock.

The octopus, showing no sign of fatigue in the slightest, hovered in place as he spoke in earnest. "So you killed the big one. Got any ideas for this one?"

"Yeah—*huff*—your turn," Lazer panted between heavy breaths.

"Me? I only weigh five stone!"

"I don't know—*huff*—what that means—*huff*. But you're a pirate!—*huff*—Do pirate stuff!"

"I was . . . technically," the octopus said, looking away.

"Technically?" Lazer asked, swallowing with a dry mouth.

"I was more of an accountant than an actual, you know, *pirate*."

"You were an accountant?" Lazer asked, finally regaining a normal breathing cadence.

"Well, yeah. Someone has to count the loot, keep records, issue paychecks, and file workers' comp claims and such," the octopus replied, waving his hook about mildly. "I've never actually stabbed anybody with this thing."

"So why do you have it?"

"It makes it easier to punch numbers into the calculator."

"Huh. You would figure space pirates would have some kind of robot for that part, right?" Lazer asked, climbing back to his feet.

"Why do you think I'm here now? Not only did they automate my job, but when I asked for a severance package, they took it a bit too literally."

The sound of rustling came from behind a set of low-hanging fronds on the other side of the boulder. Lazer silenced his companion.

"Is she still behind us?" the octopus whispered as he zoomed up against the rock.

"Where else could she be?" Lazer whispered.

"Anywhere . . . ," the octopus whispered back even quieter.

The bushes around the boulder rustled once again, louder, scraped against by more than just the gentle winds that waved the surrounding forest in a perpetual sway. A three-eyed, four-eared rodent with hot-pink fur and a stumpy foot hopped out from behind the boulder. It looked about in different directions with its pyramid of eyes, as its four ears rotated and tilted, catching sounds as they floated along the wind. It nibbled on the grasses that poked out from between the assortment of fallen leaves and twigs.

The octopus's eyes got soft as the look of dread on his face waned. "Aw, look at that. How utterly adorable. And here I was thinking that this was going to be—"

A massive fist illuminated in bright, crackling light swung from behind the bushes and grabbed the small animal. Brubnub jumped out with a roar and bit the head off of the innocent forest dweller. She spit it at Lazer, striking him in the chest.

"Dude, gross," Lazer complained, attempting to wipe the mess off his already bloody vest. The octopus squirted ink onto the ground, his expression frozen in terror.

"VENGEANCE!" screamed Brubnub as she crushed the headless body of the once-fluffy bunny and pounded its dripping fluids like a frat bro on spring break. She threw the decapitated critter to the side and turned her gaze toward Lazer.

Her eye demons hopped out and parroted her. "Vengeance shall be yours!" they cried with squeaky enthusiasm.

Lazer, the octopus, and the Porcli sprinted down the hill. Brubnub's tiny demons jumped back into their ocular burrows as the enraged brute stormed after them. Lazer glided with long steps, aided by the downward slope of the forest and advantageously lighter gravity. He kept pace with the floating octopus while the slower but determined Porcli wheezed with fatigue behind them. Over roots, under branches, over rocks, under branches, like gunning down the barrel of a neon kaleidoscope, they ran.

"Oh sh—" Lazer yelled, stopping midstride as he slid to the edge of a steep cliffside.

He shifted his feet sideways in an attempt to slow his momentum. Small rocks kicked over the ledge into the shimmering dark blue pool below. Gurgling bubbles rose from the sinking rocks as tiny *plunks* echoed out over the winding valley before them. Lazer waved his arms, flapping to regain balance as he teetered at the edge, desperately trying to keep from falling over.

The octopus reached out with one of his tentacles and wrapped it around Lazer's hand, steadying the flailing rocker. The octopus pulled, his tentacle stretching long and thin. He groaned in discomfort, pulling harder as he clasped Lazer's other hand. With an exasperated grunt, the bulbous red alien pulled Lazer back to even ground.

"Now what?" Lazer asked his rescuer, who was rubbing an over-stretched tentacle.

"I don't know." The octopus peered over the cliff to the now-still water a hundred feet below.

"Should we jump?"

"I don't know. Do humans float or sink?"

"Both?" Lazer replied with a shrug.

The Porcli burst out of the forest with a guttural squeal, skidding to a stop as he kicked up a small cloud of dust. He waved his hooves and caught his balance, keeping from going over. He coughed deeply with overtaxed lungs as he wiped the beads of sweat from his brow.

He turned to Lazer and the octopus. "Hey, guys, I know I've been quiet, but I wanted to thank you for all of your help so far. I think now is my time to contribute. I know about these things. They have a key weakness that we can exploit if we work together. It's really straightforward. All we have to do is—"

Brubnub charged out from the forest with a brilliant flash and impaled the Porcli midsentence with her protruding center horns. A spray of blue fluids ejected into the air, raining droplets of blood across the water below.

Lazer grabbed the octopus by the tentacles and screamed from the bottom depths of his being. He charged off the side of the cliff and leaped with an athlete's clearance, sailing from the ledge and settling into a gentle glide. The octopus had become something of a fleshy umbrella, carrying the two over the water.

Brubnub expelled a frustrated grunt as she pulled the limp Porcli off of her face and tossed him aside. She pounded her chest and barked, the echo of her fury reverberating throughout the Technicolor valley. She took two careful steps back and sprinted forward, leaping off the cliff's edge with a determined bloodlust. She reached toward Lazer with wanting grasp, grabbing Lazer's ankle and pulling him and the octopus down like a vengeful anchor.

The three crashed into the water below with a momentous splash as Brubnub lost her grip. The cold water was jarring but clear and vivid. Sinking beneath the surface, Lazer could see the shadow of something enormous at the bottom, settled among the flittering seagrass and craggy moon rocks. A school of tie-dye fish with stubby fins circled Lazer and sped off, wiggling their tails into the distance. He looked back up to the surface and swam, the octopus's tentacle still wrapped around one hand. Brubnub continued to sink amid the cloud of blood dispersing in the water.

Lazer climbed from the muddy bank and dragged his companion a safe distance from the water's edge. He looked down to find the octopus unresponsive, his tentacles limp and his one eye closed. Tap tap tap. Lazer lightly poked the octopus in the face with no response. He *tap tap tapped* again, harder, with the force of someone who didn't want to wait and see if the intergalactic murder rhino would climb out of the water. No response. He put his hands in the small area between the octopus's chin and tentacles and squeezed.

"Wake up, man. Wake up! We gotta go," Lazer implored.

He squeezed again as a rush of water flowed out of the octopus's underside like an emptying sponge. The floaty creature immediately inflated with air and let out a series of violently hoarse coughs. Small droplets of water expelled from his mouth, his tentacle loosening as he looked up at Lazer.

"Did we die?" the octopus asked, dazed.

"Not yet. Maybe soon. But not yet," Lazer replied as he shook his head no, then yes, then no once more.

Brubnub leaped from the water and landed on the bank, letting out another earthshaking roar. She banged her chest twice and bounded toward them, eyes bloodshot, fur dripping, a streak of molten rage caked in the blood of lesser beings. She leaped, horns forward and hands out, eager to destroy, her rage all-encompassing and pure. Her eye demons, howling from their burrows, gnashed their little jaws in anticipation. It was now, in this moment in time, that Lazer wished he'd said yes to that hunting invite he got from Ted Nugent that one night at the Rainbow Room.

A crack from the sky was followed by an earsplitting boom. A bright beam of light flew from behind Lazer and the octopus and hit Brubnub directly in the chest, punching a snare-drum-sized hole through her body. She flew back to where the water met the bank and landed in the mud, dead. Lazer turned around, then back to the octopus.

"Hey, what stops a charging rhino?" Lazer asked.

"Debt?" the octopus replied, still weak.

"Ha. Yeah, I guess. But also . . ."

Lazer picked up the octopus and turned him around. An orb-shaped ship, blinking blue and white, descended from the clouds. Rows of yellow lights zoomed around the base as it touched down in a small clearing next to them, lowering to just above the ground.

"Lasers kill charging rhinos. Lasers, man," he said, pointing to the sizable sets of guns at the front of the house-sized ship. "Get it? Funny, right? High five."

The octopus ignored Lazer's request for skin, preferring to give himself a shake and wring out some additional water from his porous skin. "I don't get it."

"My name is Lazer."

"Oh."

"With a *z*."

"Yeah, would have made more sense."

"Maybe I should have mentioned that first."

"Eh, we got busy. I'm Streek, by the way," the floating octopus said, holding out one of his nubs.

"Pleasure," Lazer replied, shaking the extended tentacle.

The hatch on the ship lowered with an exhaling hiss. The Clicklaxia woman in the fitted black suit from the auction stepped down a golden set of stairs. "Boss has some business with you. Please come aboard," she said without fanfare.

Lazer shrugged. "Depends. Are you going to eat me?"

"No," the woman said with a stone face.

"Can you take me back to my van?"

"It can be arranged," the woman replied.

Lazer thought for a moment. "Works for me."

He followed the woman up the stairs. Streek dropped his hook into the grass, pulled off his bandanna and eye patch, and cast those aside as well. He wrung himself one last time and followed the two aboard.

Behind them, a meaty barbed tongue, deep purple with a filmy sheen, slithered like an anaconda from the water and wrapped around one of the legs on Brubnub's smoldering corpse. It gave a quick tug, then slowly dragged the small giant back into the water, down into the unseen depths of the crystal blue pool, to take part in one final recipe as the creatures in her eyes gurgled their way into oblivion.

PART 6

RAISED FROM THE DEAD

QITI SCROLLED TO THE NEXT VIDEO IN THE FILE ON THE UNIVERSITY'S secret server, though before she clicked it, she paused. Her ear perked up. She heard a sound, faint but approaching. She slowly unplugged from the server and backed away silently. Footsteps, close by, the unmistakable scuff of a security officer's boot against concrete. Qiti ducked behind a nearby support column. She peeked around for a quick look; there was no one. She turned back and immediately dodged a swinging shock baton.

She stumbled back into a fighting stance, resetting herself and sizing up her opponent. Before her stood a security guard for the University of Xyzor Adjacent. He was an Olympian, stocky and short, though still a foot taller than Qiti, wearing an all-black uniform with a utility belt that held an array of less than lethal devices. He waved his shock baton with aggressive posture. Qiti ducked and dodged the attacks, blocking another before disarming the guard and taking his weapon.

The security guard jumped back, reaching for his communicator. "Command—"

Qiti moved in fast, swinging the baton over his head, cracking it down the middle of his skull, splitting his helmet in two. The guard collapsed, his leg twitching. Qiti wiped the blood from her hand on the security officer's uniform and picked up his comm.

She spoke, but used the exact voice of the now-deceased security guard. "All clear down here in the vault. I'm going to make another round back up top."

"Copy that."

Qiti dropped the comm and went back to the download; it was only halfway complete.

She returned to the files of the *Star of Zeus* and clicked on the next entry. It was more security camera footage, this time from a meeting room with three people standing around a metal table. There was a stout, middle-aged woman with tight blond braids, wearing a dark blue soldier uniform, a younger man in a finely tailored suit, and Dr. Quant. They were engaged in a heated discussion while the recently revived Dex played with a basket of toys in an adjacent room behind a one-way mirror.

The man in the suit paced back and forth, tapping on his chin. "This is bad," he said with a nervous frustration.

"What do you mean, bad?" Dr. Quant asked, taken aback.

"What do you mean, what do I mean? She's going to throw the whole study. You know how long it took to put this whole trial together? I've spent years as project director of this study, putting the pieces in place. Years!"

"Res, we've witnessed a miracle here. This girl has been practically raised from the dead," Dr. Quant said to the panicking corporate representative.

"The government doesn't just let you rent orphans, lady. The gears need to get greased, and grease dries up. A lot of money went into putting all of these kids on this ship. We don't get this chance twice."

"Wait, so a little girl wakes up after being in a coma for years—the first time this has ever happened in the history of this disease, by the way— and you want to cry about logistics?"

"Damn right I do! If you have kids waking up on the ride over, how can we say that the treatments are responsible for any positive outcomes? We can't. This whole thing is instantly sharznards!"

"You don't have to use that language."

"People, calm down," the woman in the uniform interjected. "We'll monitor the girl and maintain data collection. We're only three weeks out. We're almost there, and right now we're getting off track. So please, Doctor, what happened?"

"Yes, Captain, like I said, there was the shake and the power outage. Dex and the other patients were still asleep when I went to get some equipment from the next room. When I returned, she was awake and asking for her mother."

"Isn't her mother dead?" Res asked, calming down slightly.

"Her whole family is dead. All of these kids' families are dead. Their whole planet was hit really hard. I'm sure you care a whole lot about that," Dr. Quant replied, her reply dripping with passive aggression.

Res rolled his eyes.

"Do you think the interference had something to do with her waking up?" the captain asked, getting them back on track.

"Ooh! Good thinking, Captain Ponn, if there were unnatural phenomena, maybe we can strike her from the study," Res exclaimed with the spark of optimism.

"But wouldn't its very existence in and of itself endanger your study?" Dr. Quant replied.

Res rolled his eyes. "Ugh, you're right. I feel like I've been kicked in the orbs."

"Mr. Voland. Again, language," Dr. Quant reminded.

"Fine. Sorry," the corporate rep said as he threw up his hands and took a seat.

Dr. Quant turned back to the captain. "No. I don't believe it was from the pulse. None of the other patients showed any signs of recovery on their post-event scans. It was only Dex . . . However—"

"However what?" the captain asked with cautious interest.

"The biological sample we found in that piece of blinking debris we pulled from outside the ship. It's . . . missing."

"When you say missing . . . ," Res Voland asked as he leaned in.

"I mean it escaped from its enclosure during the power outage and I don't know where it is."

"Great! So now we have a miracle child throwing my study and an unidentified alien slithering around the ship. Awesome. Captain Ponn, got any black holes you can steer us into so I can just end it already?" the rep ranted.

Captain Ponn ignored him. "The last time you saw it was when the power went out?"

"Yes."

"What is this thing exactly?" she asked.

Dr. Quant swiped at her tablet several times, bringing up a picture of the organism and handed it to the captain. "I'm not sure. There isn't any record of it anywhere in the logs. I don't know where it's from, what it eats, how smart it is, or most importantly, if it's dangerous. It could have been an inert stowaway on a larger vessel that broke up in space . . . or it could have gotten itself here on its own accord."

"Why did you bring this thing aboard again?" Res Voland asked the captain.

"It's charter protocol to answer distress signals. The blinking from the piece of debris qualified as such. But having said that, we need to find this thing—now," the captain said, setting the tablet on the table and pulling out her sidearm.

"What, are you just going to kill it?" the doctor asked, indignant.

"If it comes to that."

"I'm with her," Res Voland chimed in, pointing at the captain.

"But we don't even know what it is," the doctor argued.

"That's kind of the point!" the rep yipped back.

Captain Ponn leaned in toward the doctor. "We are on the final leg of a very long trip. We have a crew of a dozen and a thousand sleeping kids."

"Nine hundred and ninety-nine, really," Res zinged.

"And one who woke up," the doctor said, almost to herself, looking back through the mirror at the child who busied herself with a stuffed horse.

"Indeed. And more important things to consider than your new discovery. Now, let's go to the lab," the captain said as she cocked her gun.

PART 7

A DEEPER SHADE OF RED

PINPRICK LIGHTS TWINKLED IN THE DARKNESS, STRETCHING BEYOND the series of porthole windows above Lazer's head. The soft white orbs that floated along the ceiling bequeathed a gentle illumination upon the lavish splashes of teals, purples, and golds in the ultramodern lobby of the craft. Lazer had showered and changed his clothes, eaten a breakfast burrito provided by his host, and downed several glasses of water and a cup of coffee. He felt fresh and relaxed for the first time since the abduction. It also felt good to finally be in a place where he wasn't being chased by something angry, hungry, or hangry. The Clicklaxia woman had incinerated Lazer's outfit and replaced it with an identical one using a 3D printer, the same one that made his custom breakfast order. She even made a new white undershirt to replace the one left back on the Clicklaxia ship.

Lazer relaxed on a plush plum sofa, squinting his way through a magazine full of pictures. Streek floated above the seat beside him, holding a copy of *Sunset Distortion: Galactic Edition* in his tentacles. The cover featured a muscled Viking in a rock pose while holding a black V guitar that shot a bolt of lightning into the air. The headline read "STEED: Behind the Scenes with the Demigod behind the Summer's Biggest Smash Single!"

The Clicklaxia from earlier entered the room while they read. "It will be just a few more minutes. Would you care for any more refreshments?" she asked politely.

"I'm good," Lazer said, giving a thumbs-up without looking up.

Streek replied with a more formal, "No thank you, miss."

The Clicklaxia woman gave a slight nod and exited the room, the door sliding shut behind her. Lazer picked up his cup, took a sip, and swished the water around his mouth and through the small spaces between his teeth.

Streek lowered his magazine to below his eyes. "So I never asked, but how did someone like you end up on Gorlak's shopping list?"

Lazer swallowed and cleared his throat. "Gorlak?" he asked as he set his cup on the table, next to a thin metal coaster.

"Yeah, Gorlak, you know, the giant monster that was just about to eat you . . . Kept referring to himself as Gorlak . . . Unfortunate death from smoking . . . Predilection toward large sharp objects . . . Landlord to ravenous eye goblins," Streek continued as he raised the fleshy muscle above his eye. "Ring any bells?"

"Oh, right. That guy," Lazer said with a chuckle, shaking his head. "What an asshole, right?"

Streek picked up Lazer's drink and set it on the coaster. "Yes, that Gorlak. It's not like you know any other Gorlaks, do you?" he sassed as he held a tentacle to his face, pantomiming a phone. "Hello? Hello? Oh, Gorlak the Magnificently Amazing? Sorry, I was trying to reach Gorlak the Misshapen and Unfortunate. My apologies . . . Oh, yes, the family is fine, fine, thank you for asking. Little Billy is doing great with his studies . . . Yes. Yes. He's been working quite hard. Oh, what's that? Yes, sadly, he's still a little traumatized from that incident with the double-peniied space leeches, but the doctor said the loss of vision should only be temporary." The floating octopus looked back at Lazer with a large dose of side-eye.

Lazer shrugged. "Yeah, I don't know, man. I was playing a gig and I drank some, then I woke up and there was this big white dog that was also a spider who was eating a bunch of people. And then that Gorlak guy—he ate some people. And now here we are, and I'm just hoping whoever owns this ship is a vegetarian," he replied as he sifted through several magazines. "I don't know what there is to do about it honestly. You gotta go with the flow, you know what I mean? Shoot, you're a talking octopus."

Streek tilted his head after a few beats of silence. "What's an octopus?" he asked.

Lazer stopped sifting and looked back. "It's kinda like you, but with less face," he said, moving his palm in a circle in front of him.

Lazer picked up a magazine and set it on his lap. It read Oozeweek:

News for Ooze, by Ooze in wobbly red font across the top. The cover depicted a gelatinous algae-green blob who was wearing a boxy blue suit with a matching fedora, a crisp white dress shirt, and a light red tie. It was featureless, but in the general shape of a man, possessing a head, arms, legs, a torso, and such. Across the bottom, a caption read, "Council Member Zeb and His Plan to Dismantle the GU. Exclusive Interview!"

Lazer set it down and picked up a different magazine. *Space People* featured several paparazzi photos of Kim Kardashian. "What Did Kim's Digestive Bacteria Eat for Lunch Yesterday? Story on Page Five!" Lazer set it to the side and looked down at the next periodical. His features rose in curiosity.

"Hot Naked Amoeba Action!"

Lazer picked up the magazine and opened it, thumbing through several pages until he reached a foldout section. He opened a page that unfurled like a pinup poster, but there was more; he folded an extra page down, then an extra page to the right. The top page also opened leftward, then that one folded out left again, then another page went down from there. Lazer rubbed his chin and moved the middle page out one space to the right, then two spaces up, then one more space to the right, with the farthermost section flopping over slightly. He held the unfolded mess of pages, squinting, struggling to make sense of what he was looking at.

Streek leaned in, took hold of several pages, and tilted them at a forty-five-degree angle. Lazer looked at Streek, then back at the pages, then back to Streek one last time before giving him a nod of approval.

The Clicklaxia woman entered the room. "Boss is ready for you now," she said.

Lazer nodded and folded the pages back, messily and out of sequence. "No. That's not right," he muttered under his breath, folding one of the end pages back and forth.

"No, no, it goes like this," Streek butted in, reopening a page and folding a different section under it.

"No, that's not right either, man," Lazer replied, pulling the pages a little closer to him.

"What do you mean, that's not right?" Streek said with growing incredulity, raising his voice a little while pulling the pages in his direction. "It's fold, turn, fold, fold, turn, fold, turn, fold, fold!"

"Are you sure? I thought we folded it this way before we turned, then fold, fold, turn, fold, fold, turn, fold," Lazer replied, pulling the pages back once more.

"I'm positive! Just give it to me. You're doing it wro—"

In an instant, the magazine in their hands disappeared, turning into a small black disc that fell softly onto the carpet. The magazines on the table had all reverted to rounded plastic as well.

"What the what?" Lazer exclaimed, startled, looking at the Clicklaxia woman who had her pointer finger outward, presumably pressing an invisible button.

"You didn't think those were made out of trees, did you?" she asked flatly, turning and walking through the open entrance. Lazer and Streek got up and followed the woman down a hall to a set of ornate gold doors. There was a seal affixed in the center between them, the same rose with a thorn logo that was etched into Lazer's palm.

The Clicklaxia woman waved her hand as a circle in her glove glowed a soft blue. The doors opened inward, bisecting the flower. She waited as Lazer and Streek entered into an office. It was comfortably minimalist, walled in dark panels with golden edges that bordered lines of halogenous lights running along the floor and ceiling. Before them were two metal chairs with soft purple cushions. They sat down in front of an oval ring that stood low to the ground with a thin band of horizontal glass that wrapped along the interior like a hollowed-out coffee table. A faint ball of smooth white light hovered in the open center, suspended in nothing but the air around it. It was a logo; it said Piratech.

Across the ring sat a gracefully aged woman in a high-backed chair that twisted upward into thorny curls. She was human but not. An Olympian. Her beautiful chestnut features twinkled with rose and gold freckles that splashed across her nose and cheeks. Her hair, a tight black angular frizz, jutted backward like an Egyptian queen. She wore a fitted black pantsuit with thin white pinstripes that shimmered under the light, giving length to her already lean frame. A high collar popped up in the back in an arc with waving wisps of smoke emanating from the base like a video on loop. Fine rings with precious stones lined her fingers, hanging with the weight of their value. Behind her, two muscular Clicklaxia women held sleek gray rifles in watchful silence. Their boss, attuned yet comfortable in her fancy chair, leaned forward.

"I am impressed, and I am not someone who is impressed often," she said with a wide grin.

"Cool," Lazer responded as he took another sip of his water. He set the glass back down beside the metal coaster on the thin rim in front of him.

The woman stopped talking and looked at Lazer with an emotionless stare, waiting. After a few moments, she waved at one of her guards, who approached the table, picked up the drink, set it on the available coaster, and wiped off the faint collection of droplets from the glass surface. Streek bit his lip and shrugged in a silent apology.

The guard reclaimed her position as the woman continued, "Most humans who make it off of Earth don't live very long—what between your weak fleshy bodies and penchant for suffocating in most atmospheres. Yet here you are, sitting before me, yet to be consumed by the unquenchable maw of the universe. My name Dex Rotho. I am the proprietor of this vessel and the organization that owns it. What name do you go by?"

"Lazer," he replied with a wave.

"Are you a proficient marksman?"

"Only with the ladies." He winked with a finger gun.

"Right. And your friend?" she asked, bringing her attention to the timid octopus.

"Hello, my name is Streek. Um, actually, until very recently I worked for you, ma'am."

"I see. Were you crew aboard the *Jollier Roger*?"

"Yes, ma'am. Accounting department."

"Were you involved in or do you know anything about the plot against me?"

"No, ma'am."

"Did you sign off on the proper severance forms?"

"Not exactly, ma'am."

Dex sighed. "OK. After this, I'll put you in touch with HR," she said as she pressed an invisible button on the arm of her chair. "Karen?"

"*Yes, ma'am?*" asked a voice over the intercom.

"Prepare an exit interview for a former associate."

"*Right away, ma'am.*"

"Now then, on to more pressing matters," Dex said, turning her attention back to her guests. "A recent turn of events has left me shy a piece of property. You, my dear Lazer, have the capacity to help me find it. In exchange for your cooperation, I will provide you and your friend with passage back to the planet of your choosing and fair payment for services rendered."

"So you can take me back to my van?" Lazer asked.

"Indeed," Dex replied as Lazer nodded with simmering excitement. "But first, you must do something for me."

Lazer slid back in his chair. He propped his ankle on his opposite knee while leaning toward one of the armrests. "I don't know, I'm not exactly the best when it comes to, you know, doing stuff," he replied.

"Oh, but you've already done so much."

"Like what?"

"I will tell you all about it if you agree to my terms—compensation and a ride home for your assistance. Do we have a deal?" she asked.

Streek's brow furrowed. "Could you spell out the terms of the—"

"Yeah sure, no problem," Lazer said, cutting off Streek as he stood and stretched his open hand across the table.

Dex snapped her fingers as one of her guards approached Lazer and generated a holographic form projected from the palm of her glove.

"Please sign and initial the liability release form," she said. Lazer signed with his finger on the line. Streek sighed and followed Lazer's lead. "Excellent. Now, to begin, you must first give me your hand bearing Qiti's mark."

Lazer looked down at the rose tattoo and held it to his host. "This one?" he asked, pulling his hand back to examine it.

"Considering how you are the only one on that side of the table with hands, I would say yes, that would be the one."

The other bodyguard approached Lazer, holding a small black cloth, which she draped across his palm. A slight buzz reverberated through the fabric as it melted into the contours of his hand, seeping with purpose. It wrapped around his fingers and formed taut into the shape of a glove. Its adherence to every nuanced line felt like a second layer of skin as a faint blue light flashed and then disappeared.

"Cool," Lazer said, admiring his new accessory. "What is it?"

"This is a product I am developing called the LE drive, short for liquid eye. It's a silicone-based smart substance that can mold into any shape. A substantial leap from my current model, it processes, stores, and transmits data while interfacing with any type of technology it comes into contact with. When it is activated, you can read writing in a language you don't know, control programmed mechanical functions remotely, or in your case, have an entire conversation over the course of a simple handshake."

"Can it help me play guitar faster?"

"It can do many things."

"You don't say . . ."

Dex waved her hand as the hovering light within the table expanded into a projection of star clusters, twinkling dots hanging ornamentally amid floating galaxies in three dimensions. Its rendering was breathtaking and alive, like the first time Lazer looked out the window of the Clicklaxia ship . . . or that time Lazer and his bandmates ate edibles at the Long Beach aquarium.

Dex cleared her throat. "Two days ago, one of my transport ships, disguised as a missionary vessel, was returning from a successful covert mission while carrying a very valuable piece of technology. The ship, which you yourself were a passenger on, was raided and captured by Captain Izzit, a once top-performing employee in Piratech's privateering division who has now gone rogue. I believe his betrayal was motivated by a desire to acquire my new artificial intelligence and the information contained therein. It is a prototype called the Quantum Interception and Translation Interface, but you would better know her as Qiti," she said as she brought up a holographic representation of the blue woman.

Lazer scratched his chin. "Wait, so she's not real?" he asked in surprise.

"Of course she's real. Just not organic."

"Like expensive fruit?"

"Like an expensive computer. Please keep up." Dex tapped her finger as the picture of Qiti deconstructed to a skeletal frame. "Qiti's sole purpose in existence is to translate the information contained on an ancient piece of technology," she said as she changed the hologram to a black orb with a white bilateral line. "This is the Bakuma Key. It is the item Qiti was created to understand."

"Cool. So what's it do?" Lazer asked as he moved some of his hair behind his ear.

"It is a hard drive protected by a famously unsolvable cypher. It was found five years ago, floating in the orbit of Ortoba 4, bearing a message from the dominant terrestrial species of that world, even though said species had never developed spaceflight. While it was initially postulated that an advanced civilization had made contact in violation of the GU charter, its cypher is wholly unique from all known languages in the history of the universe," Dex answered as she brought up a projection of unfamiliar symbols beside a line of white dots.

"To your left is Ubu. It was the common language of a race of mamma-lian bipeds called the Baku, who were wiped out by a comet thousands of years ago. It has been fully translated and catalogued, with examples of its ubiquity scattered across their home world. To your right is a text known as 'the dots.' It is seemingly indecipherable and only found in the data taken from this artifact and nowhere else. With the exception of a single introductory line written in Ubu, the entirety of the information on the drive was recorded in this unknown code."

"So what does the line say?" Lazer asked.

"It says, 'You will find the Aperture Parallax in the pyramid at the end of the world.'"

"The pyramid at the end of the world? Oh, that's a good album title," Lazer responded as he contemplated the artwork.

"Think of it as the celestial equivalent of your lost city of Atlantis."

"Georgia?"

Dex paused, choosing how to respond when Streek chimed in.

"I think I remember seeing a documentary about that not too long ago—not the pyramid part, but the Aperture . . . Parathingy."

"Oh yeah, what's the Aperture Parathingy?" Lazer asked, cutting his mental meanderings of epic pyramids short.

"The Aperture Parallax. It was the central artifact of the Baku religion and was claimed to give whomever possessed the object infinite life. The course of Baku history was steered by the unrelenting search to find it. Even thousands of years later, many comb the barren dirt planet using all manner of technologies. None have succeeded in finding this treasure."

"Wait, so by infinite life, do they mean if you have it you never die, or you die but then come back over and over?" Streek asked.

"And if they do come back over and over, is it a zombie-type thing or more of a Super Mario thing? You know what I mean?" Lazer added.

"Nobody knows with certainty—at least, not yet. The Bakuma Key sits in the antiquities vault at the University of Xyzor Adjacent, with its contents contained on the university's secret server, which is also located inside the vault. After several well-advertised search expeditions failed to procure the Aperture Parallax, the university regent made the first five dots of the code public. This unique puzzle challenged the brightest minds in the GU—geniuses, entrepreneurs, historians, and linguists. They all failed, humbled by their glaring inability to decode the dots."

"So nobody can solve it?" Streek asked.

"Nobody except me."

"You solved it?"

"Easily."

"How?"

"Simple. I am smarter than everyone else who has tried thus far."

"No, I mean, how did the dots work?" Streek elaborated.

Dex smiled, swimming in her own genius. "Using the QITI AI, I was able to discover that the dots existed in contrasting shades of white that are impossible to detect using most available technology. Once I verified the scope of the spectrum, I found that the gradients created pictures, each dot becoming its own painted message once adjusted to a more familiar light spectrum," Dex said as she tapped her finger.

The five dots phased into their own symbols. The first was a chrome swirl breaking apart into a three-armed spiral, set against a background of orange, black, and violet. The second was a rose-tinted flush that started as a circle in the middle and cascaded outward in pixelated dots. The third was an amber hue with scattered flecks of stonewash gray. The fourth dot was a bright red dot at the center surrounded by a cube made of white lines. Streaks of light emanated in all directions, each a different color. The final dot was a gray triangle located in a black triangle set against a blur of greens, purples, and browns.

"So what do those mean?" Lazer asked, squinting at the five projected dots.

"I have several theories, but none can be verified at this moment. The most obvious answer is that they are hieroglyphs. While these first three are difficult to understand, the fourth one here appears to represent the Aperture Parallax with its clear depiction of the famous dot-within-a-cube symbol. The final dot could have something to do with this pyramid at the end of the world. But what is the pyramid within the pyramid? Or maybe these dots are not a language but some type of visual cues to a deeper riddle? I would need to get the rest of the contents of the Bakuma Key to truly understand."

"The thing in the vault at that one place?" Lazer asked, doing his best to follow along.

"Yes. And while decoding the dots would be a challenge, getting the remaining information off the university server would prove to be the more difficult endeavor."

"But aren't you famous for being able to beat people up and steal well-guarded treasures? I mean, that's how Piratech got started, right?" Streek asked.

"That was many years ago." She sighed. "And besides, I'm not someone who can be implicated in the theft of state property—not anymore, at least. I would need a single operator with abilities far beyond anyone under my employ—someone who could enter without detection, download the contents, and get the information out of the university, even if compromised. I would have to do the next best thing to doing it myself . . ."

"Get stoned?" Lazer asked with a shrug.

Dex stopped her monologue. "I am going to go out on a limb and assume that this is a common solution to your problems."

"Nah, you'd be wrong."

"Wrong that you engage in substance abuse?"

"No, that I have problems," Lazer replied with a wink and a smile.

Dex paused once more.

Streek chimed in. "So what was the next best thing?"

"To build someone competent enough to do the job for me. Qiti is my ultimate creation. She is cunning and strong and harbors an emotional intelligence normally reserved for the living. With her AI and robotics married into a single unit, I sent her on the mission with an escort of Murderfist-division contractors. They were dressed as missionaries operating under the guise of attendees at a campus debate on robotic evolution. During the event, Qiti slipped out and was able to gain access to the heavily fortified wing of the university that houses the secret server.

"Using her hacking protocols, she was able to pass all security clearances, disable the saw-blade-wielding guard-drones, crack the multistage password programs, disarm the floor-mounted electroshock sensors, access the server from its storage safe, download and translate all contents, reengage the safe, rearm the shock sensors, bring the drones back online, and finally, return to the extraction point without leaving any evidence of her presence."

"I'd watch that movie," Lazer chimed in again.

"Definitely," Streek agreed.

"Right? And that's a pretty rad college. If I went to college, I would go to murderbot saw-blade college," Lazer said while he pantomimed shooting projectiles from his fingers. *Pkew Pkew Pkew.*"

Dex cleared her throat loudly, cutting the conversation short. "Do you understand the information I have given you thus far?"

"Yes, I think I follow. You solved this riddle," Streek said with a swirl of his tentacle.

"Correct."

"Using an AI you designed that was good at code-breaking."

"Also correct."

"And then you built her a super advanced body to steal a thing."

"Borrow."

"And she got the information off this Bakuma Key server thing for you."

"Downloaded and translated."

"Escaped."

"Free and clear."

"Until she was captured by a rogue Piratech captain?"

"Yes. But not before sending me a very important message."

"What was that?" Streek asked.

Dex leaned forward in her chair. "Glad-hand protocol activated," she said as a quick flash of blue light looped around Lazer's palm. "If anything were to go wrong at any time, Qiti was programmed to imprint the data she gathered onto organic matter as a secondary retrieval protocol. It was intended for use on any of the members of the mercenary team in order to increase the odds of success should Qiti become compromised. As her mercenary escorts had since been eliminated, however, she used you."

"Huh. You could say I came in . . . handy," Lazer quipped, looking toward Streek for validation. He got nothing. "OK, but for reals, this will tell you where the Aperture Parathingy is?" He waved his gloved hand.

"Indeed. The download has been in progress since the LE drive grafted to the imprint on your skin."

"OK. So I'm still a little confused," Lazer stated, rubbing the stubble across his chin.

"Yes?"

"These people figured out infinite life, right? Then why are they all dead?

"Baku."

"Bless you."

Dex tapped her finger several times. Two sets of aviator-style glasses rose from a small compartment on the side on the table. "Perhaps some context is in order before we proceed any further. Please put on these glasses and you will be able to see, hear, smell, and feel the educational presentation," Dex said before turning her gaze toward Lazer. "Sometimes, a more complete sensory experience helps with conceptualization in primitive species. No offense."

"None taken," Lazer replied casually, inspecting the sleek pair of glasses as Streek struggled with his.

"Hey, this only works if you have ears," the floating octopus complained, waving his pair of glasses.

Dex tapped her finger, causing the arms of Streek's glasses to reach back and wrap around. Streek put the glasses on his head once more and moved about. They fit perfectly.

"Thanks," he said with a nervous smile as he floated above his chair, a variety of colors swirling on his lenses in mesmerizing psychedelia. Lazer slipped on his pair of aviators and was met with infinite darkness. Instead of the office, he was now nowhere. It was a full blackout like a hotel room in Vegas with the curtains closed. In from the void came a blue screen superimposed by a white triangle.

A calm, feminine voice spoke. *"This unit of culture is brought to you by the Department of Basic Languages and Symbols."* The letters D.O.B.L.A.S. were spelled out in white block lettering along the bottom of the shape. The picture hung still for a moment, then faded back out into black.

In the absence of sensation, Lazer noticed the high-pitched ring of his tinnitus was gone. The teleo-healing-toaster-box thing had fixed his hearing too. Lazer had forgotten what silence actually sounded like; it was jarring.

While he was lost in thought, Lazer was zapped into a humid jungle in a blink. He was nowhere, then he was there, the sun warm on his skin, the air thick and dewy. He was still sitting in his chair while Streek hovered above his, but the chairs were all that remained of Dex's office. They were surrounded by spectacular emerald trees, as if painted with a master's touch, rising above an endless color palette of flowers and fauna amid the effervescent buzzing and chirping of life.

A Siberian husky in a canvas harness and bubble helmet trotted by. She sniffed at a plant, barked at it, and continued on, playfully engaging with her surroundings. The dog's mouth stayed closed as she spoke in an enthusiastic Russian accent, the sound emanating from a small dot on her collar. *"Hello, I'm clone Laika, the cuddliest cosmonaut! Come with me as we explore the legends behind some of the biggest mysteries in the Galactic Union!"*

A peppy, keyboard-driven theme song jingled along with the occasional burst of saxophone as Lazer and Streek were immersed in a variety of exotic locations, following the dog as she playfully walked and sniffed across them all. A bright, female alto began to sing.

A Russian pioneer, she was shot into space.
Scanned by a saucer, her genetics were saved.
They cooked up a body and gave her a brain.
Come along, Laika, show us the way!
The truth will be found, oh, once we give chase.
And look at that super cuddly face.
Into the caves and under the sea.
It's Galactic Mysteries! Galactic Mysteries!

Lazer caught himself humming along to the tune as the run of locations Laika explored faded into a panoramic view of a desert landscape. The air was sprinkled with dust carried along by the midday breeze. Smooth copper hills lined the horizon as a distant sun hung in the pale-orange sky. Lazer scanned his desolate surroundings, catching Laika trotting out of a tiny rocket that was parked behind him.

"On today's episode, we look for traces of the Baku, who were a mysterious race of beings who died out long ago. A moderately advanced species, they warred among themselves until they were wiped out by a massive comet that left little behind, save for the mechanical detritus of their globe-spanning war machine. Neat!"

Everything went black once more. An image of a brawny man with leathery skin splotched in a kaleidoscope of greens faded in. A bright shock of neon-orange hair waved faintly atop his rounded head, his ragged fur loincloth running from his belly to his knees. He bent down and picked up a crude spear with a calloused, four-fingered hand. His nails were flat across the tips of his stubby digits with lines of dirt under the edges. The blackness surrounding him faded as he rose, replaced by an overgrown marsh. He spun his weapon with dexterity and hurled it at some unknown target beyond the thicket while Laika sniffed around beside him.

"The Baku lived thousands of years ago on the planet Ortoba 4. It was a temperate sphere full of trees and water and animals to chase—kind of like my home planet, Earth!"

A small rodent hopped out from behind one of the many low-sitting ferns. Laika turned her attention to it and growled, her eyes following the vermin until it disappeared between the roots of a stalky, fronded tree. Laika looked back toward the Baku man and wagged her tail as she panted.

"*Skeletal remains show they averaged one meter in height. Cultural remains show they were very devoted to their religious beliefs. And technological remains show that they existed on that particular part of the intelligence spectrum where they were smart enough to devise methods of mass devastation but not smart enough to take them back apart—kind of like my home planet, Earth!*"

Laika looked back to the Baku man, who now crouched, painting his face with the white mud of the bog. She continued, "*The Baku lived in small hunter-gatherer communities for hundreds of thousands of years, subsisting off the land, trading with each other in times of abundance, and pooling resources in times of famine. Much of their history refers to a simple, sustainable way of life that remained unchanged for many generations . . . until the founding of the Crimson Empire.*"

An ominous horn rang out in stereo as the Baku man stopped painting his face and looked up. A meteor careened from the sky and crashed beyond the tree line, a trail of smoke in its wake.

"*The Crimson Empire was said to be founded when the creator of all things fell from the world beyond the sky. Local folklore foretold of such a being, who would deliver the people from the old ways and usher them into a new world of health and plenty. The new ruler called himself Bakuma, which translated to 'First Baku.' It would be the name and title of all the leaders that would follow.*"

The man and his surroundings faded out, replaced with a new scene. It was now daytime, bright, with a cloudless blue sky hanging calmly over a sprawling city of white cobblestone courtyards and ivy-covered spires that reached up like arms embracing the heavens. A multileveled waterfall rushed over a craggy, moss-laden cliffside in the distance, the faint sound of water blending among the murmur of voices.

Lazer and Streek sat on a balcony overlooking a large crowd who all wore crisp white tunics with wispy flows of fabric that danced in the breeze. Their brightness glared like the images imprinted on your eyes after a quick stare at the midday sun. Lazer himself had stared at the sun a few times more than he probably should have as a child. And teenager. Only once as an adult though, on a bet. Lazer won . . . and yet somehow, still lost.

The thousands in attendance simultaneously turned toward a central pyramid. It was stepped with levels of white brick until the top section, where it opened up into a columned temple with a pointed top. Black banners displaying a crimson dot within a white cube hung from the flat portions. A platform jutted out toward the crowd, wide with a carved railing.

A tall Baku man with brown freckles scattered above his weathered gray-and-orange beard looked out across the gathered crowd. A bright red stone hanging from a simple string around his neck sparkled when the sun caught it at the right angle. His crimson robe, the only among the sea of white garments, draped across his wiry frame.

Bakuma took a deep inhale and raised his hands high with fingers spread wide. With an exhale, he brought his arms down, palms facing the ground. The people collectively knelt as the faint murmurs of the crowd gave way to an instant, deafening silence. He held up a blade, curved with ornamental stones, and walked back into the temple. He was followed by a Baku juvenile in a white robe, who nervously looked over his shoulder at the silent masses until the door closed and sealed behind him. After several moments, the boy returned, his white tunic splashed in blood, the red stone around his neck. He held the blood-covered blade in one hand, and the decapitated head of the Bakuma in the other. He presented them to the waiting crowd. They cheered wildly.

Laika sat beside Lazer, who lounged comfortably in his chair as he stared out at the sea of cheering subjects. She scratched behind her ear with her back paw, only to hit her clear helmet as she continued her narration. Lazer reached down to pet the excitable pup, but his hand went right through her.

"Oh right, not real," Lazer whispered to himself before resetting to his previous slouch.

"*One peculiar aspect of the ruling dynasty, known collectively as the Crimson Throne, was their succession ritual. The heir to the kingdom would assassinate the sitting ruler with a blade said to be forged from the very meteor that heralded the new empire. This blade would transfer the spirit of the first Bakuma and guide their rule forever. Also, the ritual was not complete until the white robe of the new Bakuma was stained with the blood of the old ruler. Decapitation was common. Cool, right?*"

"Actually, yeah, that's kind of badass," Lazer replied to the dog's rhetorical comment.

"Yeah, they didn't mess around," Streek concurred.

"But for however brutal the Crimson Throne could be, they were much, much worse on their neighbors. Ooh, look, somebody's getting annexed!"

An ominous drumming, deep and rhythmic, rumbled as Lazer and Streek rose into the sky and soared over a grassy knoll to a valley quaking with the force of the empire's armies. A line of men with hide-bound vestiture held their ground with obsidian-tipped spears. Their mud-caked clothes and rugged manes were starkly contrasted by the pristine red-and-white fabrics and gleaming black armor of the oncoming legion.

The front wave of the empire's army lined up. They wielded metal lances, saddled atop short-haired mammoths shaded in tennis-ball green. The muscled beasts bore two pairs of tusks that were capped with serrated metal points, sharp and ready for destruction. The spearmen chanted and taunted their much larger adversary as the riders waited. With the blow of a horn, the mammoths kneeled to the ground, ducking forward as a volley of arrows soared upward from behind them. The projectiles looked like a clutter of faint dashes, penciled into the daytime sky before raining down upon the unprepared phalanx of defenders with maximum devastation.

Hundreds of spearmen collapsed to the ground with arrows sticking through their unarmored bodies. They screamed and grunted as a second horn blew. The cavalry charged with the deep trumpeting of the rushing mounts. The wall of lances lowered, pointed at a downward tilt in a unified front. They were long, sharp, and many. As the mammoths clashed through the wall of warriors, bodies were tossed aside, in the air, or trampled underfoot. Soldiers armed with glimmering swords and oblong, lacquered shields followed the mammoths, engaging with the shocked spearman with brutal efficiency.

Now Lazer, Streek, and their canine guide were elsewhere. It was another battle, or, rather, a slaughter, as battles implied armaments on both sides. The soldiers of the Crimson Empire raided villages as children cried for their missing parents. Pitch and fire burned houses of wood and grass, the rising black smoke amid the destruction getting lost beyond the pale moon.

"Run to the hills . . . Run for your li'hives . . . ," Lazer sang as he drummed to the Iron Maiden classic on his lap. Streek cracked a sliver of a smile but hushed Lazer.

"From village to village, Bakuma's armies laid waste to any resistance and placed the survivors in work camps. They were forced to dig and look for the cube

depicted on the invader's banner. The conquered labored in rows that stretched to the horizon, meticulously overturning every square meter of land by hand. It was the project of generations."

They were now beside a hardscrabble camp, dirty and in disrepair at the edge of a dug-out crater. A small child, naked but for a red necklace, held a spade and slapped at the soil as her father labored in the distance. He collapsed into frailty and from there to bones. The child grew to a woman, the spade to a shovel. She dug in the same spot as her father, while her young son stabbed at the dirt beside her.

It was now the future. Massive machines with treaded wheels tilled and removed chunks of land, humming along in synchronicity as they executed their tasks in unbroken formation. Steam rose from smokestacks that jutted like spikes from faded, grime-worn buildings, as an endless supply of dirt was dropped onto a field of automated sifters. Rocks and bones, chalky and fractured, popped up from the wire mesh along with broken shovels and long-lost weaponry. They bounced on the spaced wires as the dirt filtered out below to different chutes. Posters of a new Bakuma lined the busy work site. He was taller, darker, and more imposing in his stature. The same sparkling jewel hung from his neck. In blocky white font, the posters read: *To dig is to serve. To serve is to love. To love is to dig.*

An older worker, wrinkled but stout, slowed down and pulled off to the side of the dirt road. He exited his vehicle and bent over on one knee, coughing, gripping at his chest while contorting his face in pain. Two soldiers in maroon plated body armor and black cloaks rushed to the struggling worker and attempted to help him to his feet with no success. The worker let out a final lung-splitting hack before going limp and lying motionless on the soil. One of the soldiers procured a cue-ball-sized sphere from his pocket. He shook it several times, and the ball opened like a fist becoming a hand. It crawled down his arm to the fallen worker's foot and drilled a magnet into his boot. It pressed its back against the magnet, locked into place, and slowly pulled the worker's incapacitated body away from the idling vehicle.

"The Crimson Army was now the police force, having run out of people to conquer about five hundred years after their first battle. Every square meter of Ortoba 4 had been united under Bakuma's banner, so now they mostly marched down streets in a show of force while the conquered dug," Laika narrated as a parade of soldiers stomped in unison down a wide urban thoroughfare, the tromp tromp tromp of their boots echoing out between the buildings. Laika wagged her tail in excitement. *"Oh! I love going for walks. Anybody want to get my leash?"*

The walls of the brick-and-mortar storefronts were plastered with posters of determined-looking peasants holding up their various implements of servitude in pride. A shovel, a trowel, and a gun, bold and white in clean simple shapes against blocky splashes of black, yellow, and red. Somewhere along the street, around the corner, and down two-and-a-half flights of stairs, a group of people pored over maps. They collaborated and planned, surrounded by rows of firearms lining the walls, polished and ready.

"In the history of great military powers, a combination of hubris and inattention to detail have undermined even the most formidable of dynasties. Bakuma was like the wolf, strong, cunning, occasionally eating from the herd of goats that chewed upon the landscape. It was an apex predator without worry. But the line of leaders, through collective obsession with the lost relic, would bring about the end of their rule. Its search had bankrupted the government. People were hungry. And when the hungry protest, they do not do it with signs; they do it with bricks."

The marching army encountered a line of dissenters, who waved clubs and farming equipment as they shouted. As the opposing sides in the video engaged in their standoff, a young woman in fitted urban attire walked briskly along the side of the busy thoroughfare. She avoided eye contact with a passing soldier and pressed forward, gaze locked downward. At the end of the road was a checkpoint with soldiers searching a nervous family with a crying child. She tossed her backpack under a metal cart armed with a mounted gun and casually passed by. She took an immediate sharp turn down an alley, followed another, and inconspicuously walked down a set of stairs. A rusted door slammed behind her with a clink.

"It was then that the goat ate the wolf."

The backpack exploded, throwing the artillery gun into the sky with a cloud of fire that came back down as a rain of ashes and fragments. The nearby soldiers ran to the wreckage. A siren blared out from a tin speaker mounted on a tall wooden pole as civilians dressed in their matted coveralls and cold-weather coats surrounded the soldiers. They held knives, blunt metal objects, and other instruments of the mob.

One of the soldiers held out a small pistol, waving it wildly as she attempted to keep the increasingly numerous and agitated crowd at bay. Her hand shook in fear; they were the tremors of the outnumbered. She panicked, and the gun went off, hitting a young woman in the stomach. With stained hands clutching the wound, the civilian collapsed forward, crumpled and bleeding, whimpering in pain and helplessness. A roar swept through the crowd like a shift in the flight pattern of a flock of birds. They charged on the soldiers, drowning them in a fevered rush of swinging limbs and weapons.

The scenes of civil insurrection broke out across the globe as Lazer and Streek watched the reenacted fighting and bloodshed. From cities to work camps, the Crimson Empire's flags of the Aperture Parallax were replaced with rags bearing the green four-fingered handprint of the resistance.

"Though while the dissenters fought and recruited greater numbers into their rebel army, Bakuma's concerns lay elsewhere. In a far-flung province, a thousand kilometers away, the Aperture Parallax was finally found."

A six-legged dog with glittery stone scales looked on with her pups as a caravan of military vehicles and several large beasts maneuvered through the arid flatland at the bottom of a dry lake bed. Across arid dunes and fetid marshes, the detachment of agents of the empire escorted a mysterious metal crate.

"The Aperture Parallax was carried across the world, traversing through patches of wilderness while snaking around rebel strongholds. The empire's agents were bloody. They were exhausted. After suffering losses from skirmishes, nature, and disease, the caravan, now a fraction of its initial size, made it back to the capital with its cargo intact."

A different Bakuma, aging and emaciated with mottled grayish-green skin, stood before a healthy and regal representation of his youth portrayed in the life-size portrait hanging on the wall behind him. His robe, crimson and unsullied, swept dramatically behind his wiry frame as the silver crate was wheeled in by several guards. One of them cracked the box open as the weathered ruler gazed in awe, a twisted smile slowly creaking across his cracked green lips. A red reflection painted his eyes from the beaming glow radiating from the box.

Bakuma closed his hands over his unseen prize and scurried to the balcony, the guards holding the doors wide while hanging their heads in an unworthy grovel. He stepped out to the same riser overlooking his city as the original Bakuma had done so many years before. But now the city was grander, with a taller pyramid and a wider courtyard filled with even more devotees eagerly awaiting his anointed words. Bakuma walked to the edge of his platform and held the shining object to the sky in silence. The crowd dropped to their knees and bowed in a show of unified deference.

"This event was the last recorded piece of history by the Crimson Empire before the Aperture Parallax, Bakuma, and nearly a hundred thousand of his followers all vanished forever. And forever is a long time, trust me. I swear, every time my human left the house . . ."

Images of broken machines and broken bodies flashed like a flip-book. Fires raged through cities as the empire's mechanized soldiers collapsed amid rubble and ruin. A woman, young and strong with a spear dripping with the blood of her enemies, climbed up the side of a massive bipedal tank as it ambled across a charred field of wreckage. She pulled herself to the top, her muscles tensing as she ripped open a hatch.

Pkew. A shot from the cockpit. The warrior dodged it and dropped down the side, swinging with the war engine's movements. She clasped the rim with one hand and produced a small orb from her breast pocket with the other. She pressed a button, tossed it in, pulled herself back up with a grunting exhale, and kicked the hatch closed before the device detonated. She grabbed on to the hatch handle and rode the exploding tank as it crashed to the ground, sending a wave of dust in all directions that chased the backs of the fleeing soldiers.

"Without the presence of Bakuma and no announced successor, the Crimson Empire fell into disarray. The military dissolved as districts splintered into factions, each possessing different pieces of the globe conquering weapons, which were, in turn, used on each other to devastating effect. And just like that, an empire that lasted a thousand years imploded."

Cities were consumed in fire. A ruby statue of a past Bakuma lay on its side amid the crumbling affects of the dynasty. The same warrior from before stood atop a pile of dead Crimson Empire soldiers, her spear on one side, her gun holstered on the other. Overhead, a comet streaked across the sky and landed beyond the horizon. A massive wave of dust and smoke rolled out, enveloping the scene of triumph.

"A piece of recorded music called 'The Ballad of Lolo' was discovered on a recent excavation. It was a poem with accompanying sheet music that was dated back to the first years after the collapse of the empire and the extinction event that followed, detailing a rebel leader who chased the last Bakuma to hell. The

song has been recreated and recorded by famous singer-songwriter Jim Junkpan. Woof, what a hottie, right?"

The dust faded out to reveal a soft white room. A shaggy werewolf wearing blue jeans and a black jacket sat upon a stool that matched the wood of his acoustic guitar. He strummed and hummed a few notes in warm-up as Laika's tail wagged enthusiastically. She barked and rolled onto her back, exposing her belly, looking toward the musician with focused adoration as he started his song with a simple chord progression.

> A rebel leader, her story told
> Came from nothin', out in the cold
> Her future, nothin', long since sold
> Dig with this shovel until you're old
> So dig she did, along with her kin
> They did what they're told, women and men
> To stop would be an unforgivable sin
> So dig she did, along with her kin
> Just workin' folks in the heat and flood
> Then new machines all drank our blood
> Us old machines, just flesh and mud
> Crimson don't trust nothin' that feels love
> So one day they struck her pop down
> Then her brother, shot to the ground
> Then her mother, who wailed aloud
> Left Lolo alone in that digger town
> Oh, by day she dug and after she'd fight
> She trained and spied and resisted by night
> But kept up appearances, nothing outright
> Just bidin' her time till things just felt right
> The minions of the master of war
> Dug then found what they were lookin' for
> Hurried along with the loot they scored
> But Lolo, this is what she was waitin' for
> She followed through unforgiving terrain
> Mines with dead miners, pits in the plain
> Deserts and thirst and its unquenching pain
> Swamps with their monsters, you don't come back the same

> They finally got there, the bastion, the mountain
> The evil's true source, guarded by machines that they
>   mounted
> The battle, such blood ran just like a fountain
> The death toll itself could never be counted

"The death toll itself could never be counted," Lazer grunted out in his best death-metal growl with a clenched fist shaking in front of him. Streek snickered. The song continued.

> With an army behind her, they charged in and fought
> Gave the Crimson all that they got
> Inside the mountain, the door then slammed shut
> Was this to be where they all died and rot?
> A hiss, then a twinkle burst in the sky
> A crash, then a wave and everyone died

"Everyone dieeeeeeed!" Lazer sang with his best Ronnie James Dio impression. Streek chuckled, his buttoned-up posture eroding. Lazer smiled, satisfied with his ability to shake Streek from his rigid stance.

> Those plannin' in bunkers or decided to hide
> Were the only ones who came out alive
> And now here we are, the world's all gone
> The people died too, so here's my song
> A ballad for Lolo, who avenged the world
> We aren't locked out of there . . . they're locked in with
>   her . . .

Jim Junkpan strummed the chord progression a few more times as he wailed on his harmonica, finishing on a bright chord that rang out on the steel strings of his instrument. Laika barked and panted, her tongue hanging out of her smiling canine mouth. The white room faded and brought them back to the barren desert landscape from the beginning of the episode. Laika sniffed at where the singer was just sitting as her voice came back from her collar.

"*No one is quite sure where the Aperture Parallax, Bakuma, or his city of followers disappeared to. It is also unknown if Lolo and her vanguard actually managed to confront Bakuma or were merely lost in the comet's impact with the rest of life on Ortoba 4. However, with new information coming to light from the variety of artifacts being discovered, there is still some story left to reveal. Hey! Maybe I can find out where they went myself!"* Laika furiously dug as dirt piled up behind her while she panted away.

"Thanks for watching. Tune in next time when we visit Tar and look for an uncontacted tribe of Eldermoles living in the center of planet . . . then put them on our network's new reality dancing show So You Think You Can Rhythmically Spasm! *OK, everyone, see you next time!"*

"The Eldermoles of Taaaar!" Streek sang, completely putting his bashfulness aside, if only for a brief moment. Lazer cracked up, patting his friend on the back.

"OK, OK . . . I'm good. I'm good," Lazer said, wiping a tear from his eye.

The talking dog resumed her dig as the theme song kicked in, three-dimensional credits scrolling behind her at a speedy clip. Lazer took off his glasses and set them down on the table with one hand, rubbing his eyes with the other. He blinked a few times and looked back at Dex, who was waiting patiently, albeit slightly annoyed.

Streek removed his glasses as Lazer picked up his water and went for a sip. As the rim touched his lips, his glove vibrated, shaking like a paging coaster telling him his table was ready. Lazer dropped his glass onto the ground, which bounced, spilling his water across the floor.

"What was that?" Lazer blurted as he checked out the mess around his feet.

Dex leaned in. "It means the download is complete."

She tapped her finger. A small logo of the white cube with a red dot in the middle beamed from a rainbow spectrum projecting from the table. Three rows of white dots three dots across scrolled beneath. Faint lines of contrasting white emerged from the blank circles. Colors swelled in, revealing an image on each surface. Some were the same images from before. New ones included a picture of a row of the cubes with dots, all lined up. Another was a simple arrow pointing down. The pictures swirled together into a single dot, then typed in English. It was a menu:

1. To Gray
2. The Aperture Parallax
3. Maps

4. Defenses

5. The Pyramid at the End of the World

Dex chose the Aperture Parallax option. A line of dots scrolled along, becoming pictures, those pictures becoming words. The information branched out like trees, creating a forest of vocabulary that unfolded in all directions as it translated, flashing along faster than Lazer or Streek could read it. Dex smiled with a wide grin, her immaculate white teeth beaming in betrayal of her intimidating detachment.

She waved her hand slightly, scrolling through various prompts before clicking on an icon of the white cube with the small red dot. It zoomed in. The dot took shape as it grew larger, becoming a ribbon of origami plasma, deep red and curving in on itself as it swayed in ethereal rhythm. Dex read the string of text flashing alongside it. "Hmm," she said to herself before looking toward Lazer and Streek, who waited for the anticipated reveal. "Interesting."

"What's that?" Lazer asked with a shrug.

"It seems the Aperture Parallax does not give you infinite lives."

"No zombies?"

"No. It gives you access to your infinite *life*."

"What's the difference?"

"You don't become infinite going forward in time. You become infinite going sideways through probability."

"Yeah, still confused."

"According to these notes, the Aperture Parallax is an animal that exists in ten dimensions of space. Why we are able to detect it in our three-dimensional universe is not revealed here. Hmm." Dex stopped to read some more. "It says making physical contact with this creature allows its possessor to access the thoughts and knowledge of every version of itself through a fifth-dimensional plane."

"Um, that's a lot of science," Lazer responded, overwhelmed.

"Imagine you, Lazer, and every version of you that exists through the web of choices and circumstances weaving through your life. What if all of the yous could be unified by a single thread? The Aperture Parallax is that thread."

"Like different notes on a string?" Streek asked.

"Yes, but all of the notes are playing at the same time."

"I've gigged with a few bands that sounded like that," Lazer chimed in.

Dex elaborated, "No. This being is flawless—the symmetry, the grace in its very existence. It is more beautiful than the clumsy medium of language allows for. From a mathematical standpoint, it is perfect."

"It looks like a barnacle," Lazer replied.

"Oh, I love barnacles!" Streek exclaimed. "Do you have any? They're great with butter and toast."

"It's not food," Dex snapped.

"Right, sorry. Not food," Streek replied sheepishly.

"So where do we find this 'not food'?" Lazer asked with air quotes.

Dex returned to the primary menu and clicked on the maps. "Here," she responded as a row of dots morphed into a map of hilly terrain with a blinking red dot. Dex scrolled through the dots further. "Hmm. There should be more schematics somewhere among these notes, but . . ." A slight buzzing sound emanated from the table every time the woman waved her hand. "Odd."

"What's that now?"

"I can't access any type of building layout beyond the location of the entrance. It seems some of Qiti's information did not transfer over. Let me try again," she said, tapping her fingers as the buzzing continued. She clicked back to the menu and chose the Traps prompt. Buzz. She chose the Pyramid at the End of the World prompt. Another buzz.

"No, this isn't right. Lazer, be a nice human and bring me your hand."

Lazer stood, walked over to his host, and placed his hand forward. Dex tapped her pointer a few times as the glove melted off of Lazer's hand and returned to a cloth-like state. She inspected the LE drive as Lazer rubbed the sweat from his hand on the side of his jeans and smelled it. He had a tendency to smell most things coming on or off his body. It was one of the habits his ex-girlfriend pointed out when she dumped him, and one of a litany of things that made them incompatible. Dex took Lazer's now-ungloved hand and studied the image. She walked the tips of her fingers along the grooves of Lazer's tattoo.

"The LE drive is in working condition. Perhaps there was perspiration buildup, or worse, your cellular regeneration undid some of Qiti's work. I had anticipated that the initial download would give us . . . more. Let's try again," she said, putting the cloth back on Lazer's hand.

The LE drive reverted to its liquid state, remelted, and formed back into a glove. Dex flipped through more prompts. The buzzing returned. She grunted to herself in frustration, focusing intently on her troubleshooting, though was met with the continued rejection of her request. She ceased and turned back to her guests. "OK, I have good news and bad news. Which would you prefer to hear first?"

"Good news."

"I am doubling your compensation."

"Sweet."

"Um, what's the bad news, then?" Streek questioned with hesitance.

"Your friend will be beta testing the LE drive in the field."

"Wait. We have to come with you?" Streek asked in a cautious panic.

"Well . . . he does," she said, pointing at Lazer. "Whether the imprint was not completely successful or my drive needs further debugging, we will be entering blind, without a map to follow or any way to find this pyramid. As such, I will require access to the remaining information, should it become available."

"But that wasn't part of the deal," Streek pleaded.

"Until I get the entirety of the download, your end of the bargain remains unfulfilled. Though I suppose I could always just amputate Lazer's hand and leave you both stranded on the nearest asteroid. Your call."

Lazer and Streek looked at each other and back to Dex.

"Nope. We're good," they said in unison.

"Wise choice," Dex replied as she waved to her guard again, who stepped away from her post and returned with a small silver gun. She walked around the table and placed the tip of the gun into Lazer's neck. A tiny click preceded a faint pinch.

"Hey, what was that?" he said, rubbing the site of the sting.

"We will be going underground and may encounter a variety of hazards to your fragile state of being, not to mention the probable presence of the fifty or so armed contractors working under Captain Izzit. In order to increase your chances of survival, I have injected you with my latest iteration of nanobots. They will aid your immune system in fighting off foreign pathogens, assist with clotting and healing time, allow you to breathe in a wider range of atmospheres, and even slow your aging processes."

"Um, thanks?"

"You're welcome. Last chance to back out," Dex said as Lazer looked at his hand.

He clapped and stood. "Come on, Streek, let's go find this nice lady's time barnacle."

"Thank you for your cooperation," Dex replied.

PART 8

THE GIRL WITH THE SWISS CHEESE BRAIN

QITI OPENED THE NEXT VIDEO ON THE FILE. IT BEGAN IN THE SHIP'S lab, which was a total mess after the energy wave had knocked everything about. Captain Ponn opened cabinets and rifled through supplies, looking for the missing organism while Res Voland poked around at the remnants of the tiny ship on the table. The doctor pulled out a UV stick and flipped off the lights.

"It left a trail behind," she said, pointing the light at the holding tray.

They followed the slimy discharge down the table, across the floor, and into the wall. They followed the trail into the next room, where it oozed across the floor, all the way up the side to the open top of Dex's cryochamber.

"Yeah, that's not good," Res Voland said with a bite of his lip.

Captain Ponn brandished her weapon and turned toward the door, which was now being blocked by the doctor. "Wait," she pleaded with the much-larger captain. "Don't do what I think you're going to do."

"Protect my ship?" the captain barked, mildly pushing Dr. Quant out of the way to get down the hall.

"You can't hurt her."

"Ship charter says otherwise."

"But you're missing the bigger picture!"

"And what's that?" the captain asked with shrinking patience.

"This whole trip's purpose is to provide a cure for the Ravage. We may have just found it. That girl, so innocent and alone in this world, isn't a problem to be solved. She's the solution."

Captain Ponn contemplated for a moment. All of her life, she had been a shoot-first-and-ask-questions-later type. It was one of the primary reasons she was captaining an escort ship and not her bomber-class vessel back in the service. Today wasn't going to be any different. She turned back and continued down the hall, Dr. Quant pleading with no breakthrough.

"Wait," Res Voland called to the captain, who stopped. "You're a subcontractor on this operation, so technically you work for me. You're not allowed to kill the girl . . . yet." He turned to the doctor. "So what's this now?"

"Whatever happened to this girl, she went from suffering irreparable brain damage—and I mean core function shutdown—to standing about, asking for her mother, in under five minutes. That's how long I was in my lab before returning. We don't know what happened, but we know that something special did, and you will be the one to have found it."

"OK, I may be able to get behind that. What's your ask?"

"To study her. To find out why she woke up and if there is a potential link with the missing organism."

"Do you think that thing had something to do with it?"

"I can't say for sure, but it's a growing likelihood, and that's what I aim to find out."

"OK. So here is the deal I'm offering: you get to study the girl, and I retain the rights to any findings you make. Additionally, if something goes bad while you check her out and she must be, ahem, terminated, you will strike her from the study as if she were never on this ship. Deal?" Res Voland asked, hand out.

Dr. Quant lowered her head and accepted. With a sigh, the doctor left the hall and walked back to the holding room where Dex sat, playing quietly. Dr. Quant entered and sat cross-legged with the child on the floor, leaning in with a smile. "Hello, Dex, how are you today?"

"Good," the girl responded, looking down at her toys.

"My name is Dr. Quant, but you can call me Auntie Borgia. Does that sound OK?"

"OK."

"Good. Now I am going to ask you a few questions. Do you think you can try to answer them?"

"OK."

"Good. Are you feeling any headaches?"

"No."

"Before you woke up, did you have any unusual dreams?"

"No."

"Do you feel any memory loss?"

"I don't think so," Dex replied, somewhat unsure.

"Good. Good," Dr. Quant said in a soothing tone, smiling as she tapped into her tablet. "I want to show you some pictures. They may be scary or startling, but I want you to try to answer, OK?

"OK."

Dr. Quant flipped to a picture on her tablet and held it up to Dex. It was a photo of the creature, magnified and texturized. She scrolled through additional photos from different angles and distances.

"Have you ever seen this before?" Dr. Quant asked, motioning toward the gray-and-brown leaf of tissue.

"No."

"Are you sure? It's OK if you're scared."

"No."

"Does it scare you?"

"No. It's pretty."

"Would you tell me if you ever did see it?"

"Yes."

"You promise?"

"Promise."

"Good. Can I get you anything?"

"My mommy?"

"She's . . . not here. I'll be taking care of you right now."

"Where is she?"

"She's . . . away. Hey, do you like frozen cream?" the doctor asked as the girl looked up and nodded. "Great, let's do a quick little exam, just to make sure you're not sick anymore, and then we'll go get some frozen cream in the mess hall. We have different flavors here, you know."

"Do you have norfberry?"

"Of course, that's the best kind! OK, follow me, let's give you a checkup."

THE VIDEO RESUMED IN THE medibay. The chirps and beeps of the ship's tomography machine worked in a steady cadence while Dr. Quant,

Captain Ponn, and Res Voland looked at the array of screens showing varying perspectives of the inside of Dex's body.

"What are we looking for, Doctor?" the captain asked, squinting at a screen.

"We are checking for any change in organ function, brain regeneration, and as discussed . . . any passengers."

A screen showing a rendering of Dex's brain rotated. It was bored full of holes with signs of atrophy and scarring. Dr. Quant tapped into her tablet, which moved the brain into a top-down view, showing a healthy layer of tissue.

"Huh," she said, looking down at her tablet, then back up.

"Is that a good huh or a bad *huh*?" Res chimed in.

"So it appears that all organ function is normal, while her brain damage remains unchanged from prior scans . . . except for this." She tapped at her tablet as the screen zoomed in on the top portion of the brain.

"What? I'm not a doctor, but that looks normal to me," the corporate rep said, rubbing his chin.

"Precisely. These holes should continue on through the top of her brain, but it's almost as if she has regenerated a layer across the top and, oh my Zeus, did it just . . . move?" The top layer of Dex's brain shifted slightly and swelled with blood. Dr. Quant typed into her tablet. "I'm shifting to EMR scale."

"What's that?"

"I'm checking beyond our visible light spectrum."

"What do you think you'll find?" Res asked as the doctor tapped a few more times at her tablet.

"That," the doctor said as she pointed at one of the screens.

It was subtle, but the layer of regenerated tissue had a cooler thermal output than the rest of the brain, possessing the slight incongruity of a chameleon on a branch.

"So do you think that—" Res began.

"Is not actual brain tissue," the doctor cut in.

"Is it . . . ?"

"There's only one way to find out," the captain interjected, grabbing a bone saw off a table.

"What are you doing?" Dr. Quant yelled.

Res held a hand up, bringing the captain to yield. "Whoa, there. No damaging the goods," he said before a wave of light flashed across all of the screens. It was a magnificent oscillation of colors and textures that melted into each other. Dex's brain lit up region by region in response, playing off the initial bursts as if in conversation with the quilted mass lying atop it. It became brighter. Brighter. The three Olympians recoiled from the blinding white light. They held their hand in front of their eyes, protecting themselves from the glare.

Then, as soon as it began, it stopped. The screens went black, then reset to the original images. The three looked at each other. The chirps and beeps of the machine the only sound to puncture the silence. Dex remained in the full body scanner, eyes closed and unassuming.

"What just happened?" Res asked his shipmates.

"Doctor?" the captain seconded.

"I . . . I . . . In regards to the light just now, I have absolutely no idea. I'll have to run more tests," she said as she rubbed her eyes. "Though as far as the child being awake is concerned, I may have a few theories."

"Shoot."

"OK, maybe the creature, by nature of its positioning, enabled Dex's brain to compensate for the widespread damage by using disparate parts of its matter in cooperation to achieve waking consciousness—think like a trellis in a garden giving the vines a chance to bridge the gap."

"Or?"

"Or perhaps they have a more . . . symbiotic relationship."

"So what do we do now?" Res asked out loud, not even necessarily ready to hear an answer. Captain Ponn tapped her fingers across her holster.

"I'm curious about the repeated use of her visual centers here," Dr. Quant said, motioning toward the posterior end of the displayed brain image. "It's used more often than any other part. The activity here would be remarkable for a healthy person, let alone someone with such sustained damage. It may be coincidence, but she may possess higher levels of perception that we can't really understand."

"Like what?"

"Like depth perception, acuity, things of that sort. Maybe the way she experiences color is different. Again, there are many unknowns here."

"You're saying she's sharp?"

"I'm saying, we may need to find a better word than that."

"Then maybe it's time I ran my own kind of test, Doctor," the captain said as she cracked her knuckles.

THE FIRING RANGE WAS BRIGHTLY lit with a long table covered in weapons. Dex stood, her hand holding Dr. Quant's as she gripped a stuffed doll in the other.

Captain Ponn walked up to Dex and handed her a small pistol. "We are going to play a game, little one. Do you like games?"

"Uh-huh," Dex said, looking up at the captain, who towered above her.

"Excellent. Here is how this game works. Small targets of different colors will streak across that far wall. Can you see that far wall at the end?"

"Uh-huh."

"Good. When you see the lights flash across, you will use this pistol to shoot them. You will only shoot the color I call out and not any other color. There is no live ammo in this weapon; it only uses pulses of light. Can you do that for me?"

"OK," Dex said, inspecting the weapon in her hand.

"Just squeeze the trigger with your pointing finger, OK?"

"OK," she said, looking up at Dr. Quant for a nod of approval, which she gave.

"Good. This is a timed exercise. Hit the targets as quickly as possible."

Dex was led up to a small platform. A horn went off, and everybody stepped back.

A woman's voice spoke over an intercom. *"Targets activate in three . . . two . . . one . . . Sequence engage."*

"Blue," Captain Ponn called out.

A string of slowly moving blue dots lobbed across the far wall. Dex fired the pistol, hitting all four. She smiled and looked back at Dr. Quant, who shooed her attention back to the live exercise.

"Green."

A second string, longer and green with one black dot in the middle moved faster than before. Dex hit those as well, sparing the sole black dot.

"Yellow."

Another string, yellow with an orange dot in front and at the end leaped across the wall faster. Dex calmly hit every appropriate target.

"Red."

A grid of dots, scattered and populated with a dozen different colors, crossed while blinking. Dex, again, hit them without effort.

"Black."

Hundreds of small, randomized dots crossed the wall in a flash. Hit. Hit. Hit. Dex missed none. She was focused, firing faster and faster, her arm waving in coordinated movement with the flow of the dots. A loud buzzer rang out, and the gun stopped firing. Dex looked back up at Dr. Quant as a single drop of blood fell from her nose.

"Oh, sweetie, let me get that for you," Dr. Quant said with motherly concern, reaching out with a tissue. As the soft fabric made contact with the small girl, she rolled her eyes toward the back of her head and reached forward, snapping the doctor's arm in half with lightning-fast reflexes. Dr. Quant howled in pain and shock. Res Voland recoiled as he screamed. Dex fell to the floor, sobbing.

The captain looked at the chaos about her and shrugged. "OK, that's enough for today."

The video ended.

Qiti backed away from the server and looked blankly, her thoughts racing. She spoke under her breath. "Mom, what did they do to you? Is this why you are the way you are? Is this why you are so . . . cold?"

She heaved a heavy sigh and opened the next video.

PART 9

WORST GIG EVER

A MATCHBOOK-SIZED BEETLE WITH AN AMETHYST SHEEN AND A twiggy horn plodded a tightly rolled ball of dung along the small stones and clumps of dirt of a barren hill. Using its wiry back legs for leverage, it pushed upward, climbing in sustained effort with the ball moving at the behest of the tip of its centered antler. It reached a small plateau as the dung ball rolled to a stop. The beetle looked ahead to see a larger specimen of its kind.

The bigger insect scraped its legs against the dirt and reared back in an aggressive show, releasing a pitched *squee* as it waved its weapon from side to side. The first beetle stepped in front of its odorous prize and waved its horn back before lowering into a defensive crouch. The larger beetle charged at the interloper, kicking up small flecks of dirt as it rammed its horn into the hard exoskeleton of its foe, pushing it back to the edge of the elevated landing. The smaller beetle dug in its hind legs, stopping itself before tumbling off the side. It skirted around the edge and charged, striking the large aggressor, pushing its horn beneath the incumbent's thorax, and lifting with the sum of its might. The larger beetle flipped over, writhing on its back, its dozen legs wiggling in vain. The smaller beetle returned to its dung and resumed pushing it farther up the hill.

It reached the summit in one of the prouder moments of its remarkably short lifespan. The victory, however, was premature. Another beetle, an alpha and bigger than its neighbor, stood guard in front of a small opening in the dirt. It reared its horn in a display of dominance toward the intruder and circled in anticipation of battle. The large beetle charged, its horn low, the underside carving a small line into the dirt as it plowed forward like a freight train on legs. The smaller beetle jumped behind its dung ball, dodging the attack. It grabbed the prize with its front two legs and pushed with urgency away from the larger insect. The alpha beetle charged once more, horn down, full speed, forcing the smaller beetle to abandon its clod of poop and grasses and scurry down the hill in retreat.

The alpha beetle approached the dung ball and claimed its winnings. It nudged it away from the ledge with a tap. The clod was stuck. The beetle tapped again, attempting to roll the ball over the small pebble that was holding it in place with no success. It lowered its head and dug beneath the dirt, nestling its head to shift the pebble and enable a little give. It pulled its head out to give it another push when a darkly plumed bird with sharp, angular feathers swooped down on four wings and snatched the alpha beetle in its spaghetti tendrils. The bird flew away with its meal writhing in its grasp as the ball of dung rolled back down the side of the hill, coming to rest at the base before its original owner, who reveled in its fortune with an exuberant *squee* before pushing the dung ball up the hill once more.

In the cloudless night sky above, Dex's ship descended into the atmosphere flanked by several smaller craft. Two moons shone brightly among the confederation of stars and galaxies as they touched down on the hard dirt ridge that cut into the night sky. The hatch of Dex's ship opened with a hiss as her party disembarked. Dex exited first, her pantsuit glimmering in the generous moonlight as she inhaled slowly through the black breathing apparatus strapped to her face. She was followed by ten Clicklaxia guards in sleek, midnight-black space suits with matching masks. Each had a small arm patch with the Piratech logo. Lazer stepped out after, wearing a space suit and breathing mask similar to the ones used by the Clicklaxia. The suit was tight but movable, with the right amount of give in the midsection. Streek floated out last, protected within a clear beach-ball-sized orb.

A contingent of mercenaries stepped out of the two smaller craft. They were like bears but with a more human affect and proportionality. They were tall but not huge, strong but not hulking. Their deep-blue uniforms were tight, emphasizing their developed, muscular contours. They all wore breathing masks with goggles and had a variety of armaments strapped to their waists, legs, and arms. Each had a patch over their chest that read Murderfist Mercenary Services LLC superimposed over two crossed fists. They congregated around Dex, followed by a hovering supply cart emblazoned with the line Guns and Butter.

"Is everybody present?" Dex asked, looking around at her party.

A mercenary with a red bar over his patch stepped forward. "All ready, boss," he said with the gravelly tone of a heavy smoker recovering from the flu.

"Good. Wait here," Dex said as she left the group and walked alone to the edge of the ridge, looking out at the valley below. The plains were windswept and lifeless yet striking in a scarred and naked beauty. In the center of the dusty expanse sat an unremarkable hill, rounded over with the erosion of wind and time. Its slopes rolled gently into the surrounding earth, smooth save for a concealed breach. A faint gust ruffled the edges of Dex's collar as its patterns moved in liquid flux. She remained standing, staring, silent. She turned back and returned to her crew.

"The underground city will be dangerous. There will be traps and hazardous impediments to our undertaking. We will have enough water and rations for three days, so we must move quickly. Beyond Captain Izzit and his crew, we do not know what lurks in the depths of the mountain. Be alert," Dex said to her waiting security team, who nodded at the instruction.

"Hey, boss lady Dex," Lazer called out from behind the wall of mercenaries.

"Yes?" she replied.

Lazer squeezed in between two of the murder-bears and asked his question. "Hi. Yeah, do I get a laser gun or anything?"

"No."

"How about me?" Streek asked as he floated up beside Lazer.

"No."

"What if something tries to eat me again?" Lazer asked with a half shrug.

"Run."

"But what if they are, you know, really fast?"

"Be faster," Dex said coldly.

Lazer and Streek looked at each other in silence for a moment, then began stretching, Lazer going into a deep lunge as Streek pulled at the base of a tentacle.

"You do get overlays however," Dex continued as an assistant offered them each a tiny black sticker. "Place this near your visual centers and you will be able to link up with the rest of the team. Lazer, you can control your prompt with the liquid eye. I will give you a more thorough walk-through when the time calls for it."

Lazer placed the sticker on his head. A layer of lights and buttons superimposed atop his normal field of vision. There were coordinates and a list of the twenty other members of the party in off-white text.

"Is everybody on?"

"Yes, ma'am," her lead mercenary replied.

"Excellent. Let's go find ourselves something priceless."

THE ENTRANCE TO THE CAVE was low and subtle, blending in with the surrounding wasteland of monochromatic dirt and rocks. From above, it was invisible, indistinguishable from the wider landscape.

A Clicklaxia with a scanner headed up the front of the group as they entered the threshold of the cave. A screen of symbols projected on the overlay, giving Lazer live readings of everything the lead henchwoman was picking up, with text contrasting against a blackness that only got darker the farther they descended. The scanner pinged and showed an object nearby. Everybody stopped.

One of the mercenaries pulled a compact triangle from his belt and tapped the top with a muscular finger. It lit up in white florescence as he tossed it forward. It took several bounces before coming to a rest, illuminating a skeleton-riddled floor. They were comingled with rusted weapons and busted machines, piled atop each other in a testament to the magnitude of violence that had occurred here so many years prior. A trodden path leading from the cave entrance to a distant opening only confirmed Dex's intuition that someone had gotten here before them.

The CEO and her corporate army moved cautiously, anticipating at-tack. Lazer crouched down and picked up an intact skull. Its face was small and oblong and fit in the palm of his hand like a maraca without a handle, the empty sockets staring at Lazer with the detached accep-tance of the long-dead. He looked around at the remains of carnage and returned the skull to the greater pile of bones before continuing on in silence.

At the end of the cave lay a deep shaft with elevator-wide dimensions. One of the mercenaries produced another incandescent triangle, acti-vated it, and dropped it down the shaft. It disappeared instantly, silent in its fall. The mercenary gazed off into the distance, lost in thought. He checked his watch, scratched his stomach, and cleared his throat. His watch beeped once as a three-dimensional rendering of a dark corridor popped up on the overlay.

"It's twenty kilometers down, boss," he said.

"Activate the drop sled," Dex replied.

A different mercenary pulled a small box from the hovercart and stepped to the shaft. He pressed a button and tossed the box over the hole. As it fell, it straightened out into a taut platform like a magic carpet and hovered in place over the chasm. It beeped like a coffee maker that just finished brewing a pot.

"Send the scouts," Dex instructed the mercenary captain.

The Clicklaxia with the scanner and several of the murder bears climbed aboard the tarp. It beeped once and disappeared into the pit in a blink, taking the guard and mercenaries with it. Lazer and Streek loitered behind the congregation, idly looking about their surroundings.

A call came in. *"Air is breathable, no life-forms. All clear."*

"Roger that," the captain replied.

The tarp returned with a *zip*, spread and sturdy, ready for the next round of passengers. Dex stepped onto it, along with her Clicklaxia guards, one of whom motioned for Lazer and Streek to come with them. It was a command they quickly obeyed without objection, finding open space near the middle. A current ran through the floor, sticking everyone's feet to the tarp like a magnet. It beeped.

"Oh bullocks," Streek lamented as the tarp zoomed down the shaft at blazing speed, leaving the octopus with nothing to hover over. Streek fell, his scream fading into the abyss as the drop sled outpaced him, racing faster than he could plummet into the darkness below.

Lazer and company landed abruptly at the bottom of the shaft, sending a wave of dust out into the iron-lined causeway stretching before them. The drop sled tilted at a slight angle, accommodating for the remnants of the smashed lift that was pressed diagonally into the dirt ground below them. One by one, they slid off into a grand earthen foyer. The walls were a reddish-mustard clay, hard and packed with spaced beams of ore, coming together at the top of the vaulted ceiling like ribs connecting to a spine. Incandescent triangles littered the floor, illuminating the massive space as mercenaries stood to the sides, weapons pointed at the imposing metal doors before them.

The Clicklaxia with the scanner led by several paces ahead of the group, her footsteps echoing softly as they tapped against the hard dirt floor. She walked forward, following the beeping markers in front of her, treading a careful path between metal and bones.

She spoke to Dex through an intercom. "It appears as though there are triggers in the ground, ma'am, but they have all been deactivated. There doesn't seem to be any type of heat signature either. I don't know if the system has aged out of use or if they were intentionally shut down. I won't be able to tell unless I find the primary access panel on the other side of those doors," she said, pointing her scanner at the fortified gates standing at the end of the wide space. *"Perhaps if I can just find some kind of cabling, I can work backward and . . ."*

A row of spikes jutted up from the ground, impaling the Clicklaxia and pushing her several feet into the air as the scanner dropped to the floor. Everybody raised their weapons.

"Nobody move," Dex said, holding her hand in signal to keep the others where they were. Lazer widened his stance in a defensive posture. Dex stood motionless, without a hint of fear.

"Are you ready for the next grouping?" a voice on Dex's intercom hissed.

"Hold, await my order," she replied.

A scream, loud and getting louder, came in fast from above. Streek's space bubble fell to the floor and rolled out like a bowling ball into the entryway, racing past the kabobed Clicklaxia with a rocket's velocity. All matter of sharp objects flew at the clear orb as it sped by. Metal bolts fired in abundance while saws buzzed up from the ground, all missing as they followed a step behind the ball's trajectory.

Roll, roll, roll . . . It crashed into the large doors at the end of the room. A crack ran up the side of Streek's ball after impact, reaching all the way to the top before the barrier shattered into a mess of tiny pieces. A pendulum creaked as it swung from the ceiling and whooshed precariously over the dizzy octopus's head. Streek rubbed a tentacle across his eyes and regained his senses.

"AIR! AIR! I NEED AIR! I CAN'T BREATHE! I CAN'T . . . Wait . . . ," he cried in exasperation before stopping to take a deep breath. "Never mind. All is well. You know, for a minute there, I thought I was most certainly dea—" Streek looked up right as the thick, curved saw swung above him once more.

"Ah! Tetanus!" the octopus screamed as he looked side to side in panic.

He reached a tentacle to the left and stopped short as a metal bolt fired swiftly across the room and hit the door, inches beside him. He moved a different tentacle to the right and stopped short as another bolt fired toward him, stopping his movement in the other direction. He looked forward, his eyes getting wide. He frantically spread his tentacles as more bolts flew his way, striking the spaces on the door between his fleshy limbs. Sweat beaded at his brow and slowly crawled down his face. He looked up, bit his lip, and carefully reached a tentacle toward the dollop of perspiration creeping southward. The others in the room hung on the moment, anxiously awaiting a final, well-placed projectile. Streek rubbed the tip of his tentacle on the interloping dot of liquid and wiped it away. Nothing happened. Streek's facial contortions relaxed into a wave of relief as Dex looked back and shot the concealed bolt-gun with her side arm, disabling it.

Streek ducked the pendulum once more and zipped forward, only to be stopped by a protruding set of spikes. He darted back, refilling his outline from the bolts against the door.

"I think I'll just stay here for the moment," he said, keeping an eye out for the flying saw.

"OK, Lazer, it's time to earn your paycheck," Dex said as she slid her blaster back in its holster. "Your glove possesses several functions, one of which is the ability to ping the density of any surface, filter the information, and project what's inside or behind it."

"Huh?"

"You can see through walls."

"Cool."

"All you have to do is hold your hand in front of you and tap your thumb to your palm twice. That will activate your LE."

Lazer tapped his thumb twice against his palm, and a menu popped up on the overlay.

"Excellent. You can tilt your hand left or right to cycle through each option until you reach the one that says Density Sync. Once there, clench your fist and you should begin to see the added dimension."

Lazer followed the instructions. He swept over the dull clay walls that adjoined the large set of doors. Beams and support structures projected in three dimensions in whichever direction he pointed his palm.

"Good. You can now find the disable switch; every room should have one," Dex said as Lazer waved his arm about.

"What does it look like?" Lazer asked, still fascinated with his gadget.

"It should be by the door. You will know it when you see it."

"OK, sure. That sounds good. Gimme a sec," Lazer said, holding his hand forward as he followed the projection that illuminated the traps in the ground and walls.

He stepped carefully and with purpose, tiptoeing lightly around the dead henchwoman, over a hidden spike trap, under a trigger for a different spike trap, and through a narrow path of smashed metal. He approached Streek, who was still holding himself in place, surrounded by bolts lodged into the door, too nervous to make any further moves. Lazer lunged deep to avoid the swinging radius of the pendulum, turned to the side, and jumped twice over triggering bricks, hopscotching himself to the wall adjacent to the door. A bright red rectangle showed itself through the glove, embedded in the wall, glowing at waist level.

"OK, I found the thing. Now what?"

"Press it."

Lazer pressed the soft dirt behind his projection and waited. "Nothing happened."

"What do you mean, nothing happened?" Dex asked, annoyed that her presumption was incorrect.

"Maybe you need Gorlak's thumb," Streek called out, still pressing firmly against the wall, forcing a nervous smile.

"Maybe it's broken?" Lazer asked, moving his hand in a wave like he was trying to activate an automatic towel dispenser. A deep groan of gears creaked as he motioned. Lazer stopped and looked around. "What was that?"

"The door. I think. Yes. The door. Or maybe something doorlike? I don't know, I can't see behind me," Streek called out again, nervously ducking into himself every time the pendulum passed. "Hey, how did you do that, by the way?"

"I don't know. It wasn't on the dirt. I just moved my hand. I think I have the force."

"The dirt. It's in the dirt," Dex muttered to herself under her breath. "Of course! Lazer, I believe your liquid eye is connecting to an undetected frequency, which, in turn, enables you to operationally interact with some kind of analog computer."

"Yeah, I've always been more of an analog guy. Recording to tape just sounds fuller, ya know?"

"That's nice, Lazer. Please move your hand once more. That sound isn't the door. I think you are disengaging the defense systems."

"So . . . I do have the force?"

"No, you are far too primitive for telekinesis. Sorry. Think of yourself more like a remote control."

"OK. That's cool too. How do I change the channel to *Cops*?"

"Not that type of remote. Stay focused."

"Right. Focused. So now what?"

"You'll need to find the precise motion that allows you to disarm the security protocol."

"So turn it off?"

"Yes. That's the plan."

"OK. I can do that."

Lazer waved his hand once more. The scraping lurch of the obscured gears briefly resumed. Lazer kept at it, maintaining a wiping motion until it settled with a loud click. The pendulum stopped. The various traps retracted, freeing Streek while the spikes impaling the Clicklaxia woman pulled back through her body, purple blood slowly draining out. The doors lumbered open.

The drop sled elevated back up to get the next wave of mercenaries. Dex walked forward toward the open door. She was followed by her corporate military and Clicklaxia henchwomen, one of whom picked up the dropped scanner on her way past it.

A handful of carefully tossed halogen triangles illuminated the next room. It was a forked hallway with scattered skeletons and freshly trodden dirt going down both lanes. Lazer's liquid eye projected a blue outline around the passageway to the right.

"I think it wants us to go this way," Lazer said.

"Good. Borta, please take the lead with our human friend."

"Aye, boss," a henchwoman replied as she hurried ahead of the group to get a reading.

"Any signatures?" Dex asked.

"No, boss," Borta replied.

"Any visible traps, Lazer?"

"Nothing," he said, several paces behind the henchwoman with the scanner, holding his hand out, looking for spikes in the walls or ceiling or floor.

"Any atmospheric—" Dex was cut off by the sound of whizzing saw blades. They came from the ground in an arc and sliced Borta off at the shins. Her scanner fell beside her into an expanding puddle of blood. The saws stopped, flicking several droplets. Dex closed her fist. Everybody stopped.

"I don't understand. I was looking at this when the weapons deployed. How did it not register? Is the sync off?" she asked.

"I don't know, but I think your friend is still alive," Lazer replied, pointing ahead at the henchwoman. She rolled onto her stomach and began crawling back to Dex and the rest of the team.

"You're gonna be OK!" Streek called out.

"I . . . I can make it . . ." Borta coughed out as she crawled several more feet. The ground dropped out beneath her as she vanished into the floor with a "Yiiiii . . ."

Dex and the rest of the group waited, listening, until they were sure nothing else would happen.

"Get the backup scanner," Dex commanded to the mercenary on the other end of the intercom.

"Right away, ma'am," the voice replied, disappearing for a minute. *"Um, ma'am?"*

"Yes?"

"It appears we did not . . . pack it . . . ma'am."

Dex pinched the top of her nose. "Glaxxor? You're provisions. We've talked about this."

"Yes, ma'am. Right here, it says on the packing list, one scanner. But it's not here."

"Do you mean the one scanner that is currently sitting at the bottom of the pit?"

"No, it says here . . . It says . . . Yes, ma'am. It appears I misread it."

"You know operating procedure. That's a write-up."

"It won't happen again, ma'am."

"That doesn't do me any good right now."

Dex looked to the merc captain behind her. "We need that scanner."

The captain, the mercenaries, Dex, and her team of personal guards all looked at the floating octopus while Lazer continued to scan the floor in his immediate area with the liquid eye.

Streek looked about his intimidating audience. "I can't fly, you know; I float via self-generated air propulsion. I use the resistance from the ground to glide along at—"

"We need that scanner," Dex said again, cutting him off.

Streek waited to see if anybody would chime in. Nobody did.

"Any day now," Dex prodded.

"All right, fine," Streek said in resignation, muttering under his breath as he floated toward the scanner. "Stupid scanner, can't scan for things that are going to kill you . . . pointless . . . absolutely pointless . . ."

He hovered to the pit and used his suction cups to walk his way down the wall of the shaft. "Hey! I think she might be alive down here!" he called from inside. Streek reemerged back up from the hole with the scanner in one of his tentacles. "She's alive, definitely alive. I could hear her down there. She needs some rope or some kind of chain so someone can lower down and pull her out. There!" Streek exclaimed, pointing at a chain that lay serendipitously in a coil on the floor near the wall. "Here, let me get it. Somebody help me!"

Streek floated to the chain and pulled. A groan exuded from the ceiling as a spike-covered block of metal dropped from above, flew down the shaft, and crushed the security guard.

"Ack!" yelped the henchwoman as Streek curled his tentacles and winced. He pointed the scanner at the hole and looked back to Dex and her mercenaries.

"My mistake."

Streek floated back to the group and tried to hand the scanner to one of the henchwomen. They all declined, holding their hands up in recusal. Streek looked to a rifle-wielding space bear standing beside them. The mercenary stepped back; his associates followed suit.

"Oh, come on. I don't want to be scanner guy. Scanner guy always dies!" he said as Dex maintained her indifference. Streek gazed at the scanner clutched by his frontmost tentacle and sighed.

Dex moved past Streek's objections. "Lazer, it appears there is a limitation to what your drive is able to show us. You will be in front with your friend."

"It's Streek . . . ma'am," the octopus replied unnecessarily.

"OK, Streek. You're in front."

"But I—"

"And hold the scanner outward. We need to know if we lose breathable atmosphere."

"I—"

"And try not to die."

"OK," Streek said, deflated. He floated to the front of the group and pointed the scanner down the hall. "All clear, ma'am."

Dex shooed him forward as the group followed Streek and Lazer down the path. After a short trek, they reached another set of doors. Lazer used his LE drive to locate and turn the gearworks, their creaking shudder echoing down the hallway.

They entered the new space. It was a museum of cultural artifacts, portraits, and tapestries. A metal statue of a Baku warrior riding a saddled mammoth as it trampled upon a dead enemy stood in the center of the room. His spear, long and pointing toward the sky, carried a banner bearing the four-fingered handprint of Lolo's resistance.

"Magnificent," Dex said aloud as she entered, awestruck at the works they discovered.

"Yeah, that would be a sweet album cover," Lazer replied, pointing to the scene on a tapestry of a gearwork soldier firing rockets into the air. "This whole place is giving me ideas."

"But wasn't this Bakuma's city?" Streek asked, looking around.

"It was . . . at least, for a time. I need a scan," Dex said.

"Already workin' on it," Lazer replied with a nod and a shrug, sweeping his arm from side to side.

"You too," she said, looking at Streek.

Dex's guards and the military contractors all took a step back.

"Aw, come on, guys," Streek said as he pointed the reader at the room. He sighed again. "Clear."

Dex stepped up to the massive statue and was dwarfed by its incredible size, only coming up to the foot of the work of art. Beneath the iron behemoth was a marble plaque, obsidian black and in the shape of a spearhead, imprinted with Ubu text.

Dex looked to Lazer, who was poking at the dusty glass covering some unknown object. "Lazer, kindly translate that."

Lazer approached it and wiped off a thick layer of dust. He squinted, focusing intently on what he was looking at. He wiped a bit more, took a step back, and cocked his head. He looked back at Dex. "Yeah, I can't read that."

"Your liquid eye. Scroll to translate and hold your hand palm out in front of you, please."

"Oh, that makes more sense."

Lazer tapped his thumb, tilted his hand, and found the option. He clenched his fist and opened his hand, palm out. A hologram leaped out toward Lazer, scrolling text like the lyric crawl on the bottom of a karaoke video. It was in English.

"It says, 'We erect this monument to who we were, as a gift for those yet to come. May we never forget what once was and what could have been, as we slide slowly into an inevitable darkness,'" he read aloud.

"Interesting," Dex said.

"Yeah. And a little metal too."

"It's made of some sort of marble," she corrected.

"I'm talking about the musical genre."

"I am not familiar with this 'metal.' I have heard selections of Earth music. I am partial to a well-conducted concerto."

"Cool, cool. It's kind of like classical music. Maybe a neighborhood over . . . Definitely louder. Probably the party house on the block."

"That's nice. Maybe you could show me later after we retrieve the—" Dex said before getting cut off by Lazer, who pointed to a small wooden instrument beneath a glass case adjacent to them.

"Oh! I can show you now. Check it out," he said, stepping over to the encasement.

Streek floated up beside him. "Now really isn't the time."

"But it's got strings on it. How can I not play it? Just a sec. It'll be worth it, promise," Lazer said, lifting up the dusty glass top. He reached in and pulled the boxy, ukulele-sized instrument from its display. It was pastel green with a white-trimmed neck with three wire strings. He held it with his left hand on the neck while cradling it in the crook of his right arm. Looking down, he hit each string, letting them ring out in long-neglected dissonance.

Streek winced. "Maybe just a little out of tune there."

"Don't worry, I got this," Lazer assured, holding his ear to the hollow body of the instrument. He twisted the wooden knobs at the top, striking each string individually before tightening them up. "Almost there," he said, twisting a knob slowly as the notes melted together. "There. Tuned to standard. I'd drop it to E flat but that low string feels a little loose to me."

"Get on with it before I take away your new toy," Dex said, rolling her hand.

"Cool. OK, here's an oldie but a goodie," Lazer announced with excitement, leaning forward to look at his fingers on the unfamiliar fretboard.

He banged out a series of chords. Dun Dun Dunnn, Dun Dun Dah-nunnn, Dun Dun Dunnn, Dah-nunnnn. *Dun Dun Dunnn, Dun Dun Dah-nunnn, Dun Dun Dunnn, Dah-nunnnn.*

"Smoooooke on the waaaaater . . . a fire in the sky," he sang in his on-key, yet less than fantastic timbre. Lazer's vocal abilities were generally more suited for backups and the occasional harmony, though it did the job.

Dex raised an eyebrow. "This is metal? I would have expected screeching and grinding sounds."

"Nah, you'll get that when you start getting into black metal and whatnot. I'm more of a fan of thrash and the classic stuff. More toward the rock side of the family tree, you know? But it's all good, really," Lazer said as he resumed his chord progression.

"I'm sure I need to hear it on the intended instruments."

"Sure thing. Tell me if you see a guitar lying around anywhere."

"I'll keep an eye out. In the meantime, do you see where to go from here?"

"No . . . Maybe . . . Oh wait. I see a thing. Yeah."

Lazer walked toward a highlighted section of wall in the shape of a door by where Streek innocuously hovered. The octopus was looking at a piece of art depicting the same type of plains from the documentary they saw back on the ship.

Streek looked at Lazer. "Do you suppose any of these people are still alive somewhere down here?"

"Nah, man, that was a long time ago. They're all dead by now," Lazer replied.

Streek looked at him with an eye roll. "I mean their descendants. Do you think they could have survived down here somehow? After all of this time?"

"I'm sure we'll find out on the other side of this door," Lazer said as he pressed a glowing brick beside the outline. The sound of shifting gears opened a yawning gap beneath them. Lazer reached up and grabbed Streek, holding tightly on to his tentacles as they both disappeared into the trapdoor below.

Lazer and Streek slid down an endless chute. Bits of light popped out of Lazer's glove from the few areas not gripping on to Streek's tentacle. They flashed and blinked in chaotic spurts, illuminating the slick narrow confines as they sped ever downward. The visual overlay disappeared, Lazer's link disconnected. They yelled, loud and terrified, harmonizing their respective Wilhelm screams, belted out from the bottommost depths of their lungs—or at least Lazer's lungs. Streek didn't quite have the same biological setup.

They screamed and slid and screamed and slid, and when they were out of breath, they inhaled deeply and screamed some more. Small bits of water vapor hugged the surface of the tunnel, which soon became droplets and eventually a trickle. The water pulled into their chute from tiny porous holes along the carved stone. The slick surface ushered the pair along even faster, deeper into the belly of the mountain.

Lazer hit a curve in the shaft and slid out into an open hallway. He lost his grip on Streek and skid along the smooth, wet floor until he lost his inertia, coming to a gentle stop. Streek slid up directly behind him, bumping Lazer slightly with the scanner that remained tightly wrapped in his tentacle. Lazer stood and wiped the small amount of water from his hands onto his jeans. He strummed a few times on his alien ukulele.

"Hey, still in tune!" he exclaimed, before realizing the wobbly state of his companion. Lazer bent down and picked up Streek, who was in the process of regaining his senses.

Lazer looked at the vent they'd entered from. It was narrow, steep, and most certainly impossible for him to make his way back up. Behind the shaft was a solid slab of dead end. He turned around and stared down the hall; it was endless, fading away into an immersive wispy miasma. The walls, floor, and ceiling were all light-beige rock, moist in accumulated droplets that felt propped up in the air. Streek coughed a few times and hovered out from Lazer's arm, shaking off his slide.

"OK, I'm done. I'd like to go home now," he stated with a wobbly certainty as he hovered away and turned back. "I mean it. Let's go!"

"Sure thing," Lazer replied, engaging in a quick bend and stretch. "Lead the way."

Streek charged forward in earnest determination for a full three seconds before turning back in an abrupt panic. "I can't. We're as good as dead. Those people were our ride. I don't know what I'm doing. Can we climb our way back up?" he asked with wide eyes as he reached out and tugged Lazer's shirt. "Is that possible?"

"Maybe you can," Lazer said with a shrug. "But it ain't happening for me."

"OK, how about I go get help? I can work my way back up. It might take a while to get back up there. But maybe they have some gadget that can help you, like the gravity sled thing. Right? That would work. Is that OK? Can I just leave you? I can't do that. That would be wrong, right? I don't know. What should I do?"

"Whatever you think you've got to. But I think my only way out of here is to walk that way."

"I don't know. I hate making decisions. It gives me such anxiety."

"Yeah, you seem a little stressed."

"A little stressed? A little stressed? How many times have we almost died now?"

"*Now* now? Or like, all of the times now? Now now, maybe four, five times? I don't know. All the times now? Phew, man . . . Well, there was the time the bus almost crashed on black ice going through Montana . . . or was it Idaho? Doesn't matter. It was January. Never do a northern US tour in January if you can avoid it. Oh, and there's the time I ate at that bad Mexican spot and barfed up blood for a week and we had to cancel the tour . . . That was a different tour, of course. Or there was the time—"

"No, no. I mean, over the short tenure of our association together."

"Like, since we've been friends?"

"I mean . . . I guess . . . Wait. We're friends?"

"Sure, dude. Near-death experiences have a way of bringing people closer together. Plus, you seem all right to me."

"Oh, cool? Yeah. I mean, yes, of course we're friends. Is this how people normally become friends? I don't really have many . . . or, well, any really," Streek said with a nervous frown, somewhat ashamed of his awkward disposition.

"Really? Well, that doesn't matter. We're friends now. Boom."

"Boom?"

"Boom."

"Boooom," Streek said with a nod and a smile. "Cool . . . Wait . . . That means I can't leave now, can I?"

"It would probably be a dick move, yeah."

"OK. OK. No problem. No problem . . . So what do we do?"

"What I always do. Pick a direction and go that way until you decide you don't want to go that way anymore."

"What if it's the wrong way?"

"Then it's the wrong way."

"Then what do you do?"

"That's future Lazer's problem. Right now, it seems to me that the only thing there is to do is to just start walking," Lazer said, pointing toward the barren stone hallway that stretched before them. He looked back at Streek. "But you don't have legs, so I guess the walking's on me. You can keep floating . . . or whatever it is you're doing."

"I'm using the surrounding atmosphere to propel my . . . You know what? It doesn't matter. Yes. All right, friend, I'm with you. Lead the way," Streek said with a cautiously optimistic smile.

Lazer walked first, and Streek followed as the two proceeded onward into the unending darkness before them. There were no doors, windows, or openings of any kind. The only form of light came from Lazer's glove, which emitted a workable radiance. Lazer's shoes tapped along the hard rock as he stepped briskly yet aware, as to avoid slipping on the slick surface beneath his feet. Streek looked at Lazer and struck up a conversation with his new friend as they ventured.

"So you said you were in a band, yeah? What do you play?"

"I am. I play guitar . . . and some bass . . . a little keys, some drums . . . but only maybe four different beats and only when my drummer takes one of his long bathroom breaks. I also sing some backup vocals and I played the trumpet in fifth grade. I wasn't very good. You play?"

"Wow. Um, yeah, a little," he said, rubbing a tentacle. "I play the accordion. I'm not incredible, but you know, I can play a few of the hits."

"'Crazy Train'?"

"No."

"'Holy Diver'?"

"I'm afraid I don't know that one."

"'Raining Blood'?"

"That just sounds unfortunate."

"'Madhouse'?"

"Are these all song titles?"

"Yeah, man. Never heard of 'em? What are you into?"

"Mostly songs I've been able to learn how to play, Yes."

"Yes, songs you've learned, that's cool."

"No, Yes."

"No yes?"

"No, I mean Yes."

"Yes, you learned songs on the accordion?"

"No, Yes songs on accordion."

"Yes, I know, songs on the accordion," Lazer said.

Streek stopped and turned, showing a slight hint of frustration. "Songs by Yes, the band."

"I like The Band."

"No, not The Band. I'm saying Yes."

"Yes to what? Playing songs by The Band? I was raised on that stuff. My mom had a pretty good record collection."

"Yes the band, not yes, The Band. Though 'The Weight' is a classic, come on now," Streek said as they resumed.

Lazer laughed. "I'm just messing with you. Yes is badass. Can you play 'Heart of the Sunrise'?"

"Ooh, it's been a while with that one."

"Yeah, it took me a good few days to get it down."

"Same."

"Dude, if we don't die, we should definitely jam," Lazer said, waving his ukulele.

"Yeah? Deal," Streek replied with a smile before excitedly recalling more things to share. "Oh, I love Genesis, post–Peter Gabriel of course."

"Eh, it's all kind of weird."

"You're kidding. Phil Collins is incredible. And Elbow. I love Elbow. You should listen to Elbow," Streek gushed as Lazer looked him over.

"Do you even technically have elbows?" he asked, poking at a rubbery tuber hanging below Streek's face.

"I technically don't have any joints at all. My species possesses an elaborate system of subdermal cavities that use the surrounding air to not only keep us hovering off the ground but to give shape to our entire bodies. Without atmosphere, I flatten like a pancake. So yeah, no joints, just air and squishy stuff."

"Cool."

"Yeah, it's all right. What's it like being a human?"

"Itchy. I get hungry pretty often. Actually, I'm hungry right now. You have anything in any pockets of yours or . . . ?"

"I'm naked."

"Oh yeah, good point. Oh wait! I still have some peanuts from the bar," Lazer replied as he reached into his pockets.

"No, they reprinted your clothes, remember?"

"Right. So my peanuts should have reprinted too."

"You know, that's a fair point now that I think about it," Streek acknowledged.

"Yup, peanuts!" Lazer said, throwing a few in his mouth. "Ooh, salty. You want some?"

"Oh, no thank you. I'm not really a fan."

"Cool. Cool. So what do you eat? Not people, right?"

"No, plants mostly, some ocean stuff. Don't worry."

"That's good to know. I'm happy I met you. It's nice that there's one person out here who isn't trying to turn me into man-sausage."

"That's a pretty low bar for friendship, but I know what you mean. The so-called lunch laws of the GU can make being close to anyone a pretty dicey endeavor."

"What are lunch laws?" Lazer asked through a mouthful of peanuts.

"Essentially a rule that says that a culture's culinary history supersedes an individual's right to not get eaten. Originally, the rule was that if your species could travel off-world, you were deemed advanced enough to be of value to the community of planets beyond your caloric endowments."

"What's that now?"

"If your species could make it to space, it was illegal to eat you. But a few powerful member states with, let's just say, carnivorous tendencies challenged the law in Space Court—"

"Wait, they call it Space Court?"

"Sure, what would you call it? Planet Court? That's dumb," Streek asked as Lazer pondered the question.

"Yeah, I guess Space Court works."

"Right. It's pretty straightforward. Anyway, Space Court ruled that even while cultural history should be respected, the individual right to existence outweighed dietary preferences. Makes sense, right? But the carnivores were relentless. They called it an attack on their culinary freedom and formed some groups that lobbied their representatives, held rallies, and generally made a big fuss over it. Eventually, they got enough reps on board to pass a law to accommodate them, which said that as long as your culture had a history of eating a certain species, then you could continue to do so."

"Damn. So did your ship do that a lot? Sell people?"

"Would you hate me if I said yes?" Streek asked, wincing slightly.

"That's kinda messed up."

"It is. But to be fair, I applied to work at corporate, but they stuck me on Izzit's ship when the previous accountant became . . . unaccounted for. I was only there for a few months, and I was already thinking of quitting. I didn't have the stomach for it, and I have four stomachs! So yeah, I didn't really fit in much."

"That's why you got fired?"

"That, or because during an audit I found out Izzit had managed to blow his operating budget on frivolous expenditures like human-themed employee attire. He had to be pretty prolific on the lunch market to keep up. Those costumes weren't cheap, you know? He insisted on Earth-original attire, so they had to import it."

"That stuff was from Earth?"

"Yeah. The receipts said some boutique called Biff's Used Costume Surplus."

"I guess that makes sense," Lazer replied, scratching behind his ear.

"Hmm. Well, it didn't to me. That ship was bleeding red ink. Raiding ships under false pretenses, releasing those with insurance and vending off those without. It was just to keep up with all the waste."

"Yeah, man, merch is expensive. So what's up with the rule where I might get eaten?"

"It's not exactly at the point where you see people consuming each other in the streets or anything, but there's a market for it. Cash is king, as they say out here. Do they say that on Earth? Doesn't matter. Those raids covered payroll and then some."

"And people eat humans out here?"

"Not really. There aren't human farms or anything, though sometimes hunting enthusiasts break the law and go for wild caught. You know, like in the Predator documentaries," Streek said as he imitated the *Predator* noise.

"Wait, those were real?"

"You thought they were fake?"

"Aw, man, that's nuts! So what's up with the whole anal-probe thing?"

The two walked for what felt like miles, talking about bands, life, and which aliens to avoid if you would like to remain uneaten in the wider universe. Though after some time, Lazer needed to sit. He walked to the wall and rested his back against it, slowly sliding down until his butt hit the floor. Streek hovered beside him.

Lazer looked up. "Do you ever get tired?"

"Not really. The organ that keeps me floating is the same organ that keeps me breathing. I can't stop, really."

"So you never sit down?"

"No. Mostly it's just this."

"So you sleep while floating?" Lazer asked as he give his lower back a good twist.

"Yes. A full forty-five minutes a day, an hour if I'm being lazy."

"Yeah. You sound like a slacker."

"That's what my dad always says," Streek said, looking down. "Hey, wait a minute. Look at the wall behind your hand. Hold the light up to it."

Lazer turned to his side and looked at the wall by his hand. It was marked with faded white paint. He stood and stepped back and illuminated a fuller section of wall. It was a series of symbols. They were letters, like Ubu.

"Hey, Lazer, you think your glove can read that?"

"Maybe. I lost the head sticker that let me see all the options."

"Maybe there's a hologram mode? Tap your thumb against your palm a few times and see what happens."

"Right, yeah, the thumb thing," Lazer said as a hologram beamed from his palm. He found the translate option and waved through the symbols. Broken words in English emerged in three-dimensional rendering. It said: *Lolobaku. Beware demon Bakuma.*

"Beware demon . . . Hmm . . . Well, that's auspicious," Streek said sarcastically.

"I thought Australians spoke English?" Lazer replied as Streek made the same confused face he made every time Lazer said something ridiculous.

"No. It's not . . . Never mind. What else does it say? Keep going."

Lazer walked along the wall with his hand out. The symbols continued, their translations projecting out. *It live inside. Eat dreams. Never die. Only eat. Look like you. Know sign.*

At the end of the painting was a bold, two-dimensional white diamond. Beyond the diamond was blank stone.

"What do you think that means?" Streek asked as Lazer moved his arm around, looking for any other drawings on the surrounding surfaces.

"I think it means we've just answered your question about people living down here."

"I think you may be right," Streek agreed with a nervous look over his shoulder.

A slight splash of water echoed from farther down the passageway.

"Hello?" Lazer called out.

"Shh," Streek hushed with a poke to Lazer's shoulder. "We have no idea what made that noise."

"And I'm sure I just confused them too."

"Or maybe you gave whatever it is our exact location. Lunch laws are still valid in the center of planets, you know. You don't just have to be in space."

"Now who's being noisy?"

"Fair point," Streek whispered loudly.

Lazer walked forward as Streek hovered by. Every step was careful, conscious. The luminous glow of Lazer's glove gave enough light to see but not enough to anticipate. There was no distance to cover, no space to react. They could be attacked at any second, from any direction, and were utterly defenseless. Lazer turned as he walked, doing his best to show his surroundings. Above him, attached to the stone ceiling, a shadow lay still. Lazer and Streek continued on, and it crept, silently following.

"I guess it must have been nothing," Streek said a little more comfortably as the pair regained a more casual pace.

"Maybe it was an echo from farther down here. Maybe we're close to reaching something."

"Like what?"

"Whatever comes after this," Lazer said with a shrug.

"Actually, it is getting a little lighter. Right? Does it seem less dark to you?"

"You know, I think you're right."

"Yeah, maybe we've finally reached the end of this thing," Streek agreed with a cautious smile.

"I think we might be. What do you think is down there?" Lazer asked, squinting to make out the source of the distant brightness.

They continued on as the walls around them became visible like the sunrise, a churning gurgle murmured in the distance. They jogged, then ran, anxious to see what lay beyond the end of the tunnel.

They reached the edge and stepped atop a grated metal platform and looked out over an expansive forest of lichen. They grew in hazy patches of green, magenta, and blue, wrapping around ash-black rocks that were stacked like columns but irregular like stalagmites, reaching like redwoods through the wispy clouds that rolled like a blanket across the length of the subterranean biosphere. A faint ruby tint colored the sky, emanating outward in warm iridescence from the tip of a great stone pyramid at the other end.

The walls of the inside of the dome were smooth and earthy like the entrance above. Their color and surface were incongruent with that of the lichen forest. They were pocked with tubes and tunnels that reached out in varying lengths, depositing the running water that flowed out into streams crisscrossing through the valley below. Streek lifted the scanner and took a reading. A hologram popped up from its top side.

"So what's it saying?" Lazer asked.

"Well, I don't really know how to read this thing, but I think it's saying we're on a different planet."

"Weird."

"Definitely. There's more oxygen, less gravity, more humidity—even the chemical makeup of the soil is different. Or at least, that's what the scanner says. I honestly don't really know what we're looking at, though. I'm an accountant, remember?"

"I see water," Lazer said.

"I think so. I can hear it too."

"No, I mean, water is dripping on you," he said, pointing to several droplets that had landed on Streek's head. They both looked up and immediately screamed.

The creature was small, with splotchy green skin resembling a collection of leaves piled atop each other. He was shaped with humanoid proportions but had fingers for toes and wispy orange hair coming out of a small patch on the top of his head. He wore a pair of furry lavender shorts that were caked in dirt and held a spear in his free hand. His three remaining hands clung tightly to the cracks in the rocks above, gripping them with the dexterity of an expert climber.

The creature screamed back, baring a mouth filled with rows of tiny, sharp teeth. He dropped down, standing no taller than Lazer's thigh, and pointed his spear upward in a menacing fashion, blocking the route to the underground forest beyond. Streek recoiled in fear and threw the scanner at the homunculus in reflex. It was a poor throw, sailing high and wide into the thicket of columns below. He turned around and sped in the other direction, screaming, hovering as fast as his circulating air currents could carry him.

After a short sprint, Streek turned to see Lazer was not with him but still back with the creature, hunched over. Had Lazer been stabbed? Had

Streek abandoned his new friend already, failing to defend him in his greatest moment of need? *This is why you don't have friends*, Streek thought as he raced back, a pang of dread consuming him. He reached the human and stopped abruptly.

Lazer was kneeling, sitting on his heels with a hand forward, offering a peanut to the diminutive warrior. The creature snuck close, curious, sniffing in quick bursts. With a three-fingered hand reaching, he accepted the offering and scurried back several steps. He looked at Lazer, nibbled on the peanut, then looked back at Lazer once more. Lazer reached through his open zipper into his jeans pocket, jingled past his keys, grabbed some more peanuts, and held one out. The creature stepped closer and took the next offering. He ate this one faster, then stepped even closer still. Lazer handed out a third peanut, smiling at the curious gremlin.

The creature ate the treat and now stood face-to-face with Lazer. He was similar to the Baku from the documentary but smaller, wirier. He had regressed to something else, something primal. Everything was diminished but his brow, which pushed forward along with a jutting chin. The orange patch of hair on his head matched the fuzz around his face. The sub-Baku reached into Lazer's stubble, picking around. He sniffed at him closely, up and down, as Streek hovered to Lazer's shoulder. The creature hopped back and clutched his spear in a defensive posture.

"My friend. My friend," Lazer said as he gently pushed the spear to the ground and zipped his space suit back up.

"Yeah, please tell him I'm with you. That'd be nice," the octopus requested.

"OK. But I don't think he speaks English."

"No. But your glove speaks his language, right?"

"Oh, you're right. This thing is, hands down, the best. Hands down. Don't you think?" Lazer chuckled as he tapped and cycled his way to the translate function.

"Ubu. It was Ubu."

Lazer pressed the button and turned toward his new captive audience. "Hi. This is my friend. Please don't stab him," Lazer enunciated.

His request was followed by a string of grunts and whistles. The creature perked up and looked at Lazer in amazement, relaxing his spear-wielding stance. He reached out and touched Lazer's glove in wonder before stepping back.

He replied in his own language. The glove translated. *"Sorry. No kill stranger. Who is?"*

"We're stuck down here and don't know how to get back out. Where are we?"

"House of Lolobaku. Where from, stranger?"

"Up," Lazer replied, pointing to the ceiling.

The creature tilted his head in confusion. He chirped back, *"Nothing up. Only here."*

"I used to think the same thing, bud. But you have no idea," Lazer said.

Streek butted in, "Can you lead us back to the top? We need to get home."

"Home? Yes, Zizi take stranger."

"Zizi?" Lazer asked with an eyebrow up.

"Yes. Zizi. Zizi," he said, hopping up and down.

"Oh, you're Zizi?" Lazer realized, pointing to the gremlin.

"Zizi. Yes. Zizi. Who stranger?"

"I'm Lazer. Layyy-zurrr. Lazer," he said, patting his hand on his chest. "And this is Streek. Streeeeek." He pointed at his floating friend.

Zizi mouthed the words and attempted them in his staccato chirp. "Lah-zur. Strik. Lah-zur. Strik," he said without translation, smiling wide. Zizi hopped once more and beckoned them to follow, waving his non-spear hand forward. He resumed speaking in his native language while Lazer's glove translated. *"Come. Come. Zizi show home. Come home."*

Streek looked at Lazer. "I don't think he understood me."

"No. But at least we'll finally be out of this tunnel. What do you think?"

"I think you may change your mind after the climb down," Streek said as they peered over the ledge.

Zizi scampered down a lengthy series of shallow steps carved into the dirt, which led into the dense clutter of rocks and moss below. He stopped, turned, clacked the base of his spear against the ground, and pointed at his chest.

"Come. Home. Come," he said before turning back to the path before them.

PART 10

THE ONE-ARMED SURGEON

DEX DELVED INTO HER MOTHER'S FOLDER ON THE SECRET UNIVERSITY drive, opening another video.

Captain Ponn, Res Voland, and Dr. Quant, whose arm was in a cast and sling, sat around the metal table in the secret room behind the one-way mirror opposite of Dex, who sat on the carpet, once more playing with her toys.

"I want you to find a way to disable that thing," the captain said, pointing at the picture of the creature wrapped around Dex's brain on Dr. Quant's tablet.

"How would you recommend that?"

"Taking it out."

"Alive, if possible," the rep chimed in.

"But if I remove it, she might go back into a coma."

"That's kind of the idea," the captain replied. "Whatever is going on with that kid, I can't risk the rest of the people aboard."

"But she's just a child."

"A child who can outshoot and outmuscle literally every person on this ship. Scientific discovery or no scientific discovery, I cannot captain this ship at the mercy of a single little girl."

"Right. Emphasis on *little girl*, please," Dr. Quant shot back.

"Says the lady with the broken arm," Res chimed in again. "Look. I'm having serious doubts about this arrangement. I think it would be best if you went in and took this thing out. Be delicate and save both parties if possible, but there are major liability issues for both me and the company here. This goes beyond the study at this point. If somebody dies from this thing, all three of us could go to jail."

"I can't do it with one hand," Dr. Quant said, waving her cast. "And even if I could physically do it, I wouldn't."

"Then I will," the captain said, cracking her knuckles.

"You heard her," Res said to the doctor with a finger to his ear. "It's going to happen regardless. Your call."

"You'll kill her. Why can't we just wait until we reach the planet?"

"No. It's neutralized here, now," the captain demanded. "Whether it's surgery or a bullet, that's up to you."

Dr. Quant felt removed from herself for a moment. Throughout her career, she prided herself on saving children. She felt it was her calling, perhaps because she was never able to have any herself. Sometimes, she imagined what things would have been like had she had a family, but her path led her to spend her time saving them rather than making them. It often felt just as important, but she had no good answers here.

"I'm taking your sullen silence as acquiescence, Doctor," Res Voland said.

"You're right. It looks like I have no other choice."

"Good call. And please try to save the specimen. It technically belongs to the company now."

"You're soulless, you know that, right?"

"Look, lady. Both the captain and I are looking at the bigger picture here. That girl is simultaneously very dangerous and very valuable. Removing that . . . whateveritis . . . is the only way to ensure that nobody else gets hurt."

"But you're hurting her."

"Hardly, that girl was asleep, like the rest of them. We're just putting her back to her previous state. We're hardly monsters. No, that—her—she's the actual monster here," the rep said, pointing through the mirror at Dex.

"And what if she dies?"

"Then we scratch her from the study as if she were never on the ship, and she gets to be with the rest of her family in the afterlife. It's better than a perpetual coma if you ask me."

"I thought your goal was to cure people."

"I'm not a scientist—just a guy who makes things happen."

"I'll tell them what happened here."

"No, you won't. Both the captain and I will agree that your work was unilateral. Your career would be over, and you would face possible jail time. You want to save that girl's life? Keep a steady hand. You've only got one now."

Dr. Quant wept and nodded in understanding.

THE OPERATING ROOM HAD STAINLESS-STEEL surfaces and a wrap-around panel of screens giving readings of Dex's vital signs. The girl lay on the table in a paper gown. She had a plastic mask on, feeding her a steady supply of sleeping gas, which had evidently done its job. Dr. Quant monitored the dosage while the rep, who was dressed in a medical smock, acted as her assistant. Captain Ponn watched from closed circuit video from her quarters.

"OK, it looks like she's out. I will now begin by shaving her head," the doctor said to her assistant as she pulled out a set of electric shears. Their buzzing was constant as the little girl's braids fell to the floor one by one. Res wiped the remaining hair from the girl with a towel after Dr. Quant had finished.

"Marker."

The corporate rep handed the doctor a wide-tipped pen, which the doctor used to demarcate her intended incision lines.

"Cleaning pad."

Res handed a spongelike object to Dr. Quant, who sanitized the area.

"Scalpel."

The doctor took her instrument and moved in slowly, her hesitance a mixture of care and apprehension. Suddenly, a whisper.

"What was that?" Res asked as Dr. Quant stood straight.

"I'm not sure. Is she talking in her sleep?"

Dr. Quant stood and moved closer to Dex's face. Her lips moved faintly, pushing out a string of incoherent mumbles.

"What's she saying?" Res Voland asked, unsure how normal such a thing was during anesthesia.

"I'm not sure. It's a little difficult for me to lean all the way in with my arm like this."

"OK, hold on," Res Voland said as he moved around to the side of the operating table. He leaned in, his ear getting closer to Dex's mouth. The girl's murmurs continued, unintelligible.

"Anything?"

"I can't tell. I think she said *Mama*, but I can't be sure."

"Mmm . . . mma . . . mmm . . . ma . . . ," Dex mumbled, then trailed off, eyes still closed. Res Voland put his ear closer still, waiting for a break in the silence.

The girl's eyes went wide, and her mouth gaped open. The organism leaped from Dex's mouth and crawled into Res's ear. He screamed, grabbing at the creature and pulling at it frantically. It wormed its way farther, getting halfway in before the corporate rep was able to rip it out. It flipped and fluttered like a fish being held by the tail as he held a corner by two fingers.

Dr. Quant rushed to a table and grabbed the holding cube. She opened the lid and held it out for Res to place the writhing organism inside. The creature flashed white like a light grenade. Dr. Quant fell back from the shock of it and dropped the container. Res Voland let go of the creature and covered his eyes, stunned. The flashy leaf leaped once more, worming its way into the screaming man's ear, through the canal, and into the skull.

Res fell to the ground, shaking his head about violently in a vain attempt to remove the creature. He stopped screaming, twitched several times, and wiped the single drop of blood from his nose. He climbed back to his feet and looked upon Dr. Quant, who stepped backward. Res Voland moved his way to the table and picked up the scalpel.

"What are you doing?" the doctor asked in a cautious tremble.

Res Voland placed his finger against his lips. "Shh," he hushed as he proceeded to lean against the side of the sliding door. Within moments, Captain Ponn barged through, holding her pistol out. She made eye contact with the doctor, who cowered in the corner, before turning to see Res Voland lunge at her with the scalpel from behind. He came in quick and nicked her artery, sending a stream of blood to the floor. The captain grabbed at her wound and dropped her gun, which the corporate rep kicked across the room before stabbing her again. And again. And again.

Res Voland stepped over Captain Ponn's lifeless body carefully, as to not slip on the blood slowly spreading across the floor. Dr. Quant cried uncontrollably.

"You do not need to be alarmed. It . . . I . . . do not intend to hurt you." Res Voland said, blood dripping from his hand.

"What are you?" Dr. Quant asked through tears.

"I'm not sure how to answer that question. I'm me, still . . . but not. I'm also it now. Both."

"What . . . What is it?"

"Colors. Bright, warm. It's love . . . It's beautiful," he said, taking a deep breath in, then exhaling as if it were the first time he had ever done such a thing. "And yet . . . it is sadness . . . a deep, unfathomable despair. In my very pit, I feel it. An aching . . . longing for home . . . But where is home? Not here . . . It's telling me . . . Not here. Beyond nowhere. Its . . . Its mother . . . It wants its mother . . . or father . . . I'm not sure if either word is quite applicable. I . . . No . . . ," Res Voland trailed off and cringed as if he had been kicked in the stomach.

"It doesn't want me. It doesn't want me. It wants . . . her," he said, nodding to Dex, who remained asleep, blissfully unaware of the unfolding situation. "No . . . No . . . Please don't . . . ," Res pleaded with himself as he walked over to the pistol and picked it up from its small puddle of blood.

Dr. Quant cried, "I thought you said you weren't going to hurt me."

"I'm not," Res Voland responded through tears before shooting himself in the chest. He dropped to the floor, gasping silently. He convulsed as the creature slithered out of his ear. It slimed its way across the floor, up the operating table, and back into Dex, entering through the girl's mouth.

She opened her eyes and sat up, brushing stray bits of hair from the top of her newly shaved head. "Thank you, Auntie Borgia. I know you looked out for me as best as you could," she said.

Dr. Quant continued to cry, shaking uncontrollably.

"I'm sorry about your arm. I hope you get better."

The little girl got up and hugged Dr. Quant, rubbing her back several times before the video ended.

Qiti clicked on the next several files. One was a statement from Eir Pharmaceuticals listing the causes of death for Captain Ord Ponn and project director Res Voland as a murder-suicide. The next was a nondisclosure agreement on Eir Pharmaceuticals letterhead signed by Dr. Quant.

A small beep notified Qiti that her download was complete. She removed her cables and reattached the server panel. She grabbed the security guard by the feet, dragged him around several stacks of boxes, and dumped him into an oversize crate holding a collection of ornate masks. She closed the crate, took a breath, sat down, and leaned against it. Without shedding any tears, she put her face in her hands and wept.

PART 11

BLOOD FANG AND DEMON

LAZER AND STREEK FOLLOWED THE IMP AS HE EXUBERANTLY HOPPED his way down the winding stairway. He hunched in a partial crouch as he moved, leaning on his spear for support as he navigated the perilously steep descent. The steps were short and shallow, giving Lazer an uneasy sense of vertigo. He lagged behind Streek, who effortlessly floated along, albeit a bit higher than usual. The air outside of the tunnel had become thinner, lighter, and hotter.

They reached the barren, rocky floor. It was hard like concrete, with streaky veins of white embedded in the surface. Lazer approached the first column of rocks that stood before them, looking curiously as he touched it with his empty hand. The rocks were smooth and of varying thicknesses, with sharp edges like chipped obsidian. The stack was sturdy and seemingly placed with intention, yet there was no rhyme or purpose. Patches of moss clung to this and other vertical columns, their fine, wispy hairs swaying gently despite the lack of any sort of breeze. A snail with a charcoal softball-sized shell grazed on the plant life. Zizi coughed out a chirpy grunt and beckoned at Lazer to keep following.

They continued deeper into the forest of stone towers. The rock formations were getting taller, thicker, immovable in their heft. Some of the cracks Lazer was expected to fit through were a bit tight, requiring him to suck in his belly to squeeze between the rocks. The varying swatches of lichen were like fuzzy pancakes rooted into stone. Lazer wished he could eat some pancakes about now—a nice big stack of them, hot, with warm whipped butter and an avalanche of syrup. He thought of his mom's pancakes. They were kind of like Denny's pancakes, but better, a little crispier, though Lazer always preferred his food a little overcooked. *Oh, man, what if there were a Denny's here?* he thought as his stomach grumbled.

They walked until they reached a wall of lichen-covered rocks. The only way forward was through an oblong oval opening in the stone between two towers that leaned together. Fragments littered the ground before it, like scattered gravel atop a pad of wiry green fibers. Zizi hopped lightly over the mossy mat, followed by Streek as he floated through. Lazer entered behind Streek and stopped on the patch of fluffy morass. He looked around at the abundant splashes of color that surrounded him and marveled at the vibrant living carpets breathing softly with life. He lost himself in it, entranced by the Technicolor kaleidoscope of flora. Zizi chirped again from a dozen paces ahead.

Lazer snapped out of it and moved to step forward but found that his feet had become stuck to the ground. The soft fur of the moss had adhered to the shoes of his suit. He tried again with more force but was denied. He bent over and pulled his leg with a grunt. Still nothing. He reached down to pull the small hair strands from their grip. As he brushed his finger against the Velcro fibers of this sticky plant life, he felt the hairs pull at his finger, almost as if they were trying to drag him down. He ripped his hand up quickly, standing as tall as he could as the tiny hairs reached and clung their way around the bottom parts of his feet.

"Um, hey, guys," Lazer called out to his companions, who failed to hear him, still trekking forward. He called again, louder, "Guys!"

Streek and Zizi stopped and turned around. A startled look flashed across Streek's face as he saw Lazer being slowly dragged by his feet up the side of the stone halo. They raced back over.

"What the heck?" Streek yelled in a panic.

"Yeah, I know. What the heck, right?"

"Can you get free?" Streek asked anxiously.

Lazer pulled at his legs again. "Nope. What do I do?" he asked with a shrug and one palm up as he cradled his new instrument. His body was mostly horizontal, and his hair hung toward the floor of the forest.

"I don't know. Pull, maybe?"

"Sure, that's a good idea. Let's do that," Lazer said as he reached outward.

Streek floated up and wrapped his tentacles around human hands and pulled. He huffed and grunted and strained as he directed his airflow diagonally. Pushing. Harder. Impossible. Streek let go, his effort not enough. Lazer was still stuck.

"What's wrong?" Lazer asked, surprised at Streek's inability to free him.

"It's the gravity here or something. I can't get enough resistance off the ground to offer much help. I'm a little floatier here, I'm afraid."

"Yeah, I thought you looked taller."

Zizi screeched in his language as he pointed his spear toward Lazer.

"*Hold*," said the glove in translation.

Lazer reached out and grabbed the tip of the wooden weapon with his free hand. For being no bigger than a yardstick, it was impressively sturdy. Once Lazer's hand was firmly grasping the spear, Zizi dashed upward onto Lazer's arm and swung to his back. He gripped Lazer's body with his hands and feet and climbed across Lazer's leg to the lichen. Zizi pulled out a jagged blade and sliced at the sticky living fabric that was slowly claiming Lazer. The tiny teeth on his knife cut like shearing scissors, weakening the tenacious grip of the swampy fuzz until Lazer's first leg was freed. The moss pulled Lazer by his other foot, carrying him upward. He was now upside down, with one leg hanging outward.

Zizi steadied himself and scurried his way up the next leg, slicing moss with speedy ferocity as he grunted in labor. With a final cut, Lazer was released, falling to the ground with a thud and an "Oof!" He scooted away from the lichen and sprang up quickly for his middle-aged body. Lazer looked at his little savior and nodded in gratitude.

"What was that?" he asked.

"*It think you rock.*"

"That stuff can tell just by looking at me, huh?"

"*But you not rock.*"

"Ouch. Harsh, bro," Lazer replied, confidence partially deflated.

Streek cut in, "I believe he's saying that the moss thinks you are one of the rocks that are stacked all throughout this place."

"But I'm not a rock."

"Right, that's what he just said."

"Oh, right. So wait. That moss is what stacked all of these rocks, then?" Lazer asked, pointing at the array of vertical columns.

"It appears to be the case. Look." Streek pointed at one of the adjacent stone towers.

Lazer squinted and watched as a small, thin slab was carried up the side by a highway of interconnected patches of algae. The fine hairs worked in tandem like a colony of ants, hoisting the heavy object with the strength of their sticky tendrils.

"Ah. Got it. Keep an eye out for the fuzz," Lazer replied as he watched the slab crawl ever higher before continuing on.

After a short while, their path appeared, well trodden, winding through columns marked with hieroglyphic engravings. The sound of drums, steady and rhythmic, floated along the warm, sticky air. The farther they walked, the louder it became. *Bap bap, bap bap bap, cha-boom.* The percussion was soon accompanied by the shaking of rattles and chants of voices that echoed out from between the splotchy bright stacks.

They were here.

The trio emerged into a wide clearing ringed in red clay huts, rising with the columns and packed together like honeycomb. The ground was covered in beige silt, stretching the length of the open area of the village, which itself was no larger than a small concert arena. The drumming stopped as Zizi's fellow tribe members all froze, shocked by the alien creatures that had breached their space.

A cacophony of screeching commenced as a contingent of tiny yet ferocious warriors formed a spear-tipped line blocking off the village. A horn, pitchy and sharp, rang out overhead.

Zizi dropped his spear and held his hands up, waving for his tribe members to lower their weapons. He called out in his language as the liquid eye picked up scattered words in the standoff: *"Stop. Friend. Monster. Friend. No Blood Fang. Kill. Kill. Kill."*

Another horn blew as the warriors split themselves down the middle, stepping to their respective sides with a single coordinated step. An old, motherly goblin, arrayed in a flowing linen robe whelked with color, shuffled forward. She was the only member of this subterranean community of green-gray homunculi that was dressed in more than a loincloth.

She smiled with a welcoming calm, her features creased as if her entire face were squinting into the sun. She gently waved her arm in a circle and ended the raucous scene with a soothing hum. She approached, curious yet open as she shuffled toward Lazer and his floating companion on wrinkled little feet. She stood to just above Lazer's knee like a leathery toddler with white hair fluffed out in a wispy cotton-candy mohawk.

She spoke, looking at Zizi, as the automatic translator did its thing. *"What creatures? Where find?"* she asked, pointing at the alien interlopers.

Zizi replied, *"Tunnel to Up. Nice Monster."*

"No Blood Fang?"

"No Blood Fang. Here to fight Blood Fang."

"Prophecy of Up?"

"Zizi think so."

"Flying Head smell weird," she said, looking over to Streek with a hint of judgment.

"Zizi notice."

"Hey now!" Streek called out, surprising the elder.

The liquid eye translated. *"Flying Head know old-speak?"*

"Yes. Er, not quite. My name is Streek. Hello. Flying Head has feelings . . . I mean, *I* have feelings. My name's not Flying Head. Please don't call me Flying Head."

"Stryick?" the elder croaked out.

Streek smiled and nodded, which really looked more like a bow, as his being was largely comprised of head. "Yes! Thank you. Pleased to meet you. And by what name can we call you?"

"Burzbur," she chirped. *"She who commands."*

The elder bowed with her arms opening wide in a magnificent curtsy. Strands of lacy material flowed down in spiraled ribbons from her tiny arms, making her appear twice as big as her subjects. There were small pieces of wood knotted into the fabric that rattled as they clacked against each other like chimes. She slowly stepped forward and touched Lazer's suit, rubbing the material between her fingers.

She cooed as she looked at Lazer's liquid eye and spoke in her language. *"How talk from hand? Magic?"*

"Oh no, it's actually a prototype technology we got from our current—" Streek said before getting an elbow near the base of his tentacle.

"Yes. It's magic. We can do all sorts of cool, magical . . . stuff," Lazer elaborated, eyeing Streek, who picked up what Lazer was throwing down.

"Yes. Magic," Streek agreed. "We're magic. Listen to us, or we may smite thee . . . with our powerful . . . spells . . . and . . . lightning and hey, maybe you've seen some of our magical friends milling about, yeah? We need them to get home."

"Zizi home!" Zizi called out, hopping up and down with self-affirmation.

"Yes, thank you, Zizi. But Streek and Lazer's home. We go home," Streek said, pointing a tentacle at himself.

"No fight Blood Fang?" the elder asked, cautiously disappointed.

"Who is this Blood Fang again?" Lazer asked.

"Host of Demon. Killer of Lolo. Enemy of Lolo Tribe."

"Oh, Lolo, that's right, I remember her. From that documentary, right?"

"No understand."

"Yeah, don't worry about that. She was great, right?"

"Yes! She defeat metal demon army," Burzbur expressed with pride.

Lazer's eyebrow went up. "Metal demon army? Aw, man. I'd love to watch that movie!" he exclaimed with a righteous nod.

"You already did," Streek hissed back at him, still smiling at his host and her phalanx.

"Oh yeah, we did. The one with the robots."

"That's the one."

"You could say she Raged Against the Machine . . . Heh," Lazer deadpanned before settling into a grin, frozen in the blissful bask of an intentionally bad joke.

Burzbur shook her arms, which rattled with the clacking of wood, interrupting their tangent. "Blood Fang once warrior of Lolo Tribe, son of Burzbur," she said, touching her chest. *"Was taken by Demon Tribe. Come. Eat. Burzbur tell story of Blood Fang and Demon. Strangers tell story of Up."* She waved her hands as the pieces of wood swung by their ribbons. She turned and walked between the crease in the phalanx, who drew their spears back from their aggressive posture. Streek looked at Lazer while Lazer looked at his stomach.

"You think they know how to make breakfast burritos?" he asked. "Eggs, cheese, fries, and hot sauce in a tortilla would save my life right now."

"I don't think they have that here," Streek said with a shrug.

"You never know."

"Sure. You never know," the octopus sighed as he floated through the opening between the tiny warriors.

Lazer followed, his stomach audibly grumbling.

They came to a firepit surrounded by stones. It looked like a well with low walls and evenly placed divots etched into the top. Burzbur motioned for her people to sit, which they did without question. Lazer and Streek occupied an open section in the front ring, facing Burzbur. She picked up a handful of dusty white rocks from a satchel and threw them in the pit. The pieces sparked with tiny pops as they landed, starting a blaze on the dried moss.

A contingent of tribe members stepped up, holding lances twice the length of the warriors' spears, with dark pieces of matter lumped in sections like kebabs. In teams of two, they placed the lances atop the fire, laying them in neat little rows along the grooves in the rock. Burzbur motioned to a younger member of her community. The girl brought two large cups of water, though once one was placed in Lazer's hand, it had the scale of a child's tumbler. Lazer took a sip and nodded in approval. It was cold, refreshing, and best of all, didn't kill him. Burzbur waved her arm once more.

"Before story of Blood Fang and Demon, tell Burzbur of Up," she said as the tribe got silent, leaning in.

Streek and Lazer looked at each other, unsure of who should go first. Lazer pointed at Streek, who, in turn, pointed back at Lazer.

"You're better with talking to people," Streek hissed out of the side of his mouth.

"Sure, but you're the one that actually knows things," Lazer argued back under his breath.

"Fine. I'll give it a go," Streek replied as he cleared his throat. "Hello, I'm Streek. I come from a planet called Dylypin, but to our native tongue, it's called . . . ," Streek choked out a series of gurgles. "It's mostly water and is many, many light-years away from your world. My associate here is from a planet called Earth, which is also mostly water and is also many, many light-years away. Both planets are in the same galaxy as you and fall under the jurisdiction of the Galactic Union, which is the governing body responsible for, um . . . ," Streek stammered as his audience gazed at him with a mixture of confusion and restlessness. "I, uh . . . So I was a larva and then I went to university and then I joined a privateering firm and then I met this bloke here, who will tell you more about Up . . . ," he said before whispering a sorry to Lazer.

The collective attention of the tribe turned to Lazer, who swallowed his mouthful of water before clearing his throat.

"OK . . . Sure. You know, Up. It's . . . Up. And it's pretty different from here, but you know what? Honestly, even though I'm new to all of this, things really are a lot more the same than they are different."

"How same?" Burzbur interjected.

"Well, out there in the Up, everyone is trying to eat you. They will pick you limb from limb if they can't eat you whole first. I guess it's kinda like Earth, except back home, they want your soul too. And there's a lot of people. Tons. Everywhere you go, people. And still, surrounded by everyone, you're . . . alone. But I guess that's why friends are important, which is something I've been learning myself," he said, looking at Streek and giving a thumbs-up.

"They'll stick with you when things get bad," Lazer continued, "and only one of you can get out of the tunnel . . . And I've been stuck in a few tunnels in my time, believe me. But there's good stuff too. Everyone has music. Music is what makes life livable, you know? Everything is changing, and all I really want to do is go back to my van and just jam out. Actually, speaking of, I really liked your drum line. Hey, if you give me a beat, I can show you a song from Up. Show you a little somethin' somethin'." He motioned to the first row of percussionists. He patted on his thigh in a slow three-four waltz and pointed once more, waving his hand to the beat like a conductor. A few of the drummers mimicked his rhythm: a pickup beat on the and of three, then one, two, rest, and of three . . . Lazer stuck his thumb up and pointed at the next group, encouraging them to follow on the and of three with their higher-pitched tone before pointing to the final group of drummers.

"Good. I'm gonna come in, and you guys can take things up a notch on the chorus. Cool? Cool," Lazer asked of the confused third bench. Once the groove was steady, he picked up his off-world ukulele and strummed a melancholy chord progression along to the soft and rolling beat. The minimalism of the single stringed instrument playing above the rhythm entranced the crowd, who swayed like cobras.

"I feel unhappy. I feel so sad. I lost the best friend that I ever had . . . ," he began, nailing it so far. "She was my woman, I loved her so. But it's too late now, I've let her go."

The third row of drums came in with a six-eight buildup, rolling deeper across the varied skins that landed with a unified thump on the downbeat of the chorus.

"I'm going through changes . . . I'm going through changes . . ." Lazer played through the rest of the song before cutting off the drum line with a single swoop of the arm.

The room fell silent as Burzbur stepped forward. "*String drum look familiar. Where get?*" she asked.

"Oh, from up there. Not in Up, but below Up, but up from here . . . So . . . the middle? If that makes sense," Lazer said, pointing to the ceiling. "But yeah, you guys invented this thing—or at least your great-grandparents did. Do you want it back?" Lazer held the small instrument toward Burzbur, who smiled and accepted the gift.

"You can get there if you follow the tunnel Zizi found us in all the way to the end and climb up the semivertical air shaft," Streek interjected.

"Must show Burzbur after Blood Fang," she replied, redirecting the conversation to her missing son. She handed the instrument to a guard and turned back toward Lazer. She extended her arms and shook them in a limp, scarecrow posture.

The drums came back in. They had changed their cadence, marching in a slow, half-time chug. It was like a train beginning its departure in a tight, high-pitched *plunk*. Burzbur stopped, but the beat continued on. A procession of dancers shimmied before Lazer and Streek. They were clad in beads and rope that snaked up and down their wiry arms and legs, taut and woven, breaking up the large swatches of white body paint striped across them. They acted out Burzbur's narration in choreographed precision. They had clearly done this before.

"Story of Blood Fang and Demon is story of Lolo Tribe," she began as she gestured toward her people. *"Long ago, Lolo Tribe and Demon Tribe lived in Up. Was land above land. Was life above life. Blue and green and long like forever. Before time, both tribe one people. But demon not of tribe, not of kind. From up of Up. Beyond blue and green. Arrive in sacred stone.*

"Demon called Bakuma in Up. Live behind eyes. Eater of souls," she said, drawing a hand across her face as the dancers mimed a meteor crashing. Lazer mentally catalogued "Eater of Souls" for a future song title. The dancers leaped, twirling in a spiral around a single dancer who was painted in gray with black oval spots. She pulled a connected sheet of fabric wide, mimicking a flying squirrel as she hopped from side to side. She jumped and spun, turning away from the crowd, only to twist back as she put a sturdy mask made of dried moss over her face as she surveyed the audience.

"Demon Bakuma make much war. When die, Demon move into new Bakuma. Life after life. Lolo, child of warriors, fight to free tribe, to kill Demon. To end Demon. But Demon use great army to escape, move Demon Tribe into great mountain. Build new home, repeat cycle . . . But Lolo follow."

A dancer in dark green paint leaped forward, swinging a staff around in a show of martial skill. The chorus line marched forward like the phalanx from before, dramatically falling over and cartwheeling away in the face of the green dancer's weapon. She then pointed it at the dancer in gray with black spots.

"Lolo chase Demon Bakuma into mountain. Many die. Floor of blood."

Hmm. *Floor of Blood. Rad*, Lazer thought, cataloguing yet another song title. At this rate, he'd have a solo record in no time. The dancers mocked their mass death.

"Battle go deeper into mountain, to village underneath. Then mountain fall. Lolo stuck. Escape impossible. No more Up. In beneath, find huts tall like rock," she said as she waved her hands upward, making the jangly noise. *"But no victory. Demon Burzbur take half land. Lolo take half land. Two tribes."*

The dancers split into two sides and faced off, circling with staves out. It was like Michael Jackson's "Beat It" video but acted out by twiggy gremlins.

"War no end. Always fight. Demon Bakuma carry sacred stone. Curse land, make tall huts go. All gone. Replace with rock, moss, and boompa."

"Boompa? What's boompa?" Streek asked, looking at Lazer's liquid eye.

One of the tribe members handed Streek and Lazer their own sticks of meaty lumps that had been over the fire. Lazer inspected the items on his kebab. They were charred beetles with rows of crispy legs. Some of the lumps were oozing a light-orange mucus, which crept from the center hole opened by the shaft of the stick. The gremlin next to Lazer pulled one of the lumps off his stick and bit into the butt end of the roasted creature. He leaned his head back and sucked the innards out of the charred husk, grunting in gratification.

Lazer pulled one of the bugs from his stick and sniffed it. There was no smell beyond the whiff of charred carbon from the burnt exoskeleton, but his knotted hunger pangs, sharp with the twisting of an empty stomach awash in acid, overruled any sense of caution. He stuck his finger inside the hole and swished it around before digging out some of the slimy, jaundiced custard. He licked it, a small dab at first, then a little more. It wasn't great, but it wasn't terrible—like drinking a warm butterscotch milkshake with suspended bits of lawn trimmings.

Streek squirmed as he looked at his dinner. "Do you think I could get some of that moss instead?" he asked around to no avail. "Waiter? Hello?"

Lazer dug in as Streek breathed a disappointed sigh and set his kebab down.

"Sacred stone make new land. Air taste different. Water taste different.

Sky like blood," Burzbur said, pointing in the direction of the pyramid. *"Light bring new world. Lolo Tribe adapt. Tribe small. Now difficult for Demon Bakuma to live behind eyes. Demon Bakuma take biggest warrior. Life by life. Demon Tribe always take."*

The drum line picked up the tempo, finding a polyrhythmic groove that fit nicely behind the narration as the dancers stacked atop each other in sets of three. They moved in unison, swaying to the rhythm. The top level of dancers swung their arms at each other before faking death and climbing down the stack. Then the top of the stacks of two engaged in choreographed battle and climbed down. Now at the same height, the performers all spun and dropped to the floor. They were then dragged away one by one by the dancer in gray and black as the drums abruptly stopped.

"This life. Demon take Blood Fang, Burzbur child," she said, patting her chest. *"Burzbur want son back. Burzbur want life back. You help?"* A well of tears hung precariously in the corner of her eyes.

"Yes, um, maybe we can, you know, maybe do this on the way to finding our ride . . . if there's time," Streek said, smiling nervously on the spot.

"Burzbur send scouts, find others from Up Tribe. Lolo Tribe take strangers to Blood Fang, bring Blood Fang back," she said, clapping, then holding both hands out toward her guests to seal the bargain.

"Deal! But first, can I get another stick of bugs?" Lazer asked, holding his empty kebab spear.

Burzbur smiled her ancient, wrinkly smile. *"Bring back Burzbur son, get full hive."*

THE RIVAL TRIBE LIVED AT the far end of the biosphere in an ancient temple atop a pyramid made of obsidian rock. The pyramid at the end of the world, which this structure in question seemed to be, was shrouded behind mists of atmosphere and protected by an army of fervently religious gremlin folk.

It was there that Lazer and Streek were to capture Burzbur's warlord son and return him to be exercised of this mysterious demon that had him in its grip. The details on how that was supposed to happen were rather foggy beyond sneak in, put him in a sack, and carry him out, but the ten warriors who had been tasked to escort them seemed to know what they were doing well enough.

The group traveled along a narrow path in the stone forest for what felt like miles. Streek hovered close to Lazer. He spoke quietly, as to not activate the liquid eye.

"What do we do if we don't find Dex?" he asked nervously.

"Then she'll find us when we find the Aperture thingy," Lazer replied with a shrug.

"But really though . . ."

"Really. Trust me, this lady isn't gonna leave here without that trinket. As long as we get there first, we're good."

They wound through paths between columns of lichen-covered rocks and boompa hives until they reached a river. It wasn't nearly as wide as the Los Angeles River, but this one had water in it, and the water was flowing quickly. A narrow stone bridge crossed the gurgling waterway mere inches above the surface like a taut, earthen wire.

The first half of Burzbur's warriors crossed the bridge with agile grace, hunching low while moving with speed. Streek followed, hovering along the strip of rock as the waters below the edge rattled with the force of his propulsion.

Lazer took a step and slipped slightly but caught himself before falling into the water. It was like navigating the lip of a curb in a flood, which Lazer would probably have a better go at if he had a few beers in him. For a second, Lazer questioned why he felt his performance required alcohol, but it was soon gone as the grunts and shooing motions from Zizi and the remaining warriors behind him redirected his attention.

Lazer stepped forward, cautiously, balancing himself with outstretched arms. He squatted down, enough to lower his center of gravity but not enough to put too much strain on his knees. Step by step, Lazer moved his way out until he was at the center point of the river. Streek had made it clear across and was now beckoning Lazer forward, shouting words of encouragement to his human friend, who continued along at his cautious pace. He breathed slowly and chose his steps carefully. The slick rock was less sturdy for someone of Lazer's size. It wobbled with each movement, getting looser the farther out he went. Another step, then calamity.

A section of rock gave out underfoot, sending Lazer into the rushing water. It was hot—not scalding, but like a Jacuzzi turned to the birth control setting. He reached out in vain, flailing as he bobbed downstream. Zizi chirped out in his language and jumped in after Lazer. Streek rushed along the side of the shore, not even close to fast enough.

One of the warriors sprinted to Streek and motioned for him to stop.

"What? What? I need to get him!" Streek yelled out.

"Zizi eebeelu bouga nug nug," the warrior replied, pointing to the far pyramid.

"But I need to get to my friend!"

"Zizi! Zizi!" the warrior screeched again as he hopped up, pulling at one of Streek's tentacles.

Streek stopped, still in panic. Lazer had long since disappeared down the roaring waterway. Streek's breathing was fast, his adrenaline churning. Almost everything inside him said to race along behind. Still, it was hopeless, and the ex-pirate knew it. He was too adrift with the physics of this place, and his intention wouldn't help him . . . Still. He sighed, looked back one last time at his escorts, who beckoned him to follow, and jumped into the torrential rapids after Lazer and Zizi.

LAZER SPED DOWN THE RIVER as it snaked along the alien terrain, bobbing above the surface in spurts, gasping for air between gurgles. The surroundings were a blur of color amid the rush of hot water smothering his senses. He flailed, struggling to right himself as he tumbled along at the mercy of the forceful surge that enveloped him.

Amid the cacophony, a memory triggered. He was young, at the beach with his parents before his dad left. The roar of the ocean was punctuated with the calls of the sea. Birds cawed overhead, and a radio cranked oldies off in the distance as Lazer dug a moat for his sandcastle. His mom was upset. She was arguing with his father, who, in turn, slurred his words back at her.

"I'm fine! Look, I can walk in a straight line. See? SEE?" he yelled, louder than he'd probably intended.

"Sure, fine. That's the word I'd use: *fine*. Quite the achievement. If only you could even come close to achieving fine in any other facet of your life. I would pray for fine."

"Hey, I . . . I think I'm doing great. Pretty great, actually. I've got new ins, you know. Some opp . . . opportunit—burp—ties to tour with some bigger—*hic*—big plans . . ."

"Sure you do. Always plans. Planning to go. Playing for pocket change with your friends when you could make more money working anywhere else. And what money you do bring home, you just piss away . . . literally."

"That's not f—*hic*—fair. It's all for the boy! That's why I always have to leave. The kid is expensive!" he barked, ratcheting things up a notch.

"No, it isn't all for him. It never is. If it were, you would be here. With him."

"But he needs a new bike and a new—*hic* . . ."

"He needs a father."

"He has a father. I'm his family."

"A family doesn't magically exist because you say so—or because you share DNA. Family means being there, showing up day after day after day."

"I'm here now!"

"For how long? How long until your next tour? Playing in bands nobody cares about. Screwing strangers on the road. Is all of that for him too?" She pointed at the boy happily digging in the wet sand as she wiped a tear from her eye. "It's all just you trying to get away from your responsibilities, for good, once and for all. It's your way out. It always has been."

"You know that's not true."

"Only because you haven't succeeded yet. You're even a failure at failing . . ."

"I'll prove you—*hic*—wrong."

The yelling mixed with the crashing of the waves upon the shore, blurring back into the sound of rolling and bubbling water.

Lazer opened his eyes. He was pressed against a stone grate by the current that rushed with fervor against his back. The grate was embedded in the wall of the dome, stretching the length of the river like a grand storm drain. He was too big to squeeze between the carved slits but could see the water dropping off into the dark belly of the mountain. Lazer coughed out the bits of water sitting in his lungs and pulled himself up. He got above the surge and climbed his way to the water's edge and out, rolling over onto his back in exhaustion, his deep, satisfied breaths like the first sips for a parched mouth.

With a wince of discomfort, Lazer forced himself to his feet. He erected his posture slowly, with a steady groan that culminated in another fit of coughing. Through his mental fog and blurry sight, Lazer engaged in a round of stretching, giving some much-needed relief to his lower back, as it had taken a few shots from submerged rocks in his downstream tumble. He gave himself a shake and looked around for the first time. He was now on the other side of the river. He peered between the endless rows of rocks as he wrung out his hair.

"*Help. Friend. Help. Friend. Help,*" said the liquid eye.

Lazer looked up and around, wondering who was speaking to him. He didn't see anyone. *Maybe the thing is malfunctioning?* he thought. The possibility took Lazer back to the time a few years earlier when he dropped his cell phone into his beer on stage. He'd been attempting a much lower lunge than would normally be advisable for someone at his stage in life. As he went into a backward bend while ripping the second solo on Motorhead's "Overkill," he tweaked something. It was a tight pinch, then a seize of the muscles. He jerked forward in a natural reaction to the jolt, and his phone managed to work itself free out of his pocket, dropping into the half-full glass of lager placed next to his set list. The phone had died, but Lazer still finished the set, tweaked back and all.

Lazer turned to the river and saw Zizi in the water, clinging to the grate with one hand, an unconscious Streek in the other. He gargled and called out again, "*Help! Friend! Help!*"

Lazer made eye contact with the struggling gremlin and yelled back, "What should I do?"

"*Help! Friend! Help!*"

"Right, I've got that part. But how though?" Lazer yelled.

Zizi just gurgled back, a rush of water swarming into his mouth as he called out.

Lazer stepped back toward the grate. He set his footing to the edge of dry land and reached over. His arm stretched, and his fingers extended, but he was still too far away to be of any help. He stepped back and looked around. He was surrounded by rocks in stacks covered in moss—and only rocks in stacks covered in moss. He kneeled down and picked up a flat, moss-free stone, examining it. He tapped it on his hand while thinking before tossing it in the river. It landed with a *bloop*.

Eureka! Lazer held a single finger up toward Zizi, who was struggling to hang on to both Streek and the line of grate that kept them both from hurtling to a watery grave.

Lazer jogged to the nearest stone column and pushed it toward the river. The stack budged slightly but was otherwise stuck in place. He pushed again, harder. A single rock from the top of the stack fell to the ground. It was smooth and thicker on one side than the other. He picked up the rock and jammed it into a small space between two lower stones in the tower until it was firmly wedged in, giving it a few kicks to make sure it was really in there. He went back to the far side of the rocks and pushed again. It wobbled slightly, like a Jenga tower reaching the end of the game. He stepped back several paces, took a deep breath, and ran at full speed toward the tower.

Lazer plowed into the stack with his shoulder, giving it enough force for the tower to tip over the wedged rock. The moss kept the rocks from separating, their sinewy threads stitching the stones together like the trunk of a palm tree. It fell in a single piece into the river, crashing right before the grate like a dam. Lazer stepped out cautiously onto his newly laid bridge, making his way to Zizi, who was now slowly submerging under the water, gurgling on his way down.

Zizi looked up from beneath the foamy surface, blinking rapidly with the swollen cheeks of a final breath. Lazer's hand cut through the water and grabbed Zizi by the shoulder. He pulled Zizi and Streek out and dragged the two to the dry bank of the river. Zizi sat, dazed, coughing, but otherwise fine. Streek was puffy with absorbed liquid like a sponge on a sink. The exhausted gremlin pointed at Streek with worry and gasped out words between heavy breaths.

"Help. Friend. Stryeek."

"Don't worry, I know what to do here. Hang on," Lazer reassured Zizi as he bent over and picked up the octopus. He took a deep breath and bear-hugged the unresponsive cephalopod with a forceful push, sending a gush of water out of Streek's underside.

The octopus reinflated and woke up, regaining his hover. "Did the thing happen again?" the woozy octopus croaked.

"Yeah, buddy. It did. But you're good now," Lazer replied, patting his tentacled friend.

"*Friend. Help. Good job,*" Zizi chimed in between coughs.

"Yeah. Thanks for that. So did I save you?" Streek asked.

"Not quite. But thanks for coming after me. It's appreciated."

"*Zizi save Stryeek. Lazer save Zizi,*" chimed the gremlin, giving one last shake of his body to fling off the remaining bits of water.

"Oh, well . . . I suppose it's the thought that counts," Streek replied.

"Don't even worry about it, bud."

"I'll try. I just feel bad . . ."

"Why's that?" Lazer asked halfway between confusion and concern.

"I don't know, he saved me," Streek said, pointing a tentacle at Zizi. "And you saved me. And you saved him, and he saved you . . . What have I really done?"

"Dude, don't even think like that."

"Why not, though? It's not like I've been much help. I just blather on and on more than anything else. I mean, listen to me. I'm even talking right now about how I'm talking right now and I don't even know why I'm still going . . ."

"Streek, buddy. You could have let Dex take me out here by myself and you didn't. You came with me. You could have left me back in that tunnel and you didn't. You came with me. Besides, friends don't count favors."

"That's right. Friends. I'm still getting used to that. So much of the universe is so . . . transactional."

"Ain't that the truth."

"And thank you, Zizi, for being so great. You're the best, um, what should I call you?"

"Zizi."

"Yes, your name is Zizi. What is your species called? Baku or something like that, right?"

"*Lolobaku?*" he asked, pointing to himself.

"*Lolo Tribe?*" followed the liquid eye.

"OK. Lolobaku. You're the best Lolobaku . . . guy I've met. And don't worry to the both of you," Streek said, pointing between his two saviors. "The next time things get crazy, I'm going to save you two! Or at least one of you. I mean, I gotta save somebody, right? There's a cosmic balance to this sort of thing."

As Streek spoke, the wall of the cave rumbled behind him. A hidden door slowly climbed, shaking off a layer of dirt as it rose. Long-forgotten metal and stone groaned between the mechanical chug of working gears. Streek turned around to see an assortment of shadows moving behind the lifting gate, casting lines of black before a blinding white light. He immediately flew behind Lazer and hid.

Several of the obfuscated figures stepped out. It was Dex and her assortment of armed escorts, shy a few more. Streek peeked out from behind Lazer, who grinned at the arrival of his ride home.

"Well, isn't this . . . fortuitous," Dex said, smiling widely at her now-reclaimed consultants.

"What's that thing?" the mercenary captain asked aloud, pointing his gun at Zizi, who darted behind Lazer's leg.

"I'm not sure. Perhaps some kind of devolved Baku?" Dex replied, waving her hand for the mercenary to lower his weapon.

"Yeah. It looks like it," Lazer answered, peering down at his anxious little friend. "They're cool, though. This guy's name is Zizi. There's a few tribes of 'em that are fighting each other down here. We're going to rescue one . . . or kidnap him or something—one of the two. I'm not really sure. We'll figure it out when we get there."

"Banto Ubu?" Dex asked, glaring down at the tiny terrestrial.

"Speak Ubu?" said the liquid eye in translation.

"Oldspeak?" Zizi asked through the liquid eye, his dialect unique from Dex's.

"Yes. The language of your ancestors," she said, kneeling down to be at a closer eye level to the imp. "Do you know where I can find the house of Bakuma?"

"Demon Bakuma. Home. Yes. We go."

"You will show me?" Dex asked.

"Yeah, I think we were already going there," Lazer chimed in.

"Yes," Streek added. "It appears that this Demon Bakuma chap is currently possessing or infecting these little guys. I guess whatever it was that inspired all of the violence in that documentary you showed us is still alive down here. Now that we've been drafted by Zizi's chief, or queen—I'm not really sure what type of government they have—we are going to find its host and bring him back."

"Is that so?" Dex asked, picking up a handful of sand and rubbing it around in her hand.

"We're about to find out. He lives in the pyramid you were talking about. That's pretty badass when you think about it," Lazer replied.

"Did your liquid eye process the final piece of information?" Dex asked.

"Nah. We were just following Zizi. I think there's only one pyramid down here. We saw it on the way in. It shouldn't be that hard to find. I mean, it's a pyramid and it's that way," Lazer replied, pointing.

"Very well," Dex replied, looking at Lazer and his companions while water dripped off them down to the sandy dirt under their feet. "Why are you all so wet?"

"We took a shortcut," Streek said with a nervous smile, wringing a bit of water out from one of his tentacles. "But hey, it all worked out, right? You found us, now we can find the Aperture Parallax for you and Burzbur's missing kid and then all go home. Right?"

"Indeed. But first," Dex replied, letting the sand from her hand sift out as the particulates gently sauntered down to the ground, "I will need you to scan this place. The gravity and atmosphere are . . . different."

"Yeah, um, about that . . . I lost it. Sorry," Streek replied.

"Is that so?" Dex asked with a whiff of irritated disappointment.

"And by lost, he means he threw it down the stairs back at the other side of the dome because he was trying to hit Zizi with it," Lazer said, chuckling.

"Hey, I was defending myself," Streek replied indignantly before turning back to Dex. "But we did get one scan in when we got here. I guess something about the artificial sun at the top of the pyramid is projecting extradimensional physical properties—or something along those lines. But that's all we got before the . . . incident."

Dex looked up, her eyes widened in awe. "That is the Aperture Parallax you speak of," she said, pointing above the tree line to the glowing tip of the megastructure in the distance. She put a pair of black wraparound shades on her face and peered directly at it.

"So two questions," Streek said. "First, if that's one of the most powerful objects in the universe, what is it doing up there?"

"And second?" Dex replied.

"How do we get it down?"

Dex pressed a button on the side of her shades and looked at the floating octopus. "That is the source of the spacial disruption altering the gravity and atmospheric content. It was put there intentionally. And to answer the second . . ."

Streek raised a nubby eyebrow.

"We will need to get to the temple at the top of the pyramid."

"Sure, easy. Just, um, before we do . . . ," Streek replied.

"Yes?"

"Can we dig into some of those rations? The only thing they have to eat down here are bugs, and that's not really solving my blood-sugar situation."

"Yeah, I dropped my bug in the river. I could use a snack," Lazer seconded, rubbing his belly. "I hope there's peanut butter. Is there peanut butter?"

"*Zizi snack!*" chimed the gremlin.

"Very well. I suppose a hungry guide is a careless one," Dex replied, punching a button and summoning the hovering supply crate. From there, snack bars made of optimized nutritional products were distributed. Lazer was pleased to find that there were, in fact, peanut-butter-flavored bars with little, tiny peanut butter chips. He enjoyed it thoroughly, munching away as Zizi led the newly reunited expedition through the rock columns and toward the pyramid at the end of the world.

FOOD HELPED WITH THE TRUDGE through the stone forest in wet clothes, though the distance between the access door Dex entered from and the base of the pyramid was an easy ten minutes. The stairs to the top, however, felt endless.

The pyramid was stepped and hosted scattered splotches of moss. It climbed at a sharp angle, culminating in an open-sided temple with spaced columns and a clear, pointed top displaying the Parallax. The structure was impressively large, considering the size of its builders, about half the size of the Luxor in Las Vegas, give or take a story. Lazer stayed at that hotel once. The singer from Three Dog Night bought him shots of tequila until he blacked out. Nice guy.

Lazer whistled the melody to "Mama Told Me Not to Come" as he took his first step up the pyramid. Streek followed behind, swearing he knew the song but couldn't place who sang it. Maybe he saw it in a commercial or something. Maybe a movie preview? Probably. Streek would never remember, though he did spend a good portion of the ascent chewing on it.

Mercenaries and guards stood at the ready at the top of the pyramid, keeping watch from outside of the temple while Dex looked out at the forest of stacked stones below. She spotted the rising smoke from the village in the distance before bringing her gaze upward to the crimson stone, shining from the pinnacle of the monument. She adjusted her shades and got a better view. The light source itself was a pinprick, the wider glow a refraction from angled glass. She stared at her prize, falling deeply into its splendor. A violent huffing broke the spell.

Lazer pulled his panting and sweaty body up the final few steps to the plateaued landing. His unexercised thighs burned as he huffed, swallowing dry mouthfuls of air while Streek hovered effortlessly beside him.

"You know, you would be surprised what thirty minutes of exercise a day will get you," Streek said as Lazer put his hand on the octopus's face, slightly pushing the floating red alien as he rested his other hand on his knee. Lazer coughed.

"I'll take that as a maybe later," Streek said as Lazer's fingers ran down the octopus's face.

Lazer looked ahead. "Whoa."

The temple face that greeted Lazer was open, with a row of thick, chiseled rock supports that separated the sanctum from the pyramid steps. The pink atmosphere sprinkled into the front of the temple from the artificial sun above, casting shadows that stretched inward from the backs of the columns.

Dex approached them from behind. "Go on, little canary."

Lazer entered the temple first, holding his hand out, searching for traps in the floors. The ceiling was tall and arched and lined with faded frescos depicting different Bakumas. Tufts of moss ran through the cracks that split the paintings like veins, branching through the inside of the ancient shrine. Burning torches were spaced between the paintings, emitting an amber glow.

The mercenaries covered Dex as she led her team through rows of statues to the center of the temple. The carvings depicted cloaked priests, kneeling in anticipation of divine acceptance. Their stone arms reached toward the heavens, rising above the heads of Dex and her crew. The middle of the temple was open and decorated with a tile mosaic of the Crimson Empire's dot-within-a-cube symbol. The dot itself had a small slit that looked like an eye within a pupil. Dex kneeled down and collected a handful of dirt off the slit. She slowly released the grains from her hand like sand in an hourglass.

Lazer felt like something wasn't right. It was like that time the cashier at Mexberto's restaurant had charged him for the breakfast burrito combo even though he only asked for water, which everyone knew was free and therefore not subject to the same pricing scheme as the soda-and-entree combo. Suddenly, his hand buzzed. He looked at his liquid eye display, which blinked. It said the download was complete, 100 percent information exchange.

"The gravity has reverted back to normal," Dex said to her team as she stood back up.

"You're right," Qiti said as she stepped out from behind one of the inner-row statues lining the long end of the temple. "The Parallax's power only carries as far as the artificial sun will take it." She was wearing a tightly fitted black space suit with shimmering sky-blue trim. She fiddled with a knife, curved and elegant. It was the ceremonial blade used by Bakuma in the documentary. Behind her, Captain Izzit and his band of pirates emerged in a line that spanned the width of the room. They outnumbered Dex's crew several times over. The buccaneers fanned out, armed with projectile swords, glowing pistols, and one very hungry-looking Vithrax.

Captain Izzit waved his pistol at Dex. "Drop 'em."

Dex's guards looked to their employer, who nodded to do as they were told. They set their weapons on the floor and stood back up with their hands raised.

Qiti smiled. "Thanks for that, Mom. Now, please take a seat so I can remove the alien parasite consuming your brain."

PART 12

IT HIDES BEHIND THE EYES

FIVE THOUSAND YEARS EARLIER

ON A SMALL PLANET IN A DIMENSION PARALLEL TO OUR OWN, A paper-shaped creature slid out from beneath a mossy stone. Its smooth silver sheen was splattered with symmetrical black dots blasted across its surface like a Rorschach test. In human terms, the nameless creature was small, no larger than a CD case, no thicker than the liner notes within. It possessed no audible name, as this species communicated through flashes of color expressed by microscopic pigments on the surface of their skin. On their terms, the species was called *A chrome swirl breaking apart into a three-armed spiral, set against a subtly flickering background of soft orange, ash black, and violet.* The image reflected their self-conceptualization—life, always moving amid the rhythm of nature and the colors that surrounded them.

The terrain of the creature's home world was humid and sparse, with the tiniest bits of water floating about its low-gravity surface. The planet had been thoroughly colonized by patches of sentient lichen, which crawled about slowly like magenta pancake starfish. These mossy Technicolor carpet swatches organized their communities by wrapping around the flat stones that were regularly belched up from the fiery fissures dotting their world. They would stack these stones atop each other, one by one into columns that reached like a million fingers into the sky. The towers would always inevitably topple, despite the low gravity, though the lichen would just restack the collapsed heap once more. This species of cooperative plant life, colorful and industrious, was only troublesome if you happened to catch yourself on the wrong side of a falling stack.

The paper-shaped creatures were a bit higher up on the totem pole of consciousness. They lived in the gaps between the stones, in family units of single parents with children born of asexual reproduction, peeling off small layers of themselves that would, in turn, grow into new individuals. The creatures worked together to sustain their communities by piecing together like quilted silos and hooking to the yawning mouths of the steam vents that dotted the land like gateways to inferno. They would absorb the particulates spewing from the fissures, floating along like strands of kelp in the ocean. The particulates both fed them and initiated their duplication, which they would repeat once a year until they died. This, in turn, fed the soil that fed the lichen that housed them. Everything was in its right place . . . But chaos always seeks to destabilize balance, as nature demands.

One day, a small crimson orb fell from the sky and landed upon some bristly moss with an unremarkable foop. And there it sat idle, without notice, until the day it was happened upon by one of the ink-dotted, silver-sheen beings. This particular individual's name was *A rose-tinted flush that started as a circle in the middle of the squared-off leaf and cascaded outward in pixelated dots to its taut edges.* Let's call it Rose.

Rose folded itself forward and scooped the marble-sized curiosity up like fingers cupping water, cradling the new find in its moist, stretchy skin. With just a touch, the living sheet was flooded with feelings of love and elation and pain and grievance. These unfamiliar sensations pulsed through in waves, coloring its pigments in blinking shades of red. Still images of Rose flipped like a book through its conscious mind, showing the endless parallel lives it was living simultaneously in unseen realms. The sound of an infinite existence roared in cacophony, like standing beneath a low-flying plane full of radios set to different stations. Rose had never experienced anything plane related, so the comparison would not have occurred to it, but the noise did make the sheet drop its new discovery in shock all the same.

Rose was terrified yet enthralled. After a moment of hesitance, it picked up the object once more, returning to the deluge of memories the creature had never actually experienced, and yet had. Changes to the land, to the sky, and to its own sense of inner self opened Rose to foreign concepts such as spoken language, music, bureaucracy, and happy hour. But even with the newly attained knowledge of the existence of late-afternoon drink specials, there was darkness on the horizon.

In life after life, everything on the planet was about to be destroyed . . . over and over and over again. In addition to seeing sideways through possible realities, Rose could see forward and backward in time. It was less like skipping ahead on a song than it was hearing all parts of all of the songs ever written simultaneously. The wave of memories was overwhelming, blanketing its consciousness with the minutiae of lives not lived. The sheet buckled and collapsed to the ground, reacting to both the physical sensation provided by the quick jolt of omnipotence as well as the pang of fear that comes when someone reckons with their impending death . . . And death was coming, indeed.

The solar system hosting Rose's home was a binary one. Its planet, in particular, revolved around the smaller star, which, in turn, revolved around a bigger star in an oblong and irregular dance. This arrangement, while yielding stunning seasonal views, brought Rose's planet perilously close to an encounter with a metropolis-sized chunk of space rock every one thousand years. With Rose's premonition indicating the next flyby as being the fatal encounter, it knew it had a monumental problem to solve. But how? The entire concept of planetary orbits and mass extinction events had been foreign only a moment earlier.

Rose pondered. Perhaps a different version of itself had already figured out how to stop the comet . . . somehow. Would it be successful? Was this Rose even the first Rose to try? How many other versions of Rose could even be in this unique situation? Were these thoughts even Rose's own? Echoes of this mental process blinked across the void. The attempts and failures put forth by the other Roses revealed themselves. Success would be difficult.

Rose's options were limited. It could not build a nuclear device to intercept the comet in space, nor could it simply move its species off-planet. The community of organisms Rose belonged to wouldn't have those abilities in time. The species was too content for such a massive intrusion upon their steady way of life. Their inertia would be their doom. Only one understood this fact. The other creatures lived free of worry in their daily routine of sleeping under rocks and absorbing steaming particulates. The burden was to be Rose's alone. Then there, somewhere along one of the timelines, it was a path forward.

The only feasible answer for this dimension's version of Rose was to shoot itself into low orbit and use the power of the crimson orb to move the oncoming comet through a wormhole into a parallel reality outside of Rose's field of view—an empty space of matterless void, lacking the basic building blocks of reality. Nobody would get hurt.

Rose dedicated itself to the work, using its newfound knowledge to smelt the metals found in the abundant rocks littering the ground. It made tools with the metals and a crude rocket with the tools. The others of its kind paid no mind to Rose, whose changed behavior did not compute with their largely benign paradigm of existence, all save for Rose's offspring, a half-size square of soft-hued, warm amber glow with flecks of gray scattered across its body. Let's call it Gray.

The disruption in Gray's life from Rose's consistent absence was difficult for the cocktail-napkin-sized child. It needed to be near its preoccupied parent, to know it was OK, and to understand its fascination with the small crimson orb. But Gray lacked the context to understand the reasons behind why Rose labored, day after day, season after season. So it just watched, helping when it could, as Rose's obsidian alloy craft was slowly assembled. The ship was small, pyramid in shape, and reached into a fine, angular point at the tip. To launch the craft, Rose would use a platform built of beams and rings that were networked across the widest, most powerful of vents. The craft would use the sporadic eruptions from the fissures for its initial thrust, then detach the lower portion to enable a system of fans and rudders to steer the craft once in low orbit. When Rose was ready to return to the surface, it would eject itself from a thin escape capsule with a parachute in the top and sail gently back to the ground.

For years, Rose watched the night sky with a crude telescope made of bent glass and shaved rock, waiting for the comet to arrive. Rose never shared the knowledge of infinite possibilities, leaving its kind to remain blissfully unaware of the impending disaster hurtling through space.

How could it even be explained? Rose thought with colorful inner monologue as it gazed skyward one evening. The only way to fully articulate what it was doing was to share the orb and open the new paradigm with the others. That was out of the question. Beyond the potential dangers, something about the orb beckoned. It was a song only Rose could hear, a slight, never-ceasing tug on a string. It was as if the object possessed its own personal agency, and this thing wanted Rose and only Rose. Yet little did the living sheet know, Gray, too, had touched the jewel. It was only once, and only for a moment, like a flicker of a spark from a lighter in the dark. But the moment revealed its own secrets.

When the day had come and the comet had arrived, Rose wheeled out its craft to the launchpad. It climbed aboard with its crimson prize and slid itself into the control center. The ash from the vent wafted in plumes as soupy magma tossed about below, both building to a magnificent crescendo. A burst of gas and particles sprayed skyward, sending the pyramid blasting through the waving sleeve of Rose's neighbors. As the craft flew beyond the tallest heights of the mossy stacks and billowing daisy chains, it exited the limits of the planet's atmosphere. The back half of the ship detached and fell back to the surface as a tail affixed to a fan extended downward from the inner chamber. The fan rotated and engaged, buzzing as it pushed the rest of the pyramid ever upward. Farther. Farther. Everything was going according to plan.

Inside, a bright yellow metallic flash distracted Rose from its task. It was Gray. The child's repetitive blinking pulled its parent's attention. The young creature was stowed away in the craft, locked in the escape capsule. It was here to help with the mission. Rose's parental instincts beckoned, pulling its attention to its offspring. But there was no time to focus on Gray, not yet. Rose had to pay attention.

The comet rotated in a loose forward spiral, hurtling directly toward the tiny craft and the planet behind it. Rose waited, the seconds ticking by, holding off until the last moment. It took the crimson orb into its grip and focused the sum of its thoughts and energy upon a different timeline. The empty timeline. The void. A rapid blinking of colors flushed through Rose's surface as it squeezed tighter.

A deep-red light enveloped Rose, highlighting its tiny square form before shooting out in every direction. Yet the comet still approached. Would Rose have to abort? It rose a corner of its flat surface and struggled its way to the eject button, reaching.

If the plan fails, Gray must at least be saved, thought Rose.

The space rock was now directly before them, casting a shadow across the red glow of the ship as it continued on its direct course with Rose's planet. Rose focused once more, harder. It thought of the alternate realities with strange things like oceans and winter and top-forty pop radio. They blurred by, shadows and sounds, but nothing happened. The orb was not working. Meanwhile, the pointier edge of the comet was rotating directly into the ship. Rose flashed a wave of blues, deep and dull, the color of dusk and sadness. And with that lingering sense of despair, the living sheet accepted its fate. There was no time to steer away from this massive celestial mountain. It was over.

Rose let go of the crimson orb and released the escape capsule. The two sections of the ship pushed off one another as the capsule floated off, weightless in space. The fuselage dropped back into the planet's orbit as the comet narrowly split the space between them. Rose looked out of its window as the capsule slowly vanished like a lost balloon, sailing farther and farther away into space. In the distance, Gray blinked a pattern on repeat. It was saying, "I love you."

The orb blinked with strobe-light staccato as its red hue returned. It burned brighter and brighter with lighter and lighter shades until it abruptly went dark. The stars had changed in alignment, and the planet below them was new. It was green, smaller, but closer as well, rotating in the opposite direction. The comet fell into the gravitational pull of the world below but at a new trajectory. It missed the planet, got caught briefly in its orbit, and whipped around, back out into space, setting up another rendezvous sometime in the future.

Rose panicked, its edges fluttering as its side of the craft fell out of orbit. The small stretch of skin pressed against the ceiling of the component as it hit reentry, chased by a string of asteroid debris, dropping closer and closer to the surface of the planet.

Panels from the sides ripped off in sections and disappeared into the light of the day. The wind, harsh and punishing, whipped the crimson orb from its base and sucked it out into the sky. Pieces and parts tore from their welds as fast-approaching patches of green and blue came into view. The remaining piece of spacecraft tumbled through the sky planetward in a rapidly spinning free fall.

The husk of the craft landed in a bog with a muted *thwot*, the impact largely absorbed by the bubbling peat, as other bits of space rock landed in the distance. Rose crawled through the hole of a missing panel and slowly rolled across the mud, becoming caked in warm, sludgy goop. The dirty sheet of living paper picked itself up, woozy but alive and scraped off the unfamiliar bits of brown gunk. It hopped up, attempting to catch a gust of wind to help it travel above this unfamiliar muck. But the air was heavy. It pushed downward, unlike anything Rose was used to. In fact, everything was different. The colors were wrong. The water in the air was missing. There were no fissures in the ground or stacks of moss-covered rocks. Most importantly, Rose couldn't float.

Moving now meant trudging. Using the corners of its lower squarish feet, Rose walked in wide swings, like a cowboy sauntering into a bar before ordering a whiskey and punching somebody. It ambled its way along the muddy banks, tiny step by tiny step, leaving a trail of shallow imprints behind. As Rose moved, it felt weaker, sick. Its color faded to a jaundiced green before it dropped to the ground in a convulsing flutter. The lack of moisture and air-based nutrients only compounded the effects of the crushing gravity.

Rose could go no farther, lying along the soft muddy stretch of pathway that was set between rows of weeping aqua fronds that climbed sandy stalks. Lights bobbed and hovered beneath the shaded canopy as curious insects surmised the status of their next meal. Rose's skin, now drying and crusting at the edges, had degraded to the blackened stain of a smoker's lungs. The first bug landed, lightly stepping its tiny petal feet on this newly immobile foodstuff.

An omnipresent rumble shooed away the curious insect. A trunk, fleshy and curled, poked at Rose. It snorted, blowing and inhaling hot, wet air, kicking up the dying sheet of skin in the process. Rose, startled, curled in reflex into the shape of a rolled dollar bill. The trunk and the furry green mammoth it was attached to reared back. The beast was a mountain to Rose, her trumpeted breathing a gale.

The trunk snorted again, sucking Rose up through the length of the moist, vertical shaft of skin and muscle. It whizzed past hairs and through bands of mucus, bouncing its way upward before slamming into the bony skull of the massive beast.

Confused, Rose scurried around inside of the face of the now-terrified creature, who stamped around on the soft wet dirt, unsuccessfully attempting to throw the burrowing creature out. Blowing and swinging, she shook as Rose crawled along the inside of the nasal cavity, unsure of where it was going but certain in its need for hydration. As it got farther inward, Rose noticed a small fracture beneath the front of the mammoth's brain casing. It writhed its way inward, clawing softly through bone and sinew, following the radiating heat of the massive beast's brain. Once inside the skull, the living sheet unfurled across the top, hooked into the squishy matter beneath it, and drank.

Rose felt better. It was stronger, feeding off the bits of plasma it extracted while touching the moist surface. The top layer of the unsuspecting mammoth's brain was now coated by Rose's blood-moistened skin. It pulsed with shocks of energy relayed by the web of synapses firing away in futile chaos. The beast's eyes twitched as a drop of blood oozed from the tip of her trunk.

The mammoth's life up until this point in time was largely dedicated to eating grasses and being chased by the local indigenous population. Neither this mammoth nor any others in her extended herd had ever worried themselves with things like plans or expectations or taxes. But in a flash of lights and fuzz, she had a new priority: to find the orb in the box. This object was now more important than eating grasses or running from the local indigenous population.

The levers of dopamine and adrenaline that typically steered the mammoth's decision-making process had been superseded by Rose's preoccupation. The mammoth looked up to the sky and back toward the tree line. Flashes of memories of the orb and its exit from the craft played like a reel in her mind's eye. The mammoth didn't know where the mysterious marble went or why she even wanted to find such an odd object. But she did have an idea as to which direction to go, so go she did.

On the other side of the skull, birds and bugs chirped and buzzed their way around the hurried mammal. She splashed and splatted her way forward in single-minded necessity. As she stomped along the mammoth was hit by a small, crude arrow that became wedged in her natty hide. The mammoth reared back as a dozen more arrows flew in from the trees, forcing Rose and its host to turn abruptly into an open pathway that led deeper into the thicket. Additional arrows flew from behind them, mostly missing, with a few lodging into the fleeing beast.

Together they ran, Rose and the beast. Their wills were intertwined, their imperatives blurring into one. The dry dirt of the path was stamped beneath flat feet as the mammoth hurried her five-ton frame. They stumbled along, cutting down a narrow path into the vegetation as another wave of arrows narrowly missed. They were confused and scared, fleeing until they flew, Rose and the beast, parasite and host, off the side of a cliff.

The drop was steep, and the mammoth stood no chance. She landed on a pile of craggy rocks, crushing them with her forceful impact before the pressure of the fall caused the furry behemoth to smash into pieces like a watermelon dropped off a roof. Blood splattered into the sky and rained back down in a splash. The mammoth was dead. Rose was rendered unconscious from the impact, still wedged between the mammoth's skull and gray matter.

A horn blew as a tribe of short humanoids with primate and rep-
tilian features scurried out from behind the tree line. They picked up
the assorted pieces in teams, placing the smaller bits into baskets and
disappeared back into the forest, chattering away to one another as they
carried the carcass back to their village.

Rose awoke, rattled but alive. It detached from the bit of brain to
which it was pressed and crawled back through the underside of the
skull. It shuffled its way like a caterpillar through its blood-coated exit as
quickly as possible. With a final push, Rose squeezed through the exposed
opening in the side of the trunk and fell onto the dirt floor. A thin layer of
dust coated the mucous skin flap as it reclaimed its bearings. Rose was in
a storage tent, surrounded by chunks of hairy flesh waiting to be salted.

One of the natives looked down at Rose, who quickly dropped to the
floor and fluttered in its signature red hue. He was a boy, a little older,
with a vertical orange sprout of coarse hair coming out of the top of his
scalp like an upside-down goatee. He cocked his head sideways in curious
wonder and squatted down to Rose's level. He picked the blood- and
dust-covered oddity up off the floor and held it closely to his intrigued
eye. Rose fluttered again. The boy wiped some of the blood and dust off
with his finger and watched as shimmers of silver and purple pixelated
themselves into a reflection of himself.

The boy smiled, enjoying his little mirror as he made a series of faces.
He puffed out his cheeks and then sucked them in, crossing his eyes and
sticking his tongue out. He shook his face side to side and made warbling
noises. He laughed at his cleverness as he squinted his eyes and opened
his mouth agape, saying, "Ahh."

Rose snapped to attention and rolled into a tube. It lunged aggressively
into the boy's yawning orifice and jammed itself up through the roof of
his mouth. It extended the short hooks along its sides and chipped its
way in, bit by bit, clawing into the terrified child's skull. From there, it
was an easy wiggle up to the top of the new host's brain.

The boy collapsed and convulsed, his eyes rolling into the back of
his head as milky froth dribbled from his quaking mouth. Inside the
cranium, Rose adjusted itself to this new, less-spacious arrangement. It
chaotically touched parts of the young brain, creating a series of invol-
untary reflexes from the boy. Rose twisted once more, then settled into a
diagonal posture, reaching both the frontal lobe as well as the brain stem.
The spark of connection from the contact woke the boy from his spasms.

The mammoth had been a vehicle, prodded in this direction or that by the direct hijacking of motor function. But the boy, with his perfectly sized lump of gray matter, was different. They had merged. All of the child's memories, dreams, wants, and fears were now Rose's. The Technicolor sheet was not in control of the boy; it had become him. It lived his life and did his chores and learned to eat, breathe, and exist.

For Rose, being a biped had its challenges. There were aspects of life that it had taken for granted, things so routine that they were simply farmed off to muscle memory. Sometimes, Rose's avatar would jump, expecting to catch a low-gravity breeze before being pulled right back to the ground. The boy often fell over and mumbled nonsense, bleeding from the nose in occasional drips. The rest of the village believed that he had fallen under the spell of evil forces. They blamed him for the recent crop failures and pointed to how his strange behavior coincided with the recent meteorites. The shaman proclaimed he was cursed.

Their pagan religion worshipped the forests around them. Like the forests, the boy would be cleansed with fire. In the night, he was taken from his family and tied to a wooden stake at the center of the village, the sound of chanting and drums echoing along the valley. A shaman laid wreaths of dried branches and leaves among the restrained child, who twisted and turned in vain. Without the orb, Rose felt powerless. How could it escape this turn? Where could it go? Rose, the living sheet cradled atop the squishy young brain, had no answer. Yet deep in the recesses of gray matter, the boy had. Tucked between a memory of a stolen piece of meat and a swat on the behind from his mother, this new concept for Rose would be the answer: lying.

Rose, as the boy, claimed that the village deity had entered his body and granted him powers to deliver his people from the pains of famine and disease. The villagers, cautious but receptive, freed the child and awaited the fruits of the boy's proclamation. They expected magic and wonder. What they got instead was agriculture and basic hygiene. Rose's knowledge immediately elevated the village's standard of living. Grateful, they made the boy their king and worshipped him as a prophet. He was henceforth called Bakuma by his people; it was both his name and title.

Bakuma told his subjects the story of the orbiting comet and the holy orb in the clear, white-lined box. It was called the Aperture Parallax and was a relic that arrived from the sky but was lost to the swamps and forests of their world. It would be the key to their salvation, but first, it had to be found. Bakuma's forges developed tools to dig and sift and his followers used them happily.

Rose spent many nights looking up to the stars, wondering if Gray survived, out there, alone . . . somewhere. The brain-saddled sheet would reflect on the comet, if it were coming back, and if so, how destructive would it be? If the orb was never found, what then? Would all of this be for nothing? Rose's actions had saved its home world but doomed another. Would it have been better to just enjoy the time they had left back home? And where was home? Rose indulged in these thoughts in its quieter moments, but even among this anxiety, a new truth emerged: it was good being king.

Seasons passed, and Bakuma was now an old man. His skin was patchy and withered, thin against the opulent red robe he wore ceremoniously. The village had grown to a kingdom, with a stone pyramid and rolling farmland planted over tilled dirt. The search for the Parallax had stretched to their borders, and there was no sign of the missing jewel. As Bakuma's final days approached, Rose realized that it was not aging. There was time but no consequence. No decay. No mitosis. Rose would need a new body. The search for the orb could continue.

The day of the first official succession was cloudy with a slight drizzle that came down on the gathered crowd of believers wearing their matching white tunics. Bakuma had found the heir to his rule—a new leader in both state and faith. The elder ruler waved a wiry, spotted hand holding a ritual blade and introduced the next in line to the masses. The heir was young and virile with a fluffed orange mane. Bakuma chose this boy to carry his legacy, and his subjects accepted it without question.

The ceremony was brisk, with a procession of clergy and soldiers leading the boy up the carved stone steps of the pyramid to his aging forebearer. Bakuma ran his leathery finger down the boy's cheek, peering into the child's eyes, finding his reflection in deep black pools. A wide smile creaked across Bakuma's face as he turned back to the waiting audience of thousands.

He spoke. "This child is now Bakuma. He is I and I am he. Tomorrow, I will be no more. Yet I will always be, through him. And when his days wane and his pulse grows weak, he too shall follow me as one becomes him. As Bakuma sayeth."

"As Bakuma sayeth," replied the crowd en masse.

Their beloved leader raised the finely sharpened dagger. "It is time for the sacred transfer."

The rear guard opened a thick wooden door to a sealed chamber. Bakuma escorted the boy into the room and sat on a throne adorned with plush fabric and jewels and sat, laying the ceremonial knife across his lap. The door closed, and an iron bar locked the door from the outside. They were alone. Bakuma looked at the young man.

"Are you ready to lead your people, boy?" he asked, a dribble of spit living in the groove between his lips.

"Yes . . . yes, my lord."

"Good," Bakuma said as he stood from his chair and drove the blade directly into his heart. Spit gurgled, chased by blood. It ran down the side of his withered mouth. He fell to the ground, gasping for air, bleeding out.

The young Bakuma-to-be panicked. He pounded on the door and yelled to the guards, "He's hurt! He's hurt! Come help him!" His cries were met with silence. The boy turned back to his dying leader and rushed to his side. "Are you OK? What can I do?"

Bakuma looked at the concerned heir, blood pouring from the deep gash in his chest. "Listen to my breath," he said before releasing a final exhale.

There was silence.

The boy leaned in close to the lifeless ruler. He poked at the body and got closer. He put his ear up to the lips of Bakuma, waiting for the faintest of sounds. He held his breath to make everything as quiet as possible, silencing all but his heartbeat.

Suddenly, a quiet hiss came from behind Bakuma's eyes. His lips moved, a tremble at first, then a full, open snap. Rose leaped from Bakuma's mouth into the young man's ear. It squirmed and writhed its way through as the screams of the young man could be heard outside of the iron barred doors. The guards on the other side stood at unflinching attention as the screams carried on for a few moments before they stopped entirely.

A knock, three times, signaled to the guards to open the door. With a creak of wood and iron, the new Bakuma stood before the crowd. He wiped a drop of blood from his nose and approached the masses, raising his arms up as the sea of people rejoiced. Horns blew, and dancers worked their way back down the stairs, throwing confetti into the throngs of people. They sang and celebrated as the new Bakuma stood from his perch, smiling the same wide, crooked smile as the last. This was to be the first of many successions.

As the centuries unfolded, Bakuma became the avatar for terror upon nations. His followers dug and fought wars and made the losers of those wars dig and fight too. This process repeated across the planet through generation after generation and layer upon layer of sediment. And with every passing generation, Rose thought less and less of Gray, the original mission to find the child blurred across the minds of Bakumas long since dead. The brain rider had lost more of itself with every succession, each Technicolor piece replaced with the tarry blackness of obsession.

Rose yearned for the Aperture Parallax. It was a churning hunger that had become a means unto itself. And yet, despite the wars and digging, the prize was still out there, hiding in the groves and marshes, somewhere beneath the soil, forever out of reach. Yet while the God-King and his puppeteer remained fixated on the elusive prize, many of the empire's subjects considered a prize of their own: freedom. Most were the great-grandchildren of the conquered, only knowing labor with no purpose and war with no end. Over time, they became like weakened cells of the body public, turning cancerous, their ideas spreading.

Pockets of unrest bred dissent, which rippled out into the surrounding communities and metastasized into revolution. The occupying forces of Bakuma were overthrown, province by province, governor by governor. Surviving soldiers and loyal citizens alike were forced behind a ringed barricade around the capital district. There, they hid behind a massive wall as the rebellion tore the empire and its war machine down. Attacked from all sides by the rebel leader Lolo and her guerrilla armies, Bakuma was trapped.

Then one day, in a swamp over a thousand miles away from Rose's original crash site, the Aperture Parallax was found. It was boxed up and returned to the capital, making it into the withered and shaking hands of Bakuma. The old ruler retired to his chamber alone and dropped the jewel from its case into his eager, open palm.

He violently inhaled, his head thrashing backward as the orb contacted his skin. It was revelation. The comet, hurtling ever forward, was a single generation from colliding with the planet. All life on the surface would be obliterated, and the Crimson Empire would turn to dust. Bakuma focused on the orb, attempting to phase into a new dimension. Nothing happened. Rose was immortal in this place, as healthy as the day it arrived, yet its spark was gone. The orb's power was limited to sight. It was trapped.

Building a new rocket to escape wasn't feasible. Even if Rose were to survive the trip, how would it survive from there? Life would be wiped from the surface, if not immediately, then long enough for it starve out beneath clouds of dust and acid rains. Inaction would be the embrace of death, though after thousands of years, would finality really be the worst thing? *Yes*, Rose thought with a detached clarity. It remembered life before Bakuma, before the never-ending parade of primitive hosts and the fruitless search for the little red gem. Rose remembered Gray. Home. The life before becoming a perpetual tyrant.

No, death would wait as Rose had a better answer. Bakuma would direct his loyal citizenry toward a cause it already knew much about: digging. They would be quick, or all would be for nothing.

As the Crimson Empire maintained its fortified border, its citizens built a subterranean metropolis many miles below their capital. It was massive, with housing for half a million, a self-sustaining water and atmosphere generator, arable land, and an artificial sun. There were schools and hospitals, parks and a museum dedicated to the Crimson Empire built directly into the walls of the cave, and most importantly of all, a grand pyramid, the standing legacy of Bakuma.

ON THE EVE OF DESTRUCTION, Lolo's armies had breached the final redoubt of the empire. There, they found the place deserted—a Potemkin village of industrial might, hollowed and barren. They searched, moving through houses and shops, floorboards groaning beneath thick boots. The soldiers tore through Bakuma's capital, pilfering valuables and vandalizing statues, and still, not a soul. Lolo examined a stand built into the rail that looked out from the same holy mezzanine that Bakuma had when he addressed his people for the first time, all those years ago. She looked back into the temple at her men and called.

"These are the people's antiquities. They do not belong to you."

"Sorry, ma'am," one apologized, setting a gold-plated replica of the pyramid down. It had a mirror pyramid extending beneath it, crafted in chiseled ruby. The shape together made a wider diamond, which wobbled slightly when placed onto the floor.

"Wait a minute, pick that back up," the general said as the partisan paused.

"That one?"

"Yes. Where did you find that?"

"Over here." He motioned toward a stand identical to the one Lolo was leaning against.

"Bring that here."

The solider did as instructed, handing the double pyramid over. Lolo approached the stand and flipped the replica upside down, ruby portion hanging down like a reflection on water. She centered it on the display and looked out at the extended gathering space below. The weight of the object sunk the stand into the stone floor.

The shifting of gears startled a gathering of winged amphibians with droopy neck skin congregating on a nearby roof. They cawed and fled to the skies as a set of metal hatch doors in the center courtyard opened, blooming like a flower saying hello to the day. Lolo climbed down the pyramid steps to the entrance, its elegant curvature folding in layers. She flashed a light down the wide ramp into darkness, focusing but seeing nothing. Several dozen soldiers peered from behind her.

"What's that?" someone from behind Lolo yelled out, pointing upward. She looked to see a bright flash of fire and rock, streaking through the sky as small bits broke off and charted their own descent.

"Everybody, inside!" Lolo yelled as she fled into the subterranean passageway. Her army followed behind her as a rumbling whoosh roared from above. Partisans hurried along before the shuddering clank of the entry resealed behind them. An explosion shook the earth, sending bits of dust raining down from above.

Lolo broke open a flare and descended farther, flanked by hundreds, into the darkness. She traversed the stone pathway deeper into the abyss, the hiss of the low flame carried above the breathing and footsteps. They trekked downhill for hours until they reached a formal entrance with grand metal doors. Lolo's partisans readied the siege cannon and aimed it at the barricade. A gunshot.

They were ambushed. Automated heavy guns fired bolts alongside soldiers at hidden perches who sent streams of projectiles into Lolo's armies. With no ability to fall back, the rebel force engaged, returning fire in all directions. Defenses were destroyed, and many were killed as Lolo pushed forward. The bodies of the dead piling atop each other, maimed and broken, screaming then silent. The battle raged deeper, Lolo driving Bakuma's forces backward until they reached the underground city.

It was magnificent, with buildings and rivers and wispy clouds shrouding a large pyramid carved into the far wall of the inside of the mountain. Onward, they advanced as bullets and gas canisters flew through the air while robe-clad followers scrambled to escape the melee.

BAKUMA HUFFED IN HIS FRAIL state as he gripped the sleek case carrying the Aperture Parallax with his bony, spotted hands. He peered out from the temple at the summit of the pyramid, overlooking the battle as it raged below. Lolo's rebels moved through the streets, the gunfire erupting in bursts, scattered throughout the subterranean city. Bakuma hurried back inside to a crystal orb that sat at the center of the space, wheezing and choking on his filmy spittle. Bakuma pulled the orb from its case and held it tight.

He made an intention, focusing as the wrinkles across his brow furrowed together. He placed it in a specialized compartment made of diamond and watched the Aperture Parallax ascend upward through the ceiling and into the transparent tip of the pyramid. He closed his eyes and was met with flashes of images. Home. Gray. The comet. Life before, with carefree days of floating along in the breeze and sentient moss and stacked rocks and warm vents with their delicious particulates. He took a final, dry gasp and collapsed to the floor, dead.

The crimson hue of the orb flashed bright above the pyramid, blinking rapidly, faster, faster, until the entire city, buildings, armies and all, simply vanished. They were replaced by columns of moss-covered rocks. The laws of physics had changed, as small droplets of water floated about the air, suspended in the soft red light emitting from the pyramid, the only structure left from what stood before. Those who remained were those still in the tunnels, submerged underwater, or inside the pyramid, untouched from the initial sweep of interdimensional reshuffle.

Rose emerged from Bakuma's nose, crawling to the edge of the temple to witness its home for the first time in a thousand years. It reached a corner of its square out into the new atmosphere. The artificial sun now projected crimson, refracted through the tiers of layered diamond

mirrors making up its protective case. The Parallax within remained perfectly in place in the smallest chamber inside the artificial sun. The design
had been perfect, slicing along the edge of the pyramid with precision,
leaving little but the dust on the edges of the steppes outside its angle.
But the effects were inverted. Rather than transporting the pyramid back
home, the Aperture Parallax brought home to the pyramid. All things
save for the pyramid and the natural surfaces of the cave were replaced
by Rose's home world. It was a subterranean diorama.

Outside, among the stone towers and snails and vents, Rose found
its kind. They were there, just like before, clinging in towers, waiting to
drink particulates. There were thousands of them, all confused by their
new surroundings, flashing waves of designs and colors to one another in
growing worry. While they weren't the exact individuals Rose had known
in its first life, as too many years had passed, it would be good enough.

But the universe rarely settles for such clean finales. The fissures that
had appeared were purely cosmetic, as the cave's original surfaces remained, the vents were nothing more than pockmarks. The colony of
living paper with a silver sheen, unable to feed on particulates, starved
to death. Unable to communicate the concept of living in a host, Rose
was forced back into the skull of a Baku, the only of its kind once more.

Inside the Baku, Rose attempted to retrieve the Aperture Parallax from
its resting place in the tip of the pyramid, but was rebuffed, seemingly by
the jewel itself. The artificial sun would not lower, nor would the glass
surrounding the jewel break. Worse yet, this new Bakuma would be a
prisoner in his own temple, unable to touch the light of the new sun
without dying by old age. Bakuma would be forever forced to rule from
the shadows.

The remaining Baku, descendants of the empire and rebels alike,
adapted to the new ecosystem. They learned to eat the snails living on
the moss and shrunk in size over time to be a better fit for their new
home. The armies became tribes, and the tribes continued with their
skirmishes, slowly devolving in technology and means. From guns to
swords to wooden spears, the cycle of warfare continued, the dead becoming fertilizer for the moss.

Over time, the only person who remembered a world any different
to this one was Rose. It was alone, trapped, and devolving alongside its
hosts in its own personal hell. Their shrinking brains were becoming a

problem for Rose, making the fit tighter and more uncomfortable. There was only one thing left that Rose could do: find Gray.

Somewhere, out in the reaches of space, Gray could still be alive, aged not a day, just like Rose. Like its first time a thousand years prior, Rose built a spacecraft. But this craft was smaller, only large enough for a message on a flash drive. It was skinny, able to squeeze through the small hole Rose bored through the top of the mountain. The message was an SOS. It was a plea for forgiveness.

PART 13

THE PYRAMID AT THE
END OF THE WORLD

INSIDE THE PYRAMID AT THE END OF THE WORLD, ONE OF QITI'S pirates tossed a dead Baku toward Dex and her guards. Its mottled green skin was covered in splotches of dusty white paint, its scalp peeled back, revealing copper-colored blood vessels.

Qiti spoke to Dex. "I've already been practicing my brain-slug removal skills on a few of the locals. I can't exactly botch the job here. It's important I do this right. You *are* my mom, after all."

"What . . . What is happening? You were captured," Dex asked, cautiously eyeing the situation.

"No, no. Mom. I wasn't. These guys are working for me. *For* me," the robot replied, speaking slowly the second time around as she pointed to her sternum, or, at least, where a sternum would be.

"I don't understand."

"It's OK. It was bound to happen at some point in your life, right? To finally not be the first to figure something out. But to tell you the truth, there are parts to this that I don't understand either," Qiti said, waving the ceremonial blade about for emphasis. "Look, you made me. You created me from your own will and genius and the hundred thousand pieces you fabricated and welded together. I am from you, so I am a part of you. And yet, for years, I couldn't comprehend why I existed. Sure, there was the mission to find the Aperture Parallax, obviously. Duh. It's all you ever really talked about.

"But why did *I* exist? Me, the collection of thoughts and feelings and wants and needs and personality quirks speaking to you right now. If I was a tool created as a means to an end, why do I feel? What purpose does it accomplish for me to experience longing or sadness or joy or the crushing disappointment of being unloved?

"Maybe I was meant to be something more. A person? A daughter? Were you my mother or my owner? I don't know if you intended for me to have these thoughts or if this is some programming error . . . And I don't know if that even matters anymore. I do feel those things and I can't deny them, so here I am, your loving daughter, your creation . . . here to save you."

"Save me from what?"

"From the alien leech that's drinking the blood from the top of your brain. Duh."

An uncharacteristic frown settled across Dex's previously stoic face. "It's not like that," she said, looking down.

"I know about the parasite. There's an entire chapter on its home world in the Bakuma Key files you had me fetch for you. Fascinating animal, that multidimensional starfish in your head. Oof," Qiti said, tapping at her forehead. "Apparently, there are only two of them in this entire dimension, and from the looks of things, they've been trying to reconnect for a very long time. I'm actually looking forward to seeing one after I take it out."

"You can't."

"Mom, come on. You need me to take it out. This thing steered you all the way to this vermin-filled tomb at the edge of nowhere. You're rich and a genius and can literally do anything you want, whenever you want. Why are you really here?"

Dex took a deep breath and looked at Qiti with the solemn eyes of the relenting. "When I was young, I got very sick. The fever liquefied parts of my brain, and I fell into a coma. I was placed into frozen quarantine like the others who survived. We were all ghosts of the flesh. We were alive but never living.

"I was chosen to be a part of a study and shipped to the edges of Olympian space. Nobody had ever woken once they slipped into the endless sleep. Yet one night, against all probability, I did. I woke up. I woke up because of it, the nameless, unexplainable thing that communicated in pictures and feelings and purpose. This thing brought me back from the never-ending void in which I was trapped. But I was not the same; I was better. Dex, the orphaned girl from Alpha Olympus, died like the rest of the slumbering masses wiped out by the Ravage. With it living inside me, I was new.

"Its life, its memories—they became my memories. I remember the sensation of shifting through dimensions in a rickety pyramid-shaped shuttle, though I, as Dex the little girl, was in a coma at the time. I remember holding the Aperture Parallax in the slack of my shifting silver skin, and yet I have hands. I also remember a time before being sick. I remember my family and how they once smiled. Everything was full of love, and then one day it was not. The crushing weight of their pain was my last sensation before falling asleep. I had destroyed them, and all I did was close my eyes. When I woke up, it was they who would be sleeping.

"Without the thing, this symbiotic bypass of synapses, I will fall back asleep. Without me, it will suffocate in our atmosphere. We exist as one or not at all. To separate us is to kill us both. The Parallax—its power was always a means to an end. I just wanted to find my missing family."

"I am your family!" Qiti yelled, stomping her foot and cracking the tile beneath her.

Dex stopped. She raised her palms and stepped forward, alone. Her guards remained behind her, hands up.

The pirates behind Qiti collectively pointed their weapons at Dex, though Qiti motioned them down with the wave of her hand. Qiti stepped forward as well, the two meeting in the middle. Dex towered over her child, whose head only approached her naval. Dex squatted down and came face-to-face with her diminutive creation. She reached out and placed her hand on Qiti's face.

"You're right. Your love for me is no less valid than anything I feel. I've searched for thousands of years to quiet the pang of loss that haunts me like a phantom limb. I see now, the hurt in you. My single-minded pursuit may very well have both given and taken away my family. I could have been better. You deserved better, and for that, I am sorry," she said as a glimmer of tears welled in the corner of her eyes.

Qiti's chin rose in a restrained show of emotion. She hugged her kneeling mother, not quite wrapping her arms around Dex's back in her embrace. Dex placed her hand on the back of Qiti's head, showing her first outward expression of affection toward her fabricated daughter.

"Let us take what we came for and go home together," Dex said, releasing Qiti.

"Yes, and with the Parallax, there will be no limits. But first," Qiti said as she waved the blade about, looking at her reflection in it, "the brain slug has to go."

"I can't accommodate that. I will die," Dex said, standing back up.

"No, no, you won't. We've got one of the teleoboxes from the ship," she said, pointing at the squishy pirate gripping the shiny medical unit between two tentacles. It held the object upward in display. Dex's face tensed in disapproval.

"Oh, and don't worry. I'm not using this," Qiti continued, looking at the blade. "No, this is for something else." She put the blade in a compartment in her leg. "I'm using this," she said with a smile as she whipped the tip of her pointer finger off. A thin red laser beamed out several inches from a pinprick beneath her nail. She smiled and flipped her finger back in place, like closing a Zippo lighter. "Though cutting your skull open and taking the slug by force is only the backup option. I'm willing to bet that it will leave you voluntarily."

Qiti summoned a pinkish brute in the back. It lumbered forward and stopped at the front row of motley pirates and let out a deep, guttural gurgle. The single arm protruding from the center of its chest was pointed outward, carrying a Baku's limp body like a wet towel. The diminutive gremlin was weak but breathing.

"*Blood Fang!*" Zizi gasped as he reached out.

Qiti stood beside the subdued Bakuma and lightly tapped her hand on his face as she spoke. "While I appreciate your dilemma, I don't believe you are in control of the parasite. The Bakuma Key was very clear; it and it alone determines who is in control. And considering how this thing dragged you all the way here for a family reunion, I really don't see how it'll pass this opportunity up."

Qiti whipped her finger back and ignited the laser. The sharp beam of light sliced along Blood Fang's scalp, melting the skin, tissue, and bone in an even slice. She peeled back the skin and hair first, revealing blood vessels crisscrossing above tissue. She peeled that part next, the wet *shloop* of the layer sounding like wet Velcro. From there, all that remained was the still-conscious creature's chalk-white skull.

Qiti removed the top portion of the homunculus's brain casing and tossed it onto the floor beside her. It landed with a clunk and a rattle. She reached her hand in and, with the quick motion of a Band-Aid removal, ripped Rose from her host. Rose's skin pulsed in panicked shots of blood-orange as Qiti whipped it back and forth like a Polaroid picture. The fibrous tissue that clung to the interdimensional leaf flicked off with each whip.

"You can drop him now," Qiti said as she waved to the brute, who obliged.

Dex's eyes went wide as she fixated on the fluttering creature hanging from Qiti's fingers. "Don't hurt it," Dex cried, a tear rolling down her cheek.

"No problem, no problem," Qiti replied, ending her wrist motion. "All I want is what's best for everybody."

"What about that guy?" Lazer chimed in, pointing at Blood Fang, who gasped for air like a fish out of water on the painted stone floor.

"You want me to check you for parasites too?" Qiti yelled at Lazer as her finger laser reignited. She turned back to Dex. "OK, here's my offer. You and I leave here together without the brain slugs, but with the Aperture Parallax. They can live down here together in a place that's just like home and they can drink lizard brains for eternity and do whatever brain slugs do for fun. Meanwhile, I can use the teleobox to fix you, and we can go be evil geniuses. Mother and daughter. We can conquer planets and do crime or whatever, but it won't matter as much as that we'll be a family, together. Everybody gets what they want; nobody gets hurt."

Everyone looked at Blood Fang as he struggled on the ground with his brain exposed, then at Qiti.

"Oh, you know what I mean!" Qiti yelled with a sigh of annoyed frustration. "So, slug, here's your . . . mom? I don't know. Do brain slugs have genders? Doesn't matter. It's all yours. All of that searching can end today."

Dex shook her head. "I already told you, we can't separate. We will both die."

"No, no. Mom. You're wrong. I've run the models; this will fix you. It will repair your brain. Trust me."

"No."

"But don't you see? I'll be freeing you."

"No."

"Please. I don't want to do this. We outnumber you three to one."

"For now."

Qiti sighed and shook her head.

"As you wish, let's get this over with, then."

"Let's," Dex said with a slow bow before springing into a back hand-stand, picking up her pistol along the way. She fired a round of shots across the room, going over Qiti's head but hitting several of the pirates beside her.

Qiti put Rose's quivering body in one of her compartments and took cover. The room erupted into melee. Weapons fired off, sending out sprays of dust and blood as the projectiles connected with pirates, mercenaries, and statues. Red Scale dodged one of Dex's shots and returned several rounds, all narrowly missing the nimble CEO as she dove behind a statue that kicked out chalky dust as it was hit by a string of bullets.

Lazer and Streek ducked behind the closest statue as a purple beam of energy singed the tips of the musician's hair.

"What do we do?" Streek exclaimed over the cacophony of pistol fire.

"Try not to die!" Lazer yelled back.

"Right, but then what?"

"Well . . . aren't we supposed to take that guy back to the nice Muppet lady?" Lazer asked, pointing at the scalped and gasping Blood Fang, who lay incapacitated in the open center ring near a statue. A pool of viscous red liquid seeped from above the fading gremlin's eyes.

"But he's dead," the octopus argued.

"Not yet, man," Lazer replied, pointing at the teleobox lying in a pool of translucent green soup a dozen feet away.

Streek's face lit up before tumbling back down to reality. "We have to save him! Shit, we have to save him," he said, first to Lazer and then to himself.

"I know, that's what I just said! So what's the plan?"

"Um, I'll grab the box; you can get the Blood Fang fellow."

"OK," Lazer said with a nod.

"And don't forget his skull piece."

"Totally. Skull piece. Got it!"

"See you back here in one minute!" Streek yelled.

"Cool!" Lazer called back. They turned in opposite directions and moved out. Laser beams and bullets stopped them both the moment either of them moved from the cover of the statue. They turned back to each other.

"Let's say two minutes," Lazer said, leaning away from the edge as another projectile whizzed by.

ACROSS THE ROOM, DEX DUCKED and fired with precision, tumbling nimbly between the front row of statues. Red Scale's pirates were picked off by the white-hot beams of energy fired from her pistol. One by one, they fell to the ground, some shrieking, others silent. She signaled at the mercenary captain for him and two of his men to circle around the back side of the statues and flank Qiti.

A roar bellowed above the cacophony of battle as the mercenaries tossed several smoke-grenades across the room, which sent plumes of white fog spraying upward. Another roar.

The Vithrax charged through the thick cloud at one of the mercenaries and impaled him through his armor-padded stomach with a slicing uppercut. The spider-legged monster spun around and flung the mortally wounded soldier into one of his cohorts, knocking the hired gun into the statue behind him and onto the floor.

A Clicklaxia guard charged forward and tossed a small black disk at the massive arachnid, which stuck to the matted tuft of fur bordering the black exoskeleton of its legs. It swatted off the sticky puck and kicked it with a spindly appendage. The disk slid beside a statue and exploded, sending pieces of stone flying into the air along with blood and bits of the mercenary who was hiding behind it.

As the small hail of dust subsided, the Vithrax raised its nose to the air and sniffed.

Qiti peered out from a statue in the first row and immediately dodged one of Dex's light beams. "Pretty impressive that you can get that close through the smoke," the robot yelled.

"You're assuming I want to hit you," Dex called back.

"You'll have to at some point. I'm not stopping until the slug is gone."

"There has to be another way," Dex yelled out, aiming her pistol through the thickening shroud of gas.

A shot rang out, knocking her pistol from her hands. It fell to the floor, partially melted on the barrel where the beam had hit it. Izzit pulled his gun back and hid behind his statue, which was at the end of the row to her left.

Dex sprinted back several rows and pulled at a rifle still strapped to a downed Clicklaxia. She struggled to pull the weapon out from the dead guard's arms, hunching over to keep low. She freed the rifle and rolled to the side, narrowly dodging the swinging cutlass of a one-armed pirate and blocking the follow-up with her new weapon. She kicked the pirate in the stomach, who stumbled back, collected his senses, and charged once more. Dex swung the butt end of the rifle at the base of the sword, connecting with the pirate's fingers. The swarthy ogre groaned and dropped the cutlass.

Dex pointed the rifle at the unarmed privateer and pulled the trigger. *Click.* The gun was out of ammunition.

She sighed and dove toward the sword, rolling in a summersault as she grabbed it. She jumped, slicing upward with the charged blade, and removed the pirate's only arm. He screamed in shock as the tentacles on his back flailed about. Dex parried the sweeping lunge from the rightmost tentacle and dodged a strike from above. She ducked and spun, swinging the sword across the brute's knees. The pirate fell forward, his tentacles reaching in a desperate attempt to grab at Dex's glowing sword. She kicked a tentacle that came in from the side and punched the pirate in the face with the handle.

The pirate swung a tentacle downward, which Dex sliced off. He swung another, with that one being removed as well. Thick, gooey puss oozed from the wounds as the injured pirate flailed about. With a final thrust, Dex sliced through the center of the pirate's chest, discharging the current of electricity stored in the weapon. The pirate popped, sizzled, and collapsed to the floor. Dex pulled the sword from the fallen pirate's torso and moved her way through the now-impenetrable fog.

As the battle waged, fewer shots flew through the air with each fallen participant. Lazer and Streek had their chance. Streek floated as fast as he could to the slime-covered teleobox as Lazer sprinted to the barely conscious Baku, dragging him by the shoulders to a hiding spot behind the furthest row of statues. Streek arrived right after with the piece of regenerative technology and pulled out the connecting hose.

"Where's the skull?" Streek anxiously asked.

Lazer looked around and peeked back out to the lonely blood puddle where Blood Fang had just lay. Zizi was behind the nearest statue, barely visible through the shroud of smoke, avoiding a stream of purple streaks of light that were coming from Dex's side of the temple. He stepped out, hesitated, and ducked back behind the stone figure, dodging another wave of projectiles. Zizi and Lazer made eye contact through the mist, Zizi conveying his lack of options with a wide stare.

Lazer sighed and, tapping into the agility of his youth, darted up the rows of statues, hiding behind each one before making his next sprint closer. With a final burst of speed, he made it to his pinned-down friend. Zizi showed Lazer his singed shoulder, the blast had cauterized the hit and didn't look life-threatening, but it was clearly painful.

Lazer looked at Zizi and pointed toward his eyes, then pointed out to the hazy center of the temple. Projectiles and their bombast filled the air. Lazer brought up his liquid eye menu. He scrolled through and activated a holographic projection of himself, illuminating the fog beside him in a bright blue outline. He waved his hand in a forward motion and sent his decoy into the center point of the enshrouded open space. The holographic Lazer jogged to his intended place as projectiles flew through him. Lazer's bright blue doppelgänger patted around his body as Zizi used the opportunity to dart forward, grab the skull fragment, and scurry back.

As Zizi whipped his way around the statue providing them cover, the Vithrax leaped from the side and sliced the decoy with its front appendages. It spun around and hopped, looking for the crushed body that should have been beneath it. It raised its head and howled as the illuminated figure disappeared. It took a laser blast to the chest and grunted, leaping toward an unseen triggerman.

Lazer grabbed Zizi by his uninjured arm and ran to the far back row of statues, where Streek awaited with the goopy cellular regeneration box. Streek was hovering low, supporting the back of Blood Fang's head with a tentacle. Lazer took the skull piece from Zizi and placed it on one of the octopus's open suction cups.

A grenade exploded nearby.

"We've got to make this quick," Lazer said in a hurried nervousness.

"Yes, yes of course. We need to get out of here, but this is important," Streek replied, placing the fragment in its perfectly carved slot. The hose was already hooked up, the machine activated with a whir and a beep. Streek pressed on the top, and the teleobox buzzed in reply.

The tissues and fibers along Blood Fang's scalp churned with energy. Spindles of bone reconnected like bridges, plastering the carved portion of his skull back together. Streek pulled the unconscious gremlin's scalp closed over the naked yet regenerating skull. Veins pulsed as they reached like vines, pulling the loose flap of skin and hair tight and stitching them back together with sinew and fiber.

An errant blaster shot hit the top of the stone figure Lazer and company were hiding behind. Dust rained down above them as they waited anxiously for the regeneration machine to finish.

ACROSS THE TEMPLE, DEX CREPT through the rows of stone-carved priests. The fog rolled gently, having fully dispersed through the vaulted hall in uniform thickness. She stopped at the end of the final row and cocked her head, listening to the room—every shot, every scream, and every gurgle. She could hear their steps, their hearts beating, the nervous swallowing of someone close. She rounded the corner swiftly, grabbed a Porcli pirate by his mouth, and sliced his throat. He fell to the ground and was dragged behind the column with a hushed gurgle. Dex took the Porcli's gun, pointed it down the row, and waited.

The bang of another grenade rang out a half dozen rows down, sending Izzit running from the explosion. Dex fired, catching the fleeing captain with a single shot, who dropped immediately to the ground with a yelp. Dex approached slowly through the mist in a cautious crouch, weapon ready.

With a flash in the corner of her eye, she ducked, narrowly avoiding Red Scale's silver cutlass. The serpent followed through on the swing, losing his balance. Dex rolled backward and sprung up, firing her pistol as fast as her finger could pull the trigger. A single shot blazed, followed by a string of ammo-less clicking.

Red Scale stumbled back, recoiling from the blaster shot that had opened a smoldering hole in his abdomen. He roared from the shock of pain before regaining his balance. He breathed with labor as he waved his cutlass in an X before him, challenging his employer. Dex pulled her knife from its sheath and held it upside down, the blade running parallel to her forearm. She kept her left hand out, waving in measured anticipation.

"Yar, 'tis an honor to face ye," Red Scale croaked as he circled his opponent.

"I know," Dex replied.

Red Scale sliced downward with the weight of his body behind it. Dex leaped to the side, then ducked as the serpent followed with a heavy swing. Dex moved close and kicked the pirate in the burning wound in his abdomen, sending the scaled beast into a howl as he staggered back. He recovered and returned to his fighting stance, coughing and spitting to the side. With a growl, he swung wide and missed with his sword, then followed through with a whip of his tail.

Dex dodged it with a backward cartwheel, then jumped close once more, kicking the serpent in the same, raw spot. Red Scale bellowed in pain and took a lumbering step back, snorting between heavy panting. Dex waved her hand toward her, challenging the pirate.

Red Scale roared and spread his leathery wings that had been concealed beneath his coat up until this point. He raised his arms high, appearing to triple in size with the wingspan, waving his weapon in a circle. With a heavy grunt, he lunged with his sword, sloppily. Dex blocked it with the blade lining her arm, grabbed the serpent's wrist with her free hand, and stabbed her knife through Red Scale's forearm. He roared again as he dropped his cutlass.

Dex caught the sword mid fall and spun, running the blade through the pirate's belly. As Red Scale's hands instinctively pulled toward his midsection, Dex pulled her dagger from the serpent's scaly arm, leaped vertically, and planted the blade into the side of Red Scale's skull.

He fell as dead weight, his long neck landing in a natural coil. She retrieved her knife and wiped the blood off on the dead pirate's coat. She sheathed the knife, picked a blunderbuss off the corpse of an Olympian pirate, and continued onward toward Izzit's downed body.

Her steps were light through the fog, a ghost among the cacophony. She reached where Izzit went down; all she found was a small puddle of blood. There was a set of boot prints leading back into the rows of statues, showing a clear stagger. She followed them, taking cover behind one of the outermost stone priests. She pulled her appropriated blunderbuss out and pointed it down the open row. She began squeezing the trigger when the mercenary captain popped from around the corner.

"Don't shoot!" he yelled, holding one of his wounded subordinates along his side.

"How are you doing?"

"I'm fine," the mercenary captain replied before getting shot in the back by the gray alien standing behind him. The captain collapsed as he shot the other soldier and jumped back behind a statue.

Dex pointed the blunderbuss in the pirate's direction and fired, a ball of white light blasting a large chunk out of the side of the statue. A cloud of dust kicked into the air and settled, exposing Izzit, who ran to the next carving and unloaded a series of shots, singeing Dex's arm. The hit interrupted Dex's aim, sending her next blunderbuss shot high, taking off the top half of the head of an adjacent carving. She retreated behind her statue and tended to her wound.

"Oh, I'm sorry," the captain condescended from behind his cover.

Dex grunted and pulled her gun close. She closed her eyes and took a deep breath, allowing everything to slow for a moment. She leaned out quickly and fired, hitting the base of the statue beside the one Izzit was hiding behind.

He erupted in laughter. "Ha! You can't even hit me with the blunderbuss? How bad of a shot are you, lady?" he taunted.

"I'm the worst," Dex replied over the crumble of fissuring stone.

The statue beside Izzit tilted over and collapsed on top of him, burying the alien in rubble. Nothing but elongated gray fingers peeked through, limp and caked in a layer of mineral powder. The fog from the grenades began to clear. While it was difficult to say for sure, Dex thought she saw Qiti standing in the open center of the temple. She contemplated her approach.

AT THE BACK OF THE temple, Blood Fang opened his eyes. His skull had completely healed, the previously cauterized laser lines now invisible. He gazed around in a confused state as he lay against Lazer's leg. A blaster shot from across the room snapped him out of it.

"*Where is?*" Blood Fang asked Lazer, who looked down upon the gremlin, his long hair framing his face while the liquid eye translated.

"*In temple,*" Zizi replied, stepping into Blood Fang's field of vision.

"Zizi!" the resurrected Baku rejoiced before pointing at Lazer above him. "*What thing?*"

"*Friend of Zizi,*" he replied, patting his chest. He pointed to the hairy guitarist. "*This* Lahzur."

Lazer waved. "'Sup."

"*And this Strrryyykk,*" Zizi croaked in his best English thus far.

"Hello," Streek said with a wave.

Blood Fang looked to his friend in confusion. "*Just face?*" the Baku asked, wiping his hand across his face.

Streek's demeanor twisted slightly in umbrage. "Hey, I'll have you know my mother thinks I have a very lovely face," the octopus retorted.

"Sorry. No offend. Nice face. Agree," Blood Fang said as he helped himself to his feet. *"What happening?"*

"Monsters from Up kill each other. We run now!" Zizi exclaimed as a series of blaster shots rang out several statues down.

The group moved quickly but quietly toward the unguarded front of the temple, when suddenly, it dropped from the ceiling behind them—the Vithrax. It was bleeding from the abdomen, the result of being sprayed by laser fire at close range. A knife protruded from its shoulder—a mere toothpick in comparison to the massiveness of this monster—the owner of which most certainly one of the many corpses littering the temple. Splashes of blood from a variety of species matted to the creature's fur and dripped from its nimble legs, down to the floor, slowly pooling in places. The furry arachnid towered above them, rearing upon its back legs and bellowing its static screech.

The Vithrax swung a hook forward, missing Lazer but knocking the teleobox out of his hands, sending it back toward the center of the room. It snarled. Lazer, Streek, and the two Baku scurried several steps backward. The monster stalked closer, waving its hooks wide. Behind them lay the exit and the stone forest beyond. Lazer and Streek continued to back up with Blood Fang and Zizi behind them.

"So when do we run?" Lazer asked, eyeing the edge of the step as they slowly approached it.

"If we run, it'll easily catch us," the octopus replied, eyes darting back and forth.

"So . . . are you going to just talk it to death, then?"

"Ha ha," Streek laughed with overt sarcasm. "Not quite. I want you to promise not to judge me though. OK?"

"What's that?"

"When I say *now*, please jump leftward with the utmost of intention. And again, no judgment."

"OK, but I—"

"And don't forget to grab the Baku!"

The Vithrax screeched once more and galloped with its multitude of legs, rushing toward the group. It leaped through the air, scissor arms swinging.

"Now!" Streek yelled as Lazer leaped, holding Zizi with one hand and Blood Fang with the other.

Streek took in a massive inhale and pushed. He squeezed with all of his might and shot a stream of viscous black goo from his undercarriage in a puddle before him. The Vithrax landed on it and slid as Streek floated quickly over the monster with a propulsion of air.

The massive arachnid skid along the stone ground at an incredible speed, flew out the entrance of the temple, tumbled down the mountain of stairs, and careened into a stack of rocks at the forest floor.

"Run!" Lazer yelled as they all fled around the side of the temple entrance and ascended the steps to the top. They climbed, the screech of the Vithrax raging in the distance below. Lazer, despite his churning flight reflex, noticed his stamina was getting a little better. *It's probably all of the cardio*, he thought.

INSIDE THE TEMPLE, DEX STEPPED into the tiled center. The smoke had cleared, revealing the carnage of what had transpired. Every member of her security force was dead. The mercenaries were also dead. The pirates, dead too. All that remained was Qiti, standing uninjured with a hand on her hip.

"So that happened," Qiti said, shrugging at her mother.

"Is this what you wanted?" Dex asked, still holding her blunderbuss.

"Me and you, here? Yeah. I've run simulations on this scenario many times, and every time it ends the same way."

"With you carving into my skull?"

"Well, that's not how I'd describe it, but more or less, yes. I'm sorry, but sadly, this seems to be the only way."

"So it seems."

"And just to be clear, I understand that you will have to use lethal force against me. I will only go as far as it takes to remove the parasite. Once it's gone, all will be forgiven," Qiti said, clasping her hands

"How kind," Dex replied as she cocked her weapon. It didn't charge. She looked down, looked at Qiti, shrugged, and tossed it to the side. She pulled out her knife and moved into her combat stance, lean and fierce like a praying mantis. Qiti smiled and pulled into her own fighting position. The moment of stillness was brief.

Dex sprinted forward and leaped at her automaton. The tip of her blade angled downward, aimed at the meeting point between Qiti's neck and shoulder. The robot blocked the strike and steered the attack to the side. Dex flipped back and regained her balance. Their standoff resumed.

They circled around the open center of the temple, calculating their next moves. Dex slowly crept forward, knife held in a reversed grip, parallel to her arm. She stood at nearly double the height, a lean and muscular juxtaposition to her rounded metallic creation. Dex struck again, swinging through a back kick aimed at Qiti's chest.

The force sent Qiti flying backward through a pile of rubble. She stood and dusted off the chalky particulates of broken statues. She picked up a hand-sized rock and hurled it at Dex, who, in an impressive feat of agility, dodged to the side. It crashed against the statue behind Dex, exploding into fragments and dust.

Qiti charged forward and sent a flurry of punches to Dex's midsection. Dex deftly blocked and diverted them one by one. Dex grabbed Qiti's wrist and flung her into a statue. The force of the densely packed robot against the stone caused it to explode into rubble.

Qiti climbed to her feet, dusted off, and approached once more. "OK, clearly this fight could be a little fairer. What say we even it up a little bit, hmm?" she said as her arms and legs opened like hatches under an airplane.

They retracted and folded back as sturdy metal poles extended out, adding length to her limbs and bringing her height closer to Dex's. The extended limbs were segmented and thick, bending at joints halfway down, giving Qiti's arms something of an ape's proportions. Her hands were now three-pronged clamps with curved fingers that were sharp at the tips. They spun like a blender as she sized Dex up from her new vantage point.

"Remember, after this, we are leaving here together," Qiti reiterated, the buzzing of her sharp fingers revving in spurts.

Dex waved her opponent to come forward, the rhythm of her fight stance slow but shifting. Qiti obliged with a buzzing forward punch that Dex blocked in an outward direction and followed with a swift series of kicks to the robot's unprotected core. Qiti grabbed at Dex with her claws, carving slightly into Dex's shoulder. Dex grunted and pushed the tubelike limb away and swung her arm back, blood running down her sleeve.

"Don't worry, I'll fix that when I do the brain thing. Though maybe something a little more nonlethal would be better right now," Qiti said as her blade fingers retracted and turned into electric prods. They sparked with lights and the cackling hiss of electricity as she bumped them together like a boxer ready for the next round. Dex took several steps back and picked up a stun-cutlass from the ground. With one hand holding the sword and the other her knife, she charged. Qiti ran forward in kind, prods buzzing.

They fenced, sparks scattering to the floor every time their weapons connected. Dex spun around, launching a kick to Qiti's bulbous torso. Qiti's legs extended, sending her body upward, dodging the strike as Dex's feet swung between elongated metal legs. Qiti retracted downward with speed, bringing the butt end of her prod directly down upon Dex's head. Dex blocked it high with her cutlass and stabbed her knife forward, cutting directly through the rib of Qiti's metal casing. She turned her knife and created a small opening, the crinkle of Qiti's proprietary alloy giving the robot pause.

Qiti stepped back. "Impossible. I'm indestructible," she said with indignant shock.

Dex smiled. "Conventionally speaking, yes. But this knife doesn't cut. It vibrationally displaces. This thing can open you like a window. You wouldn't know about it. It's off the books," Dex said with a smile, flipping the knife in her hand.

"Doesn't matter. I'm still saving you," the robot cried, resuming her fighting stance.

"You are saving your idea of me. Not me," Dex replied, holding her weapons at the ready.

Qiti ran forward and flailed, sparks cascading down across the center of the temple. Strike, block, strike, block—the two symmetrical in their abilities. Dex had programmed her daughter well. Their fight was almost a dance, moving around the room, using fallen statues and the dead to whatever tactical advantage available.

Dex jumped and spun, her cutlass out in furious spiral. The moment slowed as the two women collided, with Dex's blade moving into Qiti's shoulder while the robot connected both prods to Dex's chest. Crackling veins of white streaked out as Dex screamed. The flash of light was blinding, then gone, replaced by Dex's slumped body on the ground, waves of steam rising.

Qiti stepped forward and pulled the displacer knife from her shoulder.

She tossed it to the side and pushed on Dex's body, the unconscious Olympian moved with a subtle groan. The robot folded back down into her traditionally small form. She walked over to the teleobox, picked it up, walked over to Dex, pulled the connection tube, and attached the medical unit to her mother's sternum.

Qiti whipped the tip of her finger open as the thin red laser beamed from the small hole inside. She steadied Dex's head and cut across the scalp, peeling back the first layer of skin and hair. Qiti then cut downward into the top of Dex's skull. She moved slowly, with precision, intent to not push the beam too deep. With a creak, Qiti lifted the skull piece and set it aside. She touched the soft membrane housing the gray matter and sliced through it carefully, gently cutting through the final layer and exposing Dex's hole-riddled brain and the blood-gorged Gray who lived atop it.

The sheet of conscious tissue pulsed as Qiti ripped it out unceremoniously and tossed it aside. She stood, walked over to the confused and fluttering intelligence, and shook her head. She pulled out Rose from her compartment and tossed it next to Gray.

"Here, everybody deserves a mother," she said.

Gray flashed in excited brilliance at the presence of its parent. Rose, having been confined to Qiti's compartment for the duration of the fighting, was weak but responded in kind. The two sheets of extradimensional tissue, parent and child, separated by light-years and millennia, embraced.

Rose's light patterns mimicked Gray's, their flashing syncing in coordinated display. Their conversation was brilliant, the sum of their want and suffering expressed in color. This had been a meeting that was five thousand years in the making, spanning the lengths of empires. Yet it was cut short, snuffed out with a stomp from Qiti's vengeful boot. She twisted with the ball of her foot, grinding them into the stone floor.

"But I can't have either of you trying to live inside Mom again."

She scraped the matter stuck to her boot against the base of a statue. The remains of Rose and Gray peeled off and stuck to the vertical ledge for several moments before falling to the ground lifelessly.

Qiti returned to the task at hand and pressed a button on the teleobox, which beeped and emitted a low hum. Inside Dex's open skull, the disconnected pieces of the brain filled in and regenerated. The decayed state of gray matter from the deadly flu so many millennia before had been wiped anew. Dex's brain had regrown. Qiti put the missing piece of skull back into its slot, and the cuts reconnected. From there, Qiti folded Dex's scalp back over and watched the cauterized wound across her forehead disappear back into her face. After the final bit of tissue healed, the teleobox beeped.

Qiti disconnected the unit from Dex's chest and tapped her face gently. "Mom . . . Mom . . . It's all OK now. I did it. You're free, just like I promised," Qiti announced with a face of genuine love.

Dex opened her eyes. The sparkles of purple were the same but dimmer. She coughed and leaned up.

"Who are you?" Dex asked the smiling Clicklaxia robot standing above her through the grog of regained consciousness.

"What do you mean, Mom?" Qiti replied with a bewildered twitch.

"Mom? Where am I? I . . . don't understand."

"You just went through a traumatic experience. It's OK. You're OK."

"I don't . . . I don't like this," Dex said, getting to her feet as she looked around. "Where's Mommy? Who are you?"

"I'm Qiti. I'm your daughter. Don't you remember?"

"Daughter? I'm a daughter. I don't have . . . ," she stammered, backing into a dead pirate behind her. She startled and caught herself on a half-destroyed statue. A wave of panic set upon Dex's face.

"It's OK . . . It's OK . . . ," Qiti reassured her visibly upset parent.

"Who are all of these people? How did— How did I get here? Why is everyone . . . dead?" Dex asked as tears ran down her cheeks.

"Mother, what's the last thing you remember?"

"I . . . I was at home. I got the virus. I was sick and in bed. Everyone was scared and sad."

"Tell me, where is home?"

"Alpha Olympus."

"Alpha Olympus? . . . How old are you?"

"Eight," Dex replied, wiping a tear from the small set of crow's feet with her sleeve.

Qiti paused for a moment. She looked at Dex and then to the smear of crushed blood and tissue that had once been Gray. She picked up the interdimensional sheet by the edge of its form and peeled it off the ground. She inspected the dead creature, peering closely at the finer details of its shimmery coat before putting it in her pocket. She looked back at Dex.

"It's OK, I can fix this. I just need the Aperture Parallax. I can get another one of those things, just like it, with the same memories. Then I can just plop it back in your head. Easy. We just need to do that. That's it. Then, when it's all done, you can say 'I told you so.'"

"What did I tell you?" Dex asked, now backed against the statue, trying to avoid the minefield of the dead.

"That I was being very bad. And that you were right. But of course you were. You always were. But for me to fix this, we have to go. There is a very special jewel that will make everything better. Do you want to help me get it?"

Dex nodded like a child needing reassurance. "OK."

"Great, all I have to do is use this blade here, and the Aperture Parallax will reveal itself."

"What's a Aputre Parallalax?" Dex asked, wiping her last tear.

"It a special . . . magic marble that grants wishes," Qiti replied.

"Oh, I'd wish for Mommy," Dex said.

The light of optimism within Qiti snuffed out somewhere within her code. She looked down. "Me too, kid. Me too."

Qiti approached the center tile of the open circle in the middle of the temple. She pulled the ceremonial blade from the compartment in her leg and placed it in the slit. The handle poked out of the floor, which Qiti twisted like a lock. A chorus of gears extended out from the center tile. They creaked and chugged as the statues rotated by row, sliding along the ground in a Rubik's Cube ballet, forcing the dead to twist and move in the shuffle.

Creak. Chug. Groan. Dex looked at Qiti with innocent worry as the room shifted. Everything lurched to a stop, followed by silence. Qiti looked at her mother, who was still bracing herself in a low crouch, nervously looking around.

"OK, Mom, we're going to the top."

MEANWHILE, AT THE TOP OF the pyramid, Lazer, Streek, Zizi, and Blood Fang climbed the final steps to the pinnacle. Lazer peered over the side, looking for the Vithrax.

"Do you think it's dead?" he asked.

"I don't know. Probably not," Streek lamented.

A howl came from the forest floor as the Vithrax appeared.

"Hey, look, you were right," Lazer said with a point downward.

"Yay?" Streek replied.

"So what do we do now? More ink?"

"All out."

"Hmm. What about that thing?" Lazer asked, pointing at the Aperture Parallax, which floated rather conspicuously behind Streek. Streek turned around and took stock of the elegant object levitating behind him. It was housed within the apex of the structure—a smaller pyramid, clear with refracting angles, no larger than Lazer's van back on Earth. It was solid prism, with three round hatches like fish eyes, one for each face. The pyramid apex was the source of light, channeled from the energy that cackled out of the Aperture Parallax with hairline static.

Streek tapped the glass with his tentacle. "So you would touch it and find out a way to stop this thing? I mean, that's how it's supposed to work, right?"

"Maybe? I was only half paying attention. Does it shoot lasers or anything?" Lazer asked with a shrug.

"I'm not sure."

"Maybe a parallel me knows how to make it shoot lasers and then I can make it shoot lasers, because he made it shoot lasers, which was really me after all, shooting lasers."

"I guess we'll just have to find out," Streek replied, peering through the glass at the brilliant speck. "So how do we get in there?"

On cue, the glass shifted with the creaking of gears. The casing at the apex of the pyramid rotated at its base, twisting one full revolution and clicking into place. The three bubble hatches silently swung open.

Lazer looked at Streek. "Probably through the door," he replied, pointing out the obvious.

"Wait. How did that happen?" Streek asked as he looked back down at the Vithrax, which skittered its way ever higher up the pyramid.

Lazer shrugged. "Does it even matter?"

"Suppose not. Hurry, get the thing, please."

Lazer climbed in. It was cramped, which made sense considering the size of the people who built it, but he made it through easily enough.

Warm energy pulsed in rhythm, crackling with whips of static among a swarm of unintelligible voices swirling in song over the padded hum that sounded like an air conditioner in Death Valley in July. Killer Orca had played a show in Death Valley in July once. It was a great idea on paper. In practice, not so much.

Lazer climbed in and stood before the Aperture Parallax. It was the deepest red he had ever seen. It was as if the entire concept of red was unable to adequately prepare him for being in its presence. It was magnificent, if a word could even justly be conceived to explain what he was experiencing. It floated in suspension as a mere speck within the marble that housed it.

Lazer thought it was pretty awesome.

He reached his gloved hand out, hesitant to touch the object. His fingers moved closer, inching to a near hover, shaking a little. He stopped. He shook his arms and hands out and took a step back, collecting his senses. He stretched out his arms.

"OK," he said softly to himself as he stepped forward again. "It's just a space barnacle. It's just a space barnacle."

He reached slowly, then quickly snatched the marble from its resting place. The light around him immediately shifted from pale red to a bright, whitish yellow. The red hue drained into the crimson glow of the Parallax, like a genie shoved back into its bottle.

The air was different now as well. It was heavier but drier, without the faint sensation of water droplets misting through. The unique climate and gravity were gone as Streek dropped down about a foot, back to his normal floating height. Lazer climbed back out of the compartment in the tip of the pyramid, clutching the marble.

"What just happened?" the octopus asked, looking about.

"You got shorter," Lazer replied, taking a fresh look at his surroundings.

"Did anything happen for you?"

Lazer patted up and down his body. "No."

He looked at the object up close, peering into pure crimson. He squinted and focused. The tiny floating gem twinkled like a satellite, alive in its presence. Streek peered back down the front face of the pyramid.

Lazer spoke as he maintained focus on the Parallax. "It looks pretty cool. Maybe it's like tinted glass frames or something, making the sky red and stuff? But nothing else happened. Maybe this thing's not as special as they say it—"

"Hey, where's the Vithrax?" Streek asked, cutting Lazer off.

Lazer looked over the side. It was gone.

"Maybe it went back in the temple?"

"Or maybe . . ."

A low snarl reverberated above them.

Lazer and Streek craned their necks. The Vithrax was perched atop the apex casing, leaning over toward their direction. It sniffed the air and roared, slicing its arms about in an aggressive show.

"Ahh!" Streek, Lazer, and the Baku cried in unison.

"Go away!" Lazer yelled as he threw the Aperture Parallax at the Vithrax, hitting it directly on the snout. The instant they connected, the Vithrax vanished. There was no smoke, sound, or special effect; it was as if the monster simply ceased to exist. The crimson jewel fell from the impact point, hit the face of the clear pyramid apex, and bounced down several stairs before coming to a rest in a groove on a step.

"Oh, damn!" Lazer yelled as Streek peered over the other faces of the pyramid to make sure the Vithrax was really gone.

"Where did it go?"

"I dunno. Where'd all of my guitar picks end up?" Lazer answered, climbing down several steps and picking up the Parallax with his gloved hand.

"*Cursed!*" Zizi yelled as he and Blood Fang quickly moved down several steps of the pyramid, away from the frightening orb.

"Wait!" Streek called to no avail.

Lazer looked keenly at the jewel again. "I don't get it," he said.

"Maybe it's voice activated?" Streek asked.

"Maybe. Parallax thing," he addressed the crimson marble, "take us back to the village so we can take Red Fang . . . It was Red Fang, right?"

"*Blood Fang*," Zizi buzzed as they paused their descent.

"Right. So we can take Blood Fang back to his mom."

Nothing happened.

"Shoot, that didn't work. OK. Next idea?"

Streek shrugged. Lazer sighed as he tossed the jewel in the air and caught it with his other, ungloved hand.

PART 14

THE CHOICE

LAZER WAS KICKED VIOLENTLY INTO WHAT FELT LIKE A POOL OF frigid water. He went limp and curled into himself as if in utero, floating in the vacuum of space. His senses were deprived of everything but the all-consuming blanket of nothingness.

He spread his arms and legs out, looking around the void, twisting his body, unable to make sense of up from down. Suddenly, the sensation of falling overcame him. Down, down, into the darkest black, he plunged. A light—faint, but getting closer—rapidly approached as if his descent were accelerating. First whites and yellows, then reds, blues, purples, and more. It was a growing kaleidoscope beamed out in high definition. As he fell toward the source of light, the horizon became a band of colors and sounds that wrapped around him like a sunrise in 360 degrees. More lights climbed from below, empty outlines winding like vines up his legs.

Lazer was now enveloped in a seed of brilliance, standing in the center like the nucleus of an atom. The place buzzed like a thousand different conversations in a thousand different languages all being had at the same time, while every single song ever written played in the background.

He continued in his fall. The lights became brighter, the sounds got louder. The cacophony of it all nearly overwhelmed Lazer before it abruptly stopped the moment he landed with a thud onto a bed of soft grass. The lights spread out and dispersed in all directions, flittering away like bubbles in the wind. He ran his hands through the grass beneath him and gathered his senses. Every blade he touched lit up faintly with contact.

Lazer stood and took stock of his surroundings. He was at the base of a small hill, alone, with only a single oak tree at the top of the hill as company. The tree was ancient, with a wide network of branches and lush foliage going up and wide, sprawling out in unencumbered majesty. The hill sloped down behind Lazer to a small grassy valley, beyond which dropped off a cliff into nothing. He made the short trudge up the hill and peered over the other side to find only more empty space. Where there should be sky, there was inky darkness, as if everything beyond the borders of his atoll ceased to exist.

"Hello?" Lazer called out, scanning the area for anybody. There was no reply.

Lazer approached the oak. Its mighty branches dwarfed him, stretching into the sky with victorious architecture. He placed his hand on the trunk and ran his fingers along the grooves. A gentle hum resonated from the tree, pulsing slightly like a drink sitting upon a guitar amp turned to ten. When the tree pulsed, so did the blackness of the void. Like a lifting dimmer, the touch revealed the atoll's surroundings, if only for a flash.

Lazer touched the oak again. The space beyond the grass revealed a rotating series of Technicolor strings—multihued threads of unfathomable numbers, vibrating slightly as they rotated, weaving in and around each other as they breathed with life. It was like being on an island in the middle of outer space, surrounded by a twinkling spool of firmament instead of the heavens. It reminded Lazer of the rubber-band ball he'd made in fifth grade. He gazed in wonder at the breathtaking display, gave one more look around, then removed his hand from the trunk. The space beyond the island became void once more.

He stepped his way down the knoll toward the expanse of grass, small glowing footprints quickly fading out behind him. Lazer walked a little farther out from the base, heading toward the perimeter when he looked back toward the tree. An image, too quick to identify, twitched and vanished. Lazer turned around and squinted. It appeared again like a projection, everything around him changing except for the tree, the grass, and Lazer himself.

The void vanished, replaced by a beautiful afternoon sky. The sun was warm but not overbearing, breaking through in shards between the leaves of the great oak tree. A different Lazer sat on the soft grass that sloped along the shady side of the hill. He was not as Lazer knew himself. This Lazer was the same age but thinner and balding in the back. He meditated as his beard, long and streaked with gray, enjoyed a soft dance in the breeze. His sun-bronzed chest held mild contrast against his loose linen pants as he sat cross-legged. He breathed with calm circulation as a smile crept across his face. His eyes remained closed, the only sounds being the faint gurgle of water from a brook that had appeared nearby and the calm exhale of a man wholly at peace with the world and himself.

A small boy, no more than five years old, ran up to the meditating Lazer. The child with a dirty shirt and jeans giggled, holding up a worm that tossed itself back and forth as it writhed in the child's fingers.

"Dad! Dad! Look what I found!" the boy exclaimed with giddy delight.

The man opened his eyes and smiled slightly. "I see," the alternate Lazer said, holding his hands out to his son. "Give it here."

The boy did as he was told and handed the worm over. The man put the worm in one cupped hand, and he dug with the other, tilling up a small amount of soft, coffee-colored earth.

"You must respect that which intrigues you, as your enthusiasm can affect others more than you realize. Remember to be gentle," the man said, placing the worm in the small hole and covering it softly with dirt.

"Sorry, Dad," the boy apologized.

"Oh, never be sorry for being fascinated by the world around you. Just be aware . . . ," the man replied, trailing off as the scene flickered and faded out.

The alternate Lazer and his son disappeared as the sky turned to twilight. The leaves on the oak all fell and withered into dust. The naked branches of the tree allowed the stars to shine through. They were brighter than usual, then they moved. They approached, getting larger. They weren't stars; they were ships, black, jagged, and asymmetrical.

"Aware. Be aware," a muscular and armed Lazer said to the small militia behind him.

This Lazer was different. It was not Lazer's normally hard-rock, leather-vested self, nor the tanned Buddha he just saw. This Lazer wore blue jeans and a blue-jean jacket, with black boots and his bleach-blond hair slicked back. He had a scar that ran down his left eye, which was broken up by a pair of black shades. He carried a rifle with a combat knife attached like a bayonet and wore bandoliers that crossed like an X across his dusty white T-shirt. They held rows of metal stakes with fine-tipped points.

The grizzled alternate Lazer waved at his small contingent of fighters and brought them close together. He spoke in hushed urgency. "Be aware. These sons of bitches have been stalking this hillside for weeks. Any minute now, they'll come from their burrows to feed. You gotta hit 'em in the center of the chest, from mid to close range. If the spike doesn't go through the eye and disconnect the cerebral node, then it'll keep on coming."

"What do we do if they keep coming?" one of the conscripts asked with a quiver in his voice.

"Shoot 'em again until they stop," Grizzled Lazer replied.

A different conscript raised his hand. "Um, sir. I heard the worms are super messed up looking."

"Only if you've got a problem with repossessed body parts, kid."

"Why are they coming here?" the first conscript asked.

"The same reason why your ancestors did. They could."

Everyone got silent, acknowledging a mutually understood horror. A snap of branches was followed by a moist slither.

"What was that?" one of the young recruits yelped, his eyes darting around. A screech, high-pitched and wet, reverberated through the night air.

"W-Was that one of them?" one of the conscripts asked, gripping his rifle close.

"Shh," the grizzled Lazer hushed, tilting his head to get a better sense of the sound's direction.

He tapped the handle on his weapon, slowly raising it before spinning around quickly and pointing it toward the air over the heads of the militia members behind him. He fired his weapon, sending a sharp metal bolt into the sky at the shadowy creature that was dropping in. A screech, loud and immediate, rang out, then faded away with the rest of the scene of the battle-hardened Lazer and his soldiers.

Everything was now void once more. All that remained were the original Lazer, the grass, and the old oak tree, which had reverted back to its previous state of verdant abundance. The leaves rustled despite there being no wind as a loud hum rang out.

"Hello!" Lazer called out once more.

Still nothing.

He climbed back to the top of the hill and stood next to the base of the tree, dwarfed by its substantial mass. He reached over and brushed his fingers along the weathered grooves in the bark.

With the slightest touch, he fell into himself, alone once more in a void of nothing. Lazer could see himself, from his birth until now, winding like a snake through childhood into his middle-aged self. The snake of Lazers through time then formed into the trunk of the oak, with every branch playing through a variety of scenarios, with the branches of those branches playing possible scenarios off the original clips of routes Lazer's yet-to-be-lived life could take. The hidden coil of illuminated strings revealed themselves once more with a pulse.

One by one, the strings detached from their fixed positions and dropped down toward him. He was enveloped, the rush of possibilities coursing through his brain. Lazer's body went limp and rose from the ground, almost as if he were back in the alley behind Love on the Rocks, getting abducted all over again.

Flashes of alternate lives flitted across his eyes like a reel. It was an overload of information, cramming itself into Lazer's mind. Lives lived of love and loss and failure and of nonexistence. The life he lived if he never played music. The life he lived if his dad never left. The life he lived if his mother survived. The life he lived if he settled down and got married. The life he lived if Killer Orca became the biggest band in the world. All of it.

As he rose higher, Lazer's hand came off the oak. The instant they separated, the lights vanished, and Lazer fell back to the grassy knoll beneath him. He ran his hand across his face and regained his senses. He was woozy getting back on his feet, the memories that weren't his still flashing in his mind—snippets of songs he heard long ago but never did, names and faces of people he never met but did. His mind cleared, and he stepped away from the oak.

Suddenly, the ground rumbled. The tree shook, the branches swayed, the leaves hushed as they brushed against one another with the orchestral abundance of a field full of crickets. Lazer stumbled backward and scurried down the slope to the valley below.

Plumes of smoke rose from pockets in the ground, the rumble of earth preceding every new gaseous release. Mountains of skeletons grew from the depths of the nothing, piled atop each other, bleached and dry. The screams of a terrorized unseen being surrounded him as fire rained across the void. The leaves on the tree combusted into flames, burning vividly in orange, yellow, and red. The colors danced and flitted into the sky, rearranging into a face.

The face was massive and skinless, showing muscle and connective tissue. Its features were firm, serious, with an anger that exuded beyond the unbearable heat that pushed in oppressive waves. Lazer felt a gnawing pang at the center of his very being. The face looked directly into Lazer's essence; it spoke without moving its lips.

"*I see you,*" its voice said in an omnidirectional gravel before the face exploded into a scattering splash of fire. It screamed in a rage that felt layered infinite times over. It seeped into Lazer, draining into his pores, vibrating on the minutest levels before building into a torrential pummel. A fireball landed beside him, sending him over the edge of the island and into the abyss.

LAZER SNAPPED BACK TO REALITY. He fell over, catching himself before taking a short tumble down the steep face of stairs, dropping the jewel in the process. He looked up to see Streek and the two Baku cowering behind him.

"Erm . . . what did you see?" the octopus asked with nervous concern.

"Everything?" Lazer replied, half a question in and of itself, squinting and scratching the back of his head.

"So now what?" Streek asked, looking around for any additional signs of danger.

"I think we were supposed to take that guy home." Lazer nodded toward the chieftain's son as he climbed to his feet.

"Right. But what about Dex?" Streek asked, still anxious about his ride home.

"*Take the jewel,*" a voice called from within Lazer's head.

"What?" Lazer asked aloud.

"I said, but what about Dex?" the octopus reiterated.

"You wanna go back in and find her right now? I think we should worry about one thing at a time," Lazer replied, dusting off his jeans.

"Are you mad? She'll leave us!" Streek yelled.

"*Take the jewel,*" the voice repeated.

"OK," Lazer said back to the voice.

"OK, you are mad?"

"Um . . . No. No, I'm good. We're good. We just need to take this," Lazer replied as he bent down and picked up the Aperture Parallax with his gloved hand.

The Baku took another step back.

"I suppose you're right. Off we go, then," Streek said.

Lazer looked to the two nervous Baku. "It's OK, guys. I'm fine," Lazer said, waving for his companions to follow.

The two Baku nodded and led the trek down the steps with Streek behind them. Lazer slipped the marble into his pocket and carried on, following behind them.

QITI FOLDED BACK OUT INTO her larger, battle-ready form, her extended appendages ending in husky claws. She hoisted Dex onto her back and walked to the open face of the temple.

"All right, Mom. All we have to do is go to the top of the pyramid and get the magic marble. Sound good?"

"OK," Dex replied, arms hugging Qiti's collar.

Qiti stepped out and immediately noticed that the sky was no longer red. Shocked, she looked up to the top of the pyramid, her vision zooming in with increasing resolution. The jewel was gone.

"Impossible!" she yelled.

She looked back down the pyramid and scanned the forest through various spectrums. Near the bottom, moving through the stone columns, the glow of the Parallax shone through Lazer's pocket.

"Oh, you're so dead!" she yelled from the top before beginning her descent down the mountainous stair.

"I'm scared," Dex said, clinging to Qiti with a nervous grip.

"It's OK to be scared, Mom. Just whatever you do, don't let go."

ZIZI, BLOOD FANG, AND STREEK raced through columns of moss. Lazer huffed behind them, wheezing as if his lungs were attempting to escape his body. Everything was more difficult with the added gravity. Lazer paused for a moment and placed his hands on his knees, swallowing through a dry mouth. A red tentacle reached back, grabbed his hand, and pulled him onward.

"No time for that!" Streek yelled to his winded companion.

"Almost home!" Zizi called out.

Lazer followed through the towers of rocks and saw the narrow passes becoming wider and more well trodden. They weaved around several larger columns and into the wider clearing of the village. Lazer collapsed to the ground, attempting to regain his breath between hoarse coughs.

A phalanx of guards scurried into a row and pointed their spears out toward the white-painted Blood Fang. Zizi leaped between the previously rival Baku and his people and waved his arms.

"Stop! Stop! Get Burzbur!" he exclaimed.

Blood Fang held his hands up.

The wizened leader of the tribe stepped through the wall of guards and approached her son. "Blood Fang?"

"Mother Burzbur?"

"No more Demon?"

"No more Demon," Red Fang said, his voice cracking with emotion.

The two embraced in an extended hug whose time had long since come. Burzbur held her reunited son as tears slowly ran over the grooves in the woman's wrinkled and weathered cheeks. She looked at her son again, caught between wanting to hold him and wanting to see him. She wiped a tear from her face with her sleeve and looked at Lazer, who was now back to his feet, Streek hovering beside him.

"Many thanks. Gratitude of Burzbur stretch length of great cave."

"No problem," Lazer said with a smile and a final, post-run cough.

"We were happy to do it," Streek followed up.

"Yeah, actually, it was really this guy," Lazer said, pointing to Streek. "He's the one who knew how to use the teleobox thingy."

"Thanks, Lazer, but really it was Zizi over here. He's the one who got us there and back."

Zizi tapped his chest twice and pointed at Lazer. "Zizi thank Layzur. Save Zizi life."

"Aw, no worries, little dude. We made a pretty good team, the three of us, huh?" Lazer replied. "Hey, high five, little buddy."

"High five?" Zizi replied, confused, looking at his three-fingered hand.

"Ah, yeah, that might make less sense for you. Here, just put your hand up," Lazer said, holding his hand up for Zizi to mime. Zizi raised his scale-lined palm and digits. Lazer tapped it softly with his open hand. "High five!"

"Maybe you should average it out and meet at a high four," Streek suggested.

"Nah, the high five is about more than the count of the fingers, dude. It's about feeling it in here," he said, pointing at his sternum. "And here."

He pointed at Zizi's sternum. He turned to Streek. "And h—" Lazer said before stopping, aiming his pointer finger in a wavering circle around Streek's chin as he tried to determine just where Streek's heart, or heart-equivalent organ, resided.

"Looking for this?" Streek asked, opening his mouth to show a beating heart encased in layers of mucous tissue.

"Gross. But cool. Yeah, for the most part, that thing."

"You shouldn't celebrate quite yet though," Streek warned.

"Why's that?" Lazer asked.

"While I'm happy, thrilled even, that we didn't die during the rescue, we have to figure out how we're actually getting out of here. I mean, is Dex even still alive?"

"I don't know. There were a lot of bodies in there . . . Oh, that's a good song title."

"Focus, Lazer. What do we do?"

Lazer thought for a moment. "What if we just went back to where we first found her?"

"That's actually not a terrible idea. Worst case scenario, we can get out to the surface using the way she came in. Good thinking."

"You know, I'd swear that teleobox thing shook something loose in my brain. I definitely feel smarter . . . ish."

"Are you sure that isn't sobriety?"

"Hmm. Could be part of it."

"But wait . . ."

"What?" Lazer asked, surprised that wasn't the end of it.

"Do you know how to fly any type of spacecraft? You know, in case we can't find Dex."

"I don't know. I don't think so."

"But doesn't touching the jewel make you know everything?"

"I don't feel like I know everything. Though you're the space alien, right? Shouldn't you be the one who knows how to fly a UFO?"

"I count numbers, not fly ships."

"Maybe Zizi knows how to fly it."

Streek looked at Zizi, who was trying to eat a butterfly that flitted past him, then back at Lazer. He raised an eyebrow. "Ugh. We're doomed. We'll never get out of here. Dex is probably dead, nobody can fly a ship, and I'm going to have to eat bugs for the rest of my life."

A loud crash interrupted them, a fallen column heralding the arrival of

Qiti. Dex had her arms wrapped around Qiti's shoulders and held on like a terrified backpack. The enraged robot flailed her arms, whipping them around like a pair of morning stars, flinging a half dozen Baku across the village. She rampaged through waves of warriors, searching, smashing.

She saw Lazer close to the center of the village, standing out fairly conspicuously among his much-smaller company.

"You!" Qiti yelled, pointing a claw at Lazer.

Lazer pointed at himself, mouthing, "Me?"

Qiti's claw rotated once. She bashed another wave of Baku warriors and charged with a burst of speed, jarring Dex from her position. The confused Olympian fell hard to the ground and got the wind knocked out of her. She silently coughed as she scurried away, back toward the stone forest. Qiti, oblivious to her fallen mother, raced toward Lazer. She was a bull after the matador, narrowly focused on the jewel inside Lazer's pocket as it shone like a beacon through a shroud. Her inattention to her surroundings cost her. Several Baku had extended a trip wire made of dried woven moss, catching the robot's foot and sending her careening into the fire.

Burzbur pulled at Lazer's sleeve as she spoke to Zizi quickly. *"Take friend of Lolobaku back to Up. Protect. Zizi job now,"* she instructed her warrior.

The imp nodded and tightened his fist around his spear. He pointed at the rocker and his floating companion and motioned for them to follow. *"Back to river."*

Lazer nodded as he and Streek ducked behind a row of dwellings and escaped through the stone forest at the opposite end of the village. As they fled, Qiti raged, crawling out of the fire as spear-wielding Baku surrounded her.

Lazer and Streek sped through the narrow columns of moss-covered rocks, following Zizi as he darted his way through the forest. Streaks of color surrounded them as they raced their way toward the spot where they had encountered Dex hours before.

"So you're sure you can get us out of here?" Streek called to Zizi as they hurried.

He didn't answer.

"I don't know about you . . . but I'm following regardless," Lazer panted from behind him.

Streek thought about it for a moment and realized Lazer was right. His options were limited: run or die. Over rocks and around narrow passes, the three made it to the river. Zizi hopped across the bridge as Lazer and Streek followed without issue. They turned south and trekked along its bank, all keeping an eye out for Qiti or any other surprises.

They made it to the door that Dex and her security had entered through. Lazer waved his liquid eye and brought up the menu. He tapped a few prompts and twisted the lock open behind the secret exit. The door rose upward, revealing a long series of twisting ramps with a hollow gap in the center, like a stairwell without the steps or railing. Up and up, they climbed the winding path, all the way to its end—a thick metal slab. Lazer held his hand out, waving it around as he searched for an exit while catching his breath.

"Now what?" Streek asked through anxiety.

"Let me see," Lazer replied, inspecting the dead end.

A crashing sound from the ground floor echoed its way upward as the trio peered over. It was Qiti. Her claws pinched as she clinked and clanked her way upward, her extended metal limbs grabbing onto the ramps as she ascended.

Streek looked at Lazer and Zizi in panic. "Quick! Do something!" he yelled.

"I'm trying, but I think we're stuck. How long does it take for you to make more goo? Can you squirt some?"

"Maybe a little, but not enough to stop her," Streek exclaimed as he pointed a tentacle toward the opening. "That's a lot of ramp surface to cover!"

"Not for that. Here," Lazer said with a snap of his fingers, pointing at a narrow seam between walls. "Squirt there!"

Streek floated over and pushed. A small spritz of oily liquid hit the crease and trickled down. Lazer put his gloved hand out and turned. The metal slab groaned as it rose like an opening garage before getting stuck a foot off the ground.

"Yeah, it looks like something's jamming the door. Hit it again!" Lazer yelled, straining.

Streek floated over to the other side and took a deep inhale, inflating his body before giving the biggest push he could muster. With a sustained and final grunt, Streek managed a weak spurt that dribbled out, not even so much as misting the stuck section of the door. "Sorry, mate, that's all I've got."

Zizi scurried under the small opening and disappeared into the next room.

Streek exhaled all of his air and squeezed as best he could under the opening. Despite his best efforts, he was unable to get anything past the front part of his face into the crack. He pulled himself back. "I think I see a chain. Maybe if Zizi pulls it, the door will go up?"

Lazer looked through the wall with his liquid eye and saw the chain Streek spoke of. It was wrapped around the foot of a dead mercenary near the floor and unable to rise any farther. Lazer stuck his gloved hand into the next room and spoke, letting the glove translate.

"Zizi, buddy, pull the chain," Lazer said.

There was no response.

"Zizi, mate, do your friends a solid and open the door a bit farther, please," Streek pleaded. Still no response.

The crunching of claws into stone grew louder as Qiti got closer up the ramp. She called out from about halfway up the winding path. "I know you're up there, Lazer! Just give me the Aperture Parallax and I'll make your death quick. I promise," she yelled.

"That's not a very good deal. What if I give it to you and you let us leave? That's cool, right? I don't even really want it, honest!"

"Maybe under different circumstances, Mr. Lazer with a z. But I've got this overwhelming urge to murder you. I mean, like, it's really strong. I think I'm going to indulge in it. Sorry," Qiti replied, getting closer.

Lazer turned back to the door. "Hey, Zizi, how are we comin' with that door? . . . Zizi?" Lazer asked, jogging back and peering through the crack.

Zizi was pulling as hard as he could on the thick metal chain but couldn't move it. Zizi's strength wasn't enough to pull the foot out or untie the chain. It was firmly stuck.

"What do we do?" Streek asked in panic.

"Hey, Zizi, listen to me, bud," Lazer said calmly to the inside of the next room. "I have to give you some bad news."

"*What?*" Zizi asked as he stopped trying.

"You're gonna have to chew through his foot."

"*What?*" both Streek and the liquid eye said at the same time.

"Yeah, man. I know you're more into bugs and stuff, but I really need you to take one for the team here, buddy."

Zizi's face expressed concern, followed by disgust, followed by sadness.

He ripped the sturdy, composite shoe off the mercenary and raised his pant leg. The corpse of the muscle-bound bear was incredibly furry and most certainly on the gamy side. Zizi opened his mouth wide in hesitant acceptance and leaned in. He sunk his sharp rows of teeth into the skin covering the mercenary's ankle. As Zizi's jaws compressed tightly, the chain around the corpse's foot climbed vertically, lifting the body and carrying Zizi along with it. The large metal slab creaked its way fully open. Lazer and Streek rushed in to find Zizi firmly latched to the foot of the dead mercenary, hanging several feet off the ground.

"No time to be hangin' around, man," Lazer quipped as he helped pull the shark-toothed gremlin down.

Zizi massaged his jaw and spat to the side.

"OK, close the door! Close the door!" Streek yelled as a snaky appendage rose from behind them.

"Got it!" Lazer shouted back as he twisted his glove, shutting the door closed as Qiti's claw narrowly missed its opportunity.

They took a collective breath and peered down the dank, stone hallway before them. Circular metal grates running the length of the ceiling dripped water while wisps of haunted miasma hung in the air. Streek realized this was most likely the service tunnel used by Bakuma's people to move large items in and out of the underground city. Lazer, meanwhile, considered how great it would be to shoot a music video here.

They ran down the hall, following the guidance of Lazer's holographic projection. The clank of Qiti banging on the door behind them echoed out down the corridor. The metal caved in slightly with every blow from the other side.

"Here!" Lazer called, motioning to a hall to their right. They turned and continued their pace. Left, forward, right, forward, right again. Streek and Zizi kept up with Lazer's navigation as he whipped around turns without stopping to look where he was going. Another left, another right, left again into an extended corridor. They moved as fast as their legs and atmospheric propulsion systems would allow them, respectively.

Lazer turned another corner and collided with a massive metal door. A low tone splashed like a muted gong as Lazer fell back onto the floor. He looked up and marveled at the engraved work of sculpted artistry. It was just like the door he saw when they first descended into the mountain.

"Hey, is that the door we saw when we were in the museum?" Streek asked.

Lazer looked at the projection that had been guiding him. "We're on the other side of it, but yeah, looks like it."

"That's great! Open it!"

"Right. Right. Hopefully, no trapdoors this time, right?" Lazer asked with a chuckle.

"That was traumatizing, you know." Streek frowned.

Lazer took a deep breath and held his hand out. He waved and drew in his arm like a mime pulling a rope. A hidden set of gears bisected the doors, drawing them open toward Lazer and company as they all stepped back to make room. They hustled through the doors and into the museum, through the long tunnel, and into the lower mouth of the cave.

"The drop sled!" Streek yelled.

A rumble shook the ground as Qiti crashed upward into the space behind them from a hidden shaft. Her arms were extended, climbing out of the hole with clawed fingers gripping into the old, worn stone.

"Are you kidding me?" Streek yelled as he hurried toward their exit.

"*Seriously,*" Zizi buzzed.

Lazer made it to the thick black tarp first and cued up his liquid eye. Streek followed as Zizi lagged a step behind.

Qiti, now entirely out of the chute, lunged forward with a metal claw. Her arm slithered like a snake in the grass and snipped at Zizi's foot. She narrowly missed the leaping gremlin, who made it safely onto the black tarp, which then shot upward through the vertical shaft.

The drop sled launched into immediate lift, leaving Qiti alone at the bottom. The raging murderbot began her climb, moving up through the shaft in chase behind her orb.

As the drop sled elevated, Streek's face fell into panic. "Oh, balls."

"What? We got away . . . ish."

"How are we supposed to breathe once we get to the top?"

"Oh, um, in small sips?" Lazer asked.

"*What is problem?*" Zizi asked.

"No air in Up," Streek explained.

"*How no die?*"

"I . . . I don't know," Streek said, his face now blank with shock.

"I got it," Lazer exclaimed with a snap of his fingers.

"Should I be worried?"

"Yeah, maybe a little . . . Just go with it."

Lazer unzipped his suit. He bear-hugged Streek, compressing the air out of him like a deflating mattress, and put the octopus's collapsed body into his suit like he was smuggling a Frisbee under a jacket. He motioned for Zizi to jump in on the other side. Zizi took a deep breath and climbed in, shaking around before finally nestling in like an oblong love handle. As Lazer zipped his jacket back up over both of his companions, the drop sled reached the top of the mouth of the cave. Lazer put his breathing mask on and moved as fast as he could with both passengers inside his suit. Suddenly, he stopped—a familiar chill. His keys were missing. He turned back to see the glimmer of his key chain sitting on the drop sled. He ran back.

"Wait, what's happening?" Streek muffled through Lazer's space suit.

"One sec," Lazer replied, getting closer to the drop sled. He got right up to the platform.

Beep. The drop sled descended, keys sitting in the middle.

"No!" Lazer yelled, reaching in vain as they disappeared down the shaft. He stood at the mouth of the opening, looking down. His breathing elevated.

"Is everything OK up there?" Streek followed.

Lazer stood in silence, gazing into the abyss.

"Should I be scared?" the octopus continued.

Lazer looked back out toward the entrance of the cave.

"No, buddy. I've got you," he said to Streek as much as he said it to himself.

He huffed his way along the pathway between the dusty corpses of the original Baku warriors and broken machinery and out the mouth of the cave. At the top of the hill were all of the ships. None of Dex's soldiers of fortune or her security detail had made it out.

Lazer scanned the vehicles and found a small passenger vessel that felt appropriate to acquisition. He projected the hologram from his glove and picked the digital lock safeguarding their new getaway vehicle. The ship beeped, and the hangar door opened. Lazer ran inside, making a bee-line to the control console. He waved his hand across the dash, scrolled through a projected menu, and pressed the option for cabin atmosphere.

With a hiss, the door closed, and air rushed through the vents that ran along the sides. Lazer unzipped his suit halfway. He pulled Streek out and wobbled him a few times until his air and form returned. Zizi jumped out and ducked behind the nearest seat. Lazer sat in the pilot's chair and looked at the array of buttons, levers, and screens with holographic projections.

"Hmm," Lazer muttered to himself as Streek regained his senses and joined Lazer up front.

"What?"

"Oh, um, nothing really . . . just, what do I do next?" Lazer asked with a drumroll across the steering mechanism.

"I think flying us out of here would be a good option."

"Yeah. I get that. I just don't think I know how to fly this thing. Comin' up blank here. It's weird. I was able to seal the cabin like I'd done it a hundred times before, but now . . . nothing."

Streek's face settled into a nervous frown. "You touched the Aperture Parallax; you got us in here. We're alive because of you. You can do this . . . Or fake it till you make it, right?" he said, growing a small smile as he tapped his human companion on the shoulder.

"Story of my life, dude. Follow me into oblivion?"

"Straight into the heart of the sun, mate," Streek replied.

Lazer grabbed the steering mechanism as a burst of memories erupted in his mind; pictures floated by, playing reels of a different life. Lazer could see the controls and feel the stitched grip of the throttle. The sound of engines firing up and the smell of leather finishing sparked neurons to life. A muscle memory returned, one which had never originally been there. Passive knowledge seeped into his thoughts; his hands gripped with the familiarity of repetition. He knew how to fly the ship. Lazer threw on his aviators and looked toward his copilot.

"Good news."

"What's that?"

"I fly spaceships now."

Lazer pressed a series of buttons and flipped a large switch. The turbines beneath the wings hummed to life. He pulled the steering mechanism inward, giving lift to the craft. After a slight wobble, the ship stabilized. Lazer swiped along the holographic interface, bringing up a variety of navigational maps.

"Where are we going?" he asked, sliding around the menu.

"I think up would be a good start!" Streek yelled, pointing through the windshield before them.

Lazer looked forward to see Qiti charging across the dune in his direction. He pulled the control wheel toward him as the ship rose. Qiti jumped, her metal claws tensing as she soared upward. With a loud clank, she caught the nose of the ship. Her arms pulled her to the windshield as she came face-to-face with Lazer on the other side of the glass.

"Give me the Parallax!" Qiti yelled from outside.

"OK!" Lazer yelled back as the ship continued to rise.

"Do not give it to her," the voice whispered.

"How do I give it to you?" Lazer asked loudly.

"Just hand it to me," Qiti yelled through the glass.

"But you're outside!"

"Not for long," Qiti yelled back with a smile as she punched the windshield.

"What are you doing?" Streek exclaimed in panic.

"Getting what's mine," she replied.

"I'll throw it out the window," Lazer yelled back, pointing to the outside of the craft.

"If you open the window, we'll lose cabin pressure," Streek chimed in.

"Just a crack. It's that or the windshield," Lazer replied to his friend before calling back to Qiti. "I'm gonna give it to you now."

"Do not do that," the voice inside Lazer's head rebutted.

"Where's the fun in that?" Qiti yelled with a smile as she punched the windshield again, creating a small crack in the glass.

"Here, I'm going to toss it outside. It's all yours."

"Do not lose the jewel," the voice demanded.

Lazer pressed a button, and the window to his side hissed open slightly. The air whipped around the cockpit, pulling light debris out as the deafening flutter of a slightly ajar window wubbed loudly. He pulled the orb from his pocked with his gloved hand between his thumb and pointer finger as Qiti punched the windshield again, widening the blast radius of the crack in the glass. The ship rose higher still. He waved the tiny glowing orb in front of him to show Qiti what he was doing before reaching over to the small opening in the window. Qiti scurried toward him like a spider, cracking the edge of the glass as her claw jammed the window farther open and grabbed Lazer's hand by the wrist. They looked at each other, then back to the Aperture Parallax, which sat nestled between Lazer's fingers.

"Give it to me," Qiti yelled.

"That's what I'm trying to do, lady! Give me my hand!"

"What if I just take both?" A manic smile grew across Qiti's mouth as her claw gripped tighter.

Lazer yelled in agony as he let go of the steering wheel and grabbed the jewel with his ungloved hand.

LAZER WOKE UP IN HIS van, lying on his bed, still wearing the clothes he'd been wearing when he was abducted. He sat up and scratched at the sweat behind his neck. It was daytime, and the inside of the van was stuffy. He rubbed his hand across his face and picked up a bottle beside him. He unscrewed the cap and took a sniff. It was water. He took a swig, swished it around, and swallowed. He took one more swig, coughed, and rescrewed the cap. He cleared his throat and pushed the back door of the van open.

He stepped out to Love on the Rocks, the shade from the roof cast toward him. It was afternoon, threeish. The white noise of passing cars hushed along in the background, punctuated by the stray horn as Lazer looked around at his surroundings. All of the same buildings were there, as were people walking about the neighborhood. He slammed the back door shut and headed into the bar.

The black vinyl door swung open as Lazer's figure cut against the light coming in from behind him. He entered, stepping up to the bar and giving the bartender a once-over. It was Rebecca, sporting the same inviting smile as always.

"The usual?" she asked as she pulled a glass from the freezer.

Lazer took a seat at the bar and looked down the row, spotting a single man in a black shirt, black jeans, and black cowboy hat sitting at the end of the bar, sipping on a bottle, his beard hiding most of his face. Lazer had never seen him at the bar before, so he gave him a smile and a nod. The stranger looked up slightly, winked, and turned back to his drink.

Lazer turned back to the bartender. "Sure, I'll take the usual," he said, climbing onto a barstool. He leaned in. "So you know what's weird?" he continued, lowering the tone of his voice.

"Shoot," she replied, pouring from the tap into the glass.

"I had this dream, right? I don't know. I wouldn't know where to start, really. It was really vivid. It had aliens and robots and these messed-up brain leech things that would control your mind."

"Definitely weird," Rebecca replied, setting Lazer's beer down in front of him.

"Yeah, but the really, really weird part is that I had made some friends in the dream and, honest to God, I sort of expected them to be in here when I walked through the door."

"Did you eat anything off last night?"

"Maybe? Everything was pretty blurry," Lazer said through his first sip.

"Yeah, you were on a good one last night."

"It happens."

"It can happen forever if you want," she said, her face going blank, her voice becoming the unsettling rasp of the voice of the Aperture Parallax.

Lazer spit out his sip of beer across the bar. "What?" he asked, a chill creeping up his spine, concurrent with the realization that he wasn't actually home.

"This is what you want, right? I can give this to you," Rebecca said again, rubbing the side of her body slowly. *"Do you want your old life? Do you want me? I see how you look at me. You want me to come to your van with you? We can have some . . . fun."*

"Who are you?" Lazer asked, standing quickly and backing away from the bar.

"I'm you. I know what you want. I know everything about you. I know every-thing about every version of you. You want this life back, right? It's what you've been wanting ever since it was taken from you. So unfair. Your van can always be just right outside that door." She pointed past the man at the end of the bar to the employee door in the back.

The man at the end of the bar drank his beer in silence, paying no attention to the conversation.

"What about Streek and Zizi?"

"What about them? You don't need them anymore. You've got me," she said, stepping out from around the bar. She approached Lazer as he slowly retreated.

"Well, I mean, they're my friends. And Qiti was . . . *is* about to down our ship."

"Is she? Time doesn't exist here. Every day can be today, or tomorrow, or a different Lazer's tomorrow, in case you get bored of this. Or if you get bored of me," she said, winking toward the front door, which opened on cue.

The light outside gave shape to a shadow, which stepped into the door one high-heeled foot at a time. It was Lazer's ex-girlfriend. She was done up, nicer than she had ever bothered to get during the tenure of their relationship. She approached Lazer, biting her lip in the confident hunger of a woman ready to pounce. Lazer backed up farther, facing the two women, who continued their advance.

"This doesn't feel right."

"Doesn't it, though?" the women said in unison, both with the voice of the Aperture Parallax.

Lazer's thoughts raced through his head. Was this actually so bad? His van *and* two beautiful women. On paper, this was Lazer's ideal scenario, like a fever dream out of the mind of his fourteen-year-old self come to life. This was really what he had always wanted—or rather, what he always told himself he wanted. Was there even a difference? But what happened when the things you knew in your heart to be the core of what made you no longer suited you? What would it mean to look at those things, as available as reaching out your hand, and to have it feel so wrong—and not just wrong but incongruent, out of key?

Lazer bumped into something. He turned back. It was the push bar for the employee door, cold and creaking slightly. He looked back at the women, their faces mere inches away, their breath warm against his neck. They giggled and moved in, like vampires about to slake their thirst.

"This is what you've always wanted," they said in unison.

Lazer stopped his retreat, his face going calm. "You're right," he replied, slowly pressing them away. "But it's not what I want anymore. I think it's time I moved on . . . Besides, I think I'm still wrestling with a robot, and my friends are probably going to die if I stick around for too long. You girls are nice, so . . . maybe next time?" He winked and smiled, backing into the door, swallowed by his surroundings as he fell into the bright daylight of outside.

LAZER SNAPPED BACK TO REALITY. He paused for a moment and looked at the Aperture Parallax as it glowed in his fingers. It illuminated brighter, shining out with burning intensity. He yelled and gritted his teeth through the pain of Qiti's grip as he forced his hand toward the window. A little more. Release.

He threw the Aperture Parallax out through the open slot over the glass and watched it fall away. Qiti reached for the falling jewel, pulling Lazer's wrist out the window. He screamed as he reached, grabbing the control wheel, turning it violently in their struggle. The ship rolled. Qiti reached for the falling orb as she swung. She missed.

"Why did you do that?" Qiti yelled. She punched the side of the ship in frustration and leaped off, diving through the sky after her prize.

"We're losing all of our air!" Streek yelled to Lazer, who was looking out the side of the ship at the falling robot.

"Right," Lazer yelled back, returning his attention to the console. He pressed a few buttons and brought a thick metal plate up like a second window, sealing the cockpit once more. Streek gasped a breath of air and looked back at Zizi, who gripped the metal edge of one of the seats in tightly wound terror. Lazer took the wheel and pressed forward, shooting the ship quickly out of the atmosphere.

"What's going to happen to Qiti?" Streek asked, looking out the front of the ship as they zoomed off into the night sky.

"That's a pretty long fall. Maybe she'll explode?" Lazer offered.

"Or burst into a bunch of pieces?" Streek replied, half a question.

"Or maybe catch the Parallax on her descent and teleport to a parallel universe and go after other versions of us. Then after she's murdered not us, she'll find herself, team up, and come back for real us . . ."

Streek took a nervous swallow and replied, "Or maybe if we're lucky, even if she does catch it, she'll be unable to use it since it only seemed to work when it touched something organic."

"Yeah, then she yells 'Noooo!' as she falls back to the planet," Lazer said, leaning forward in slow motion, slowly waving an arm.

"I suppose we'll never know," the octopus replied with a sigh.

"She hit the ground."

"What?"

"See that little cloud?" Lazer said, tilting the craft slightly and pointing below.

"Boom?" Streek asked.

"Boom," Lazer said with a definitive nod, giving his octopus friend a fist bump.

The ship exited the upper atmosphere and hovered in orbit.

Lazer wiped at the navigation index and brought up a projection. "So now that we're not being chased by anything . . . where do we go?" he asked.

"Maybe somewhere that has more than bugs to eat?" Streek replied with a slight wince.

"Do you have breakfast burritos in space?"

"Only the best."

"OK. Sounds good. Let's start there," Lazer said as he pressed a few more buttons. He tapped the Spaceberto's icon, flipped the autopilot switch, and leaned back. The ship blasted off, taking Lazer, Streek, and Zizi onto their next adventure: a burrito run.

EPILOGUE

A SNAIL CLIMBED A MOSS-COVERED ROCK AS A SOFT VOICE CRIED from behind it. It was the sniffling sound of a lost child. Dex sat on the ground, back against the lower section of the rock stack. She hugged her knees and sobbed. The crunch of footsteps on moss alarmed Dex, who raised her tear-soaked face.

Burzbur stood at head level with the sitting woman, who wiped her forearm across her eyes. The wizened gremlin cooed, holding her hand out to Dex, who sniffled once more. Dex looked at the diminutive chieftain and stood, towering above Burzbur once on her feet. The light of the artificial sun shone bold and warm from atop the pyramid in the distance, casting its rays upon the pair as they entered the village clearing, hand in hand.

A THOUSAND FEET ABOVE, THROUGH tunnels and bedrock and sand, Qiti lay in a crater, smashed and shattered, mechanical components spilling out in all directions. Her eyes were closed, black scuff marks streaking across her face. Wires protruded from bent metal, sending the occasional spark into the thin night air. The Aperture Parallax remained clutched in Qiti's hand, though her arm was detached and lay several feet away. A shooting star flew across the night sky, zipping by over Qiti's lifeless body. Her eyes twitched as a low whir struggled from within her casing. Another spark, then the motor turned over. A hum pulsed from within the broken robot in static waves, reaching through to her scattered pieces. Another spark, then her eyes opened.

PAUL BAHOU is the author of *Sunset Distortion: The Pyramid at the End of the World*. He holds a B.A. in Political Science from Cal State University Long Beach with a minor in music. He began his career writing grants while playing in his rock band, eventually moving out of music and into the sustainability sector. He lives in Southern California with his wife Melissa, daughter Sophie, and son Harrison. He writes fiction, music and the occasional dad joke in his spare time.

Made in the USA
Las Vegas, NV
23 April 2021